# THE EDGE OF NOWHERE

## C.H. ARMSTRONG

central
avenue
publishing

2019

Second edition published by Central Avenue Publishing,
an imprint of Central Avenue Marketing Ltd.
First edition published by Penner Publishing.

www.centralavenuepublishing.com

THE EDGE OF NOWHERE

Trade Paperback: 978-1-77168-161-2
Epub: 978-1-77168-162-9
Mobi: 978-1-77168-163-6

Published in Canada
Printed in United States of America

1. FICTION / Historical / General   2. FICTION / Family Life

1 3 5 7 9 10 8 6 4 2

In Loving Memory of Edward Joseph Hedrick.
November 18, 1931—January 13, 2018

*November 12, 1992*

*To My Grandchildren,*

*I know you refer to me as "the meanest woman you've ever known." I've heard you joke behind my back that I'm too mean to die—that even Satan wouldn't have me. This is probably true. I'm not like other grandmothers and, frankly, I have no desire to be. I'm neither warm nor approachable, and I don't bake cookies to keep on hand for your visits. As my daddy would say, I'm "meaner than a cottonmouth, and not nearly as predictable." And I'm okay with that. But what you probably don't know is that I love you.*

*The struggles I've endured, and the choices I've been forced to make, have shaped me into the woman I am today: opinionated and aggressive, with very little patience for sentimentality. At my core I am a survivor, and for that I have no regrets. I neither need, nor desire, forgiveness; and I sure as hell don't want pity.*

*My doctor has discovered a tumor on my pancreas. There is no cure this time. No amount of hard-headedness or sheer determination can change my future. The best I can do is say my goodbyes in my own way, by my own rules.*

*Before I go, there are some things you should know—secrets I've kept hidden these last fifty years. Secrets that have shaped me into the woman I am today. I share them with you now in hopes you might know me in death better than you knew me in life. Remember me not as your hostile and overbearing grandmother, but as a woman unwilling to be a victim, and dedicated to protecting her family at all costs.*

*Victoria Hastings Harrison Greene*

# PART ONE

## DECEMBER 1913

# CHAPTER ONE

"VICTORIA?" MAMA'S EYES SHONE WITH LOVE as she stepped away from the Christmas tree we'd placed in the corner of our small sitting room. "Are ya almost done with that string? I'm just about ready for it."

Jumping to my feet, my face flushed with pride, I placed the long rope of cranberries and popcorn I'd created into her outstretched hand. "I'm finished!"

"Oh, Victoria! It's perfect!" Standing on tiptoes, Mama placed one end near the top of the Douglas fir Daddy had brought home the previous week. After some time, she stepped back and assessed her work through narrowed eyes.

"It fits!" I said.

"Of course it does!" Mama smiled. "You did a nice job, baby girl."

Singing a familiar Christmas carol, she again stood on tiptoes and adjusted a glass ornament of a red cardinal. Though I didn't know the words to her song, I hummed along with her, mimicking her every motion.

Though the tree looked perfect to my young eyes, Mama continued her circle around its circumference, adjusting an ornament here and the rope of cranberries there, taking care not to knock it over. Sadly, at nearly eight months pregnant, it was an impossible task. In slow motion, I watched our tree tilt, first to a forty-five degree angle, then topple to the floor.

"Aaaaa!"

I giggled at Mama's surprised screech.

Thrusting her hands on her hips, she bit her bottom lip to hide a smile. "And what do you find so amusing, young lady?"

"Mama!" I gasped between giggles. "Your tummy is huge! Are ya sure there's only one baby in there?"

Lifting an eyebrow, she reached down and heaved our tree upright. "Yes, Miss Smarty Pants. Just one baby, thank you very much!"

"It's so big, though! Will it be here for Christmas?"

"Oh, I hardly think so. He needs a bit longer to grow and get stronger. Six or eight weeks more, I think."

"How can ya be sure there's only one? Jeannie Herrick's dog had puppies, and there were *nine* in there! There could be at least two, couldn't there?"

"Not likely," she laughed.

Mama snapped a broken branch from the tree then stepped close once again and straightened two more ornaments, but left the tree leaning visibly to the left side. Stepping back now, she nodded. "Well, it's not perfect by everyone's standards, but it's perfect for us."

"Perfect for us," I agreed.

Together, Mama and I admired our tree. In addition to the missing branch and the noticeable lean, it was flatter on one side; but it was the perfection of those imperfections that has stayed with me these many years. We snuggled together in Mama's favorite rocking chair as she picked up the strains of the forgotten carol. Christmas was only a week away.


THAT CHRISTMAS IN 1913 was my last with Mama and Daddy. At only eight, I knew nothing about death and hardship. I knew nothing beyond the love of my two parents.

I don't remember much about Mama and Daddy before that Christmas. What I remember most was a beautiful couple, deeply in love. I remember my mother had the most beautiful fiery-red hair. She and I sat for hours each day as I brushed through its long length. Each strand slid through my fingers like grains of fresh-cut wheat during harvest season. Almost too beautiful to touch, it appeared electric in the sunlight. Each downward stroke awakened her fragrance, cocooning us in the scent of vanilla. Always vanilla. Not overpowering, just a subtle reminder of long hours spent in the kitchen baking for Daddy and me. To this day, the smell of vanilla reminds me of her love.

More than anything, perhaps, I remember the sound of Mama's voice. Our home was always filled with the music of her laughter, the cheerful cadence of her voice in conversation, and the sweet melody of whatever song was escaping through her soul. I remember her moving around our home, her voice lifted in song to keep her company while she worked. Mama's voice was the sound of love and happiness. Hers was the first voice I heard upon waking in the morning, and the last I heard before closing my eyes at night. Mama was everything in the world I'd hoped to be, and nothing I would ever become.

Daddy had been energetic and fun. His job with the Rock Island Railroad kept him away from home about as often as he was with us, but I remember him playing his banjo while Mama and I danced around his feet after dinner. Though quick to smile, he was more reserved than Mama. He spoke when spoken to, but was perfectly content listening to Mama carry the conversation. I still remember the love in his gaze as he looked upon her, as if she were the center of his universe.

Daddy was a strong, robust man with eyes the color of a blue Oklahoma sky on a clear day. His golden-blond hair was wavy and, though always trimmed neatly, a small piece constantly worked its way out of its neat combing to hang over his right eye. Mama was forever threatening to take a pair of scissors to that wayward lock. Daddy and I would just grin, sharing our secret knowledge that Mama didn't really mean it. We both knew she loved that rogue strand almost as much as she loved Daddy.

Mama and Daddy were everything I had in the world. They came to each other without families, insisting they had become each other's family when they married. Both only children, Daddy's parents had died long before I was born; and Mama's family had promptly disowned her when she defied them to marry my daddy. With nothing to keep them in St. Louis, they relocated to Oklahoma to begin their new life. Mama never regretted it. She'd told me often that all we needed was love and each other. She was wrong. I needed my own family. Losing Mama and Daddy would leave me orphaned and completely alone in the world.

SITTING DOWN TO dinner that night, I was confused at Mama's quiet demeanor. Always a blur of movement, her laughter had been a constant in our home. That evening, she was strangely quiet—her discomfort evident by the taut grimace of her lips, and the dimness of her normally bright green eyes. I thought little of it at the time. She'd frequently suffered contractions from false labor and, though painful, Dr. Heusman had assured us it was normal.

"How much longer 'til Santa comes?" I asked, hoping to distract her from her discomfort.

"Now, that's at least the twelfth time you've asked today." Mama smiled. "Seven more days."

"Will Daddy be home in time?"

"Yes. In fact, I expect him in another day or two."

"Can I stay up late to see Santa? George Holly said he's not real. He's a big fat liar. This year I'm gonna prove it to him!"

"Ya know ya can't, Victoria. Santa skips the houses where the children aren't sleeping."

"But . . . is he real?"

"He's real if you believe in him, sweetheart. What do *you* think?"

"Oh, I definitely believe in him!"

"Then there ya go." Mama smiled, but it didn't quite reach her eyes.

Silence descended upon us, and I could feel the thickness in the air. "What's wrong, Mama?"

"Nothin', sweetheart. I'm just a little tired is all."

As we collected the dinner dishes that night, Mama moved at an unusually sluggish pace. Each step was carefully placed, one foot in front of the other, as though crossing over a layer of thin ice. I studied her covertly for the longest time, noticing how she caressed her extended belly and her occasional wince of discomfort. Was the baby kicking? Was Mama soothing away pain? I could never tell, and she never complained. Her only explanation was to say she'd "overdone it that day."

Drying the last dish, Mama turned to me, her lips tilted in a tired smile. "Victoria, I think we're gonna call it an early night. Why don'tcha take that book we've been reading together and see how much of it you can get through on your own before bed?"

"But ya always read to me," I whined.

"I know, darlin', but I'm not feelin' well so I'm gonna turn in early. You're a good reader—take your book with you and read it to yourself for awhile. But not too long—it's almost bedtime. Only six more sleeps until Christmas." Smiling, she ruffled my hair to soften the disappointment of her directive.

"Okay, Mama." I reached my arms around her large stomach in my ritual goodnight hug. "I love you."

"I love you, too, baby. Goodnight."

Back in my room, I had no patience for reading. Giving up, I placed my book on the bedside table, and turned out the light. Within moments, I was sleeping soundly.

# CHAPTER TWO

THE NEXT MORNING, I WAS AWAKENED BY A
strange sound; almost like that of a mewling kitten. Listening intently, I tried
to puzzle through the sound that had awakened me. Impatient, I crawled out
of bed and tiptoed down the hall until I found myself standing in front of
Mama's open bedroom door.

"Victoria?" Mama's voice was barely a whisper.

I approached her and found her lying on her side with her eyes closed. If
not for her flushed cheeks and sweat-matted hair, she might've been sleeping.

"Mama?" I touched her fevered cheek. "Are ya okay? Can I get you some
water?"

"No, darlin'. But I need you to be my big girl and help me, okay?"

"Okay, Mama. What can I do?"

"Go find Dr. Heusman. D'ya remember where he lives?"

"Yes, ma'am," I whispered. "What do I say?"

"Just fetch him, and tell him to come quickly. Tell him the baby's comin',
and it's too soon. Can ya do that?"

"Yes, ma'am. You'll be okay while I'm gone? You look really sick."

"Oh, honey, I'm okay. Don't you worry none about me. Women have babies all the time. Now go find Dr. Heusman—and put on some warm clothes
first. It's cold out there."

"Yes, ma'am," I said, racing out of the room.

Still in my nightclothes, I paused to throw Mama's wool cloak over my
shoulders and step into her too-large boots in my bare feet. Racing into the
street, my feet crunched on the fresh snow that had fallen the night before.
On another day, I might've stopped to enjoy the beauty. That morning, I
needed to find Dr. Heusman.

I ran every step of the three blocks to Dr. Heusman's house, only slipping
twice on the slick sidewalks. Before I even reached the front door, though,

I knew: he wasn't home. The windows were darkened with no light shining from within. A blanket of untouched snow surrounded the house, proving my theory. If Dr. Heusman were home, his boys would surely have stomped through the yard in a quest to build a snowman or beat each other in a snowball fight. Hoping I was wrong, I leaped onto the porch and banged on the front door.

"Dr. Heusman! Dr. Heusman!" I banged my fists until they ached with pain. "Dr. Heusman!"

No answer.

I crept around the side of the house and peeked through the windows.

"Victoria Hastings!" The crotchety voice of old Mrs. Simmons, the town librarian, called out from across the street. "What in the world are ya doin', child? Dr. Heusman ain't home—can't ya see that? You're fixin' to wake the whole neighborhood with that terrible racket! Now what is it ya need, young lady?"

"Mrs. Simmons!" I cried. "My mama's not feelin' good, and she told me to fetch Dr. Heusman. I think she's havin' the baby!"

"Ah honey, she'll be alright. Women have babies all the time. Dr. Heusman's in Oklahoma City visiting Mrs. Heusman's people for Christmas."

"But Mama needs a doctor! What am I gonna do?"

"Don't you worry, child. She just needs a good midwife. Go on over and fetch Mrs. Kirk. She'll help ya out. She lives right down from Lincoln School. D'ya know which house is hers?"

"Yes, ma'am."

"Then go on and fetch her. Tell her I told ya to, and that your mama needs help bringin' a baby. She's as good as any doctor, and probably better. Women are always better at bringin' babies anyhow, so don'tcha worry none. Now get goin'."

"Yes, ma'am! Thank you!" I called behind me.

"Don't you go a-thankin' me. You just let your mama know I wanna see that baby as soon as she's up and around!"

"Yes ma'am, I will!" I shouted as I raced through the street toward Mrs. Kirk's house.

By the time I arrived, my face and lips were numb from the cold. Jumping the steps onto the porch, I banged on her front door. "Mrs. Kirk! Mrs.

Kirk! Please open up!"

The front door opened so quickly my raised fist failed to connect with the door, and I stumbled forward into Mrs. Kirk's solid arms.

"Victoria Hastings!" she gasped, steadying me. "What in the world's goin' on, child?"

"Mrs. Kirk!" I said, catching my breath. "I need ya to come with me. Dr. Heusman's gone, and my mama's havin' the baby. She says it's too soon. Mrs. Simmons said to fetch you and that you'd do a better job than Dr. Heusman anyhow on account of you bein' a woman and all! Will you please come and help my mama?"

"Okay, Victoria . . . slow down a second. Everything'll be alright." Mrs. Kirk ushered me into her home. "Let me get a couple things together, and we'll go, okay?"

I nodded—I was too out of breath to say more.

"Julianne," Mrs. Kirk turned to an older girl with beautiful long, golden hair. "I'm goin' with Victoria to see about her mama, and I want ya to look after Jacob while I'm gone. Your daddy oughta be back soon but, if he's not, feed Jacob some of that leftover ham for lunch. Tell Daddy I'll be home as soon as I can."

"Yes, ma'am," the girl said.

"Now, Victoria," Mrs. Kirk turned to me. "You sit tight for a quick second while I get my things together. Have ya had breakfast?"

"Yes ma'am," I lied.

"Okay, then. Just one more minute and we'll go." She nodded, then left the room in search of whatever necessities she'd need.

Waiting for Mrs. Kirk, I tapped my foot. It wasn't that I meant to be rude; I was really worried about Mama. I needed to get home. The second Mrs. Kirk returned, I nearly bolted out the door in my anxiousness.

"Victoria," she scolded. "Please slow down. These sidewalks are slick, and I'm not gonna get there any faster if I fall and twist my ankle. Your mama will be okay. I've helped bring dozens of babies with no problems."

I slowed my step to match Mrs. Kirk's slower stride, but inside I was an anxious wreck. So much time had passed since I'd left to find Dr. Heusman, and I didn't want Mama worried about me. More than that, I didn't know what bringing a baby entailed. The only thing I knew was I needed to get back to Mama. Reaching our house, I opened the door and raced inside. As quickly as I could, I removed Mama's wool cloak and boots, taking a moment to put them away properly. Though I was in a terrible hurry, I didn't want to make Mama unhappy with my carelessness.

Following my lead, Mrs. Kirk found a peg by the door for her cloak; then stomped her feet on the woven rug in the foyer, removing the excess snow from her boots. Taking her hand, I led her to Mama's bedroom where we found her in much the same way I had left her—her cheeks still flushed, her eyes closed, and her damp hair stuck to the sides of her head.

"Mama?" I whispered.

"Did ya find Dr. Heusman, baby?" She asked without opening her eyes.

"No, ma'am, but I brought Mrs. Kirk instead. Dr. Heusman's in Oklahoma City."

Mama opened her eyes. "Elizabeth—thank you for coming."

"Now, Anna. Ya know better than to thank me for comin'." Mrs. Kirk smiled then turned her attention to me. "Victoria, see if you can find me a big pot like your mama uses to make turkey soup. Fill it with water and put it on the stove to boil; then bring me some clean sheets and towels. I'm just gonna sit here and talk to your mama for a bit."

"Yes, ma'am," I responded, relieved to have another adult in the house.

Leaving the women to converse, I set off to do as I'd been asked. Mrs. Kirk would make everything alright. I just knew it!

The water was boiling steadily when Mrs. Kirk joined me in the kitchen. "Thank you, Victoria," she said, removing the pot from the fire. "I'll take care of things from here. Now you be a big girl and play quietly in your bedroom, okay? Your mama and I are gonna be busy, and I need ya to stay outta the way unless I call you. Can ya do that for me?"

I nodded and headed obediently toward my bedroom.

THE NEXT SEVERAL hours were the longest I'd ever lived through. I'd tried reading, but the words ran together, and I couldn't remember a single word.

The grandfather clock chimed from the living room, reminding me I'd missed lunch. It was now dinnertime, but I was too scared to bother Mama and Mrs. Kirk; so instead, I listened to the indistinct chatter of the two women in the master bedroom. Not loud enough to hear their words, their voices were calm and left me reassured everything would be okay. With nothing left to entertain myself, I crawled into bed and pulled my blankets high over the top of my head. My stomach growled, but I soon drifted off to sleep.

SOME HOURS LATER, Mama's high-pitched scream startled me from a deep sleep. Rubbing my eyes, I adjusted my vision in the darkened bedroom. Confused, I pulled back my curtains and discovered night had fallen. My stomach grumbled, but my hunger was forgotten as another scream pierced the silence. Without thought, I stumbled out of my room and raced to Mama's bedroom.

"Mama!" I threw open the door. "Mama? Are ya okay?"

Near the head of Mama's bed, Mrs. Kirk turned to me with flushed cheeks and eyes narrowed in concern. "Victoria, I'm gonna need some help. Will ya help me?"

I nodded, but my feet stayed rooted to the floor.

"Don't be afraid, sweetheart. C'mon over here next to me and hold your mama's hand. I just want ya to talk to her, okay? Use a soft voice."

"What do I say?" I asked, moving to her side.

"It doesn't matter. I just need ya to distract her with the sound of your voice. Tell her a story, maybe. What would she do to soothe you if you were sick?"

I thought for only a second. "She'd sing."

"Then sing to her. Don't be afraid—she'll be okay."

Taking Mama's hand, I hummed the strains of the Christmas song she'd sung to me the night before. At the sound of my voice, her eyes opened and she lifted her lips in a smile. "Victoria, darlin', you ought not be in here right now. Go on back to your room, please."

"No, ma'am. Mrs. Kirk needs me. I wanna help."

"Sweet girl." Her hand tightened in mine, and I waited while she breathed through another strong pain. "This isn't something you should see. Now be my big girl, and go back to your bedroom."

"No, ma'am." I shook my head. "I'm stayin'—I can help."

"Don't argue, Anna," Mrs. Kirk interrupted. "Ya don't have the strength, and I could use some help."

Mama stared between Mrs. Kirk and me for only a moment before nodding and closing her eyes again. "Fine."

For what seemed like hours, I sat next to Mama alternating between singing, retelling the stories we'd read in my books, and reminding her of my love. I talked until my mouth was parched and each word scratched like sandpaper on my throat; and I bit my lip in my own pain as she squeezed my hand each time a contraction gripped her in agony. She gave no indication she heard anything I said; instead she lay with her eyes closed, dozing in and out of consciousness, until the next pain overtook her.

Some time later, Mrs. Kirk turned to me, her eyes kind and almost apologetic. "Here we go, Victoria. Ready?"

I nodded, but I had no idea what I was ready for.

"Anna?" Mrs. Kirk turned back to Mama. "On your next contraction, I need ya to push, okay?"

"Yes," she replied. One word: a simple "yes."

In the next moment, Mama's stomach tightened and her body heaved as she pushed toward her goal.

"That's good, Anna," Mrs. Kirk encouraged. "Now, on the next one, I need ya to push harder and don't stop 'til I tell ya. Okay?"

"Okay," Mama replied. Again, just one word.

Mama's hand squeezed mine as another contraction seized her, this one sharper and more painful for both of us.

"Keep goin', Anna. It's almost here." Mrs. Kirk's voice was pitched high with excitement. "I can see its head. Keep pushin'!"

Mama pushed until it looked like there was nothing left in her, but she didn't give up.

"You're doin' real good, Mama!" I whispered.

When her belly relaxed, Mama fell back onto the bed. I prepared myself for her next contraction, but a chill went through me at Mrs. Kirk's next words.

"Oh, God." Her words were a frantic prayer. "Oh, God. Anna, ya gotta keep pushin'. Don't stop now—keep pushin'!"

"I can't," Mama cried.

"Ya have to! Sit up, Anna! Push! The cord's slipped out, and the baby's head's pressin' on it. I need your help—he'll die if we don't get him out right now. Push!"

Mama lifted her shoulders and let out a long, low groan as she pushed with everything she had in her. She pushed and heaved long past the point when she should've been out of strength; and, through it all, Mrs. Kirk issued orders in her strong, steady voice. Just when I thought it couldn't go on another second, my baby brother slipped into Mrs. Kirk's waiting hands.

"Oh, God," she whispered. "Please let him be okay—please let him be okay."

Moving efficiently, Mrs. Kirk cleaned the mucus from his mouth and nose, then tapped his feet and spanked his little bottom. I waited in the near silence, confused.

*Why isn't he crying?*

*Aren't babies supposed to cry?*

"Elizabeth?" Mama whispered.

Mrs. Kirk continued her ministrations without pause. Beside me, Mama let out a keening moan filled with so much grief the hairs on my arms stood straight up—but not a single sound came from my baby brother. He was gone—died before he'd ever entered this world; before taking his first breath; and likely while I was still lending Mama encouragement through those last contractions.

"I'm sorry, Anna," Mrs. Kirk whispered, but I don't think Mama heard her through her own cries.

Mrs. Kirk wrapped the baby in a soft cloth and handed him to Mama where, for the next hour, she refused to let him go. She lay there with my brother, singing him a lullaby tinged with so much sadness it hurt my heart to hear.

Mrs. Kirk approached Mama. "Anna, I need to take him and get him cleaned up."

Mama refused to let go. Screaming at Mrs. Kirk to leave her be, she thrashed in her bed until most of her blankets fell to the floor. Still she clutched the body of my baby brother tightly to her bosom.

With no other solution, Mrs. Kirk left the baby in Mama's arms, took my hand, and led me out of the bedroom. As the door clicked shut behind us, I once again heard the soft sounds of Mama's sad lullaby. For the last time, she sang to what remained of my baby brother.

"Victoria," Mrs. Kirk said. "I can't leave ya here by yourself with your Mama. She's not herself right now. I'm gonna need to stay the night to keep an eye on the both of you, then we'll figure out what to do in the morning. Is that okay?"

I nodded, secretly relieved. I'd never seen Mama the way she was that night, and I was scared. I gave Mrs. Kirk my bed then curled up on the floor with a pallet of quilts.

Neither of us slept that night, though we both did a good job of pretending for each other. Several times I was awakened as Mrs. Kirk sneaked from the room to check on Mama, each time returning only moments later with her head bowed and the weight of the world upon her shoulders.

# CHAPTER THREE

THE NEXT MORNING CAME EARLY. AFTER crawling out of my pallet, I padded down the hall toward Mama's bedroom, hoping the previous night had been a dream. I opened Mama's door to find her exactly as we'd left her the night before, my baby brother still in her arms. Seated beside her in a rocking chair was Mrs. Kirk.

I studied Mama, praying for signs of improvement, but little had changed. She uttered nothing more than a low keening. I stood statue-still, terrified of the woman in the bed. She looked like my mama; but the light in her eyes had dimmed, and the song in her voice had been silenced. She simply lay there, moaning the same dry note, over and over again.

"Anna," Mrs. Kirk approached Mama's bedside. "It's time to say g'bye. I'm so sorry, but I need ya to let me take the baby."

Mama didn't move, nor acknowledge she'd heard Mrs. Kirk.

"I'm gonna take him now, okay?" Mrs. Kirk whispered.

Still Mama didn't respond. Indeed, she seemed to not even realize Mrs. Kirk was in the room, much less talking to her.

Mrs. Kirk leaned over and gently pried the baby out of Mama's tight grip. For a moment, I thought she wouldn't let go; but then her arms dropped weightlessly to the bed, and Mrs. Kirk stood upright with the baby cradled in her arms.

"See now, Anna?" she whispered. "That wasn't so hard. Now, I'm gonna take good care of him while you rest, okay?"

Again, Mama didn't respond. She just stared blindly at some distant point on the wall.

Mrs. Kirk's lips tipped downward, and she let out a worried sigh. Then, with one end of the baby's small blanket, she covered his face and walked on quiet feet toward the door. Reaching my side, she took my hand and guided me out of the bedroom, closing the door behind us with a quiet click.

"Victoria," she whispered. "I need to prepare the baby for burial. D'ya think you could go find Reverend Patterson. I think we're gonna need his help with your mama. With Dr. Heusman gone, I'm not sure what else to do."

"Yes, ma'am. Is Mama gonna be okay?"

"I think so. She's had a terrible shock, and it's gonna take her some time to recover; but I'm hoping Reverend Patterson can help with that. And your daddy oughta be home soon, so that will help. For right now, she just needs some time to grieve."

I nodded my thanks, and headed toward my room to change my clothes.

*How could our world could change so quickly?* I wondered. One minute we were decorating for Christmas and excited about the pending birth of a baby, and the next minute, everything was taken away—stripped from us without warning. They had all said it would be okay—Mama, Mrs. Simmons, Mrs. Kirk—all of them!

*She'll be okay,* they'd said.

*Women have babies all the time,* they'd told me.

If that were true, why didn't my mama have a baby?

Changing into my dress and warm stockings, I was consumed by these thoughts. I didn't have any answers, and I didn't even understand enough to ask the right questions.

"Mrs. Kirk?" I said softly, closing my bedroom door behind me. "I'm leavin' now."

"Thank you, darlin'," she said.

Her back turned to me, Mrs. Kirk stood in our kitchen. My brother was nowhere in sight but, beside her on the table, was Mama's wicker laundry basket with a yellow crocheted blanket peeking over the side. Mama had completed the pattern only a few days earlier in anticipation of the baby's birth. Now, with no baby, we wouldn't need the blanket anymore. We would bury it with him, I guessed.

Tears misted my vision, and I swiped at my eyes. Without another word, I donned Mama's wool cloak and too-large boots, then stepped out into the cold winter morning.

ST. JOHN'S METHODIST Episcopal Church stood at the corner of Barker and Russell Streets, about seven or eight blocks from our home. While not the only church in town, it was the largest. It was also the best-attended among Mama's friends, and it boasted the most busybodies of any in our small town. The moment Reverend Patterson was summoned, every female member of the congregation would swoop in offering words of kindness and support. But I knew what each one really wanted was firsthand information they'd quickly pass along to others. I knew this because I'd seen it last summer when Jimmy Howard drowned in the North Canadian River. He and his brother had gone riding on the riverbanks when his horse got spooked, throwing Jimmy some distance. His neck broke when he landed, and the swiftly-moving water carried him away. A search team found his body two days later, several miles downriver in the next town over.

Sure as anything, the Howard home became a beehive of visitors. Curious church-goers descended in droves. Most came bearing food in exchange for information, and each departed with heavy hearts at the sad tale they would no doubt share. The same would happen with our family, I knew, but there was no help for it. Still, I walked slowly toward the Reverend Patterson's home, delaying the inevitable as long as possible.

Reverend and Mrs. Patterson lived in a tiny, white, one-story house on a small plot of land adjacent to the church. I hoped to find Reverend Patterson alone—the last thing I wanted was the prying ears of Mrs. Patterson or the congregation. Rounding the corner, I spotted the church ahead and realized my mistake. In all the turmoil, I'd forgotten it was Sunday. My stomach sank with dread. It would be impossible to speak privately with the reverend on a Sunday. I wavered. Should I leave and return later? No, I would sit through the service. At least if I stayed, I knew where I'd find Reverend Patterson.

I eased open the church door and slipped inside. A few heads turned to discover the identity of the latecomer but, having little interest in a child, they quickly returned their attentions to the sermon.

"So it was that Joseph and Mary, unable to find shelter at an inn, continued their journey until they came upon the only shelter available to them: a stable. A home for animals. Sheep and cattle." Reverend Patterson's baritone voice echoed throughout the room.

Breathing in a deep breath, I squeezed my hands into tight fists and waited impatiently for the sermon's end. To my dismay, Reverend Patterson enjoyed the sound of his own voice and he droned on for the longest time. I tuned him out, allowing my thoughts to wander. I thought about Mama and the day's service. Normally, we would've attended together. Mama loved Reverend Patterson's sermons, and looked forward to them all week. I closed my eyes, wishing I could turn back time. I wondered what the future would hold.

*When would Daddy get home?*

*What would he say about the baby?*

*Was Mama gonna be okay?*

Time ticked by slowly until Reverend Patterson called upon attendees to sing one last hymn. Standing with the congregation, I bowed my head; but, while Reverend Patterson asked God for peace, harmony, and the remembrance of the true meaning of Christmas, I prayed for Mama.

"Amen," said Reverend Patterson.

"Amen," repeated the congregation.

"Now shall we go forth with peace and joy in our hearts as we celebrate the birth of Jesus Christ our Savior. May God bless you, and keep you in good health and good cheer, this Christmas season." With those words, Reverend Patterson left the pulpit and walked to the back of the church where he greeted parishioners as they exited. Too scared to move, I waited on that bench until the last person left the church, and even then I sat, waiting.

"Victoria Hastings," Reverend Patterson said. "What a pleasure to see your face this mornin'. I must admit, I'm surprised to see ya alone. Where's your mama? Is she feelin' well?"

"No, sir." I shook my head. "Mama's not feelin' good, and I need ya to come with me to see her."

"What seems to be the problem?"

"Please, sir," I whispered. "I need ya to come with me right away."

A line formed between his bushy, gray eyebrows. "Ya can't tell me what the problem is?"

"Yes, sir, but please don't make me explain here. Mrs. Kirk sent me to fetch you since Dr. Heusman is outta town. She thought ya might be able to help."

"Well then, that sounds urgent. One moment while I let Mrs. Patterson know I'll be gone."

He stepped outside into the cold winter air and, within the minute, came jogging back in. Retrieving his heavy overcoat, he followed me out the door.

Neither of us spoke. I was too upset, and Reverend Patterson finally understood I couldn't be tempted to talk.

The walk home was miserable. At every corner and every intersection, we were waylaid by neighbors and friends offering greetings to Reverend Patterson. To his credit, he didn't dally. He just smiled, tipped his hat, offered brief greetings, and continued on his way.

Approaching my front door, Reverend Patterson reached for my arm and stilled my progress. "Victoria, I need ya to tell me what's wrong before I walk into that house. I don't need details, but I need some idea what I should expect. Can ya do that for me, please?"

I stared into Reverend Patterson's eyes for a long moment. It wasn't that I didn't want to tell him; it's that I wanted so badly to be brave. If I told him, I'd cry. Brave girls didn't cry. But I was only eight, and the battle was lost by the kindness shining from his brown eyes. Squaring my shoulders, I wiped away the first of my tears.

"My mama . . ." I inhaled a breath. "My mama had the baby last night. Mrs. Kirk—she came to help 'cause Dr. Heusman's gone."

I swallowed hard, but the tears continued heedlessly down my cheeks.

"Go on, Victoria—is the baby okay?"

"No, sir," I whispered. "The baby died. And Mama isn't actin' right. She wouldn't give the baby to Mrs. Kirk 'til this mornin'. And she won't talk. She just lays there starin' at the wall, not seein' anything."

"Oh, sweet girl." Reverend Patterson placed his arms around me and pulled me close. "I'm so sorry. Let's go inside and see what can be done. It'll be alright."

I nodded and opened the front door. Stepping inside, we found Mrs. Kirk pacing the length of the small sitting room.

"Victoria!" She rushed to my side and pulled me into her embrace. "Thank God you're back! You were gone so long, I was afraid somethin' happened!"

"I'm sorry." I stepped out of her embrace. "Reverend Patterson was givin' his Sunday sermon, and I had to wait 'til he was through before I could tell him."

"His Sunday—Oh gracious! Of course it's Sunday!" Mrs. Kirk turned to Reverend Patterson. "Thank you for coming, Reverend."

"Mrs. Kirk." He nodded. "I'd say it was my pleasure, but there's no pleasure in these situations. Tell me what's happened, and I'll see what I can do to help."

"Thank you," Mrs. Kirk replied then turned toward me. "Victoria, you've not eaten a thing since I've been here. I made some biscuits and gravy, and left them warming on the stove. Please eat while Reverend Patterson and I talk for a few moments."

"Thank you, ma'am."

Mrs. Kirk offered Reverend Patterson a seat in the sitting room while I went to the kitchen. Instead of eating, however, I stared at the gravy-covered biscuit and strained desperately to hear the conversation in the next room. In the end, their words were indistinct, but their concern was evident in the intensity of their mumbled conversation.

After several minutes, Mrs. Kirk led Reverend Patterson to Mama's bedroom where she left him inside and gently closed the door behind her. Returning to the kitchen, she sat beside me. Clearing her throat, she lifted a napkin from the table. "You must be very confused, Victoria, and maybe a bit frightened by all that's happened here since last night. Would ya like to talk about it, or ask me any questions?"

I pushed the biscuit through the congealed gravy and shrugged. "I don't know what to ask. I don't understand any of it. Why did the baby die? And why won't Mama talk? She doesn't even seem to know that people are in the room with her."

"Oh, darlin'," Mrs. Kirk sighed. "There was an accident when your baby brother was bein' born. It wasn't anything anybody did, and there was just no way to predict or prevent it. There's a cord connectin' the baby to the mother in the womb. It's how the baby gets food and oxygen. When he was bein' born, that cord slipped out before he did, and his head pressed against it, pinching it closed. It's a terrible, terrible thing that's happened."

Mrs. Kirk stared down at the table and dabbed her eyes with the napkin. When she looked up again, her eyes held almost as much sadness as Mama's. "These things almost never happen. I've delivered scores of babies with no problem. I just never imagined it might happen to one of mine."

"If Dr. Heusman had been here, could he've fixed it?" I asked.

She shook her head. "I don't know—maybe, but I doubt it."

I thought on her words, tossing them around in my brain and hoping to make some sense out of them. "Why won't my mama talk?"

Mrs. Kirk sighed again. "It's the brain's way of dealing with traumatic events. She looks awake, but her brain's asleep. She'll wake up when she's strong enough to handle it."

"So she won't be like that forever?"

She shook her head again. "I don't think so. When her heart doesn't hurt so much, her brain'll wake back up so she can think about everything again."

I thought on this for a long time while Mrs. Kirk waited for me to ask other questions. But I had no other questions. I only needed to know my mama would be okay.

"Okay," I said, standing.

Mrs. Kirk stood and opened her arms. As I stepped into the warmth of her embrace, the door behind me opened with an enthusiastic shove. Daddy stood in the doorway, a huge grin spread across his handsome face.

"Merry Christmas, darlin'!" The words had barely escaped when he noticed Mama's absence and Mrs. Kirk's stricken expression. His forehead creased as his gaze roamed back and forth between the two of us. "Elizabeth? Where's Anna?"

"Stephen." Mrs. Kirk cleared her throat. "There's been an accident. Anna went into labor last night, and there were problems with the delivery—"

"Anna!" Daddy headed toward their bedroom door.

"Stephen, wait!" Mrs. Kirk grabbed his arm before he could open the door. "Wait—let me finish! Anna's fine—I promise!"

Daddy jerked loose of her grip. "Then what? Where is she?"

Mrs. Kirk took a deep breath. "Anna's fine—that is to say the delivery doesn't appear to've harmed her, physically. But Stephen, the baby didn't make it, and she's takin' it pretty hard."

Daddy stiffened. "Didn't make it? Oh, God—I need to get to Anna."

"Yes—but wait!" She grabbed his arm again. "She's havin' a hard time copin'. It's like she's escaped inside her own head. She hasn't spoken a word since last night, and it took me 'til this mornin' before she'd let me take the baby."

"And ya left her alone?" he accused, turning back toward the bedroom door.

"Reverend Patterson's with her. I didn't know what else to do, what with Dr. Heusman gone. I thought maybe the preacher could help—he's been in there with her for about twenty minutes."

"Thank you, Elizabeth." Daddy said, his lips in a tight line.

"Daddy?" I whispered.

He stared at me a moment, almost as though he didn't recognize me. Then, collecting himself, he breathed out a breath and lifted his lips in a barely recognizable smile. "Victoria. C'mere and give your daddy a hug before I go in and say hello to your mama."

With a huge sob, I flew into his arms.

"It's okay, baby," he said, patting my back. "It's gonna be okay. I know it is."

Still embracing me, Daddy addressed Mrs. Kirk over my head. "Elizabeth, you've done so much for us already, but d'ya think maybe Victoria could go back home with you for a little while 'til we figure things out here?"

"Of course." Mrs. Kirk smiled and took my hand as Daddy released me. "Victoria, you've been such a big girl, and I'm so proud of ya—and I know your mama is too. Let's go back to my house, and you can play with Julianne and Jacob for a little while."

I couldn't form the words to thank her, so I nodded and followed her toward the door. As she opened the front door, I turned back and raced to my daddy once again. Wrapping my arms around his hips, I held on tightly. "I love you, Daddy."

"I love you, too, darlin'. Now go with Mrs. Kirk. I'll come get ya in a bit, okay?"

"Okay, Daddy."

Reluctantly, I returned to Mrs. Kirk's side where we paused only long enough to don our cloaks—Mrs. Kirk in hers, and I once again in my mama's. Then, together, we headed out the door.

# CHAPTER FOUR

MY BABY BROTHER, WHOM MY FATHER NAMED Stephen Andrew Hastings, was buried on December 23, 1913, in the El Reno Cemetery located at the farthest edge of town. Reverend Patterson led the service and, despite the frigid temperature, every person we knew came to pay respects. I stood between Mama and Daddy on that cold Tuesday morning, holding each of their hands within my own.

Mama hadn't spoken since the night of Baby Stephen's birth, and the silence in our home settled over Daddy and me like dark, heavy clouds in the hours before a storm. Mrs. Kirk and some ladies from the church took turns visiting our home, where they cared for Mama and cooked for Daddy and me, but Mama never acknowledged their presence. She did only as she was bid, and nothing more. Each morning, they helped her dress and spoon-fed her a bite or two of food, but she never uttered a single word, or even made eye contact with any of us. Mama's bright light had been extinguished.

In the days that followed, Mama spent most of her time in her rocking chair in our small sitting room. There she'd sit for hours, rocking back and forth, as though keeping tempo with a sad ballad.

*Creak-creak-creak-creak.*

The painful sound of the chair rocking in the silence of our home was almost more than I could endure.

Mrs. Kirk and Julianne often invited me to play at their house; but, no matter how hard they tried to engage me in games and painting, I never stopped worrying about Mama. When I was away from her side, I longed to be with her. Somehow I thought my presence could wake her. So I sat with her for hours, watching her rock back and forth in her chair, all while staring silently at the nothingness in front of her.

Completely lost in my thoughts, I was startled at Daddy's elbow nudging me to pay attention. Glancing around, I realized I not only hadn't heard a word Reverend Patterson had said, but I was the only one with my head not bowed in prayer. My face flamed, and I dipped my head.

"Our Dear Lord, Jesus Christ in Heaven," Reverend Patterson prayed. "Please wrap your arms around this precious child as we return him to you ..."

I closed my eyes and prayed a prayer of my own.

*Dear God, please bring Mama back to us. She's so sad, and I'm so scared. Please don't let her forget she still has me and Daddy. I promise I'll be good if You'll give her another baby. Or, please help me find a way to make her happy so she'll smile again. But please, God, bring my mama back to me.*

"In Jesus's name we pray. Amen," Reverend Patterson said, concluding his prayer.

"Amen," replied the mourners.

Daddy reached down to the pile of overturned earth next to the small hole where my brother's tiny coffin now rested. Scooping the red Oklahoma clay into his hand, he stood up straight and walked to the edge of Baby Stephen's grave. There he stood for a long moment, staring down at the tiny casket containing my baby brother. Reluctantly, it seemed, Daddy bowed his head and opened his palm over the casket. The sound of dirt sifting through his fingers and onto the closed casket below seemed to break him. Daddy wiped away a stray tear, leaving behind a smudge of the red earth on his cheek. With his hand now empty, he reached down a second time and scooped another handful of soil into his palm. Turning back toward Mama, he approached her slowly, as though careful not to frighten her. Mama stared straight ahead, not acknowledging his presence.

"Anna," he whispered. "Time to say g'bye."

Mama didn't move—she just stood there, staring far off into the distance. Daddy lifted one of Mama's hands and held it palm up within his own before slowly pouring the rust-colored grains from his palm to hers. Still Mama stood there, now with the Oklahoma dirt staining her hand. Daddy never showed impatience. Rather, he took Mama's free hand and rested it in the crook of his elbow before leading her over to the edge of the grave. Dropping her arm, he stepped away and returned to stand beside me.

We waited, wondering what Mama would do. Did she even understand what was expected of her? How far inside her own head had she hidden?

The funeral-goers filed away, allowing Mama privacy. Daddy and I stood waiting, watching for Mama's next move. After some time, she opened her tightly clenched fist and turned her palm face down. With her fingers now outstretched, she wiggled her fingers and released the last remaining evidence of earth between each digit. Dropping her arm, she turned toward Daddy and nodded—a silent communication signaling she was ready to go home.

As they turned toward me, a lone tear escaped and slid down Mama's pale cheek, and onto the wool of her dark cloak, where it quickly blended into the fabric and disappeared as though it had never existed. Without a word between us, I followed Mama and Daddy out of the cemetery and toward the awaiting wagon in the street nearby.

SANTA DIDN'T COME for us that year. As I got older, I realized Mama's grief left her incapable of playing the role. For Daddy's part, Mama's pain became his own, and he didn't have the heart to celebrate in the midst of so much heartache. December 25, 1913 came and went. There were no gifts under the tree, and no music filled our home. Our traditional Christmas feast consisted of the leftover food from our generous neighbors, brought to us in our time of grief.

# CHAPTER FIVE

THE DAYS FOLLOWING CHRISTMAS AND THE early weeks of 1914 were quiet in our home. Gone was the sound of Mama's voice and, with it, the joy I'd always known. Mama spent long hours each day in her rocking chair and, as the days passed, she showed small signs of joining our world once again. Though she never spoke, she sometimes smiled. Slowly, she shed the vacant expression that had come to define her after Baby Stephen's death. She was silent, but aware—going through the motions of life, doing what was asked of her, but nothing more. The way she navigated the world had changed entirely. She moved with calculated precision, leaving us with heavy hearts.

Daddy consulted with Dr. Heusman, whose only advice was to give Mama time. "Time will heal all," he'd promised. He wasn't concerned about her continued silence, instead considering the resumption of her old routine of caring for us and the home a good sign. He assured us Mama would return to normal by the next year. He made a lot of promises, and failed to keep any of them.

Despite Mama's supposed progress, Mrs. Kirk checked in with us daily, frequently inviting me to her home to play with Julianne. Sometimes I wondered if her invitations were atonement for Baby Stephen's death; but, regardless of her motive, I was happy to accept. Her presence soothed me, relieving the constant quiet and loneliness of my own home.

February arrived and Mama's melancholia remained, leaving Daddy desperate for a solution. For maybe the fourth time in as many weeks, I sat on the floor in the corner of Dr. Heusman's sitting room and pretended to play with my baby doll. In truth, I was listening to his conversation with Daddy.

"I don't know what more to do," Daddy told Dr. Heusman. "She's just not gettin' any better."

"I told ya, Stephen," the doctor replied. "Ya need to give her more time.

Losin' a baby is hard on everyone, especially the mother. Some just need longer to recover."

"I understand that. But it's been two months, and she still hasn't said a single word. Hell, she barely smiles much less acknowledges we're standin' right next to her. Somethin' just ain't right, and I can't keep leavin' Victoria home with her every time I go out on the tracks. There's gotta be somethin' more we can do."

"But she's made some improvement, Stephen. True, she's not talking; but she's takin' some interest in life. She's carin' for Victoria's and your needs, you said. That's progress."

"Yeah, she is. But I'm not sure it's enough. I can't shake this feelin' that if we don't do somethin' soon, all hell's gonna break loose."

Dr. Heusman thought for a moment before replying. "I'll tell ya what: I really think she just needs more time, but I can see you're worried. And, with things as they currently stand, I can see leavin' Victoria alone with her isn't a good situation. There's a sanitarium over near Norman. It might do her some good to spend some time there—maybe see some doctors who specialize in the type of melancholy she's experiencing."

"Norman," repeated Daddy. "That's what—forty miles?"

Dr. Heusman nodded. "About that."

Daddy ran his fingers through his hair. "Damn. That's a far piece. How long're we talkin'? Victoria can't stay home alone while I'm out workin'— that's even worse than stayin' home with Anna."

"Hard to say," said Dr. Heusman. "Best case scenario is just a couple months. Of course, it could be much longer."

Tapping his index finger against his upper lip, Daddy looked far off into the distance and tossed the idea around in his head. Squaring his shoulders, he focused his attention back on the doctor. "Okay—let's do it. I'll go by the Kirks' and see if they'll take Victoria for a spell. You can set things up with this place in Norman?"

Dr. Heusman nodded. "Shouldn't be too hard."

"Okay—let's get it done. The sooner we get Anna some help, the sooner we'll have her home. Ya sure this is a good place?"

"From all I've heard," Dr. Heusman replied. "They have the latest technology, and some of the best-educated doctors in the state."

"Okay, then." Daddy stood and extended his hand to shake the doctor's. "We'll talk in a couple days?"

Rising to his feet, the doctor met Daddy's hand with his own. "Yes. We should be able to get her moved by the end of this week—early next week at the latest."

Daddy nodded. "Much obliged to ya, Doc."

"Think nothin' of it."

Walking toward the door, Daddy motioned me to follow him. He held the door as I slipped outside, then followed behind until we reached the street. Side-by-side now, we walked a full block before either of us spoke.

"Victoria," he said. "Ya heard the conversation I had with Dr. Heusman?"

"Yes, Daddy."

He paused, as though trying to find his words. "Ya understand, darlin', that I don't wanna send your mama away, but this is the best thing for her? Norman's not as far away as it sounds. It's about a day's drive, but she won't be gone long—and we'll visit her. When she gets back, she'll be right as rain again."

"Can I go with ya to take her over there?"

"I don't think so, baby. I'd like ya to stay with Mr. and Mrs. Kirk, if they'll have ya. I won't be gone long."

"But I'll miss Mama, Daddy."

"Me too, baby. But ya want her to get better, right?"

"Uh huh." I bit my lip.

"Alright, then. Let's go see Mr. and Mrs. Kirk."

Hand-in-hand, we approached Mrs. Kirk's house. For the first time in weeks, my heart lifted. We were finally doing something. If Dr. Heusman was right, Mama would be back to normal by summer.

THE CONVERSATION WITH Mr. and Mrs. Kirk was short and took no convincing. In fact, Mrs. Kirk was relieved to know we were doing something. She and Mr. Kirk assured Daddy I could stay as long as necessary to see Mama well.

After saying goodbye, Daddy and I walked back toward our house. As we rounded the corner and caught sight of our front door, I pulled him to a stop. "Are we gonna tell Mama?"

Daddy nodded. "I think we should, don't you? It wouldn't be right to drop her there without warnin'. She needs to know it ain't permanent."

"D'ya think she'll be mad?"

Daddy scratched his jaw. "It's hard to know what your mama's thinkin' these days. But if the doctors fix her, she won't be."

Stepping forward, I wrapped my arms around my daddy's hips and hugged him tight. "I just want Mama to be okay."

"Me too, darlin'," he said. "Me too."

WHEN WE ARRIVED home, Mama was pulling a dinner roast out of the oven. Daddy and I sat down at the table then dug in the moment it was served. As usual, dinner was a quiet affair. With Mama not talking— and Daddy accustomed to Mama carrying the conversation—dinner had become an awkward thirty minutes each night. The sounds of our forks clinking against our plates echoed throughout the room, breaking the silence.

"May I please be excused, Daddy?" I asked when I'd completed my meal.

He nodded. "Yes, sweetheart. Why don't you go ahead and get your things ready for bed while I talk to Mama for a bit. When we're done, I'll come read with ya for a while."

"Okay, Daddy." I pushed my chair in and carried my dish to the sink before heading toward my bedroom.

Knowing Daddy planned to tell Mama about the sanitarium left me anxious. Instead of going to my room, I rounded the corner and knelt low behind the wall. Peeking at them, I watched Daddy rise and move closer to Mama. Lifting her hand in both of his own, he spoke softly. "Anna, honey, I'm worried about ya. Ya haven't spoken a word since Stephen Andrew's death, and I don't know how to reach ya. I don't even know what you're thinkin'."

Mama sat as still as a statue, staring at the table and saying nothing.

Daddy blew out a breath. "I saw Doc Heusman today. We don't want this gettin' any worse, and he thinks we should act now to get ya better. This sadness ain't good for ya, and it ain't for Victoria."

Mama's head remained bowed, still uttering not a single sound.

"There's a hospital over by Norman that specializes in melancholy," Daddy said, forging on. "We think it'd do ya good to visit there for awhile. They have doctors trained to help ya."

Still Mama said nothing.

Daddy lifted his hand toward her face and, with his index finger, tipped her chin so she was looking directly into his eyes. "Anna, I wanna help ya, but I don't know how. Gimme some sorta sign that ya wanna get better. Go to this place—please. Go for me, and Victoria. Get better for us. Will ya do that? Will ya try to get better?"

For the longest time, Mama sat staring at Daddy without any acknowledgment she understood. Finally, with the tiniest movement, she nodded. If I hadn't been watching so closely, I would certainly have missed it. But she did it—Mama had said yes!

I rose from the floor, careful to remain unseen, and eased my way toward my bedroom. Releasing a deep breath, I wrapped my arms around myself in relief. Mama was gonna get better! I closed my eyes and said a prayer.

"Thank you, God," I whispered. "Thank you!"


THAT NIGHT I slept better than I had since before Christmas. I dreamed pleasant dreams of Daddy playing his banjo while Mama and I danced around his feet. Mama's voice was clear and melodic as the room filled with the sweet strains of a long-forgotten song.

The music played through my head all night, and I awoke the next morning with a grin. After slipping from my bed, I padded on bare feet toward the kitchen. A shiver of excitement raced through me—it was the beginning of a new day, a new chapter! Mama would see a doctor and get the help she needed. Soon she'd be the Mama I'd known before that terrible night.

Except she wouldn't. As I rounded the corner to the main room, I came up short. There, hanging by a thin rope attached to the lowest beam, was my mama. Beside her, lying tipped over on the rug, was the stool I often used in the kitchen to help her with cooking. Her body hung like a rag doll, her eyes vacant, and her bare feet just inches from the floor.

A horrible scream pierced the silence. I later realized that awful howl was coming from me.

# CHAPTER SIX

IN THE WEEKS FOLLOWING MAMA'S DEATH, Daddy changed. Gone was the fun-loving, kind man I'd always known. In his place, was an angry stranger who drank to dull his pain. It was just like Mama but worse. They'd both left me behind; she for another world, and he for alcohol. Only weeks before, Daddy couldn't imagine leaving me alone while he worked the rails. Now he disappeared for days at a time. Sometimes he'd return in the dead of night, stumbling and stinking of stale sweat and alcohol. On those nights, I helped him to bed and hoped he'd sleep off his binge. I always thought he'd awaken the next morning ready to begin life once again, but he never did. Mama's death broke him in much the same way Baby Stephen's had broken Mama. By mid-morning, Daddy was always gone—back to the bottom of a bottle in whatever hellhole he spent his days and nights, never giving me an extra thought.

By spring, I was filthy, bedraggled, and hungry. My hair hung to my waist—unwashed, and knotted in tight snarls; and I was stealing food from neighbors late at night after their families were asleep. Even at eight, I was too proud to ask for charity.

Mrs. Kirk continued checking in on us once daily; but, with Daddy absent, I hid in Mama's bedroom and refused to answer the door. Mrs. Kirk would knock several times, sometimes trying the doorknob, which I kept locked. Other times, she'd peek through the windows, hoping to catch a glimpse of movement. But with no sign of life within our home, she always gave up and moved on her way.

May of 1914 arrived and brought torrential rains, causing the North Canadian and Cimarron Rivers to overflow their banks. Homes were flooded in the lower-lying areas, and entire wheat crops were destroyed. As the waters receded and families searched for lost loved ones and property, neighbors pulled together to return our town to rights. During this time, Daddy never came home. I hadn't seen him since before the rains came, and he never returned to check on me in the days after the flood waters receded. Two weeks later, a trio of boys out fishing on the banks of the North Canadian River found his bloated body floating downstream, some twelve miles from our home.

The discovery of Daddy's body ignited desperation in Mrs. Kirk. In the two weeks I was completely unaware of my father's death, Mrs. Kirk checked on me with increased persistence. Twice each day, she rapped on our front door, sometimes calling my name from beyond the safety of my home. I never answered—I was too scared.

Four days after Daddy's body was recovered, Mrs. Kirk rallied her husband and three neighbors to her aid. After banging on our door until it shook on its hinges, Mr. Kirk kicked it open. After a quick search, they found me squatting on the floor in Mama's bedroom, wedged between a side table and the wall. I was cold and shivering; but I sat there with my head tucked into my arms, hiding. I wore nothing but some flimsy underclothes and Mama's wool cloak, wrapped tightly around me.

# PART TWO

1924-1932

# CHAPTER SEVEN

AFTER DADDY DIED, JULIANNE KIRK BECAME my sister and best friend. When Mrs. Kirk found me squatting on the floor in Mama's bedroom, she and her husband adopted me as their own. I hated the idea of charity, but where else was I to go? My mother and father were dead, and I had no means of caring for myself. Mrs. Kirk blew in like a tornado, and accepted no argument. I was moved into her home that very day, and her family became mine.

Julianne was the perfect sister. We shared everything—clothes, secrets, and no end of trouble. But the years had transformed us into young women, and we both knew things could not stay as they were. Julianne had agreed to marry Earl Sykes, a local farmer whose land was approximately five miles northeast of town. I was excited for her, but I hated the idea of losing my best friend; yet another person leaving me behind. Despite my sorrow, I kept a smile on my face.

"Turn around a bit, Julianne," Mother Elizabeth (as I had come to call Mrs. Kirk) said with a mouthful of straight pins. "I can't seem to get the length on this hem right."

Julianne stood on a small stepstool in the middle of the kitchen. At her mother's request, she turned a quarter turn to her right. Placing one more pin at the hem near Julianne's ankles, Mother Elizabeth sat back on her heels and narrowed her eyes before turning her smile on Julianne. "That should just about do it, I think. Now, go on in and take this dress off so I can hem it. Victoria, go help her—and be careful not to drag it on the floor. We don't want it dirty before the weddin' on Saturday."

"Thank you, Mama." Julianne stepped off the stool and headed toward our bedroom.

Tears misted Mother Elizabeth's eyes. "Of course, darlin'."

I followed Julianne into the bedroom we shared, then unbuttoned the back of her dress and helped her pull it over her head.

"Three more days." Her eyes shone with excitement. "Three more days, and I'll be Mrs. Earl Sykes."

"Three more days, and I guess I'll have this bedroom to myself." I grinned.

"Oh, Victoria! Don't tease! I'm gonna miss ya somethin' awful, but I'm so excited to be gettin' married! Aren't ya the least bit excited about findin' some man and settlin' down? Maybe havin' a couple babies of your own?"

"No! I'm not like you, Julianne. I don't ever wanna marry, and I don't need children of my own. I can just be auntie to your babies."

"Oh, but you'll have to marry. You're eighteen now. Mama and Daddy are gettin' older, and ya can't live with them forever."

Through all the preparations leading up to Julianne's wedding, I'd never imagined my turn was next. I hid my fear behind a smile. "Oh, I don't know about that. Don'tcha think they'd like to keep at least one of us around to keep 'em comfortable in their old age?"

Julianne's eyes widened. "Surely ya don't mean that, Victoria! Ya know ya gotta get married."

"Oh really?" I quirked an eyebrow. "Why?"

"Because all young ladies must marry! Think of all the things you could do in your own home. Ya wouldn't have to do as Mama and Daddy tell ya anymore. You'd be your own woman—independent!"

"But then I'd have to do whatever my husband directs," I retorted. "How is that any better?"

Julianne grinned. "But what about when your husband is out doin' whatever it is men do? It'll be you making the decisions. You'll get to run things your way."

I hadn't thought of it that way. Could I really gain freedom through marriage? I had sworn off love, but I wasn't so sure it was integral to marriage. Could I make a man comfortable and, in return, gain some semblance of independence? It was worth considering.

OVER THE FOLLOWING days, I pondered the conversation I'd had with Julianne. I'd passed my eighteenth birthday, and many of the young women I knew were already married, or at least had a beau in mind. I didn't really want to marry, but I also didn't want to burden Mother Elizabeth and Father Caleb. They'd done so much for me already, didn't I owe it to them to move on and stop relying on their charity?

# CHAPTER EIGHT

THE MORNING OF JULIANNE'S WEDDING AR-
rived, and the house was a flurry of activity. Mother Elizabeth wanted everything perfect, and had planned every moment with exacting precision.
Nothing was left to chance, and I was committed to ensuring the same.

Julianne's gown was made of pure white linen with tiny cap sleeves,
a modest bodice ending in a dropped waist at her hips, and finished with
an elaborate floor-length lace overlay skirt. She had argued endlessly with
Mother Elizabeth over the length, insisting on the more modern mid-calf;
but Mother Elizabeth was scandalized at the idea, and would not be swayed.
Seeing Julianne now, I knew she'd been right—the floor-length skirt was
stunning.

In place of a traditional veil, Julianne wore a cloche hat with an oversized
brim wrapped with a long ribbon of linen that extended around the crown,
over the edge of the brim, and all the way down to her waist on one side.
Mother Elizabeth had argued for a traditional veil; but, having won the battle
of the hem, was resigned to cede victory to Julianne over the hat.

Escorted down the aisle by her father, Julianne's clear green eyes sparkled
with joy. Her excitement was tangible and, coupled with her natural beauty,
she was the most beautiful bride any of us had ever seen. My heart swelled
with joy on her behalf.

Waiting at the end of the aisle was her groom, Earl Sykes, with his best
man, Will Harrison, at his side. I knew Mr. Sykes well from his association
with Julianne, but I'd only briefly met Mr. Harrison a few weeks before in the
chaos of wedding preparations. As a result, we'd not had time for a proper
conversation. I studied him now, assessing his tall frame. At six feet and four
inches, Mr. Harrison was a good match for my own five-foot eleven-inch
frame; but otherwise, he was my polar opposite. Where I was pale-skinned

and lightly freckled with dark auburn hair, he was deeply tanned with thick hair the color of newly harvested wheat. Though some years older than myself, I found him quite handsome; and I'd heard from Julianne he was recently widowed with several children. Not that I was interested, but I wondered where those children were now.

I sneaked a glance at the groom. Mr. Sykes, like Mr. Harrison, was a handsome man. Though not nearly as tall, he still towered over Julianne's petite frame. His unruly hair was the color of sable, and the dark stubble on his cheeks implied that keeping a close shave throughout the day was difficult for him.

Julianne completed her journey down the aisle and was greeted by Reverend Patterson and a smiling Mr. Sykes. I retreated slightly with the best man so as not to detract attention from the bride and groom.

"Dearly beloved," Reverend Patterson bellowed. "We are gathered here, in the sight of God and these witnesses…"

The expression of pure pride on Julianne's face left me almost envious. I wondered what it was like to be so much in love, and to be loved the same in return. It wasn't something I ever expected to know firsthand, and it certainly wasn't something I sought. Mama and Daddy had both been victims of love lost and, standing there, I promised myself again I'd never suffer the same fate. I would never be broken, and I would not fail.

I was surprised out of my silent musings as Julianne turned my direction and extended her bouquet to me for safekeeping. Accepting it, I closed my eyes and inhaled the strong aroma of the orchids within the beautiful arrangement. Lifting my eyes, my gaze locked with Mr. Harrison's. With an arch of one eyebrow, he assessed me for a moment then tilted his lips upward into a teasing grin. Surprised, I turned my full attention back to the bride and groom, but was unable to stop seeing Mr. Harrison's smile in my mind.

*What did he find so amusing?*

*Was he laughing at me?*

As the ceremony concluded, I begrudgingly accepted Mr. Harrison's arm and, together, we followed the new Mr. and Mrs. Earl Sykes back down the aisle and out the sanctuary doors. When we reached the narthex, I stepped back and removed my hand from the crook of his elbow.

"Thank you," I said politely. "If you'll excuse me…"

With a small tip of my head, I escaped into the crowd of wedding guests departing the church.

THE RECEPTION FOR Julianne and Mr. Sykes was held on the back lawn of our home. Mother Elizabeth and several neighbor ladies had created a sumptuous meal for all to share, and an area in the far back corner of the yard had been cleared and designated for dancing. It had been some time since our last town social, and Julianne's wedding reception gave the young men and women an excuse to make eyes at each other. I wasn't interested in any of that for myself, but I found great amusement watching many of the young ladies make fools of themselves as they attempted to gain the attention of the young men nearby.

"What, I wonder, must you be thinkin', Miss Hastings?" A deep baritone voice wrenched me out of my silent musings.

"Mr. Harrison!" My hand flew to my chest, and covered my pounding heart. "Ya startled me!"

"I can see that." He grinned. "But tell me: what in the world is on that brain of yours? You're studyin' Miss Barker and Mr. Hurst with quite a lot of intensity—and no small amount of amusement, I might add."

"I can assure ya I'm doin' no such thing," I replied. "I'm simply enjoyin' the reception. And you? What do you find so amusin'?"

Mr. Harrison gazed at me, his lips lifted in amusement, as though we were sharing some secret. "I was just wonderin' whether ya planned to stand here on the sidelines all night, or if ya were gonna dance. I can't imagine you've not been asked. So tell me, Miss Hastings, why aren't ya dancin'?"

"I'd rather not," I stated simply.

"And why is that?"

"Mr. Harrison." I blew out an unladylike breath. "You ask a lot of questions for a gentleman I hardly know. Now, if you'll excuse me."

I turned to make my escape, but was brought up short by Mr. Harrison's deep laugh. Turning, I opened my mouth to give him a piece of my mind, but he surprised me by throwing his hands palm-up in a gesture of defeat.

"Ah." He grinned wider. "Now I see."

"What d'ya see?"

"Why ya aren't dancin'."

I narrowed my eyes. "I beg your pardon?"

"I said, Miss Hastings, I begin to understand why you're not dancin'."

My irritation rising, I crossed my arms in front of me. "And why is that, d'ya suppose?"

"Because you intimidate all the young men here. They're all just boys. They don't know what to do with a young woman who knows her own mind."

My jaw dropped and I stood there, mouth agape, unable to utter a rejoinder. Flustered, I threw my shoulders back and feigned irritation. "If you'll excuse me, Mr. Harrison, I should see if Mother Elizabeth needs my help with anything."

I'd barely taken two steps when Mr. Harrison's fingertips snagged my elbow, and I was pulled gently back to his side. "Now I've offended ya," he said in my ear. "I'm sorry. That wasn't my intent. It was a compliment."

"A compliment?" I shook his hand from my arm. "That was the least flatterin' 'compliment' I believe I've ever received."

"Dance with me," he said, his grin mocking.

I lifted my chin. "No, thank you."

"C'mon, Miss Hastings. Just one dance. I don't bite."

I narrowed my eyes, trying to discover what he was playing at.

"Simply a dance." His voice, now softened, was almost a plea. "Would ya do me the honor? Please?"

"I—I'm not a very good dancer," I admitted, my own voice now softening.

"And neither am I. I'll tell ya what: you dance on the tops of my feet, and I'll dance on the bottom."

Surprised, I laughed. "Very well, then. But just this once—and only because ya said 'please.'"

Mr. Harrison extended his arm then escorted me to the area designated for dancing. I wasn't lying when I said I was a bad dancer. I was terrible; but dancing with Mr. Harrison made me feel graceful, even refined.

Dancing and talking at the same time proved impossible for me, but Mr. Harrison was a gracious partner and allowed me silence to concentrate on the steps. As the song ended, he escorted me to the refreshment table and offered me a glass of lemonade.

"I'd like to call on ya sometime, Miss Hastings," he said over the rim of his drink.

I shook my head. "I'm not sure that's a good idea, Mr. Harrison. But I do thank you. I've surprisingly enjoyed our conversation and the dance."

"I, however, think it's a wonderful idea. But tell me, Miss Hastings, why do you find the idea unappealin'?"

"Oh, I didn't say I found the idea unappealin'," I clarified. "I simply said I'm not sure it's a good idea."

"Okay, then. Why do ya think it wouldn't be a good idea?"

"Mr. Harrison, you're an attractive man, and I thank you for your attention. And, while you're considerably older than I am, you're still young. You've lost your wife recently, and I'm truly sorry. But I'm guessin' ya plan to remarry someday, and I have no wish to marry at all."

"How very candid of ya, Miss Hastings." His lips twitched, but he fought back the smile. "If you weren't standin' but two feet in front of me, I'd've sworn you were the young man and I the woman."

I bit my lip, trying to hold back my own grin. "It wasn't my intent to shock ya, but I see no point in bein' anything but honest. I have no intention of marryin', so there's no reason for ya to call."

"But I enjoy your company, Miss Hastings. Would you really say no to our becomin' friends?"

"I'm quite sure ya have enough friends, Mr. Harrison," I said, my own smile now mocking. "Now if you'll please excuse me. Thank you for the dance."

Mr. Harrison lifted an eyebrow, but took a step back, allowing my escape. "Until next time, Miss Hastings."

# CHAPTER NINE

TWO WEEKS AFTER JULIANNE'S WEDDING, I
was searching for ripened vegetables in Mother Elizabeth's garden when Mr.
Harrison unexpectedly called upon me. I'd just pulled several tomatoes off a
vine when Jacob, now thirteen, raced outside to inform me of our guest.

"Victoria," he said. "Mama said to come quick. You've got a guest."

"A guest?" I asked.

"Yeah. A gentleman's come callin' on ya. He brought flowers."

"Flowers?"

Jacob rolled his eyes. "Yeah. Flowers! Now, c'mon. Mama said to come
quick. The gentleman's waitin'."

I handed the basket of tomatoes to Jacob. "Would you please take these
into the kitchen for me? I'll be right behind ya."

Grabbing the basket from my hands, he raced into the house.

"Don't slam the screen door!" I called out as Jacob released the door, leaving it to slam against its frame.

Alone now, I brushed the dirt and dust from my hands and followed him
through the back door and into the kitchen, closing the door gently behind
me. My heart pounded in my chest, and I wasn't sure why I was so anxious. I
wasn't at all interested in entertaining a suitor, yet a thrill of excitement and
nervous energy raced through me.

Pausing in the kitchen, I wiped my hands on a damp dishrag from the
countertop and smoothed my windblown hair with my fingertips. With no
mirror handy, I studied the shadow of my reflection in the glass pane of the
kitchen door. Deciding I was as presentable as could be expected on short
notice, I pulled in a deep breath and followed the voices to the sitting room.

I recognized Mr. Harrison's voice before my eyes landed on him. Seated
to the left of Mother Elizabeth, he stood the moment I entered the room.

"Miss Hastings." His eyes smiled as he walked toward me. "It's lovely to see you again. Please forgive the intrusion; I was in town and hoped to find ya at home."

"It's no intrusion at all, Mr. Harrison," I replied. "D'ya come to town often?"

He shook his head. "Not often enough, I'm afraid. I live about five miles northeast of town, over near Earl Sykes, and I don't have nearly enough occasion to come into town. But I was here, and couldn't resist stoppin' in to say hello."

"We're glad ya did, Mr. Harrison!" Mother Elizabeth interjected.

My face flushed with heat and I cleared my throat. "Please—won't ya sit down?"

"Thank you." Instead of sitting, he advanced toward me and extended a lovely arrangement of wildflowers he'd been holding. "But first, these are for you."

"They're beautiful," I said, taking in the delicate yellow petals of the black-eyed Susans.

"They reminded me of you, and I couldn't resist," he said.

My eyes flashed to his just in time to catch his subtle wink. Surprised, I stood there unable to form a reply.

*They reminded him of me? Whatever does he mean?*

I must've stood there too long without responding because I was startled by the not-so-subtle clearing of Mother Elizabeth's throat.

"Oh!" My face heated again. "Thank you for the flowers. Please—let's sit down."

Mr. Harrison returned to the seat he'd vacated, and I selected another directly across from him, though some distance away. We talked briefly about the weather and the coming wheat harvest, when I remembered he'd mentioned living close to Julianne's new husband.

"Mr. Harrison," I said. "You mentioned living near Mr. Sykes's homestead. Are ya near enough to visit with him and my sister often?"

"Yes, of course," he replied. "Our two properties are adjacent, with our homes not more than about a mile apart. Your sister was just by earlier this week to bring me some eggs. They have far more layin' hens than they can use, so they bring me their extras so they don't go to waste. In return, I usually send one of the kids over with a gallon of milk for them, since my cows put off enough milk for a couple families."

"And how is Julianne?" Mother Elizabeth asked.

"She's doin' right fine, Mrs. Kirk," he replied. "I must admit, marriage seems to agree with them. I don't recall ever seein' Earl happier, and your daughter seems happy as well. I think they've made an agreeable match."

"That's good to know." She smiled. "We've yet to make the trip out there. Soon, I hope. The house seems so quiet without her."

"I'm sure it does." Turning to address me, Mr. Harrison said, "Miss Hastings, I wonder if ya might take a walk with me? Maybe just a short walk down to Legion Park? It's not far and, after sittin' in that wagon for the drive on up here, I could sure use a chance to stretch my legs for a bit."

"That sounds like a wonderful idea," exclaimed Mother Elizabeth. "Victoria?"

Caught between the two of them, I couldn't decline; and, judging by the twinkle in Mr. Harrison's eyes, he'd trapped me on purpose. I rose from my seat and graced him with an icy glare. "Of course—I'd be delighted."

Mr. Harrison rose from his seat and extended his arm for my escort, then turned to Mother Elizabeth. "Thank you for the coffee, Mrs. Kirk. We shouldn't be gone long."

"Oh, please!" She waved a hand in dismissal. "Take your time, and enjoy yourselves! It's beautiful out today! When ya return, ya must have dinner with us, Mr. Harrison."

My body tensed. The last thing I wanted was to spend an extra minute in Mr. Harrison's presence. I'd already told him I wasn't interested in a suitor, yet here he was calling on me despite my wishes.

Sensing my reluctance, he shook his head. "Thank you, ma'am, but I must pass this time. I'm needed home in a few hours. Mind if we try for another time?"

"Of course." Mother Elizabeth smiled warmly. "Y'all two take your walk and have fun. We'll plan for another time."

"G'day, Mrs. Kirk."

MR. HARRISON AND I walked the four blocks to Legion Park without a single word between us. Though it wasn't an awkward silence, it felt as though we'd left a lot unspoken. As we approached the park, I stopped and stepped away from him to put some space between us.

"Mr. Harrison," I began. "I'm not sure what your intentions are in callin' upon me this afternoon. Ya must realize you've placed me in a difficult position."

He lifted one eyebrow. "What position is that?"

"Mr. Harrison, when we spoke at the weddin', I assumed that would be the last time. I asked ya not to call on me."

"No, Miss Hastings." He shook his head. "Ya did no such thing. Ya only said it was a bad idea. On the contrary, I thought it was a wonderful idea."

I blew out a breath. "You knew what I meant, Mr. Harrison. Ya must realize the difficult position you've now placed me in."

"I'm not sure I do."

"Then allow me to be more clear. Gentlemen don't call upon ladies to simply be friends. So I have to assume you're here as suitor, even though I already told ya I'm not plannin' to get married. Ya must realize what Mother Elizabeth thinks!"

"Miss Hastings, you've said this before. What ya haven't said is why. How is it that a beautiful young woman of your age isn't interested in marriage?"

I tipped my chin up. "That's really none of your business, Mr. Harrison."

Any other gentleman would've allowed the conversation to end there and apologized for prying. Not Mr. Harrison; he wouldn't stop until he had answers.

"You're right. It's not my business. But I'd still like to know. Will ya explain it to me?"

I looked away, my heart clenching. I remembered the love my mama and daddy had shared, and the way their spirits were broken by the loves they'd lost. "I prefer not to."

Mr. Harrison closed the space between us and touched his thumb and forefinger to my chin, forcing me to meet his gaze. "Victoria, please tell me. I wanna know."

Perhaps it was the softness of his voice, or maybe it was the use of my given name, but something in me wanted to share with him my greatest secret and the pain of my past. Not sure how to explain myself, I spoke slowly and considered my words. "Marriage needs love to be successful, and I don't ever wanna be in love."

I expected Mr. Harrison to laugh, or at least scoff at my words. Instead he narrowed his eyes. "Why not? Never is a very long time, and you're still so young with so much life yet to experience."

"Love makes the strong weak, and I refuse to ever be weak again."

"Whatever gave ya that idea?" His eyes softened as he tucked a stray lock of hair behind my ear. "Love can be empowering. It can make ya feel invincible."

"Maybe. But the loss of love can break the spirit. It can make even the strongest weak. I won't be weak. I can't."

Mr. Harrison studied me a moment before replying. "You're referring to your mama and daddy."

Tears gathered behind my eyes, so I closed them. I had to gain control of my emotions. I hadn't cried since the first few days after my mama's death, and I would not cry now. Breathing in a deep breath, I opened my eyes and looked directly into Mr. Harrison's.

"Yes," I replied.

Leading me to a nearby bench, he offered me a seat then sat beside me on my left. Taking both of my hands, he looked deeply into my eyes. "I knew your mama and daddy—both of 'em, though not well. I was a few years younger than your daddy, but my older brother, Atticus, was great friends with him when they moved here. Your mama was never a strong woman. She never should've been brought to such a harsh land. She was raised to decorate a sitting room, not suffer the hardships of this new state. She was delicate; like a gardenia—beautiful as it grows in the garden, but bruises easily by the human hand. When plucked from a bush, it wilts quickly. When tended carefully and patiently, it flourishes; but, if planted in the wrong soil, it won't thrive. Your mama was much like that. She was a city girl from an affluent family, and wasn't suited for the harsh life we have here. She required careful handling, and your daddy did his best. You, on the other hand, are like the black-eyed Susans I brought for you today. I said they reminded me of you, and I meant that. You're strong, yet beautiful. Ya overcome adversity, only to be stronger for it. Like the black-eyed Susan, you can thrive in any soil. When the fields are barren, and no other flower will bloom, the black-eyed Susan rises from the earth and overtakes the barren land. You have that same strength, Victoria."

"What makes ya believe that?" I asked. "Ya barely know me."

"It's true we've only just met, but I've watched ya from afar for many years. I remember when Mrs. Kirk retrieved ya from the home you'd shared with your mama and daddy. You were filthy and far too skinny, but I could see you were a survivor. You were only about eight and had clearly been on your own for several months, but ya refused to ask for help. You were too strong. Ya saw your mama die by her own hand, then your daddy's self-destruction; but ya refused to be defeated. I admired the child ya were then, and I admire the woman ya are today. Adversity makes many people weak. You, on the other hand, are challenged by it. Overcoming adversity gives ya greater strength."

Embarrassed at his words, I looked away. "Thank you."

"I wonder, Victoria, whether you've considered that sometimes marriage is more than strictly about love. While love is important, I'd argue that mutual respect may be more important. Many great marriages have been built on less. But more than that, there's a lot you and I could do for each other."

I lifted my gaze back to his. "How d'ya mean?"

"I'm forty-one. I'm still young enough that I'd like to remarry and live comfortably with someone by my side. I have five children—two sons and three daughters—and I need help raisin' them. My parents and sister-in-law live nearby, but that's not enough. I need the daily influence of a woman. I need a wife to take my children, treat 'em with kindness, and raise 'em as her own. I need you, Victoria. I want them to have your strength and indomitable will. I need my children—my daughters, especially—to know they can make their way in this world, confident in the knowledge they determine their own destinies. I know ya can do that, because I've seen ya do that for yourself."

"And these children of yours? How old are they? Surely they must be close to me in age."

"Caroline, my oldest, is fourteen. Olivia is next at twelve. Then come the twins, Joseph and Daniel, at ten; and, finally, Catherine is seven. True, you're nearly the same age, but your maturity is far older than your years. I think you'd do us all a great service by settin' an example for the girls," he explained.

"And how would I benefit? I'm happy as I am. I have no children, and my only responsibilities are to Mother Elizabeth and Father Caleb."

"Victoria," he said softly. "Ya do understand you'll be expected to marry soon, don'tcha? If your parents haven't begun searchin' for a husband, they soon will. Wouldn't it be better to choose your own, rather than be forced to marry some man you could never respect? Would ya prefer a man who lies down and allows ya to walk all over him, or one who challenges your spirit and engages your mind? As my wife, you'd have the independence to do mostly as ya please—provided ya neither embarrass me, nor ignore my needs. I spend most days in the fields, as the farm is my livelihood. Once the needs of the home are met, you're free to do as ya wish. As we've discussed, your sister is only a mile from me. You could visit regularly. When she begins her family, as I suspect she will soon, you can help bring her children into the world. You can support each other through difficult times."

"I see." I cleared my throat. "It seems you've given this a lot of thought."

"I've thought of little else since meetin' ya at your sister's weddin'."

"But why me? Surely there are others who could fill this position easily."

"I'm sure there are, but I find myself quite likin' ya. You make me laugh, and ya challenge me to stay on my toes. I suspect ya won't take any guff, and my children would be in capable hands."

"Children," I said, thinking aloud. "What about children? Would ya require more, or are the five ya have already enough?"

"I hadn't given that any real thought, to be honest. But, no. I wouldn't require more children, but children are sometimes the natural consequence of marriage."

"I see. But, as I've said before, I'll never fall in love. I can't give ya the love ya deserve, and I'm certain ya must want."

"I can live with that. I've loved once before. I'd be a very lucky man to be loved a second time, so I neither seek it nor expect it. No, I believe we'd complement each other well, and that our partnership would be very beneficial for us both. So what d'ya say, Victoria? Marry me."

"Mr. Harr—"

"Will. Whether ya marry me or not, we've shared too much today to continue with formalities. Now, give me the answer I want. Marry me, Victoria."

"Will," I said. "I don't know. I need some time to think. As I said, we barely know each other. I don't know anything about your children, aside from their ages and genders. Really, I know nothin' about you. I'll need time to consider."

"Very well, then." Will nodded. "I'll be back in town in about two weeks to get ready for harvest. I'll call on ya then. In the meantime, I want ya to think about all I've said. Will ya do that?"

I nodded. "Of course. But I can't make ya any promises."

Satisfied, Will stood and extended his hand to help me stand beside him. With a smile, he said, "Two weeks, then."

With those final words, we strolled back toward my home, once again walking in silence. When we arrived, Will stopped and turned me toward him. Staring into my eyes, he lifted my chin with his forefinger until it was impossible for me to look away. "I'll be back, Victoria. Two weeks, and I'll expect a yes." Then, without permission, he leaned down and placed a chaste kiss upon my lips.

Staring and dumbfounded, I watched him walk away without a backward glance.

# CHAPTER TEN

Mr. Harrison's visit left me confused and anxious. I'd never planned to marry, yet I was seriously considering his proposal. Was it possible to marry without love?

I opened the front door and looked around for Mother Elizabeth. I found her in the kitchen, completing preparations for our evening meal. On the kitchen table, neatly arranged in a glass vase, were the flowers Will had given me. Mother Elizabeth had trimmed the stems, allowing water to move freely through the stalks.

"Victoria, you're back." She smiled.

"Yes." I sat at one end of the table, hoping she would join me. "Thank you for arrangin' the flowers. They look beautiful."

"You're very welcome. I was surprised to see Mr. Harrison come for a visit. You must've made quite an impression on him at the weddin'."

"It would seem that way."

Mother Elizabeth studied me, then removed her apron. Reaching out, she collected my hands into her own and took a seat across from me. "Ya seem upset."

"Not upset, exactly." I shook my head. "Confused is a better word."

"Did Mr. Harrison say somethin' inappropriate, Victoria?"

"No. Not inappropriate, exactly. Just surprisin'."

Mother Elizabeth smiled. "Would ya like to tell me? Maybe I can help."

I was torn with indecision. It seemed like something too personal to share until I'd made a decision, but I knew Mother Elizabeth wouldn't judge. Coming to a decision, I said, "He asked me to marry him."

Never one to easily mask her thoughts, Mother Elizabeth's face lit up with excitement, and I erupted in a burst of unexpected giggles.

"Well, Victoria! That's—that's certainly a surprise," she said. "I'd known you'd danced together at the reception, but I wasn't aware you'd spent so much time together that afternoon to become so well acquainted."

"We didn't actually. We spoke for several minutes before we danced, then for several minutes afterward; but I can't honestly say we became well-acquainted."

"But he's asked ya to marry him. Did ya give him an answer?"

"No—I didn't know what to say. I asked for time to think on it, and he said he'd call again in two weeks. But I know he's expectin' me to say yes."

"And how d'ya feel about that?"

"I'd sworn never to marry," I admitted.

Mother Elizabeth's eyes widened. "What d'ya mean you'd sworn never to marry?"

I looked away, unable to explain once again in the same day. "What should I say to him?"

Choosing not to push the subject, Mother Elizabeth drew in a deep breath. "Well, I s'pose it depends on how ya feel. D'ya love him?"

I shook my head. "No. But I don't love anyone, and I don't expect I ever will. I can't. It's not in me. It's not who I am."

"Oh, Victoria." Mother Elizabeth frowned. "Whatever gave ya that idea? You're the most loving young woman I know. You've loved Father Caleb and me well these last ten years, and I know ya love Julianne and Jacob. You love the children ya teach at church every week. I can tell."

"Those are a different kind of love. I'm talkin' about the love between a wife and husband. That I can't do. I just won't."

"I see. Does Mr. Harrison know this?"

"He does." I nodded.

"And he still wants to marry ya?"

"He says he does."

"How d'ya feel about that? Are ya tempted to agree?"

"I don't know!" A headache was forming behind my eyes, so I squeezed the bridge of my nose between two fingers to offset the pain. "I thought I knew what I wanted. I thought I knew I'd say no, but he made it sound so easy—like it'd be some sort of cure-all."

"I see," she said again.

Mother Elizabeth and I sat for a long time, neither of us speaking. Finding my words, I said, "He said he likes my strength and my spirit. He said I'd be a good example for his daughters."

"Well, Victoria, all I can say is that we've known Mr. Harrison for years, and he's a good man. He comes from a good and well-respected family. His mother's a challenge, but whose isn't? I've known his brother, Atticus, since we were children. They're all good people."

"He said his farm is about a mile from Julianne. If I married him, I'd be close enough to visit her regularly."

She nodded. "Yes. I believe his folks live about a mile or so in the other direction with his brother and sister-in-law, Veronica. I think I'd heard Old Man Harrison claimed the land in the original Land Run of '89 then divided it for the two boys when they married. He and Old Mrs. Harrison lived with your younger Mr. Harrison for a while until he married. Rumor was your Mr. Harrison's wife and his mother were unable to live under the same roof. It was quite the story when Old Man Harrison and his wife moved down the road to live with Atticus and Veronica."

"D'ya know anything about his children?" I asked.

"Not much." She shook her head. "The boys are typical boys; always looking for mischief, but good boys overall. The girls, as I recall, are pretty little things. Somewhat timid, though, if memory serves."

We sat in silence for several minutes, each of us mulling over the situation and the information she'd given me. Finally, Mother Elizabeth stood and swiped invisible crumbs from the table. "Well, Victoria, it seems ya have a lot to consider in these next two weeks. I'm here, if ya wanna talk; but I can't make your decision for ya. Just know I'm always here, and I love you. You'll make the right decision, I feel certain."

Standing, I gathered the vase of flowers in my arms and carried them to my bedroom. I had a great deal of thinking to accomplish, and not nearly enough time to get it done.

# CHAPTER ELEVEN

THE FOLLOWING WEEKS FLEW BY, AND MY two-week reprieve was almost at an end. We still hadn't seen Julianne and Mr. Sykes. Mother Elizabeth decided we'd give it two more weeks, then we'd make the trip out to see them. She'd been patient enough, she declared. She needed to see her daughter was in good health.

As the second week passed, the black-eyed Susans died and the petals fell off, scattering onto the dresser and down to the floor. Somehow I couldn't make myself throw them out. Instead, I collected the delicate petals, placed them within a folded sheet of waxed paper, closed them within the deep confines of Mama's Bible, and buried them in the back of my wardrobe next to Mama's woolen cloak.

True to his word, Will Harrison returned exactly two weeks after his first visit on a beautiful Saturday afternoon in May. Mother Elizabeth and I were sewing curtains to replace the time-worn ones hanging in the kitchen when we were startled by a knock on the door. Mother Elizabeth's eyes met mine, and I held my breath as she excused herself to answer the door. Moments later, she returned.

"Victoria," she said softly. "Mr. Harrison is here to call on ya."

I sat there, dazed for a moment. The time had come for me to announce my decision. In my mind, I knew what I'd decided; but I wasn't sure I'd be able to follow through with the decision I'd made.

Rising from behind the sewing machine, I smoothed the wrinkles from my skirt and moved toward the sitting room where Will awaited my arrival.

"Miss Hastings." Will stood in the foyer and assessed me. "Ya look lovely."

"Mr. Harrison." I nodded. "Thank you."

Stepping forward, Will handed me another stunning bouquet. "These, of course, are for you."

I smiled, remembering the last time he'd given me these same flowers. "Black-eyed Susans."

His eyes twinkled, and the right side of his lips tipped up in a half smile. "Yes. I believe I mentioned they seem to suit ya."

Holding back my own grin, I waved my hand toward the closest chair. "Thank you. Please have a seat."

Will sat on the chair nearest Mother Elizabeth, and I sat directly opposite him.

"Mr. Harrison," Mother Elizabeth said. "May we offer you some refreshment?"

"No, ma'am, but thank you. I'd actually hoped I might take Miss Hastings out for another walk, if she's up for it." Turning his attention to me, he asked, "Would ya like to take a walk, Miss Hastings?"

"Yes, I believe I will," I replied. "Mother Elizabeth, d'ya mind?"

"Not at all," she replied. "Please—go and enjoy yourselves."

Like before, we said nothing on our walk toward Legion Park, only this time the silence was oppressive. Will was clearly waiting for me to speak, and I wasn't sure what I was supposed to say. As we approached our destination, however, I found my voice.

"Mr. Harrison," I began. "Why is it ya always require me to break the silence when we're together?"

Will grinned a slow smile but said nothing for the longest time, leaving me edgy in the silence. Finally turning to me he said, "I wondered how long it'd take ya to say somethin'."

We'd now reached the park and found the bench we'd shared on our last visit. Will swept his arm forward and offered me a seat. I sat, my shoulders tense, while I waited for him to take his seat beside me.

"So then, Victoria," he said. "You've had time to consider my proposal?"

I nodded. "I have."

The silence stretched between us, each of us waiting to see who would concede defeat and speak first.

"And?" Will lifted a mocking brow. "D'ya plan to leave me in suspense?"

I bit my lip to keep from smiling "Well, before I can answer, I have some questions."

"Of course ya do, Victoria." He laughed. "Okay, then. How can I help?"

"First, I'd like to know about your children. What can ya tell me about them? How long has it been since they lost their mother, and how do they feel about gaining a stepmother? Especially one nearly their own ages?"

Will thought for a long moment, his gaze turning out toward the pond in the distance. When I thought he wouldn't answer, he turned back toward me. "In all honesty, I haven't discussed it with them, so I have no idea how they feel. Really, how they feel isn't important. At some point, they'll all leave to pursue their own lives, and I have no intention of livin' the remainder of my life alone and without companionship. So it's really not their concern."

I shook my head. "I disagree with you, but that's a fair answer. How long has it been since they lost their mother?"

"Fifteen months. Hannah—their mother—was ill for the longest time after Catherine's birth. I'm not sure she ever completely recovered, and the hardships of farm life didn't agree with her; especially in her weakened state."

"I see. What are the hardships of livin' on a farm? I've lived in town my whole life, so I know nothin' of farmin' and the like. I'm not convinced it would agree with me."

"I have no doubt you'd do fine. But, to answer your question, you'd work with the children to take care of the chores close to the house—things like milkin' the cows and feedin' the chickens, horses, goats and the hog. Those types of things. Additionally, I'd expect ya to care for the children and my home."

"But I know nothin' about farm animals. I've never milked a cow. I'm not even sure I'd know the difference between a pig and a hog."

"We'll teach ya. I have faith in your ability to learn quickly, and even greater faith in your inner strength."

"Okay, then." I nodded. "Tell me more about your children. I know their ages and genders, but tell me somethin' about who they are."

Will smiled and his eyes shone with pride as he spoke. "Caroline and Olivia are the oldest. They're quiet girls, but strong and hard-workin'. They'll help ya learn your way around the farm. The twins, Joseph and Daniel, will spend most days with me in the fields. They're good boys, but easily led into mischief if their energies aren't directed properly. Then there's Catherine. She's the most like ya, I think. Spunky and full of life. She prefers playin' with her brothers and wearin' britches, yet she works hard to please her older sisters."

"And your mother and father?" I asked.

"They live about a mile away on the adjacent property with my brother, Atticus, and his wife, Veronica. We'll see 'em once in a while since we live so close. They're our nearest neighbors next to Earl and Julianne."

"Forgive me for askin', but I heard your first wife and your mother were frequently at odds." My face flushed with heat, but I had to ask the question. "How will your mother feel about ya bringin' home a new wife?"

"It's really none of her concern," he responded.

"Yes but—"

"There are no buts, Victoria. You'll be my wife, and my mother can think about it any way she chooses. She's an opinionated woman—difficult, some would say—but I'm not really concerned with what she has to say. I care about what *you* have to say. Your opinion will always come first."

The silence stretched between us as I thought on his words. Could I go through with this arrangement? I was totally unprepared for the life he was proposing. But I was equal parts terrified and intrigued. I had to get married, that much was evident. The Kirks had given me enough already. It was time I made my own way. Squaring my shoulders, I made a decision.

"Mr. Harrison, before I agree to marry you, I have a few conditions."

Will chuckled. "Of course ya do, Victoria. I would expect nothing less. Tell me your conditions, and I'll see if I can accommodate. But first, I must insist upon a condition of my own."

"Alright, then. Go ahead, please. If I'm unable to comply with your condition, then there's no reason to negotiate mine."

Will shook his head in amusement. Now, smiling broadly, he took my hand. "Victoria, ya have to call me Will. I can't be 'Mr. Harrison' to ya anymore."

I swallowed the lump in my throat and closed my eyes to collect myself. Taking a deep breath, I opened my eyes. "Very well, Will. I can do that."

"Thank you. Now, tell me your conditions, and let's see if we can come to an agreement."

Clearing my throat, I forged ahead. "First, the children shouldn't call me 'Mother' or 'Mama' or even 'Mother Victoria.' I'm not nearly old enough to be any of their mothers, and it'd make me feel ridiculous. They've had a mother, and I'm sure they loved her. I won't have them thinkin' I'm tryin' to take her place. I insist they call me Victoria."

Scratching his upper lip, Will covered his smile with the tip of his finger. "You've given this a lot of thought."

"I have."

"Very well, then. Victoria it'll be," he said.

"Thank you."

"Your next condition?"

"Alright." I nodded. "If I'm to act as mother to these children, especially given my nearness to their own ages, I simply will not be undermined. They'll have to respect my decisions, and I'll need your support. I can't have them comin' to you to overrule the decisions I make in your absence."

Will nodded. "Another well-considered condition, Victoria. Ya never cease to surprise me. Very well. In my absence, your word will be the law in our home. I will not undermine ya in front of the children. I can't say I'll always agree with ya—in those cases, we'll work together and come to a compromise."

"I believe that's fair." I nodded. "Yes—I can live with that."

Will's lips twitched, but he held back his smile. "Very well, then. Any other conditions?"

"Just a couple. I insist on a simple ceremony, presided over by Reverend Patterson. No fanfare. Just the two of us and our families. No reception, and no unnecessary guests. Just simple."

"You're sure? You'll only get to do this once," he reminded.

"Yes. Forgive me for sayin', but this isn't a love match. A fancy weddin' would make a mockery of what we're doin' here. I prefer an intimate ceremony with only those closest to us in attendance."

"Alright then. Any other conditions?"

"Only one last condition. Ya gotta ask Father Caleb for my hand. Though you well-know he's not my natural father, he's acted as my father these last ten years. He deserves the right to give his blessing."

"I expected as much," he replied. "Of course. I'll ask him straight away. D'ya anticipate any obstacles in that regard?"

"None at all." I shook my head. "Well, perhaps exceptin' the age gap between us. However, Father Caleb has always wished to see me happy. If he believes this makes me happy, then he'll give his consent."

"And will this make ya happy?" Will asked softly.

My throat closed and I had difficulty responding. My heart beat so hard I was afraid it could be heard outside of my chest. "I believe it will," I said, surprising myself.

Using just the knuckles of his right hand, Will gently caressed my cheek. "I believe it'll make me happy as well." Leaning forward, he placed a chaste kiss upon my forehead. "Thank you."

# CHAPTER TWELVE

WILL HARRISON WAS A FORCE TO BE RECK-
oned with. Once a decision was made, he moved forward swiftly. That afternoon he returned me home, then stayed for dinner. True to his word, he
requested permission from Father Caleb, and it was granted immediately.
With only our two small families to consider, we scheduled the wedding for
two weeks later on the first Saturday in June.

Mother Elizabeth was in a tizzy. She'd hoped to celebrate my wedding
with the same fanfare as we had Julianne's, but I was adamant. I wanted a
small wedding, with only our closest family.

With so little to plan, Mother Elizabeth was fixated on the smallest
details. Most notably, my wedding dress and the bride's bouquet. To save
money, I'd suggested wearing my best dress. Mother Elizabeth was aghast at
the suggestion.

"Absolutely not! You will not be married in some old dress! You'll have a
special dress for your weddin' day, just as Julianne had for hers, and I will hear
no more discussion about it. A woman only gets married once, and I'll not
have ya rememberin' your weddin' day—small though it may be—as anything
other than lovely."

I conceded defeat, and Mother Elizabeth set to work creating the loveliest dress of white linen and lace I'd ever seen. I'd once thought Julianne
was the loveliest bride ever. Now I wasn't so sure. While I couldn't compete
with Julianne's petite frame and lovely golden features, I couldn't argue that
I looked good.

For a veil, Mother Elizabeth and I selected a handmade lace headband
with a mid-length veil in the back. It was simple, yet lovely, and I was thankful I'd allowed her such freedom with my wedding ensemble.

The only detail for which we remained at odds was my bridal bouquet.
Remembering the two bouquets Will had brought me, I decided upon an

arrangement entirely of black-eyed Susans. Mother Elizabeth, however, was dismayed.

"But Victoria," she said. "It isn't a weddin' flower. It's a prairie wild-flower—not much more than a weed, really. It grows rampant in the fields, and overtakes the crops if you're not careful. Ya want somethin' more elegant, like gardenias or orchids. Calla lilies or roses would be lovely. But the black-eyed Susan is a poor-man's flower."

"I like 'em, and that's what I want," I said.

"Very well, then," she replied dubiously. "If you're sure, then I'm sure we can make a lovely bouquet."

"Thank you, Mother Elizabeth." Taking her hands in mine, I squeezed gently, pouring all my love and appreciation into the small gesture. "Thank you. Not just for the weddin' and for lettin' me have my way with the flowers, but for everything. Thank you for takin' me in when I was a child and I had nobody else. Thank you for bein' my mother in every way that's important. You've always cared for me as your own. Ya didn't have to do that, but ya did—ya still do. I can never express how much I appreciate all you've done for me."

"My dear Victoria." She smiled through tears. "You couldn't be more my daughter if I'd brought ya into this world myself. But tell me—are ya sure you'll be happy with Mr. Harrison?"

I nodded. "I think so."

Mother Elizabeth studied me, apparently searching for the answer to an unasked question. After a long moment, she smiled and pulled me into the comfort of her strong arms. "I think so, too, sweetheart."

# CHAPTER THIRTEEN

ON JUNE 2, 1924, I BECAME MRS. WILLIAM Jackson Harrison. Our wedding was held at the St. John's Methodist Episcopal Church, now in its new location at the corner of Barker and Woodson streets. Built only two years earlier, this modern brick building gleamed with fresh paint, but was still headed by the aging Reverend Patterson. Standing as witnesses for the ceremony were Julianne and Will's brother, Atticus.

Waiting in the narthex for the ceremony to begin, I stole a peek into the sanctuary at our waiting families. Time hadn't allowed an introduction to Will's family, so I was nervous about what they'd think of me. Will's mother, Imogene, was seated in the front row on the groom's side next to her husband, Walter. Behind them, seated side-by-side, were Will's children in order of oldest to youngest. Caroline, Olivia, and Catherine were dressed in matching pink dresses. Sandwiched between the girls, and dressed smartly in matching suits and short pants, were Joseph and Daniel. Behind Will's children, in the third row of pews, were Atticus's wife, Veronica, and their three children: Gerald, George, and Robert. There was virtually no one on the bride's side—just three lonely figures, all seated in the front row: Mother Elizabeth, Jacob, and Earl Sykes.

The first strains of the bridal march echoed through the chapel. Winking at me, Father Caleb took my arm and placed it in the crook of his own. "Are ya ready?"

I nodded. "Yes. I believe I am."

"You're sure ya still wanna do this? It's not too late to change your mind, ya know."

Turning to him, I smiled and squeezed his elbow where my hand rested in its crook. "Thank you. You've always been so good to me."

"Ah, honey." His eyes glossed with tears. "You've made it easy to be good to ya."

We stood in silence for a long moment. Gathering my courage around me like Mama's wool cloak, I straightened my shoulders and lifted my chin high. "I'm ready."

Beaming with pride, Father Caleb led me down the aisle toward Will. Our eyes met, and my heart fluttered. Gone was the mocking grin Will often wore. In its place was a smile of pure joy and pride. Had I not known better, I'd have thought ours was a love match.

As I reached my destination, Will stepped forward and nodded at Father Caleb, who removed my hand from the crook of his arm and placed it in Will's. A burst of happiness shot through me when Will's attention landed on my bouquet. His eyes widened with surprised recognition, and I bit my lip to keep from laughing.

"Black-eyed Susans?" He lifted an eyebrow and his lips tipped up in a grin.

In that moment, it didn't matter that ours wasn't a love match. I knew I'd made the right decision. Everything just felt right.

Biting back a grin, I shrugged. "They seemed to suit you."

Holding nothing back, Will erupted into laughter. I tried to resist, but it was impossible. To the shock of the congregation, I joined Will's laugher with my own.

"Victoria," he said, his voice loud enough for all to hear, "this is gonna be fun."


WILL AND I had planned to spend our first night together at the nicest hotel in town, while the children went back to the farm with his family. We would have one night together before our real life began.

Preparing to leave the church, Will escorted me to his children and parents for introductions. As expected, the older girls greeted me formally, while the younger three were precocious and full of mischief.

"What are we to call ya, Mrs. Harrison?" asked one of the twins, whom I'd yet to distinguish from the other.

"Victoria, will be fine." I smiled. "And you, sir?"

The boy studied me, his lips tipping into an exact imitation of Will's mocking grin. "I believe Mr. Harrison will be acceptable."

"Daniel!" Will scolded, but it was too late. The child had his father's sense of humor, and I erupted in laughter for the second time that day.

The boy flushed crimson at his father's rebuke. Swallowing hard, he lifted his chin and said quietly, "Daniel Alexander Harrison, ma'am. Just Daniel."

"Thank you, Daniel," I replied. "I have a feeling you and I will be great friends."

My words soothed his injured pride, and his face lit up in another grin. "Yes, ma'am. I believe we will."

Will nodded his approval then took my arm and led me to his parents. "Mother. Father. I'd like ya to meet my wife, Mrs. Victoria Hastings Harrison. Victoria, my parents: Imogene and Walter Harrison."

"It's a pleasure to finally meet you, Mr. and Mrs. Harrison," I began. "I'm sorry we've been unable to meet before now."

Imogene Harrison studied me down the length of her long nose then, ignoring my greeting, turned her attention to Will. "She's not much to look at, Will. Whatever were ya thinkin'? She's plain and don't look like she's seen a day of honest work in her life. How d'ya expect her to help ya on the farm? At least if she was pretty, I'd understand."

Stepping closer to my side, Will circled his arm around my waist. "That will be enough, Mother. You will not embarrass my wife, especially on her weddin' day."

I stood there, dumbfounded. Glancing at Will's father, I wondered if he agreed with his wife, but the old man stared off across the room as though he hadn't heard a word.

"My apologies, Will," Mrs. Harrison replied. "I didn't mean to offend you."

"You should apologize to my wife, Mother," he replied, his words clipped.

Clearing her throat, she turned to me with a look of disdain. "My apologies, young lady."

Pulling my manners around me, I accepted her apology and attempted to right the situation with polite conversation. "It's quite all right, Mrs. Harrison. No harm done. As I said, it's a pleasure to meet you. What should I call you?"

Mrs. Harrison's brows pulled together until they were a straight line. "What should ya call me? Why, Mrs. Harrison, of course. What did ya think you should call me? Imogene? Mother? Absolutely not!"

Heat flooded my neck and cheeks. Twice I'd greeted this woman cordially and with respect, and twice she'd deliberately offended me.

"Enough." Will's eyes narrowed at his mother in warning. "I assume we'll see ya at Mr. and Mrs. Kirk's for refreshments, Mother? That is, if ya can behave."

Not waiting for a reply, he tightened his arm around my waist and escorted me out of the church.

MOTHER ELIZABETH HAD insisted upon serving refreshments at the house, since I wouldn't allow her to throw a proper party celebrating our marriage. Thankfully, it was brief. Mrs. Harrison behaved cordially for the remainder of the afternoon, but I was unable to get her harsh words out of my mind. The children, on the other hand, were a delight; and I soon found myself enjoying the company of the oldest two daughters.

"Please don't let Granny Imogene embarrass ya," Caroline, the oldest daughter, whispered as we sat together in the sitting room. "She was like that with our mother as well. It angers her that Daddy won't let her control him like Grampy does."

Her words soothed my anxiety.

"Thank you," I said. "I wasn't sure what to expect upon meetin' your grandparents, not to mention all of you; but her venom was a surprise."

A hand landed gently on my shoulder, and I looked up into Will's smiling eyes. "I believe it's time to make our escape."

Smiling, I blew out a relieved breath and joined Will to bid our goodbyes. We approached Mother Elizabeth and Father Caleb, the latter of whom enveloped me in his safe arms. I tucked my head beneath his chin and whispered, "Thank you."

Pulling away just enough to meet my eyes, Father Caleb tipped my chin with his knuckles. "Enough of that, Victoria. You're our daughter, and ya don't need to thank us. Remember, this is your home and we're always here if ya need us."

I nodded. Then, giving him one last squeeze, I stepped out of his arms and into those of Mother Elizabeth.

"Be happy, sweetheart," she whispered.

I nodded and stepped way, now turning to Julianne who pulled me in for a tight hug. "I'm so happy we're gonna be neighbors! I'll give ya a few days to get settled, then you'll have the devil of a time gettin' rid of me!"

"I'm countin' on it," I said.

Having said our goodbyes to my family, we approached Will's parents. Straightening my shoulders and lifting my chin, I gave them my sweetest smile.

"Mother. Father," Will said. "Thank you for comin' and seein' the children back to the farm."

Mrs. Harrison nodded regally then turned her attention to me, once again glaring at me down the length of her long nose.

"Mr. and Mrs. Harrison," I said. "Thank you for comin'. It was a pleasure to meet you."

Before either could reply, Will spirited me out the door, leaving his mother standing in our wake with a disapproving frown on her face.

# CHAPTER FOURTEEN

THE SOUTHERN HOTEL WAS A BEAUTIFUL three-story building located on Grand Avenue in El Reno. With more than one hundred rooms, and nearly as many baths, it was still one of the most modern hotel structures in the state, nearly fifteen years after its grand opening. Though I'd passed it many times, I'd never been inside; and I never imagined I would walk through its doors as a guest. As Will signed the register, I took in the grandeur before me. I never dreamed there could be so much elegance within our small town.

Closing the register, Will turned to me. "Why don't we go upstairs and freshen up a bit before dinner? I know ya must be hungry."

Will was right. I hadn't eaten anything at the reception. "Let's do—but let's make it quick. I'm starvin'."

"That's what I enjoy most about ya, Victoria." Will grinned. "Ya say what's on your mind."

DINING IN THE hotel restaurant was an experience I would always remember. I'd never eaten in a restaurant before, so the elegance and the service left me giddy with excitement. Will ordered for both of us, and we dined on roasted lamb in mint sauce with steamed asparagus on the side, then fresh strawberries with cream for dessert. Though nervous, I ate every bite. I didn't know when I'd ever have such a luxurious meal again.

Sensing my anxiety, Will carried the conversation. He told me more about his farm and the hard work it entailed; then regaled me with stories of Daniel's and Joseph's antics, often in conspiracy with Catherine. As dessert was served, I gathered my courage and asked those questions weighing heavily on my mind.

"Will," I began. "Your mother—she doesn't seem particularly pleased about our marriage."

Taking my hands, Will waited until I lifted my eyes to his. "Please don't worry about my mother, Victoria. I love her dearly, but she can be difficult. She's spent the last fifty years rulin' my father and, more recently, Atticus and Veronica. She's never been able to control me, and that infuriates her."

"I see." Retrieving my hands, I placed them in my lap.

"I'm sorry about the way she behaved today," he said. "I should've warned ya about her before ya met. I should've guessed she'd get her feathers in a fluff at my not consultin' her. Truthfully, I haven't consulted her in many years on any important matter. But I'd forgotten how cruel she can be when intimidated."

"Intimidated? By who?"

Will lifted an eyebrow. "By you, of course."

"I don't understand." I shook my head.

"Like her, you're a strong woman who knows her own mind. That, coupled with the fact that, as my wife, you have the power to influence my decisions, intimidates her. What little influence she may've had on me she lost when I married Hannah. When Hannah died, she probably thought she'd regain some of that control. But then I decided to marry you, and she could tell within seconds of meeting ya that any control she thought she might gain was lost."

"So she was destined to hate me?"

"Not hate you, I hope. But yes—she's intimidated because you're her competition."

"I see," I replied again. "Then how're we to get along?"

"I don't know that ya will. I can only tell you that what I admire most is your strong spirit and your ability to speak your mind. Ya just have to keep doin' that, especially with someone like my mother. Don't ever let anyone see they've intimidated you, or they'll walk all over ya. Remember that, okay?"

I nodded.

"As for my mother," he continued, "you'll earn her respect if you demand it, though she might never warm to ya."

"How does Veronica handle her?"

Will grinned. "Veronica is crafty. She's demurs, makin' Mother think she's in control. She's not, of course; but it's Veronica's way of manipulatin' her into her way of thinking. She makes Mother think Veronica's decisions were all her idea to begin with. It's rather ingenious, actually, but I don't expect ya to follow Veronica's example."

"And your father?" I asked. "Is he in league with your mother?"

"My father is complicated," Will said. "No, I don't believe he agrees with all Mother says and does, but he picks his battles. He's not strong in the same way as you and I are strong. He puts his foot down occasionally; but, for the most part, he gives Mother free reign. In return, she keeps him comfortable."

"What about the children? How do they get along with her?"

"Atticus's boys do well with their grandmother, fortunately. They're all quick studies and have learned how to make her think she's gettin' her way, while eventually doin' whatever they please. She dotes on those boys, which is good. It makes for a more harmonious household, since she and Father are livin' with Atticus and Veronica."

"But your children?" I asked. "How do they fare with your mother?"

"Their relationship with my mother is more difficult. She loves them, but she doesn't dote on 'em like she does with Atticus's boys. I've tried teachin' 'em to be strong and speak their minds, but Caroline and Olivia struggle with that. Hannah insisted they demur, and it's difficult to change a mother's lessons. On the other hand," Will grinned, "the boys and Catherine are much more uninhibited, and that's caused a bit of resentment—or perhaps even more intimidation—on my mother's part."

"Will we see her often?"

"I expect we will. Just treat her with respect, but don't let her rule ya. Believe me when I tell ya she'll try."

I thought on his words for the next few moments. I was grateful I wouldn't live with this woman who clearly despised me, but I was also nervous. I was only eighteen, and she was in her mid-sixties. This woman would be part of my life for at least a few more years. I'd have to learn to interact with her or she'd rip me to shreds.

Will took my hands once again, this time kissing my knuckles. "Don't let it worry ya so much. I wouldn't've married you if I didn't think ya had the stamina to overcome my mother. Now, have ya finished with your dessert?"

Glancing down, I realized I'd eaten the remainder of my strawberries and cream. I'd been so absorbed in conversation, I'd forgotten the rest of the world around me. Sheepishly, I grinned. "Yes, I s'pose I have."

Will smiled his roguish grin, making the lines beside his eyes crinkle and the dimple in his left cheek more noticeable. "Then I suggest we retire for the evenin'."

Imagining the night ahead, my face flushed. Standing now, Will moved behind my chair and pulled it out for me to stand. "Shall we, Mrs. Harrison?"

WILL HASTINGS, MY husband of only a few hours, was gentler than I'd ever hoped or imagined. I'd never lain with a man, so the mental images of what was to come left me near panic. Mother Elizabeth had talked to me before the ceremony. In spite of my embarrassment and her own, she'd even explained the mechanics of sex. Still I was unprepared. Will led me into our room and closed the door behind us.

"I felt ya shakin' all the way up the stairs, Victoria." Stepping toward me, he cradled my face in the palms of his large hands and stared intently into my eyes until I couldn't look away. "Never be afraid of me, because I'll never hurt ya. If I'm ever too rough, ya need only tell me. Understood?"

Unable to speak, I nodded. My eyes were round and my heart beat frantically within my chest. I held my breath.

Leaning toward me, Will touched his lips to mine. It was barely the whisper of a caress, but it was the first real kiss he'd given me. In fact, it was the first real kiss I'd ever received from anyone. Until that moment—and even at the church that morning—every kiss we'd shared had been chaste and unremarkable. This kiss was different—I felt it all the way to my toes.

Will slid his hands to the nape of my neck and weaved his fingers between the strands of my long hair. Holding my head firmly in place, he deepened his kiss, this time touching his tongue to the seam of my closed lips. Shocked, I snapped my head back.

"Breathe, Victoria." Will smiled. "Ya need to breathe or you'll faint. Just relax and let me kiss ya properly."

I studied him, assessing the complete sincerity in his expression. Then, breathing in a deep breath, I stepped closer to Will until there was no space between us. To the surprise of both of us, I think, I brought my mouth to his.

"That's my girl." Will grinned, then lifted me in his arms and carried me to the bed in the middle of our small room.

HOURS LATER, I lay beside Will and listened to the sound of his not-so-gentle snoring. I thought about all that had transpired. I remembered my surprise at not only the initial pain, but the pleasant feelings that followed. Will was patient, soothing me with words of comfort. Soon I was cocooned in warmth and belonging. Though I'd been sheltered and loved by Mother Elizabeth and Father Caleb, I'd always felt like an outsider—a guest. I'd never felt I truly belonged. That night, Will made me feel truly loved. I felt like I'd come home, like I finally belonged.

THE NEXT MORNING, I awoke just moments before dawn. I thought I'd sneak out of bed and complete my morning ablutions, but a movement beside me made me aware I was not the only one awake. I stiffened in surprise when Will's arm came around me. He pulled me close and into the warmth of his large body.

"Mornin', Mrs. Harrison." I knew Will was smiling. I could tell by the sound of his voice.

"Good mornin', Mr. Harrison." I relaxed slightly.

Nudging my shoulder until I lay on my back below him, Will stared down into my eyes. "You are simply stunning, Victoria."

Heat flooded my cheeks and I tried to look away, but he'd have none of it. Catching my chin between his knuckles and his thumb, Will turned my face back toward him until I had no choice but to look him in the eye. "I mean that. You're beautiful."

It's not that I thought I was ugly. It's more that I'd never considered it at all. I was taller than most young women my age, with small breasts and an unremarkable face. My crowning glory was my hair, which I'd refused to cut as most women were doing at the time. It was thick and long—a deep reddish-brown that glowed with blond highlights in the sunlight.

I shook my head. "Thank you. But I don't need flattery. I'm tall and plain. That's okay with me."

"How is it ya lack no end of confidence in any other area, but I tell ya you're beautiful and ya can't accept a compliment? I'll have to work on that."

With a gleam in his eye, Will placed his lips against mine until butterflies danced in my belly. Understanding his purpose, I pulled away from his kiss. "Will, it's mornin'."

Will glanced around the room and feigned surprise. "Well, what d'ya know? It sure is." Bringing his head toward mine again, he gifted me with another leisurely kiss.

Swatting away his wayward hands, I pulled away a second time. "Will, it's *daylight!*"

Will glanced around the room once again and grinned. "So it is."

As his head moved toward mine in an obvious attempt at another kiss, I pushed him back with the palms of my hands. "Will! Your intentions are a *nighttime* activity!"

"My beautiful Victoria," he laughed. "Ya still have a lot to learn about marriage, so I think it's best we get started right away."

I gave up. All thoughts disappeared as Will slowly made love to me again.

# CHAPTER FIFTEEN

THE HORSES MOVED SLOWLY IN THE SWELTER-
ing heat of the hot Oklahoma sun. While automobiles were becoming more
common, they were expensive, and Will had yet to find a need for one.

Now that the anxiety of the previous day's events was behind us, Will
and I conversed easily. We talked about a variety of topics, and discovered we
shared many common interests. We both loved to read, and we talked at great
length about books. I was learning that I liked this man I'd married. He was
funny, kind, quick-witted, and just a little bit devious. He made me laugh,
and he made me want to make him laugh in return. About a mile from the
farm, conversation turned to the previous day's events.

"Tell me about the black-eyed Susans," Will said.

"You didn't like 'em?"

"Actually, I liked them very much. But I'm curious why ya chose 'em."

I shrugged. "I wanted somethin' different; somethin' unique. You seemed
to like 'em, and I'd be lyin' if I didn't admit I was flattered when ya said they
reminded you of me."

Will grinned. "I wondered if that might've played into your decision."

"Mother Elizabeth almost had a conniption," I laughed.

"How so?"

"She said they weren't the type of flower young ladies chose for weddin'
bouquets. She referred to them as a 'poor man's flower.'"

Will's laughter filled me with pleasure. Somehow making this man laugh
gave me more joy than I'd had in a very long while.

"I s'pose that's a fair description," he replied. "They grow everywhere out
near the farm. In fact, you'll likely get sick of 'em before too long."

"Oh, I doubt that. They've become my favorite," I admitted.

Will smiled, but said nothing for several moments. Finding his words he
said, "And even though Mrs. Kirk disliked them, ya still put your foot down?"

"I did." I nodded. "It was important to me."

"I'm glad."

We drove in silence for many minutes before I responded. "I'm glad, too."

WE ARRIVED AT the farm in the early part of the afternoon. Waiting in the yard were all five of Will's children and three scraggly dogs. The dogs barked viciously as though to discourage us from trespassing; yet their tails wagged wildly, easing my anxiety that they might truly be aggressive.

"Damn dogs," Will muttered.

Halting the horses and pulling the wagon to a stop, Will herded the dogs out of his way before helping me down to the ground below.

"Victoria . . . Daddy!" one of the twins hollered. "Look at the frogs we found down by the creek!"

"Nice job, Joseph! Now hold onto 'em so they don't go jumpin' all over your new stepmother." Will turned to his oldest two daughters. "Are your grandparents here?"

"No, Daddy," said Olivia. "They brought us home, then headed back to their place. Grampy said . . ." she paused, apparently afraid to say something inappropriate.

"What did Grampy say, Olivia?" Will prompted. "You should speak openly in front of Victoria. She's family now."

"Well." Her face flushed crimson. "Grampy said he oughta get Granny Imogene home on account of how she'd already caused enough trouble yesterday."

Will's laughter rang out around us and sent the dogs into a tizzy of frantic barking.

"Yeah, she sure did at that!" Taking my hand, Will placed it in the crook of his arm and turned toward the house. "Daniel. Joseph. Y'all two go on up in the bed of the wagon and bring in Victoria's things. Be careful not to drop anything—ya don't know what's breakable in there."

"Yes sir," they answered together, and I wondered if I'd ever tell them apart.

"Daddy?" Catherine grinned a toothless smile. "What can I do? I wanna help the boys! I'm big and strong enough!"

"Go on, Catherine," he said. "But mind your brothers. If they tell ya something's too heavy, then ya let them carry it and stay outta their way. Understand?"

"Yes sir!" Catherine raced off after her brothers.

"Girls," Will said to Caroline and Olivia together, "why don't y'all two come with us while I give Victoria a tour of the farm. I wanna walk her through the things she'll need to learn around here. I expect you'll help her get the hang of things?"

"Yes, sir," they replied. Together we toured the farm and all the things I'd need to know to be a farmer's wife.

# CHAPTER SIXTEEN

FARM LIFE WAS LIKE NOTHING I'D EVER EXPE-
rienced and much harder than I'd ever expected. Each morning, we awoke
long before the sun rose in the sky to feed the animals nearest the house.
Then Will took the boys out to the pasture and worked the fields. The girls
and I worked together to manage the house, feed the livestock, and care for
the horses.

At the end of each day, I was exhausted and fell easily into bed; yet I
also found myself invigorated at the hard work I'd learned to do. I'd come
from town not knowing the difference between a hog and a pig. After only a
month, I'd learned not only the difference between the two, but I could milk
cows and snatch eggs out from beneath a laying hen. I still caused a ruckus in
the henhouse, but Caroline promised that stealth came with practice.

That first month of marriage passed quickly, and I loved the life I'd chosen.
I loved the quiet of the early mornings and the late evenings. Farm life meant
peaceful evenings and no nosy neighbors. Visitors were announced long in
advance by the overzealous greeting of Will's dogs, and receiving guests was
always a surprise. Most mornings I awakened before sunrise to the beautiful
music of birds chirping nearby. At night, Will and I often sat on the front
porch swing, just listening to the crickets and watching the lightning bugs
glow in the dark. I loved life, and I loved the family I'd adopted as my own.

Caroline and Olivia had welcomed me as a friend and, together, the
three of us worked to complete our daily chores. The boys and Catherine, on
the other hand, needed firmer discipline. They were good children, though,
and the entire family welcomed me far better than I'd hoped.

More than anything, Will was a surprise to me. We hadn't known each
other well before taking our vows, but I'd believed from our short acquaintance we'd be compatible. The truth was, I never expected to enjoy Will so
much. He was, without any doubt, the finest man I'd ever known—kind,

generous, sensitive, and always gentle.

Will was a farmer by birth and by trade, but he was a gentleman at heart. He never took my existence for granted. He rose when I entered a room, and always pulled a chair out for me to sit. He treated me with kindness and respect. Requiring the same of his sons, he taught them to be gentlemen through his own example.

More important than anything, Will listened to me. Every night without fail, he sat with me in the swing or held me close after we retired to our room. Together we shared the day's experiences in the absence of the other. He listened to my thoughts. He cared about my concerns. He nourished my soul by his desire to know more about my hopes and my dreams. Though I was still learning to be a farmer's wife, he never made me feel inadequate. He was tender and kind—more than I'd ever dreamed possible in a husband. He tore down my defenses and, together, we built a life based upon friendship and trust. Though the days were exhausting, we usually found energy to comfort each other as only a husband and wife can do. I'd sworn never to love, but Will Harrison made me a liar. It was impossible not to fall in love with him.

JUNE AND JULY passed in a haze of sweltering Oklahoma heat, and August arrived promising the same. The first week of August brought Julianne for a visit. This wasn't her first visit, but it was a surprise as we'd seen each other only two days earlier. She found me in the kitchen, kneading a loaf of dough for that night's meal.

"There's something I need to tell ya," she said. "I wanted to tell ya when I was here the other day, but I wasn't sure I was ready."

Brushing my hands off on my apron, I turned to her with a smile. "Well, tell me then! What is it?"

"I'm havin' a baby," Julianne said, barely containing her excitement.

The world spun around me. Julianne was having a baby. I heard the words, but I had trouble understanding them. Julianne—lovely, petite, Julianne—was having a baby.

My mind raced with thoughts of my mother—those days before Christmas, the tree, her singing while we decorated, and the eventual silence. I'd once been told childbirth was normal and nothing to worry about. But Mama hadn't been fine. A baby—a pregnancy—caused the loss of everything

I'd ever known. Now Julianne, my best friend and big sister, was having one of her own. I sat there, unable to find the words to speak.

"Oh, God, Victoria! Are ya okay?" Julianne rushed to my side and helped me sit at the table. "You've turned as white as a ghost!"

Collecting myself, I pasted a smile on my face. "I'm sorry. I just—I don't know what to say."

Julianne's joy lit up the entire room. "Well congratulate me, silly! I'm gonna be a mama, and you're gonna be Auntie Victoria!"

"Congratulations, Julianne." My voice sounded wooden to my own ears. "I'm happy for ya."

Julianne's eyebrows drew together, and she studied me. "No, you're not. Tell me what's wrong. I thought you'd be happy. This is what I've always wanted!"

Reaching across the table, I took her hands and forced myself to smile. "I am happy for ya. I'm just surprised is all. Ya took me off-guard and I just need a moment to get used to the idea. Really."

Julianne graciously accepted my words at face value, but I knew I'd hurt her. My reaction had created a divide between us, and carrying on a normal, easy conversation proved impossible. Soon after, Julianne made excuses and returned home long before she would have on any other day. Bidding her goodbye, I watched her walk down the path toward her home and life with Earl Sykes.

DINNER THAT NIGHT was quiet—I couldn't stop thinking about Julianne. Sensing my mood, Will and the children gave me a wide berth, allowing me to wallow in my thoughts.

With dinner completed and the dishes washed and put away properly, I escaped to the bedroom under the pretense of a crushing headache. After changing into my bedclothes, I climbed under the warm blankets of our bed. There I hid, and privately explored my reaction to Julianne's news. I wanted to be happy for her, I really did. But grief and fear washed over me. For the first time since Daddy's death, I cried freely—for my mama, for my baby brother, and for my daddy. I cried for Mama's pain, and I cried for my own loss at Daddy's death. More than that, I cried for Julianne, Earl Sykes, and our parents. What if history repeated itself? How would they survive losing Julianne?

I sobbed until my tears ran dry. Exhausted, I was almost asleep when the door to our bedroom opened. Moving on quiet feet, Will removed his clothing and hung them on the peg beside the door. The bed dipped with his weight as he crawled in beside me. He adjusted the blankets over his large frame, then laid quietly for several moments.

"Victoria," he said, breaking the silence. "Ya can't pretend you're sleepin'. I know you're still awake. Talk to me."

"I can't," I whispered, my throat sore from crying.

Will wrapped an arm around me and pulled me close. "Yes, ya can. There's nobody better to listen and ease your pain than me. Now tell me."

I lay there a moment, collecting my thoughts, unsure how to explain my fears. I didn't know where to begin, so I started with Julianne.

"Julianne was here today."

The silence that followed was thick. The clock on the mantel ticked down the seconds, while we each waited for the other to break the quiet stillness of our bedroom.

"I saw her leavin' earlier. What'd she have to say?" Will asked.

I swallowed a lump in my throat and pushed the tears back from behind my eyelids. "Julianne and Earl—they're havin' a baby."

Will tightened his arms around me. "I see. And this upsets ya?"

"Yes. No. I don't know! I'm happy for her 'cause I know this is what she wants. But ..."

"But, you're scared."

This man—my husband of only two months—already knew me so well. How did he know me better than Julianne, the sister of my heart? She and I had shared everything these last ten years, yet it was Will who immediately understood what motivated my emotions. How was that possible?

I nodded.

"I thought as much. Earl mentioned the news to me this afternoon. I was wonderin' when Julianne would tell ya. Honestly, I'm not surprised by your reaction."

"You're not?" I asked.

"Not at all. In fact, I somewhat expected it. We've not talked much about your mama, but I heard ya never cried, not even as they placed her in the ground. And when your daddy died a short time later, they say ya still didn't cry. You were like this tiny adult, carryin' the worries of the world on your shoulders. You refused to show weakness. I admired that in ya when you were a child, and it's what made me fall in love with you."

Startled, I pulled away from Will and propped myself on an elbow. "You love me?"

"Ya know I do. I don't know how ya could help but know."

Settling back into Will's arms, I lay quietly for some time before Will spoke again. "So about Julianne. You're worried somethin' will happen with the pregnancy?"

I nodded. "It's what I've always been afraid of. There are too many what-ifs. What if the baby dies? What if Julianne dies? I've had too much loss to go through it all again."

"But what if none of those things happen? What if Julianne delivers a perfectly healthy baby? Should she not reach for happiness on the off-chance her happiness might turn to sorrow? What kinda life would that be to live?"

I mulled his words over in my mind before responding. "That's what I've been doin', isn't it? Saying I'd never marry—swearin' never to love, and promisin' myself I'd never have children."

"That's exactly what I think you've been doin'. My job is to help ya scratch those things off your list so ya can live a happier life, one small thing at a time. I succeeded in convincin' ya to marry me, so I'm makin' progress."

"Ya backed me into a corner!" I laughed. "You painted a bleak future for me if I didn't make my own decisions before someone else made 'em for me!"

"I was right, wasn't I? Can ya say you're not happier married to me than ya were before? I know the work is harder than you've been used to, but you're not truly unhappy, are ya?"

"No!" I said quickly. "I'm not unhappy at all. In fact—I'm happier than I've been in a long time."

"I expected as much." Will smiled.

"So how do I turn off this fear I have of somethin' bad happenin' to Julianne? I just can't seem to erase it from my mind."

"I'm not entirely sure, but I think maybe ya start with askin' yourself some questions. For instance, would ya be this upset to find *yourself* with child?"

"Noooo . . ." I replied slowly. "I don't think I'd be upset, or afraid, if it was me. But then, I wouldn't be losin' anyone. If somethin' happened to me while havin' a baby, then it'd be me leavin' others behind; and not me bein' the one left behind alone. And if it was the baby, well, I think I'm strong enough to overcome the loss. Surely I'd grieve, but I'm pretty sure I could move forward—it's not like it'd be someone I know and love who's already close to me. So no—if it was me, I think I'd be okay."

"So maybe the answer is that ya stop frettin' over Julianne, and instead concentrate on your own baby."

"Oh, I don't think I'll have any children of my own."

Will didn't answer right away. After several moments, he said softly, "I don't think ya have any choice in the matter, darlin'."

"Well, of course I have a choice. I simply won't become pregnant."

Will was silent once again, carefully choosing his next words. "Has it occurred to ya that you're already expectin' a baby? Our baby?"

My world spun for the second time that day. "What are ya sayin'?"

"I'm sayin' the probability you're already pregnant exists. In fact, I suspect ya already are."

"What? Why?" I sat up again, but quickly lay back down when my head spun. "Whatever gave ya that impression? Please don't joke with me, Will Harrison. This is *not* a joking matter!"

"Sweetheart, this is one thing I would never tease ya about. It's too important, especially considerin' your feelings on the subject. But we've been married for just over two months. In all this time, we've made love nearly every night. Not once have ya turned me away for your courses."

"Oh, God," I whispered, tears springing to my eyes. "Oh, God ..."

I mentally calculated dates in my head. There could be no mistake. The last of my courses had arrived only a few days before our wedding. Will was right. In all the hard work around the farm, I hadn't even thought about it.

"Oh, God," I said again. "But how is that possible? I haven't been sick. Don't women usually get sick when they're expectin'? I'm as healthy as I was when I came here—more so, even!"

"I won't pretend to understand a woman's body, but I do know not all women are sick when they're expectin'. When Hannah was expectin' the twins, she was very ill. But she never had a moment of sickness with any of the girls. I'm not sure I'd gauge the verdict on whether or not you've been sick."

Will was right, and I knew it. In all the time we'd been together since our wedding, and the many nights we'd held each other under these same blankets, it never occurred to me I might become pregnant. I wasn't sure how I felt about that.

*Pregnant?*

*Me?*

*A baby?*

*Will's baby?*

*Our baby?*

The idea took root, and my pulse quickened in anticipation. "A baby. Someone completely mine."

"And mine, of course," Will teased. "Ya didn't do it all by yourself."

"And yours." I smiled—I couldn't stop smiling.

"So where does that leave ya feelin' about Julianne?"

I thought for a long moment. It seemed ridiculous to remain upset about Julianne when it seemed I was in the same condition. Our children could be friends!

"I guess it's pretty ridiculous, huh? Oh, but I do worry, Will!"

"It's okay to worry; we all worry. But worryin' don't fix the problem, and it often creates new ones . . . like, I'm guessin', your relationship with Julianne. Would I be guessin' right that ya didn't leave things on good terms when she left?"

"Oh, God! No, Will—I didn't. I tried, but I just couldn't be happy for her. My reaction must've hurt her somethin' awful."

"So now ya have to find a way to make amends. I have a feelin' it won't take much; you can probably just tell her your own good news, and that'll be enough."

"Thank you, Will."

"For what, darlin'? I didn't do anythin' more than help ya see a little sooner what you'd've figured out on your own, eventually."

With nothing more for either of us to say, we laid quietly together and listened to the crickets chirping beyond the windows of our small bedroom. Will alternated between stroking my arm in long, leisurely caresses, and running his fingers through my hair. His words had filled me with both confidence and joy. After nearly an hour without speaking, I turned toward Will.

"You've been rather successful with your 'to-do' list," I said.

"How's that?" he asked, his voice sleepy.

"You convinced me to marry ya. You persuaded me to have a baby. Then ya gave me no choice but to fall in love with ya."

"Of course I did. That was my evil plan all along," he said, grinning wickedly.

As the light from the outside moon shown in through the window and onto the bed, I looked at Will and waited until his eyes met my own. "I love you, William Jackson Harrison."

Will closed his eyes and smiled. "I know ya do, sweetheart. And I love you, too, Victoria Hastings Harrison."

With no other words needed, we fell asleep in each other's arms.

# CHAPTER SEVENTEEN

THE NEXT MORNING I AWOKE EARLIER THAN was my habit. I had slept restlessly, unable to erase my last conversation with Julianne from my mind. Easing out of bed in the still-dark morning, I moved on quiet feet so as not to wake Will. Just as I eased open the door to our room, he opened his eyes and propped himself up on one elbow.

"You're up early. What time is it?" His voice was still groggy from sleep.

"Go back to sleep. Ya have about another hour," I whispered. "I just wanted to get an early start. I need to go see Julianne today, and I have things to get done first."

"Thought about her all night, did ya? I felt ya toss and turn."

"Yeah. I need to go see her and make things right."

Will rolled out of bed and stepped into his pants, then pushed his arms through the sleeves of his shirt. "I might as well help ya. It's still pretty dark to be out there by yourself."

"I'll be fine—go back to sleep. You get up early enough as it is. Ya still have the fields to see to today."

"Nah. I won't be able to sleep anyway. C'mon."

Together we worked side by side on the morning chores. We milked the two cows, fed the goats and pigs, then collected eggs for breakfast. The girls could muck out the horse barn when they awoke.

Returning to the house, I prepared breakfast.

"Mornin', Daddy. Mornin', Victoria," Caroline said, joining us at the table.

"Good mornin', darlin'," Will said.

"Breakfast is just about ready," I told her. "Did ya wanna go wake Olivia, Catherine, and the boys?"

"Yes, ma'am," she replied, leaving the table to do as she was bid.

Minutes later the heavy bodies of the four remaining children entered the kitchen and took their seats at the table.

"Girls," Will said. "Victoria and I've been out in the barns this mornin'. We've already taken care of the livestock. The only thing left to do is muck out the stalls, so you'll need to do that today. Victoria needs to walk over to the Sykes's and talk to your Aunt Julianne."

"Yuck!" Catherine scrunched her nose in dismay. "I hate muckin' the stalls. It's stinky. Can I go with you and the boys out to the field instead, Daddy?"

"No you may not, Catherine," Will replied. "Ya need to stay here with your sisters and give 'em a hand. Victoria isn't sure how long she'll be, so they may need your help preparin' the noon meal for when the boys and I get back."

"Humph!" was Catherine's only reply.

I turned my back to hide a smile, and flipped the eggs to cook on the other side.

"Wasn't Aunt Julianne just here yesterday?" asked Olivia.

"She was," I said, turning to face her. "We had some harsh words, and I need to go make things right."

"I'm sorry," she replied. "I didn't mean to pry."

"Of course not. It's quite alright."

I dished the eggs onto several plates, and served them to my family.

"How long d'ya think you'll be gone?" Caroline asked, taking a dish from my hands.

"I'm not sure. I thought I'd set out right after breakfast. I expect we'll have a lot to discuss, and maybe I'll help her with some of her chores. I don't expect to stay all day, though. If I'm not home by noon, I'll be home shortly after for sure."

"Jacob. Daniel," Will said. "You boys need to hurry up 'n eat. We need to check the back five acres today. Time's a-wasting."

"Yes sir," Daniel said.

"I'm done," Joseph announced, taking his plate to the sink to be washed.

"Okay. Me too," said Daniel, following Joseph.

"Me too," Catherine said.

With breakfast completed, I washed the dishes while the girls mucked the stalls outside. I worked quickly in the quiet house, and finished my chores in short order. Gathering my courage, I walked the short distance to Julianne's.

THE OKLAHOMA HEAT was stifling, the air so thick and sticky I found myself struggling to breath. Heat waves rose in squiggly lines above the earth, but disappeared each time my feet approached their location. The flat landscape allowed me an unimpeded view for miles of this red earth I loved. I'd never been out of Oklahoma—or even Canadian County, for that matter—but I'd heard our soil was unique. The rich rust color stained the earth in every direction, lending it an unexpected vibrancy.

Preoccupied with thought, my foot struck a rock and I lost my balance, barely righting myself before my backside hit the ground. Steady on my feet again, I spied the culprit: the largest Cherokee Rose Rock I'd ever seen, easily the size of my fist. Reaching down, I lifted the rock and tested its weight in my palm. Stories from my childhood flashed through my mind—stories Mama had told, branded so fiercely in my memory they had become a part of me. I smoothed my hand over my flat stomach, imagining the day I might share those same stories with my own child.

My mind swirled through the years. Mama's voice was as clear in my head as if she was standing right beside me, retelling for the hundredth or more time of the great migration of the Cherokee people to Oklahoma. Remembering, I was once again aghast at the unimaginable hardships, yet awed by the strength and resilience of those great people as they journeyed—by force, through the Indian Removal Act of 1830—to a strange land then considered uninhabitable by the white man. Known as "The Trail of Tears," more than 16,000 of our nation's first residents travelled—most on foot and through inclement weather—approximately two thousand miles. The journey lasted many months, and an estimated 4,000 people died before reaching their destination. The Legend of the Cherokee Rose Rock held that, as their tears of pain and despair fell to the rust-colored earth below, a "Trail of Tears" in the formation of red rocks, shaped in the distinct likeness of a rose, grew from the ground at each spot a tear had landed. Mama had called the Cherokee Rose Rock sacred, and had reminded me never to forget the lives lost and tears shed as the result of an unjust government. Wiping a stray tear from my cheek, I kissed the rock and stuffed it in my pocket for another day.

About twenty yards from the house, Earl's massive black dog sounded the warning of my approach. Blind in his right eye and gray around the muzzle, Mutt danced happily around my feet, barking for attention and nearly knocking me to the ground. More like a small horse than a dog, he stood high on his back legs and rested his paws on my shoulders.

"Mutt!" Julianne yelled, stepping out of the house. "Mutt! You stupid beast! Down boy! Down!"

Earl Sykes followed behind at his wife's voice. "Get down! Down!" Overtaking Julianne, he reached my side first and pulled the dog away. "Bad dog! Bad, bad dog!"

"Oh, Victoria," Julianne said. "I'm so sorry! That crazy dog! Are ya okay? I don't think he'd bite ya, but he gets so excited when we get guests!"

"No, no," I said, brushing strands of the dog's fur from my skirt. "I'm okay. Ya know we've got those big dogs of Will's out at our house. I'm fine. Just taken by surprise is all."

"I don't know why Earl keeps that dog," she said. "He's old, half blind, and no good for anything but makin' a lot of noise."

"Which is exactly why I keep him." Earl wrapped an arm around Julianne and smiled warmly. "I don't like ya bein' out here at the house by yourself when I'm out in the field. That dog might surprise ya. He'd protect ya if you needed it. But, even if he doesn't, at least ya won't be caught off guard by somebody sneakin' up on ya."

Releasing Julianne, Earl pulled me into a hug. "It's good to see ya, Victoria."

I smiled. "You too, Earl. Married life seems to suit ya."

Earl's cheeks flamed and he rubbed his jaw, his eyes shooting downward. "It does at that."

Julianne cleared her throat. Now that the commotion with the dog had passed, she seemed to remember we'd parted awkwardly the day before. I'd have to make the first move.

Stepping forward, I enveloped Julianne in a hug. "I'm sorry."

Forgiveness was immediate, as I knew it would be. She returned my hug and we held on for long moments, neither of us ready to let go.

Finally stepping back, Julianne smiled. "Come into the house for some coffee?"

"I'd love to." I nodded.

"That's my cue, ladies." Earl pulled Julianne in for a quick hug and a swift peck on the cheek. "I gotta get on out to the field. I'll be back 'round noon, darlin'."

"I'll have lunch ready," Julianne replied, then looped her arm through mine before leading me into the house.

"So what brings ya out here?" she asked, turning to prepare our coffee.

"I came to apologize." I sighed and sat on one side of the kitchen table. "I'm sorry for the way I behaved yesterday. I have no excuse except to say the idea of you havin' a baby terrified me. If somethin' happened to you, I don't know what I'd do."

Julianne set two coffee cups on the table and sat across from me. "Ah, Victoria. I'll be fine. Women have babies all the time!"

I stared down at my hands. "Yeah, I know. That's what they said about my mama."

"Oh gosh!" Her cheeks flushed pink. "I'm so sorry! I never thought about your mama or your baby brother! I was just so excited that I couldn't wait to tell ya. It never crossed my mind that, well—that you'd think about your mama. I'm really sorry."

Reaching across the table, I took her hands in mine and smiled brightly. "Don't you go apologizin'. This isn't your fault. It's mine. I just wasn't prepared for it, and the news threw me off guard. I'm actually really happy for ya, now that I've had time to think on it."

"Are ya truly?" she asked. "You're sure?"

"Yes. Truly." I nodded. "I admit I was upset, but that was my problem, not yours. I talked to Will about it last night, and everything he said made sense. I just couldn't see it for all my fear."

"Thank you!" A tear leaked out of her left eye. "I was so worried you were gonna stay mad. I don't think I could've stood that. I'm gonna need you."

"Well, I'm gonna be here, so don'tcha worry." I bit my lip to conceal my grin. "Besides, I'm gonna need you, too."

Julianne waved a hand in dismissal. "Well of course! That's what sisters are for!"

"I was hoping you'd say that, because now I have somethin' I need to tell *you*."

She studied me a moment, taking in my flushed cheeks and barely contained smile. Her eyes narrowed, and her lips tipped up in a curious smile. "Okay—spit it out. What is it?"

"Well, ya see ..." I cleared my throat. "This is hard for me to say."

"It can't be bad—you're smilin' too much for that! What is it?"

"No. It's not bad. It's just that—well, Will is apparently more observant than I am," I began. "He—he thinks I'm expectin'."

"What?" Julianne squealed. "Victoria! I'm gonna be an aunt! We're gonna have our babies together, and they'll be best friends!"

Julianne's excitement was contagious, and I found myself giggling like a little girl. "Yeah, I think we just might."

For the next two hours, we talked about nothing but babies. What would we name them? When were they due? Would we deliver on the same day? Glancing at the clock, I was surprised at how much time had passed—it was nearly noon and Earl would be back soon! I rose from the table, intending to bid Julianne goodbye, but was interrupted by Mutt's frantic barking.

"Whatever is that dog goin' on about now?" Julianne rose and moved toward the door. "I swear he's the most irritatin' animal God put on this earth!"

Just as she reached to open the door, it burst open.

"Julianne! Victoria!" Earl entered in a blur and grabbed ahold of Julianne's arm in a bruising grip, pulling her out the door. "Come quickly! There's a twister comin'! We need to get down to the cellar!"

"Oh, my God!" I ran to the door, and searched the landscape. "I have to get home! The children are alone, and Will's gonna be worried!"

I rushed past Earl, but he grabbed my shoulder and pulled me up short. "Ya can't go right now. We gotta get to the cellar. We don't have time."

"But what about Will? I gotta get home!"

Earl shook his head and held firmly to my arm. "He'll be okay. He'll see it comin' and get the children to safety! Now y'all two get in the cellar! Now!"

Still I resisted, but Earl was too strong. With no other choice, I ran toward the safety of the underground shelter, but stopped before descending the steps, and stared in awe at the greenish-hued sky. Wind whipped around me, nearly knocking me off my feet. Less than a half a mile from us was the tornado, its base swirling toward the sky like thick, black smoke.

I'd always imagined a well-defined funnel, but this was so much more immense, and far less defined. Covering about a quarter mile in width, it blanketed the sky in pitch black. The winds picked up steadily and debris floated around the perimeter of the funnel, but it was still a good distance away. I scanned the landscape, wondering if I could get to Will and the children before the twister reached us.

Sensing my hesitation, Earl grabbed my elbow. "You'll never make it, Victoria, and Will'd never forgive me for lettin' ya try!"

"Earl, please! Let me go! I need to get to Will!"

"No! Get in the cellar!"

"But—"

Before I could utter another word, Earl tightened his grip on my arm and shoved me toward the open cellar door. "Go!"

I stumbled down the steps, falling on the last one with the force of Earl's shove. Pulling myself upright, I found Julianne waiting in a corner of the musty, cold cellar. Spider webs hung from the ceiling, and the underground sanctuary stank of mildew. The floors were nothing but red dirt below my feet, and I imagined all kinds of creepy, crawly things surfacing from the earth. In our rush, we'd forgotten to bring a lantern. The only light came from the open hole above our heads, as Earl stood on the top steps watching the storm move our direction. A few minutes passed, and the sky opened up, raining down hail the size of large fists.

"Here we go!" Earl stepped inside and pulled the doors closed, locking them with the pull-down board attached to the door on his right. "Hang on!"

With the cellar doors closed, we were enveloped in darkness. The only light was provided by the tiny seam between the two closed doors. Even that wasn't enough to see by. The darkness covered us, and the musty scents of damp dirt and mildew assaulted me. I shook violently. Finding his way in the darkness, Earl joined us and pulled the both of us into his embrace as though to shield us from harm.

We waited in the dark as the wind picked up and swirled above us. The cellar doors rattled, as the winds yanked them forcefully back and forth. I was certain that, between the wind and the chunks of ice pelting the doors, it wouldn't be long before the doors either broke free or the hail broke through.

As quickly as the rain began, it stopped. Silence surrounded us. I'd thought the worst had passed, but then the ground above us rumbled and shook. The winds picked up again, blowing more violently this time beyond the doors above. The storm roared like the sound of boxcars racing over the tracks of the Rock Island Railroad where my daddy used to work. It was deafening, yet Julianne's screams rang in my ears. Earl and I moved closer and held her more tightly.

The storm raged on. The cellar doors creaked and pulled viciously against the bar holding them shut. I was sure they would break free at any moment. Standing in the dark, I lost track of time as the wind pitched and howled for the longest time before finally slowing to a stop. Huddled together and holding each other tightly, the three of us waited in silence. I didn't know what we were waiting for. I just knew Earl would know, and would get us out safely.

After a long time, Earl pulled away. "I think it's passed."

Leaving Julianne and me huddled together, Earl climbed the cellar steps and approached the now still doors. Cautiously flipping first one door open, then the other, he peeked outside at the bright sunshine above. The storm had passed, leaving behind only the rays of the bright Oklahoma sunshine. We were blinded by the intensity after so long in the dark, yet grateful to see the sun's rays.

"Oh, my God! Oh, my God!" Julianne moaned and sobbed.

"It's okay, darlin'." Will returned to her side and gathered her into his arms. "We're safe. It's okay. Shhhh."

"It's not okay! We forgot Mutt! We left him out there!"

Earl and I froze. In all the commotion, none of us had considered the dog. He'd been there, barking at our feet when the storm began, but where was he when we ran for the cellar? If he'd been there, we surely would've taken him with us! But he wasn't there. Where had he gone?

"We'll find him, honey," Earl said. "He must be out there. Dogs're smart. He saw the storm comin'. He knew where to go for safety. I'm sure he's okay."

"No, he's not," Julianne sobbed. "He's a stupid dog, and ya know it. He's out there somewhere. It's my fault for forgettin' him!"

Leading her up the stairs and through the hole of the cellar, Earl soothed Julianne as best he could. Following behind, I had only one thought on my mind: Will and the children. I was sorry for Julianne's dog, but Earl was right. Surely he'd be okay. I needed to get home.

"Mutt!" called Julianne, now standing on the barren ground outside the cellar. "Mutt!"

Shielding my eyes from the now-bright sun, I assessed the damage. The storm had made a path about fifty yards south of the house. It had taken the roof off the barn, but had left the house standing. The trees were stripped completely bare of their leaves, mangled, broken, and filled with debris on one side. The other side remained entirely untouched.

"MUTT!" shouted Julianne, her voice frantic.

Turning to Earl, I pleaded with my eyes. "I'm so sorry, Earl. I have to go."

"It's okay, Victoria. Julianne will understand. Go."

Just as I turned to tell Victoria I was leaving, we heard barking in the distance. Julianne shouted for Mutt, her voice now a prayer. Moments later, the dog burst through the wheat field some 200 yards away.

"Mutt!" Julianne screamed and fell to her knees. "Mutt!" She opened her arms wide to embrace him. Tears of relief streamed down her face.

Not wishing to interrupt her reunion, I nodded at Earl and raced toward home.

I ran every step of the way, sometimes maneuvering through large branches or pieces of debris on my way. I ran until I had a stitch in my side. I could barely breathe in the sweltering Oklahoma sun, but I didn't stop. I ran with everything in me until I reached the path leading to our property, then picked up my pace and ran even faster. As I approached the house, its structure became clearer—the tornado had missed it entirely! The livestock barns had survived as well. The trees nearest our house were missing most of their leaves but appeared in good shape. I scanned the landscape for Will and the children, but they were nowhere in sight.

Now about a hundred yards from the house, I called to them. "Will! Caroline! Olivia!" Nobody answered, so I ran harder and yelled louder. "Joseph! Daniel!"

I was almost to the yard, still screaming their names, when the front door to our house flew open. Will ran out with the children behind him.

"Victoria! You're okay!" He met my distance and scooped me into his arms. "I was just fixin' to come lookin' for ya!"

"I'm okay!" I whispered, my voice clogged with tears. "Everyone's safe?"

"We're all good. The boys and I saw the tornado comin', and rushed in from the field to tell the girls. I was gonna take one of the horses to come get ya, but there wasn't time. It just came down so fast. We almost didn't make it to the cellar."

"I was just fixin' to come home from Julianne's when the storm hit," I said. "Earl rushed us down to the cellar so fast I barely had time to think! Oh, my God, Will! Did you see it? I've never seen anything like it!"

"We did! We stood out by the cellar and watched it for as long as we could, but we had to go underground when the hail started. It was comin' straight at us." Will scanned our property. "It must've taken a turn or lifted, otherwise there'd've been nothin' left standin'."

"Oh, God, Will! You're okay?" I examined him, trying to convince myself he was unscathed.

He pulled me against his chest, squeezing me so tight I almost couldn't breathe. "I was so worried ya might've been on the road on your way home when the tornado passed. Thank God you're okay!"

"I am. Really. But you're crushin' me." I was crying now, tears of relief mingled with fear.

Will placed me on the ground and took my face in the palms of his hands. His eyes scanned over my face, then down my body. "You're okay? You're sure?"

I nodded. "I'm fine. I was so afraid for you and the children! I tried to come home when we saw the storm comin' toward us, but Earl wouldn't let me."

Will stepped back, his eyebrows drawn together in an angry frown. "Ya tried to come home? What the hell were ya thinkin'? You'd never've made it, and could've been killed!" It was the first time Will had ever shouted at me.

"I wasn't thinkin'! I could only think of y'all! I needed to be here with you. I needed to know y'all were safe."

Wrapping his arms around me again, Will placed a kiss on the crown of my head. "Thank God for Earl. I owe him!"

Standing around us, the children were reluctant to intrude. Each had a look of combined fear and relief on their face. I reached my arm out toward Catherine, who rushed toward me. She embraced me tightly, then the other children quickly followed her lead. The seven of us stood sweltering in the haze of the Oklahoma sun, thankful to be together.

# CHAPTER EIGHTEEN

THE NEXT TWO WEEKS PASSED IN A FLURRY OF activity, as we helped our nearest neighbors rebuild what was lost in the tornado. Luckily, the damage was minimal. Earl Sykes lost the roof on his barn, but the livestock were all unharmed; and most neighbors had damages requiring similar repairs. Though the twister completely missed Atticus's place, we found it had destroyed the corral on our property that Will used for breaking horses. Everything else seemed in good shape.

During this time, Will's mother was a constant presence in our lives. Her intense dislike for me had not changed, and she'd taken to calling me "girl" rather than my given name. Will was furious, but I'd soothed him by insisting it wasn't important. His love and support were all I needed to deflect the meanness of her words.

Imogene Harrison's behavior became so confrontational that we'd chosen to withhold news of my pregnancy until my condition was obvious. I'd hoped the baby would soften her; but Will feared it would intimidate her more, causing her to lash out even more viciously. So we kept the information to ourselves, sharing it only with Julianne, Earl, Veronica and Atticus.

As the men finished assembling Will's corral, the women prepared a meal to share when the men were done. Mrs. Harrison had disappeared, so our conversation turned to the babies Julianne and I carried.

"What about names?" Veronica asked. "Have you decided on one yet?"

"Not yet. It's still too early." I laughed and turned toward Julianne. "What about you?"

"Oh no!" Julianne replied. "Earl and I decided we'd wait until the baby's born to see what he looks like. It would be just awful to decide upon a name like James, only to discover he looks more like a Charles!"

"When will you tell Imogene?" Veronica asked.

"I'm not sure," I replied. "I think I'll leave that up to Will. She's his mother, after all. She dislikes me too much for me to give her the news."

"I sure wish you'd do it soon," Veronica replied. "Imogene's gonna do whatever Imogene's gonna do. The longer ya wait to tell her, the harder it's gonna be. Ya think she's disagreeable now, just wait until she finds out you've kept this information from her. I'm tellin' ya now: heads will roll!"

"What exactly am I gonna do, Veronica? Whose head's gonna roll?" Imogene Harrison stepped around the corner of the house, greeting us with her steely gaze. "And what is it you're keepin' from me, girl?"

Startled, I jumped and my heart raced in my chest. *How long had she been standing there? What had she heard? Where in the world was Will?*

Mrs. Harrison arched an eyebrow. "I asked ya a question, girl. What is it you're keepin' from me?"

I didn't know how to respond. I was a terrible liar, so I tried for a partial truth. I hoped I could salvage some small amount of peace.

"Hello, Mrs. Harrison," I said. "Nothin', really. It's just that Will and I have some news we'd hoped to share with ya, but we just haven't found the time."

"Well, I have time right now. What is it?"

"I—we really should wait for Will, Mrs. Harrison."

"Why?" She folded her arms across her ample chest. "I'm standin' right here, and I have time. Go on with it—I don't have all day."

I looked around for Will, but he was nowhere in sight. The men had moved away from the corral, presumably to wash up for dinner. How long could I stall before she made me tell her about the pregnancy?

"I said I'm waitin', girl. Give me your news, and get it over with."

"Well," I said slowly. "I'm expectin'. You're gonna be a grandmother again."

I'm not sure what I expected from her. What I received was her laughter. She stood right in front of me and laughed in my face as though I'd told her the most amusing story.

Gaining control of herself, she narrowed her eyes at me. "Tell me, girl: who's the father?"

Veronica and Julianne gasped. My jaw dropped. Did I mishear her? Surely even she wouldn't be so cruel?

"I beg your pardon?" My voice was barely a whisper.

"I asked ya, who's the father?"

"W—Will, of course."

"Humph!" she snorted. "I highly doubt that. A young girl like you, and a man more than double your age? I wondered why he married ya, and why it was done so quickly. He never even consulted me. Now I know. If ya can't be pretty, or even strong enough to pull your weight, then at least it's good to know you're good at somethin'. It takes all kinds, I s'pose."

Hot blood rushed up my neck and to my cheeks, yet I stood there stupidly. I didn't know how to respond. I wasn't alone. Next to me stood Veronica and Julianne, both equally speechless.

I lifted my chin and threw my shoulders back. Pulling my pride around me like a cloak, I looked that nasty old woman in the eye. I refused to let her see me broken. "If you'll please excuse me, Mrs. Harrison, I have things to accomplish."

I walked away with deliberate steps toward the creek some distance off. I needed time to think, and I was afraid I might cry. The idea of crying no longer upset me as it once had, but I'd be damned if I'd cry in front of that awful woman. I wouldn't give her the satisfaction.

WILL FOUND ME some thirty minutes later. I'd been standing at the creek, near the water's edge, skipping rocks across the surface. I'd seen Will teaching the boys and Catherine so many times before, but I couldn't get the hang of it.

I heard Will approach before I saw him. He made no attempt at stealth; I think he intended me to hear him. Reaching my side, he selected a rock from the edge of the water. Pulling his arm back, he released it to skip across the water's surface. When I didn't comment, he cleared his throat. "Julianne and Earl went home."

"Oh?" I stared out at the water.

"Yup. She seemed pretty upset—said she didn't feel well, and asked Earl to take her home. Veronica packed up two plates of dinner to take with 'em."

"Hmmm." I bit my lip to keep from saying something I'd regret. "I'm sorry to hear that."

"Funny thing," he said. "After they left, Atticus was huddled in conversation with Veronica, and then he pulled Father aside. When they were done talkin', Father insisted it was time for him and Mother to go home as well."

"Hmmm," I said again. "That's strange."

Pulling his arm back, Will skipped another rock across the water's surface. "It is, isn't it?"

The silence stretched thick between us, as though Will was waiting for me to respond. When I said nothing, he continued. "The interestin' thing is, Veronica refused to make a plate for Mother and Father to take with 'em, and Father refused to wait for Mother to make 'em herself. It seems he couldn't get her home fast enough."

"Hmmm."

Will turned toward me, his eyes studying me while he decided upon his next words. "So, ya see, I finally asked Veronica what'd happened."

"What'd she say?" I whispered.

"She said it wasn't her place to say, but she sent me out here to find ya. She said you'd tell me, if ya wanted."

I swallowed hard, my throat now aching with unshed tears. "I see."

"So I'm thinkin' something happened when we were workin' on the corral. Julianne couldn't get away fast enough, and Veronica's hoppin' mad at my mother. In fact, I'm not sure I've ever seen her so angry. Then there's you. Here y'are out alone by the creek skippin' rocks—poorly, I might add—and I have the distinct impression you're upset. Maybe more upset than I've ever seen ya."

I bit hard on my lip, counting on the pain to keep my focus on not crying.

Will took my shoulders and turned me to face him. Then, taking both of my hands, he stared into my eyes. "Tell me what happened. I know it was somethin' to do with my mother."

I'd held the tears as long as I could. Will's words were the catalyst that set them free. As the first drops of tears landed on my cheeks, he pulled me into his arms and whispered words of comfort.

"Shhh—Just tell me. What'd she say? We'll work it out."

Once the first tears had fallen, there was no holding them back. To my embarrassment, they ran like rivers down both sides of my cheeks. Will's mother had not only shocked me; she'd shamed me. I knew I would never gain acceptance from this woman, and I was finally done trying.

Will leaned back and lifted my chin with the knuckle and thumb of his right hand. "Tell me what she said."

"Oh, Will," I whispered. "Ya don't wanna know. Truly. It's not somethin' ya need to hear."

"Wrong. Whatever she said has upset ya. I need to know what it is. Now, tell me."

I took a deep breath and stared at the ground at my feet. "She overheard us talkin' about the baby. I had no choice but to tell her. She asked me . . ."

"What'd she ask, Victoria? I need to know."

I took a deep breath and lifted my chin even higher, then closed my eyes. I couldn't look at Will when I said the words. "She asked me who the baby's father is."

Will went completely still, and anger radiated from him in hot waves. "She didn't."

I nodded. I was deeply hurt; but, more than that, I was embarrassed. Is that really what she thought of me? If so, how many others would she tell?

Pulling me close once again, Will kissed the crown of my head. "I'm done. This is somethin' I can't tolerate. I'm so sorry, sweetheart. If she were a man, I'd beat her within an inch of her life."

"It's fine."

"No, Victoria. It's not fine. Nothin' about the way she's treated you—or Hannah before ya—has been fine. I thought she'd eventually come 'round, but I can see that's not gonna happen. She wants me to choose? Fine. I choose you."

"What're ya sayin'?"

"I'm sayin' I'm done. She's backed me into a corner, and I don't like bein' backed into a corner. There is only one decision in this situation. I choose my wife. She's not welcome here anymore, and we won't be goin' to see Veronica and Atticus so long as they're still livin' on the same property. It's that simple."

"No! Ya can't do that. She's your mother!"

"She was my mother, and you're my wife. She should know by now I'd never choose her over you. Now c'mon. Let's go on up to the house. I need to pay a visit to my mother, and I wanna make sure you're okay."

Taking my hand and placing it in the crook of his arm, Will led me back toward the house.

"What're ya gonna do?" I asked.

"Don't you worry about that, Victoria. I can't tell ya how sorry I am, but I promise it'll be the last time she says or does anything to ya so long as I'm here on this earth." Will gritted his teeth until I thought they might crack.

"I don't wanna come between you and your mother," I said. "Really. I was upset by what she said, but I'll get over it."

"Ya might get over it, or ya might not. But I swore to honor ya. I can't honor ya if I allow my mother to get away with treatin' ya so dishonorably. What she said is reprehensible! Don'tcha see that? I could almost ignore her rudeness, but she's gone too far this time. If I don't draw a line now, where and when does it stop?"

"Let's just sleep on it," I pleaded.

"No." Will shook his head. "I should've done this long ago. This isn't your fault; this is my mother's doin'. It ends tonight."

Reaching the house, we found Veronica and Atticus cleaning up the leftover dinner that had never taken place. Veronica sent me a questioning glance, while Will addressed Atticus.

"I need to run over to your place and talk to Mother and Father for a bit. Can ya stay here with Victoria and keep her company? I don't think she should be alone right now."

"Will, I'm fine," I interrupted. "Really. Don't go. Please."

"I have to, Victoria."

Veronica stepped toward me and looped her arm through mine. "He's right, Victoria. It's been comin' a long time. Go on, Will. We've got it covered here. D'ya want Atticus to go with ya?"

"Doesn't matter what Will wants," Atticus said. "I'll go, too. Mother has behaved badly for the last time. It's long past time she understood her behavior won't be tolerated."

"Okay, then. We'll be here," Veronica said, leading me into the house.

"Will?" I said, resisting Veronica. "Please don't go. Ya really don't need to do this."

Coming toward me and taking me once again in his arms, Will held me tight and kissed my forehead. "Yes, Victoria. I really *do* need to do this. I'll be back soon."

With those words, Will and Atticus saddled the horses and rode out to see their mother.

I NEVER LEARNED what Will said to his mother. He never would say. I do know she and his father never visited again. They continued living with Veronica and Atticus, who visited us from time to time, but we never made the short trip over to visit with them. Will meant what he'd said. His mother was dead to him. As far as I know she never laid eyes on him again.

# CHAPTER NINETEEN

THE FINAL DAYS OF SUMMER CREPT TO A
close, and soon it was autumn. In late September we celebrated my nine-
teenth birthday. The girls took over my chores for the day and prepared a special meal that evening. Will found a meadow of black-eyed Susans and presented me with a lovely bouquet. Carefully, I trimmed the stems and placed
them on our table to show them off. They'd not only become my favorite
flower, but they were the only flower I ever again wished to receive.

Winter came early that year and, with it, the blistering cold. And Christmas. Anticipating my dislike for the holiday, Will took extra care to make it
unique and festive. For the first time in many years, I enjoyed the celebrations
and participated with joy; and nearly forgot the pain that, for me, had always
accompanied the season.

In March, Julianne delivered a healthy baby boy, whom she and Earl
proudly named Theodore James. I was too large with child by this time to
travel even the one mile for the baby's birth, but Veronica was summoned
and helped bring this new little person into the world. Julianne survived the
delivery with ease, visiting us only days later to show off her new bundle.
Studying his tiny face, excitement raced through me. My own baby would
arrive soon.

March bled into April, and I neared the end of my term. The chores had
become difficult, so Caroline and Olivia pitched in. They were wonderful
girls, and I felt truly blessed to call them my friends.

On April 12, 1925, with the help of Veronica and Julianne, our first
child was born—a girl. Grace Elizabeth Harrison came into the world angry
and purple, not at all pleased at leaving the warmth of the cozy home she'd
enjoyed for nine months. Her hair was fiery red, the exact shade my mother's
had been. Her eyes were the color of cornflowers, almost identical to my
daddy's. Gazing at her tiny features, the fear I'd carried for so long disap-

peared. Grace's birth brought with it healing, and I finally understood my mother's despair at the loss of my brother.

As Grace wrapped her tiny fist around my pinky, my anger vanished as though it hadn't been my constant companion for eleven years. My heart was too full of love, and there was no room left for anger to reside.

AFTER GRACE'S BIRTH, the babies came fast and at regular intervals. Jackson Ellis was born in January 1927, followed by Ethan Thomas in May 1929, and Sara Jane in November 1930. All but Ethan inherited the brilliant copper of my mother's hair. Ethan, on the other hand, was the image of Will. From the golden wheat color of his hair, to the deep dimple in his left cheek, that boy was his father's son.

Julianne only had one more baby, Constance Marie, born in April 1930. As we'd hoped, our children were playmates and the best of friends.

In the spring of 1929, Caroline and Olivia—now twenty and eighteen—began courting brothers from a neighboring farm, about three miles down the road. The young men, John and Jefferson Janicek, were the grandsons of Czechoslovakian immigrants who'd staked a claim in the original Land Run of 1889. They had recently inherited that same land from their grandfather, who had raised them, and soon erected a second house some quarter of a mile away from the first. Now settled and searching for wives, their attentions turned to Caroline and Olivia, who both eagerly returned their affections.

Late that summer of 1929, Caroline and Olivia married John and Jefferson Janicek in a dual ceremony in the back yard of our home. Presiding over the ceremony was Reverend Patterson, now bent with age, but pleased to perform this rite for the next generation.

I was happy for Caroline and Olivia, but sorry to see them leave our home. They'd both been good friends to me. They'd welcomed me and treated me with kindness, and I would forever cherish them for that love.

In the fall of 1929, Will's father suffered a stroke and never recovered his full energy. Though Will frequently visited his father to check on his health, he was always careful to arrange his visits around his mother's trips to town. The years had passed, and he still refused to see her. I didn't miss her, but I'm sure he must have. He never said.

In late October of that same year, the stock market crashed in what became known as Black Tuesday. As farmers, we had nothing invested in the stock market, so we weren't directly affected by the crash. We knew people who were, though. Many of those we'd grown up with, or who'd been my neighbors in town, lost everything.

It was now November 1931. Will and I had welcomed four children in eight years, and I was expecting our fifth in late March. I was happier than I'd ever been. Will was as excited with the announcement of each baby as he had been with the first. Together we now had nine children, with the tenth due in only a few short months.

Thanksgiving that year was joyful. We'd invited Mother Elizabeth and Father Caleb for dinner, along with Caroline, Olivia, and their families. Caroline was expecting her second child, and Olivia was due with her first in mid-April. Julianne and Earl came with both of their children; but Jacob was spending the holiday with the family of a young lady he'd begun courting, and whom we were certain would become part of the family soon. Joseph and Daniel had passed their eighteenth birthday, and Will had gifted them each a plot of land adjacent to our own. As single young men with limited cooking skills, they spent as many mealtimes at our home as they did at their own.

The house overflowed with food, laughter, and the pounding of far too many children's feet in such a confined space. Our family had grown, and Will and I were the head of this boisterous family. The joy I'd never known as a child now consumed me. The only thing missing was Veronica and Atticus with their boys. Due to the continued estrangement of Will and his mother, Atticus felt they should spend the holiday with his parents. He couldn't leave them alone, and I understood.

Dinner was a raucous affair, with each person talking over the other, and different conversations taking place in each corner. Our table was too small for everyone, so the boys carried in several sawhorses from the barn and laid large sheets of plywood over the tops to make one table that extended the entire length of the front room. We covered this makeshift table with bed linens for tablecloths. In the center of everything was a large tom turkey Will had butchered from our back acres the day before. He and the twins had plucked the feathers, then presented it to me that morning to prepare and stuff with dressing. Caroline and Olivia brought casseroles of sweet potato and green beans preserved from their gardens, and Julianne brought potatoes she'd stored in her cellar. With the cream and butter from our cows, we made fresh mashed potatoes. Mother Elizabeth supplied the desserts. It was the most delicious meal I could ever remember having.

With the adults and older children seated at the large table, and the youngest children seated around a smaller table nearby, we dined in grand fashion. All except Will, who wasn't feeling well. Though he enjoyed the conversation, and loved having the family around us, his stomach was giving him trouble. He barely touched his food, instead pushing it around his plate without eating. I watched him throughout the day with concern—nobody hated waste more than Will. The last thing we needed was for him to get sick. The boys needed him on the farm. Our family counted on him to get by.

# CHAPTER TWENTY

PREPARING FOR BED THAT NIGHT, I WAS BOTH exhausted and exhilarated. I'd never dreamed I'd have so many people under one roof, all of them my own family.

"Ya didn't eat much at dinner," I said to Will as I crawled into bed beside him.

"My belly's been hurtin' somethin' fierce all day," he said. "I wasn't sure I could keep anything down."

"I wondered at that. Doesn't seem like you not to be hungry."

"I'm sorry, darlin'."

"Don't be. I'm just sorry ya couldn't enjoy the day. That's the best meal we've had in ages, and I'm not sure we'll have another like it again anytime soon."

"Anythin' left?"

"Not much. I put a plate aside for ya in case ya felt like eatin' some later."

"Thanks. Maybe tomorrow."

Will sat up and pulled his shirt over his head then slipped out of his overalls, one leg at a time, leaving himself clad in only the long underwear he wore beneath his clothing during those cold winter months. Stretching slightly, he winced as he hung his clothes on the peg by the door.

"Is it that painful?" I asked.

"Ah, it's nothin'." He pulled back the bed sheets and climbed into bed.

Scooting over to Will's side, I snuggled up close to him.

"Careful, darlin'." He stiffened. "My gut's not feelin' right, and I don't know if I'm gonna be sick or what. Best not get too close."

"Can I get ya somethin'? A warm water bottle, maybe? Or some bakin' soda?"

"Maybe a water bottle."

I slipped out of bed, not bothering to throw a robe over my nightgown, and padded on bare feet to the kitchen. Finding a water bottle in the cabinet, I placed a pot of water on the stove and warmed it.

When I returned, Will was lying on his left side with his knees tucked up toward his chest. He exhaled and inhaled in shallow puffs. I watched him a moment then, lifting his left arm, I gently laid the water bottle next to his belly, anchoring it with a pillow to keep it snug.

"Careful, darlin'," he said. "It's pretty painful at the moment."

"Are ya sure you're okay?"

"I'm alright. It'll pass on here shortly."

Crawling into bed, careful not to jostle him unnecessarily, I scooted close behind him and draped my arm over his shoulder to share his warmth.

"Does that help any, d'ya think?" I asked.

"Some maybe," he said, but the strain in his voice betrayed him. He was in far more pain than he let on.

I closed my eyes and listened to Will breathe. Each time I thought the pain had eased, his body stiffened and his breathing became exaggerated.

"Can I do anything?" I whispered, in case he'd dropped off to sleep.

"Nah, honey. It'll be okay. If I don't feel better here soon, I'll get up and take some bakin' soda."

With not much I could do to help, I eased off to sleep.

WILL SLEPT RESTLESSLY that night, and I lost count of how many times I was awakened by his quiet groans of discomfort. Somewhere in the middle of the night, I refreshed his water bottle and found some baking soda and insisted he take it. It wasn't until nearly 3:00 a.m. before he settled down into a deep sleep.

The sun was just peeking above the horizon when I awakened. Sitting up, I wiped the sleep from my eyes. Will was resting easily, but it had been a long night for him. Slipping out of bed, I dressed in the quiet of the morning, then gently eased open our door to begin breakfast.

I'd just finished cracking the eggs when Catherine came in with Grace, Ethan, and Sara in tow. As was his habit, Jack was still asleep.

"Where's Daddy?" Catherine asked.

"He's still sleepin'. He had a hard night, so I thought I'd make breakfast before wakin' him up. I'm almost done, d'ya wanna go get him?"

"What's wrong with him?" she asked. "He never sleeps late."

"He had a bellyache, and it kept him up half the night."

Catherine paused at our bedroom door. "Should we let him sleep a bit longer? It's not like Daddy to be sick."

"Nah," I replied. "He slept well the last few hours, so I think he's feeling better. Knowin' your daddy, he won't be happy to miss half the day sleepin'."

As Catherine reached for the door, Will stepped out. He was dressed and his hair combed, but dark circles bagged under his eyes from lack of sleep.

"I was just comin' to fetch you for breakfast," Catherine said. "Victoria said ya didn't sleep well last night."

"Nah, I'm good. Ain't nothin' tough enough to knock me down for very long." Will grinned, but his color seemed off.

"Your eggs and bacon are ready," I said, setting a dish at his place at the table. "Toast'll be outta the oven in just a minute."

Will smiled weakly. I studied him, finding his skin tone slightly flushed, but attributed it to lack of sleep. He hadn't complained about his belly in hours and, though I hated seeing him under the weather, I wasn't overly concerned. Back then, my faith in Will was absolute. I was sure nothing could take him down.

Will pushed his plate away and folded his hands on the table. "Why don'tcha save this for Jack? I'm not quite ready to try anything on my belly just yet."

"It still hurts?" I asked

"Nah—it'll be okay. Just don't wanna see my breakfast come back up."

Not wanting to nag, I took the plate away and set it aside for Jack, who would be down soon and ravenous.

"Ya want some coffee?" I asked.

"Nah, darlin'. I think I'll just head on out to the fields. Daniel and Joseph will be out there already if I don't get a move on."

Four-year old Jack stumbled to the table in stocking feet, clearly having just risen from bed. Taking a seat at the table, he grinned at Will. "Mornin', Daddy. Mornin', Mama."

"About time ya got outta bed, little man." Will smiled, then rose from the table and ruffled Jack's unruly copper-colored hair before pulling me close in a hug. "I'll be back around noon." To the children he said, "Y'all best behave while I'm gone. Catherine, help Victoria with the children. She's been up half the night with me, and we don't need her gettin' sick."

Embarrassed, I squeezed Will back. "I'm not the one who was feelin' poorly last night. You're sure you're better today?"

"Positive." Will grabbed his coat from the peg by the door and threw it over his shoulders, then placed his hat snugly upon his head. "Back for lunch," he said, his smile bringing out the dimple in his cheek.

"We'll be here," I told him.

My heart beat hard within my chest. After eight years of marriage, he still made my heart beat frantically.

"GRACE," I SAID, frustrated. "I'm not gonna ask ya again. Will ya please help Catherine with Ethan and Sara, or I'll put ya to real work. I can't muck out these stalls and keep the babies from eatin' manure at the same time."

"Sorry, Mama." Grace picked up her baby sister and took the hand of her brother.

"Don't be sorry, just get 'em outta my hair so I can get some work done," I grumbled below my breath.

I hated mucking stalls. Of all the chores I'd learned, mucking stalls was my least favorite. I hated the smell, and the hard labor. More than that, though, I hated the flies!

I stood to stretch my back and heard the sound of a truck approaching. I wondered at who could be calling on us. Most folks in these parts had work to do and not much time for social calls. Leaning the rake against the nearest wall, I wiped my hands on my skirt, and walked out of the barn to discover who was approaching.

Sitting behind the wheel was Joseph, or maybe it was Daniel. I still had trouble telling them apart from a distance. Whichever one it was, he was driving far too fast. I stepped into the path, prepared to give him a piece of my mind. What in the world was he doing out here when his daddy needed him in the field?

The truck jerked to a stop. Jumping out from the driver's side, Joseph rushed to the tail bed. "Victoria, come quick! Daddy's collapsed!"

"What?" My heart dropped low in my belly. "What d'ya mean he collapsed?"

"He just fell down and is unconscious!" he said.

Appearing now from the bed of the truck, Daniel stood and spoke to Joseph. "C'mon, Joe! We can explain later. Right now we need to get Daddy into the house!"

Turning his attention back to his brother, Joseph helped Daniel heave Will's lifeless body out of the truck. Laying his body on a heavy blanket made moving him easier, but it was still burdensome work. Will was a large man.

"Catherine!" I shouted toward the house. "Catherine!" Hearing the door open behind me, I didn't look to see who was there. "Hold the front door open, then make sure the sheets on our bed are pulled down! Quickly!"

I helped the boys as best I could, but I was really only issuing orders, while they carried Will through the house and into the bedroom.

"Mama?" said Grace. I could hear the panic in her voice and had no patience for it. My entire focus was on Will.

"Out!" I yelled. "Catherine! Come get these kids, and get them outta here! I need to worry about your daddy and can't do anything with them under my feet!"

Rushing to Will's side, I held his hand in my own and studied his ashen features. "Joseph, go get me a pot of cool water and a washrag. Daniel, tell me what happened, and help me take off his boots."

"I'm not sure," Daniel began as we removed Will's boots. "We were out by the fence separatin' our property from Uncle Earl's. We were tryin' to fix that line of fence that old mare knocked down last week. Daddy just looked up at us, and his face turned gray. We asked him if he was feelin' okay, and he just collapsed. We tried to rouse him, but he wouldn't wake up. Joseph had that old blanket in the bed of the truck, so we laid Daddy out on it and brought him here."

"Here, Victoria," Joseph said, setting the water and washrag next to me.

"One of you boys run into town and fetch Dr. Heusman. Tell him he's needed quickly. Don'tcha dare take no for an answer," I warned.

"I'll go," said Joseph. He was out the door before I could even respond.

Sitting beside Will on the bed, I bathed his face and neck with the cool rag. His skin was clammy to the touch, and his complexion had taken on a waxy appearance.

"Has he been conscious at all?" I asked.

"No," Daniel replied.

"Will?" I said gently. "Will, wake up. Can ya hear me?"

Will didn't move; he just lay there. Not knowing what else to do, I continued bathing his face and neck with the cool water. Time stretched endlessly as we waited for Will to gain consciousness, or for the doctor to arrive. With each ticking of the clock, the walls closed in around me until I could barely breathe. It was taking too long!

"Daniel—help me take off his overalls," I said.

Heaving his body upright, we pulled the bib down to his waist, then lifted his hips to pull his pants down his legs. Covering his body with a light blanket, I glanced at the clock on the mantle. Twenty minutes had passed since Joseph left to find Dr. Heusman, and still no response from Will.

Finally, at nearly the thirty-five minute mark, Will regained consciousness. He'd recovered some color to his skin, but now he was too flushed. I ran my palm across his forehead and snatched it back quickly. He was near scalding to the touch.

"Victoria?" Will whispered and tried to sit up.

"Be still, Will." I placed a hand on his shoulder to prevent his rising. "Don't try to get up. I'm here. Ya passed out in the field and the boys brought ya home. How're ya feelin'?"

"Not so good. I'm cold all over. And weak. I just feel very weak."

"Don't worry about that. Ya have a fever and Joseph's gone to fetch Dr. Heusman."

"Dammit, Victoria. I don't need no damn doctor, and we don't have the money for one! I just need some rest"

"Well, it's too late. I already sent for him. We'll just have to figure out how to get him paid for later. Ya don't look good, and I don't like it."

"Just let me rest a bit. I'll sleep it off, and be right as rain tomorrow." Will closed his eyes, drifting immediately off to sleep.

Not knowing what more I could do, I sat with him, bathing his face and neck with the cool water, while we waited for the doctor. Will's appearance alarmed me, but I took deep breaths to calm my nerves. In such a short time, he'd gone from pale and sticky to flushed and fevered. I didn't know what this meant, but it was the sickest I'd ever seen anyone, much less Will.

TWO HOURS PASSED, then three, then four. The noon hour had long passed, and soon it would be time for dinner. At nearly five hours gone, Joseph returned with the doctor in tow.

"What took ya so long?" I growled at Joseph.

"Dr. Heusman was out makin' calls in Kingfisher. I had to wait around for him to get back."

"Hello, Victoria," Dr. Heusman said. "Tell me what's goin' on here."

I explained to Dr. Heusman about Will's being sick the night before, his apparent recovery that morning, and then his collapse in the field. "He seemed better this mornin'. Tired, maybe, but he didn't sleep much last night."

"All right, then. Everybody out. Let me take a look," Dr. Heusman said.

"I'll stay here in case ya need help," I replied.

"There's no need, Victoria. I'll be out in a minute."

I crossed my arms over my chest and stood my ground. "This is my house, and my husband. Not to mention, my bedroom. I'll stay right here—outta your way if ya want—but I won't leave him. If ya need me, fine. But in either case, I'm not leavin'."

The doctor shrugged. "Suit yourself, then."

Dr. Heusman did what appeared to be a thorough examination, poking and prodding until he awakened Will from his slumber.

"What the hell?" Will moaned, his eyes still closed.

"Just checkin' some things, Will. Just lay still, and I'll be done in a minute," Dr. Heusman explained.

Will opened his eyes for a few seconds, then closed them again. "I don't need ya, and I can't afford ya, Doc. I'll be fine."

Dr. Heusman didn't say anything. He continued poking and prodding, occasionally eliciting small groans of discomfort from Will.

"Tell me more about last night," Dr. Heusman said. "Tell me about the pain. You say it was gone this morning?"

"I just didn't feel well most of the day yesterday, kinda like I was fixin' to throw up, but it never actually came to that," Will said. "Then last night, my stomach hurt somethin' awful—like maybe I'd been kicked by a horse. No matter which way I turned, I couldn't get comfortable."

"But it got better? When was that?"

"I don't right recall. Somewhere in the middle of the night, I guess. The pain just went away. Almost like when ya have gas built up in your stomach, and ya finally release it. I 'spose that's the best way to describe it."

"And then you felt better?"

"Pretty much," Will agreed. "I didn't feel like eatin' none, but I felt well enough to go out to the fields."

"And that's when ya collapsed? How long had you been out there?"

"Ah hell, Doc, I don't know. Maybe a couple hours?"

"He was gray and clammy when the boys brought him home," I interrupted. "He was still unconscious, and didn't wake until about half an hour after Joseph left to get ya. Then he went back to sleep and has been restin' until just now."

"I see." Dr. Heusman pulled a chair over beside the bed and sat down. "Will, I'm gonna give it to ya straight. Based upon your symptoms and on my exam, I think you have a ruptured appendix."

"What's that mean?" I asked.

"It's an inflammation in the appendix. If left untreated, it bursts and spills infectious materials into the abdomen." The doctor turned his attention back to Will. "The pain ya had last night is consistent with inflammation. If you'd seen me right away, we might've had time to do somethin'. But I'm afraid it's too late. It appears to've burst and you'd need immediate surgery to remove it.

"Then take it out!" I snapped, as fear once again suffocated me.

The doctor shook his head. "I'm afraid I can't. I'm not a surgeon, and the closest one is in Oklahoma City."

"Fine. The boys'll load him up in the truck, and we'll leave right now. Who d'we need to go see and where?"

"Ya don't understand, Victoria," Dr. Heusman said. "It's too late for that. With the worst of his pain already past, I'm pretty sure his appendix has burst."

"But a surgeon could still fix it, right? They could make him better."

"Maybe. But it's a gamble. Even if it weren't too late for surgery, it'll take ya, what? A couple hours to get up to Oklahoma City? I'm not sure Will's good to travel in this shape; but, even if he was, it'll be past midnight by the time ya get there. They're gonna need to bring in a surgeon. D'ya have any idea what that'll cost?"

I didn't answer. I had no idea. Worse, I knew we didn't have the money for one.

"I'll tell ya," the doctor continued. "I don't think they'll even look at him for less than a couple hundred dollars, anyway."

"So what're ya sayin'?"

"Well, there's just not a lot we can do. We can keep him comfortable, and hope he recovers. The odds aren't good, but it happens."

"So he might be okay, then?"

Will had been so quiet throughout our exchange, I was afraid he'd fallen unconscious again. But, then he spoke. "No, Victoria. The doctor's tryin' to tell ya as gently as he can, and you're just not listen'. I'm not gonna make it. I've seen this before. Atticus and me had a little brother who died of an appendix rupture back when we were kids. There just isn't a whole lot that can be done."

"But we can drive up to Oklahoma City to find a surgeon," I argued.

"No," Will said, his eyes closed.

"But we can't sit here and do nothin'! We should at least give a surgeon a try, Will!"

"Dammit, Victoria, listen to me." Will opened his eyes and stared into mine. "There's no money for it. There ain't enough gasoline in the tank to get us there, and we'd barely have enough to fill the tank. And where the hell d'ya think we're gonna come up with a couple hundred dollars?"

"We could find it. I know we could!"

"Think, Victoria. You're smart, but you're not thinkin', and I don't have the energy to fight with ya. We don't have the money to spend on it," Will explained. "It's a gamble at best, and then what? I die anyway, and you and the kids are in far worse shape than we already are."

"What are ya sayin'?" My eyes moved back and forth between Will and Dr. Heusman.

"Just that," Will said, closing his eyes again. "There's nothin' more to it."

I shook my head. "No!"

"He's right, Victoria," Dr. Heusman interrupted. "A drive to Oklahoma City is nothing but a fool's errand. The poison in his appendix will eventually cause serious infection that I can't treat with medicine. I can give him some morphine for the pain, but there's just not much more that can be done. Ya need to be prepared."

"Surely there's somethin'—"

"I'm sorry, there's nothing we can do," the doctor interrupted. "If we'd caught it early, he might've had a chance. If times weren't so tough, and ya had money, he might've had a chance. Maybe."

"But it wasn't so bad earlier," I said. "At least not so bad he was alarmed."

"Will's always been as hard-headed as a mule, Victoria. You know that. I don't doubt he was in excruciating pain last night, and just didn't wanna worry ya."

"Will?" I asked.

"I didn't think it was serious," he replied, his eyes still closed.

"Damn you, Will Harrison!" I screamed.

"Leave me alone, Victoria," he whispered. "Just let me rest."

"He's right," Dr. Heusman said. "We need to let him rest. This is fixin' to get a whole lot worse before it gets better. There's really not much we can do but keep him comfortable and hope he pulls through it."

"How long?" I asked.

"Until we know if he'll be okay?"

I nodded.

The doctor shrugged. "Hard to say. He could go quickly—tonight or tomorrow, even—but it might take a few days. If he's still here after that and feelin' better, then we'll know he's pulled through. We just have to wait and see."

With nothing more he could do, the doctor left us alone with Will. The only thing we could do was keep him comfortable, and even that proved impossible. With nothing else to do, we waited.

# CHAPTER TWENTY-ONE

THE NEXT THREE DAYS WERE AWFUL. WILL drifted in and out of consciousness, becoming delirious sometime in the middle of the second day. His prognosis was explained to the older children, and they were devastated. Ethan and Sara were too young to understand, but Grace understood fully. Jack was just beginning to grasp the concept. Caroline and Olivia stayed with us every day from early morning until dinnertime. Daniel and Joseph continued working the fields during the days, but moved back into their old beds to help with their father's care at night.

Will's fever rose so high he became delirious. For three days, he tossed and turned, uttering nonsensical statements—everything from instructing the boys how to drive the truck, to confusing me with his mother. In the early morning hours of the fourth day, Will eased peacefully into death with a tiny gasp of breath.

Will was gone. With him went the last joy in my life. I was furious with him for leaving me. He was supposed to be with us for a great many more years. He was supposed to watch his children grow up, get married, and even have babies of their own.

I couldn't cry. I was too angry, and too many responsibilities were hanging over my head. Leaving the bedroom, I found the twins sleeping in their old beds. I awoke them gently.

"He's gone," I whispered. "Y'all two best get up, and help me get him prepared before the little ones wake up. I'm gonna need to go on into town to talk to Reverend Patterson, and figure things out for his burial."

Clearing the sleep from his eyes, Joseph grabbed my arm. "We've got it, Victoria. Take the truck into town and do what ya need to do. When Catherine wakes up, we'll send her over to get Caroline and Olivia, and let them know. Maybe they can let Uncle Atticus and Aunt Veronica know. And Grampy and Granny Imogene."

Imogene. I hadn't seen her since the day Will tossed her out of our lives. She'd never even met our children.

"No. Not Granny Imogene." I clenched my jaw. "Grampy's fine, but I don't want that woman in my home."

"But, Victoria," Daniel said. "She's his mother. She'll wanna know."

"I s'pose she will, but she lost that right. Your daddy cut her out of his life years ago, and he wouldn't want her here. Tell her she's not welcome, or I'll tell her. I'm not afraid of her like I once was, so I warn ya not to push me on this."

"I'll tell her," Joseph said. "But she's not gonna like it."

"It'll get ugly," Daniel warned.

"That woman pulls anything, and she hasn't seen ugly yet," I replied.

I was angry at the world, and ready to pick a fight. Let that old woman come to my home, and I'd escort her out, picking up pieces of her rear end on the way.

IMOGENE NEVER CAME to view the body, but she showed up at the cemetery for Will's funeral. I could keep her away from my home, but I couldn't keep her away from the public cemetery, where we laid Will to rest.

I didn't hear a single word Reverend Patterson said at the funeral. All I could hear were the sounds of anger buzzing in my ears. It consumed me. But I wasn't just angry, I was furious. I was furious at Will for dying, but I was more furious at myself for allowing him into my heart so completely that his loss left an empty hole. I was angry for not learning my lesson the first time, when Mama and Daddy died. Once again, I swore I'd never let it happen again.

When the funeral ended, Daniel took my arm and led me out of the cemetery. I followed quietly—I didn't have the emotional energy for much more.

Leaving the funeral, we were stalled by Will's mother as we passed. Before now, my instinct might've been to rush by her as quickly as possible, but now I was so angry that I stopped when I realized she had something to say. I was edgier than a long-tailed cat in a room full of rocking chairs. If Imogene started something, I would end it.

"Imogene?" I lifted an eyebrow. "You have somethin' ya wanna say?"

Imogene sniffed as though inhaling something distasteful. "Expectin' again, are ya? Can't say I'm surprised; some things don't change. Always said Will married ya for somethin' more than your looks. I'm also not surprised to see that not a one of 'em looks like my boy, except that little one over there." She pointed a claw-like finger at Ethan. "And even that one I'm not so sure."

"Did ya come here to insult me again, Imogene?" I asked, deliberately using her given name. I wanted her to know I held no respect for her.

"Not at all. I just came to inform ya that I'll be watching you. Don't think for a minute ya can pass those bastards off as Will's. They won't inherit his land. I won't have it."

The buzzing in my ears was deafening. I clenched my fists until the nails on both hands left half-moon wounds on my palms. Pulling my arm back, I swung at Imogene with everything I had. My fist hit her square in the face with a resounding crack. Blood spurted from her nose as she fell to the ground.

Pain shot up my arm. I examined my fist—the skin on my knuckles was bloody and broken, presumably from grazing Imogene's teeth on contact. Immense satisfaction enveloped me and, looking neither left nor right (and entirely missing the gasps of shock), I marched toward the car idling at the curb to take me home.

"Come along children, if you expect to get home," I said. "I'll not wait a single second for ya."

# PART THREE

## 1932-1934

# CHAPTER TWENTY-TWO

WILL'S DEATH BROUGHT WITH IT THE REAL-
ization I had allowed myself to become weak. Though my body was strong
from the hard work of being a farmer's wife, my inside—my heart—was soft.
I'd forgotten the cavernous empty of being alone. Always larger than life,
Will had filled our lives with his presence. He'd seemed invincible and, because of that, I'd allowed him to take my worries and fight my battles. Even
after the unexpected passing of my entire family, I'd never imagined Will
could be taken from me. I had become complacent, and now I was completely
unprepared for a life without him. I had failed myself, and I had failed our
children. And, maybe worst of all, I'd failed Will. But I would not fail again.
The world was no place for the weak, and I vowed I'd never be weak again.

In the weeks following Will's death, I stopped worrying about others,
and concentrated only on the children and myself. I now had five children
depending upon me to keep them fed and clothed. That didn't include the
baby I was carrying. I felt entirely alone. Without Will, I was dependent
upon Joseph and Daniel to work my part of the fields. I needed them; the
farm was our survival. Will had set aside a small savings, but I would need to
make it stretch. In the years of our marriage, I'd never concerned myself with
finances. That had been Will's domain. Now it was mine, and I was determined to carry on as well, or better, than any man.

Will had barely been gone a full month when Gene Blanchard drove
out from El Reno for a "friendly visit." Gene was our account manager at the
bank and held the mortgage on our farm. Will's father had given the farm
to him free and clear some twenty years before, but Will took a loan against
the farm and expanded planting the previous summer in hopes of a bumper
crop. Instead, the rains stopped, and we were left with a significant decrease
in production. At the same time, wheat prices plummeted, leaving us with
dismally small proceeds. By the end of the last harvest, we were barely mak-

ing ends meet. Paying Dr. Heusman's bill, followed by Will's burial fees, left me scrounging for money. If things continued as they were, we'd be destitute in no time. I cringed at the sight of Gene Blanchard. His visit was the last thing I needed.

"You kids stay in here," I said, walking away from the window and toward the front door. "Catherine, put 'em to work doin' somethin'. There's plenty that needs done in this house. I'll be back in a minute, and then y'all can come help me out in the barn."

Opening the front door, I stepped out into the cool winter air of mid-December and waited for Gene to approach the house. As usual, the dogs were going crazy at this unknown visitor. In no mood for Gene's visit, I did nothing to curtail their excitement. I hoped they'd shorten the length of his stay.

"Mornin', Victoria. You're lookin' well," Gene slammed his car door and sidestepped both dogs.

I wasn't in the mood for small talk, and I was less in the mood for Gene. On a good day, his presence was irritating. Today wasn't a good day. Gene's greasy hair and slick mustache did nothing toward improving it.

"Good mornin', Gene. What brings ya out here?"

"Just thought I'd come out and pay a friendly visit. Invite me in?"

"I don't think so. I'm busy, and it's been a long day already. Best just tell me what's on your mind."

Gene frowned. "We've been friends a long time, Victoria. Why the cold shoulder?"

"We've never been friends, Gene. Now, d'ya need somethin'? I have a lot to get done yet today."

"Okay then." Gene paused for a moment, collecting his thoughts. "I'm here 'cause Will owed money to the bank when he passed on. Were ya aware of that?"

I nodded. "We'd talked about it some. He was plannin' to pay it off with next summer's crop. I believe y'all had an agreement."

"Yes, of course." Gene fiddled with the end of his mustache. "We did have an agreement. I just wanna be sure you're aware of that agreement. The members of the bank are gettin' a little antsy, what with Will's death and all. They wanna make sure his bills'll be paid now that he's gone."

"I'm not clear on why you're here, Gene." I crossed my arms over my chest. "You had an agreement with Will that he'd pay off the remainder of the mortgage in what? August?"

Gene nodded.

"Then why're ya here now?" I asked. "I don't have time for these social calls if ya want the money repaid. It's only mid-December. I believe that gives me a full seven or eight months left, at least."

"Well, yes," Gene said. "I s'pose I'm here to make sure ya have a plan in place."

"I don't believe that's any of your business, Gene. I have months left to get my affairs in order before I need to worry about you or the bank sniffin' around for repayment. I'll thank ya to remember that. Now, please do me a favor and drive slowly on your way out. That car of yours kicks up too much dust, and I can't keep up with it as it is."

"Okay, then, Victoria," he said, reaching for the handle to open the car door. "Your attitude isn't gonna help ya much if ya need a favor from me."

"Goodbye, Gene," I replied. "I'll thank ya to not return before August."

Gene settled into his seat and slammed the door closed. Backing away from the house, he ignored my request. His tires spun in the dirt drive, kicking up a cloud of red dust into the air as he drove away.

# CHAPTER TWENTY-THREE

SEVERAL NIGHTS LATER, LONG AFTER I'D tucked the children into bed, I sat at my kitchen table with Joseph and Daniel trying to figure out how to make ends meet while still paying back the bank. I ran the numbers over and over. We'd need a bigger crop than last year's to pay back the bank, not to mention eat. If we didn't get more rain—and if wheat prices didn't stop dropping—I wasn't sure how we'd make it.

"Joseph and I can work your fields along with our own," Daniel said. "That's what we'd've done if Daddy was still here. They're all connected, so we'll just make one big drop after harvest. We'll sell the wheat together, then divide the proceeds based on the percentage of land we each have. Just like we did last year."

"Can y'all two handle it by yourselves with what workers we have?" I asked.

"Shouldn't be too hard." Joseph shrugged. "We've lost Daddy, but Daniel and I've picked up a good piece of Daddy's share the last couple of years. It's doable."

"What should I do? I can't just sit here and do nothin'."

"It's not like you're gonna be able to do a whole lot, what with that baby comin' in March," Daniel said. "Catherine's worked the fields before. I doubt she'd mind pitchin' in again, and Gracie's gettin' big enough to learn. Maybe we have Gracie follow Catherine for a bit. Jack's big enough to help with the babies, so he can stay here with you. Make him pick up some of what Catherine and Grace've been doin'."

"That might work," I said. "What's your gut tell ya on the crop this year?"

Joseph and Daniel shared a long look, a million words communicated silently between them in the way only twins seem able to do.

"It's hard to say," Daniel finally said. "If we have another drought like last year, we're gonna be in trouble. We're gonna need some rain, and a lot of it.

Ain't no way we can get through another year like last. We got lucky, we had some crop. The Beaumonts didn't do nearly so well."

"All right, then." I nodded. "Y'all tell me what I need to do, and I'll take care of my end. I'm thankful to ya both for stickin' this out with me."

"Ya know we wouldn't have it any other way," Joseph said, getting up from the table with Daniel. "We're family."

Tears gathered behind my eyes, but I refused to cry. Instead, I nodded. Family or not, I couldn't rely on the boys forever.

LYING IN BED that night, my mind whirled. I missed Will, and I was worried about everything. How much longer would the money last? Would the next harvest finally bring that bumper crop? What options did I have for making money? I'd never before needed to worry about money. Now, it was the one thing I worried about most. Having money meant feeding the children. It meant keeping a roof over their heads.

Food. That was my first concern. How would we eat if the money ran out? Will had taught me to use a rifle and, though I wasn't a crack shot by any stretch, I could usually hit my mark by the second or third shot. He'd also taught me to use a knife, then how to skin and clean animals. It was a messy job, and I hated it, but it was another tool to work with. So long as there was wild game, we wouldn't starve. At least I hoped not.

As skilled as I was, Catherine was better. The younger children needed to learn, so I'd send Gracie and Jack out with Catherine to be taught. If nothing else, they could bring down some quail or hunt down a jackrabbit. Even just throwing a line into the creek and catching a couple of catfish would be meat on the table.

Satisfied I had a plan—feeble though it was—my mind shifted to Will. I missed him terribly, and I hated the new me. Will had brought out the good in me, but his loss made the ugly come out. Yet I refused to back down. A woman alone had to be strong. She had to teach her children to be strong.

# CHAPTER TWENTY-FOUR

CHRISTMAS OF 1932 WAS UNLIKE ANYTHING the children had ever experienced. With no money and Will's recent death, there were few gifts and no joy. All of my happiness had been stripped away with Will's death, and I had no energy left to pretend. If I'd had any remorse over not making the holidays festive for the children, I excused myself by remembering times were difficult. Allowing the children to become any softer than I'd already allowed would be an injustice to them. I needed them to be strong. So they couldn't be coddled.

Anger was my constant companion. Caroline and Olivia stopped visiting, saying they didn't like how hard and unyielding I'd become. Their judgment stung, but I squared my shoulders and moved forward. I couldn't allow the criticism of others to compromise my goals. Surviving was my priority. Everything else came second.

Julianne, on the other hand, never judged. I knew she neither approved of, nor understood, my anger; but she remained my steadfast and only true friend. Joseph and Daniel never wavered in their devotion, but we'd begun arguing. Like their older sisters, they were concerned. I'd changed since Will's death, and they were alarmed by it. Ever loyal, though, the boys stayed with me. They worked both fields and helped provide food for our table. They wouldn't abandon me, or their younger siblings.

On a Thursday afternoon, not long after Will's death, I was mucking stalls when a vehicle approached the house. It was nearly time to prepare dinner, so I was already aggravated at the intrusion. When I realized who was approaching, however, my anger reached a new level. Imogene was driving toward my home. I didn't bother putting the pitchfork down. If necessary, I'd use it as weapon. I'd had enough of Imogene, and a feces-covered pitchfork was better than she deserved.

Stepping out of the barn, I walked quickly toward the oncoming vehicle.

Imogene stopped the car some thirty yards from the house, and stepped out to greet me. Gray-haired and fat in the middle, she'd grown age lines across her forehead and between her brows.

"What d'ya want, Imogene?" I held the pitchfork tines-up with the handle digging into the dry earth near my feet.

"Victoria." She nodded.

"So ya remember my name these days? Maybe somebody should've knocked some sense into ya years before."

Imogene stood there for long moments, just looking out across the prairie and then back toward my home. The silence stretched, and what little patience I had was wearing thin.

"Ya didn't come out here to see me or to look at my land," I prodded. "What d'ya need?"

Still not looking at me, she answered. "Walter's sick. He's not been doin' well since Will's funeral. He wants to see his grandchildren."

"What grandchildren?" I laughed. "You made it clear you didn't believe my children belonged to Will. You still have a relationship with the older kids. What d'ya want with my children?"

"Walter wants to see 'em."

"I see." Anger consumed me. Walter wanted to see my children, when he'd not come to see them once in the years since their births? Will had gone to see his father from time to time over the years, but Walter hadn't once acknowledged my children as their grandfather. He also hadn't apologized for his wife's reprehensible behavior.

"I'd like ya to bring 'em over to the house," she said.

I thought on this a moment, biting my tongue before the hate inside me spewed out onto the ground below. I lifted my chin in defiance. "No."

Imogene narrowed her eyes. "What did ya say?"

"I said, no. Not today, not tomorrow, not next week. No. Never."

"Well you ungrateful little—" Imogene took three steps toward me.

I moved the pitchfork so the tines pointed directly at her. Now only a few feet from me, if she advanced much further the tips would meet the fleshy part of her throat. "You take one more step, Imogene, and I'll stab you through with this pitchfork. How dare ya come here and summon my children to your husband's bedside? Ya both had your chance to be grandparents to my kids, and it passed when Will died. How dare you! You called my children—Will's babies!—bastards in front of fifty neighbors and friends. Don't you dare call me ungrateful! You should be grateful I only punched ya. You can be sure it would've been different if we'd not been surrounded by so many people."

"Now listen here, girl," she began.

I advanced toward her, the tines of the pitchfork still pointed her direction. The sharp tips brushed her soft flesh, leaving no doubt I meant business. "That's another thing, old woman," I said through clenched teeth. "Don't you ever call me 'girl' again. You bullied me when I was barely more than a child, and I let Will fight my battles. I've grown since then, and Will's gone. Don't underestimate me. If ya call me 'girl' again—or if ya call my children 'bastards' again—you will regret it. Now leave."

Imogene stepped back, never taking her eyes off the pitchfork in my hands. "I'll leave, but you've not seen the last of me. Mark my words: you'll regret this. Nobody threatens me."

Imogene's words hung in the air as she stomped back toward her vehicle, slamming the door once she was seated. Starting the engine, she pulled away, kicking up clouds of red dust in her wake.

Yet again, fury consumed me. I was so angry, I almost didn't recognize myself. How dare that woman summon my children after not acknowledging them all these years? My body vibrated with anger, and my ears buzzed. Walking into the house, I was thankful to find Catherine preparing dinner. She was one of the few people who could calm my anger.

"Where are the little ones?" I asked.

"Gracie and Jack took Ethan and Sara down to the creek to fish," she said.

"They're not gonna catch anything this late in the day. And they better be watchin' those babies close. Last thing I need is to bury one of my babies."

"They'll be fine. The little ones were gettin' antsy, and just needed to get out and do somethin' different." Catherine gave me a sad smile. She didn't say the words, but her look said everything. Like her siblings, she was concerned. My anger reached everyone.

"Whatcha got there on the stove?" I asked.

"Rabbit stew. Joseph stopped by earlier and dropped off two jackrabbits.

Said they was thick out in the pastures earlier, so he brought down about a half dozen and dropped a couple off here."

"Thanks for startin' dinner."

Catherine nodded.

"Granny Imogene was just here," I told her.

Catherine's eyes went wide with shock. "She was?"

"Yeah. Grampy's sick. She wants me to bring the little ones out to the house to see him."

"What did ya say? That can't be a good idea, havin' you and Granny Imogene in the same room."

"I told her no. They've not cared about the little ones all these years. I see no reason why they should show an interest now."

"I bet she was mad!" Catherine said. "What'd she say?"

"Exactly what you'd expect her to say. She threatened me. Told me I'd not seen the last of her."

"What'd *you* say?"

"Not much. She called me 'girl,' and that pretty much ended the conversation. I told her she'd regret it if she ever called me that again, no to mention my children bastards."

"Victoria! You didn't! Please tell me ya didn't threaten her! Things are bad enough between y'all two without ya threatenin' her!"

I nodded. "I did, and I meant it. She's pushed me around for the last time. I've had enough of that woman to last me a lifetime. I won't have another minute of it."

"Ya know you've just declared war on Granny Imogene." Catherine frowned. "She won't back down."

"Neither will I."

Catherine was quiet for long minutes, then said, "Caroline and Olivia are worried about ya. Actually, we all are. You've changed so much since Daddy died. You're hard. Don't take that wrong: I love you. We all love you! But you're so angry now."

"I'm well aware of that," I replied.

"But it's not you."

"I'm not so sure, Catherine." I shook my head. "I think I'm more me than I've ever been. This world is harsh; you're either on top, or you're on bottom.

128

I won't be on bottom. I can't."

"But I don't understand. You've always been opinionated. I remember Daddy sayin' it's what he loved best about ya. But you've never been mean before. Lately you're like a horse with a burr under your saddle. You seem angry all the time."

"It's because I am. I'm angry all the time. I wake up angry in the morning, and I go to bed furious at night. Some days I resent the anger, but most days it's the only thing keepin' me goin', so I hold onto it with everythin' I have."

"But why?"

"Catherine," I sighed. "I don't know how to explain this to ya so you'll understand, but I'll try. And then I don't wanna discuss it ever again. Understood?"

She nodded.

I took a deep breath, searching for the right words. "I loved your daddy. He made it impossible not to fall in love with him. When he died, everything good in me died with him. Sometimes I can forget for a few minutes he's gone; but then reality crashes back down on me, and I feel empty and vacant. It feels like I'm standin' at the edge of nowhere, lookin' out onto the land of nothing. The world is barren. It's empty without him. There's no kindness or beauty for me anymore. There's no future. All I can see are miles and miles of nothin'— just a vast world of desolation and ugliness."

Pausing only a moment, I continued. "I never meant to love your daddy. I told him I wouldn't when we first met. I'd sworn to never marry; never to fall in love. I didn't even want children. Your daddy changed all that. He knew me like nobody else ever did, and he loved me in spite of my faults. I was shocked when I fell in love with him, but I loved him more than I ever thought possible. By lovin' him, though, I allowed him to change me, to make me soft. He brought out the best in me and made me trust in love; but that love made me weak. With him gone, I gotta be strong. Failing to be strong is to fail all of you."

Tears collected in Catherine's eyes, but I forged on. She'd asked, and this was the first time I'd allowed myself to speak the words out loud. I needed to say them as much as she needed to hear them, so I continued.

"When I was a child, I watched my mama die. She'd lost a baby and, with it, her will to live. When she died, my daddy changed. He'd once been loving and kind, but her death turned him into a drunkard. He became a sorry excuse for a father, then abused himself with alcohol until he died as well. Love had done that to 'em both; love destroyed them. When they died, I promised myself I'd never love. I refused to allow love to make me weak as it had them. Then I met your daddy. He charged in like the white knight of childhood fairy tales, and he made me forget my promise. I surrendered my fear, and allowed him to fight my battles. He loved me. He made me forget I needed strength to survive. When he died, I lost the one thing standin' between me and the rest of the world. And now, I'm damn-near helpless and weak because of it. The only thing I know is that I gotta be strong at all costs. So if I've changed, well, I guess that's the price I'm willin' to pay. I won't lie down and let others walk over me."

Catherine nodded, her eyes near overflowing with unshed tears. We sat there in silence, both of us pondering my words. After several long moments, I was startled when she approached me. Placing both arms around my neck, Catherine hugged me tightly and placed a light kiss upon my cheek.

"I love you, Victoria," she said.

"I know," I responded.

Hearing that from Catherine was nearly my undoing. Refusing to cry, I bit the inside of my cheek and watched her leave the room. I was left alone in the quiet of my kitchen with my thoughts and fears; but, most importantly, with my anger. It would be the anger that would see me through the years ahead, and I embraced it with everything I had.

# CHAPTER TWENTY-FIVE

THAT NIGHT, I TOSSED AND TURNED, STEW-
ing in my anger at Imogene. Eventually I drifted off to sleep, but my dreams
were uneasy. I had horrible nightmares of large, vacant eyes—my children's
eyes. They were hungry, their bodies nothing but skin and bone. I dreamed of
Imogene and Walter stealing them away from me. I dreamed of pitchforks. I
saw myself lying in a pool of my own blood. Holes covered my body, allowing my blood to seep onto the ground until I was lying in a pool of crimson.
I cried out, hoping to get someone's attention. Nobody responded. There was
no one. I lay on the ground with my knees pulled up to my chest as the pain
radiated throughout my body. My blood disappeared into the red dusty dirt
of the Oklahoma prairie.

"Victoria! Victoria, wake up!"

I was jolted out of my dream by Catherine. I opened my eyes just enough
to see her. She was standing over me with tears streaming down her face, her
eyes wide with terror.

"Victoria, wake up!" she pleaded.

The pain of my dream consumed me. It radiated down both legs, taking
my breath away. I was dying. I looked up at Catherine and whispered, "Help
me. I'm hurt."

"Victoria! You're covered in blood, and I don't know what to do!"

"Granny Imogene," I whispered. "She stabbed me."

"Victoria! Wake up! Granny Imogene isn't here! I think you're losin' the baby!"

The last of her words penetrated through the fog of my sleep-muddled
mind. I'd been dreaming, but the pain was real. Relentless. Kicking back the
covers through my pain, I assessed my blood-soaked nightgown and knew
Catherine was right. From the waist down, there was nothing but a thick
pool of red.

"Catherine," I said as calmly as I was able. "Take the truck down to

Joseph's, and tell him to go get Dr. Heusman. Hurry. Tell him I'm losin' the baby. And be quiet—don't wake the little ones!"

"I'm goin'. I'll be back! Just stay here!" Already to the front door, she closed it with a loud thud. I winced, hoping she hadn't awakened the little ones.

Alone now, the room was silent, and the pain was excruciating. I wanted to wash the blood off. I couldn't just lie there; I needed to do something. Scooting to the edge of the bed, I paused to catch my breath. Six steps. Only six steps to the bedroom door, then another ten steps or so to the kitchen. I could do this.

Using the railing at the foot of the bed to steady myself, I pulled to a standing position. Blood gushed from my body in a steady stream of large clots onto the rug below. The room spun, and bright lights flashed behind my eyes. I needed to sit back down before I fell.

Easing back onto the bed, I sat there for a moment to gain control of myself. I wanted this blood washed away before Catherine returned. Once more using the bed railing to steady myself, I climbed to my feet. Six steps. I could make it to the door. I knew I could.

Using what furniture I could for support, I walked on shaky legs toward the bedroom door. Six steps felt like a hundred; but, if I could make it to the kitchen table, I could sit for a moment before cleaning up. Slowly, I crept to the doorway leading to the outer room. My head throbbed, and reams of sweat poured down the back of my neck. Yet I didn't feel at all warm. Instead, I was chilled through, as though I'd never be warm again. My body trembled; either from the pain or the cold, I wasn't sure.

Slowly releasing myself from the doorframe, I continued toward the kitchen. Ten more steps. The anger inside of me burst forth, giving me the energy to take another step. Nine more steps, I estimated.

My hair was thick with sweat, and blood poured from my body. I was almost there. I looked around for something to lean on, but there was nothing nearby. I'd have to do without. I took another step. Lights flashed behind my eyes, and the world spun around me. Everything went dark.

I'm not sure how long I was unconscious. I awoke a short time later in a clean nightgown, on clean sheets, and in my own bed. Sitting beside me were Catherine and Daniel, both with concern etched deeply into their young features.

Taking my hand in his, Daniel spoke first. "You're awake. How're ya feelin'?"

I considered the question. The pain was still present, but not as intense as it had been earlier. I could feel the blood hadn't stopped, but at least I was clean and not covered in it.

"I don't know. The pain's better," I whispered.

"You've been out for at least half an hour," Catherine said. "Joseph left for Dr. Heusman, and then I went to get Daniel. He cleaned up your bed while I cleaned you up a bit. I didn't get it all. I'm sorry."

"Thank you," I whispered. "Ya did fine."

"What were ya doin'?" Daniel asked. "We found ya on the floor between here and the kitchen."

"I wanted to clean up before Catherine got back," I answered.

Neither responded. There was really nothing that could be said. We all knew what the bleeding and pains likely meant, and none of us wanted to say it out loud.

"How long has Joseph been gone?" I asked.

Catherine glanced at the clock on the wall to my left. "Maybe forty-five minutes? I'd imagine he should be back soon, so long as he finds Dr. Heusman right away. At this time of night, I can't imagine where else he might be."

"Then I guess we wait," I said.

"Can I get ya somethin'?" Catherine asked. "Water, maybe?"

Closing my eyes, I shook my head. "I'm fine."

Fifteen minutes passed, and then twenty with no sign of Joseph or Dr. Heusman. Another ten minutes passed before a truck pulled down the path toward our house. Racing out the door to greet them, Daniel left Catherine sitting with me in silence.

"I'm really sorry, Victoria," she whispered.

I didn't know how to respond. I knew what she was saying. She knew as well as I did that I'd probably lost the baby. Will's last baby.

"I know."

Dr. Heusman arrived with Joseph dogging his heels. There was nothing he could do; no medicine could save my baby. Even if I'd delivered him alive, he was too early. He would never have survived outside my body. With Dr. Heusman's help, I delivered the tiny body of what would've been a boy. Will's last child, gone to join him in the Heavens. I won't lie; I was relieved. One less mouth to feed.

# CHAPTER TWENTY-SIX

MOST PEOPLE ASK GOD TO FORGIVE THEIR
sins. I prayed to Will instead. Though I was deeply relieved my burdens
wouldn't be increased, I was sorry to have failed Will. I remembered his excitement when I told him of this pregnancy. It stung to realize I'd let him
down. No matter how poor I thought we were, or how much money we
didn't have, Will was always excited at the prospect of a new child. He always
found a way to make the money stretch. My relief left me feeling wretched. I
knew Will would've been saddened at our baby's death. But how could I not
feel relief that my burdens wouldn't increase? So I prayed to Will. I asked his
forgiveness, both for the loss of our child, and for the relief I felt at that loss.

Will's son was buried on February 8, 1933 on one of the coldest winter
days in my memory. I'd withheld naming this child. Naming him made his
existence too real. Sadly, my actions caused another rift between myself and
the two older girls. Caroline and Olivia, whom I'd once considered very dear
friends, were incensed and stopped talking to me entirely. While their absence left another hole in my heart, it was just as well I experience that loss
now. Always loyal, Joseph and Daniel stuck by me. For her part, Catherine
was clearly confused, and didn't know which side to take. I was the only
mother she'd ever known, but her sisters were mothers to her as well.

Instead of a funeral, we had a simple graveside burial attended only by
me, the children, and Will's family. I could afford no more. I couldn't even
afford that. Now on top of my mounting debt, I had to find the money to pay
Dr. Heusman. Like last time, I had nothing to show for his efforts.

Will's father, Walter, rallied enough to attend the burial; but he, too, gave
me the cold shoulder. Seated in a wheelchair pushed by Atticus, he glared at
me each time my attention strayed toward him. He was furious I'd refused
Imogene's summons of my children to his bedside. I'd made yet another en-
emy.

With the burial concluded, I took Ethan's and Sara's hands and guided them toward the waiting vehicle. I assumed Grace and Jack would follow, and I hoped Catherine would as well. Passing Imogene and Walter, I was waylaid much like I had been at Will's funeral.

"Walter. Imogene." I stopped in front of Will's parents, waiting to hear what Imogene had to say.

Standing behind his father, Atticus greeted me. "It's good to see ya, Victoria. Veronica and I are both sorry for your loss."

"Thank you, Atticus." I nodded. "Thank you both for comin'."

"It's just as well," Imogene said, not unkindly.

"Yes," I agreed. "Yes, it is."

In all the years I'd known Imogene, it was the kindest thing she'd ever said to me. With nothing more to say, I continued on toward the truck idling at the curb.

# CHAPTER TWENTY-SEVEN

THREE WEEKS HAD PASSED WHEN MOTHER Elizabeth and Father Caleb paid me a visit. They hadn't attended the burial because I hadn't told them. I hadn't told anyone except Will's family and, really, Catherine had been the one to tell them.

As Father Caleb's car ambled toward the house, I smiled to myself. I'd missed them. I hadn't seen them since Will's funeral.

Father Caleb stopped the car some twenty feet away. Moments later, his bushy brown head emerged from the vehicle, followed closely on the opposite side by Mother Elizabeth. For a moment my heart squeezed . . . with love? Pain? Regret? I wasn't sure. I massaged my chest to ease the ache.

I stepped out onto the porch and was brought up short by the tears in Father Caleb's eyes. Reaching for me, he enveloped me in a hug. "You didn't tell us. Why?" His voice cracked on the last word.

"I couldn't," I said. I couldn't because I didn't know how to tell them. I couldn't because I didn't want them to know. I couldn't because telling them made the loss more real. So many reasons why I couldn't.

Father Caleb released me and Mother Elizabeth pulled me into her arms. She cried openly. "You've had so much loss in such a short time. Ya should've sent word. We could've been here for ya."

"There's nothing ya could've done." I pulled away from her embrace. "Come in for some coffee?"

Mother Elizabeth took my arm, while Father Caleb followed behind. Seating them at the table, I turned to make the coffee I had promised.

"Where are the children?" Father Caleb asked.

"Catherine, Grace, and Jack are at school," I said with my back to them. "Ethan and Sara are sleepin'. It's nap time."

"I forget they have school," he said. "It's been so long since we had little ones in the house."

"For how much longer, I'm not sure." Returning to the table, I set down three cups and pulled out my chair to sit. "Things are gettin' harder here, and I'm gonna need the three older ones to help the twins out in the field. I'm tryin' to keep 'em in school as long as I can, but I'm not sure how much longer this can go on. We're gonna need all available hands here soon if we're gonna be able to eat."

"Is it that bad?" Mother Elizabeth asked.

"Worse," I answered. "Will had some money set aside before he died, but I had to use most of it for Dr. Heusman, and then for Will's funeral. And then . . . then there the baby's burial."

Father Caleb shook his head. "I'm so sorry."

"Me too. We're just barely scrapin' by until harvest season. The twins are hopin' for a bumper crop to pay off the bank."

"Will owed money to the bank?" Father Caleb asked.

I nodded. "Remember that equipment he bought a couple years back? He needed it to plow up another of the fields that wasn't bein' used. He was hopin' the extra wheat would bring in more income, but then we didn't get much rain. All but a little bit of the crops dried up. He took what he could to sell, but we didn't get nearly what it was worth, and we were lucky to come out on top. Not much on top, but more than some."

"How're ya managin' to get by?" he asked.

"Day by day." I shrugged. "The twins have been a godsend. They bring us a few jackrabbits when they can. They said the rabbits have gone plum nuts, and they're all over the place right now. So that's helped put a little meat on the table. We've still got that last sow, but I'm savin' her for an emergency; then we have the cow, but we need her for milk. We've butchered all but the rooster and two chickens. But even they're eatin' more than they're givin' off in eggs, so they'll probably have to be the next to go. We've got a herd of young cattle out grazin' the front forty, but the twins are hopin' to sell those off this summer to make up whatever comes up short from the harvest. If it's a good one, we can keep the profits from the sale of the cattle, and we'll be in much better shape."

"And what about cash on hand? How much do y'all still have?" he asked.

"Not much. Some loose change, mostly. Last week Sara got into the can I've been using to save what we do have, and she swallowed two dimes.

Damn that child!" I shook my head, remembering. "Catherine and I set her on a bucket every time she needed to use the toilet 'til she finally gave up those dimes."

"For two dimes?" Mother Elizabeth gasped. "How long did it take?"

"Two days."

"Victoria, I just don't know what to say!" she said. "Why didn't ya tell us?"

"I didn't want y'all to know. What good would it've done? Y'all two are doin' okay, but I know ya don't have any extra; and I know you'd go hungry just to make sure we didn't. I didn't want that. I still don't. I'm just tellin' y'all 'cause ya asked, and you've been too good to me to lie to ya."

"What can we do?" Father Caleb asked.

"Nothin'. I can't think of anything that'd make this better, save havin' Will back or God droppin' money from the sky. Not likely either's gonna happen, so we just keep on keepin' on."

"I know it's soon, but have ya thought about remarryin'?" Mother Elizabeth said.

I shook my head. "I don't wanna remarry. I didn't wanna marry the first time. You know that."

"I know, but times're hard. If ya had a man around here to handle the farm and do more of the hard labor, it might help," she said. "It's not really about what ya want; it's about keepin' the kids fed and clothed, and a roof over their heads. Just think about it."

I didn't respond. She'd planted a seed in my brain, but I wasn't ready to acknowledge that it might be the answer to our problems. I hated the thought of remarrying. But I also knew I'd do anything to survive.

# CHAPTER TWENTY-EIGHT

MARCH PASSED, AND APRIL ARRIVED. WITH the change of seasons came spring, but she'd forgotten to bring the proverbial April showers. We'd made it through winter, but just barely. The chickens and rooster were now gone; and we'd eaten every piece of meat off the bones then used the carcass to make soup. We butchered the sow only the week before, and that meat would last us awhile if we were careful. We still had Will's dogs to look after, but we'd stopped feeding them. They'd have to find their own food wherever they could. The only reason we still fed the cow was because she gave us milk. Otherwise, we would've left her to her own resources as well. Harvest was coming soon, and I hoped it would bring us some financial solvency.

I loved April. The cold of winter was over, yet the summer season hadn't quite set in. On a warm afternoon, just as I'd finished milking the cow, I heard the children screaming and the dogs barking wildly some distance away. I couldn't imagine what those children were up to now. Tired and sweaty, I wasn't in the mood to settle another dispute.

I stepped out of the barn, prepared to scold them for their incessant squabbling, when I was stopped dead in my tracks by the sight before me. Racing toward me, with Sara cradled tightly in his arms, was a man I'd never seen before. He was tall and broad-shouldered, with black hair. Catherine met his strides and, close on her heels were Grace, Jack, and Ethan—all screaming as though Satan was chasing them. I met their distance and took Sara from the man's arms, then raced back toward the house to set her down.

"What happened?" I called over my shoulder.

"Cottonmouths! A nest of 'em down by the creek!" he replied.

We reached the front door, and the stranger yanked it open for me. I ran straight for my bed and placed her on the quilts.

"Show me. Where's she bitten?"

Lifting Sarah's skirts, Catherine pointed out several pairs of holes on her sister's upper thigh.

"Mama," Sara cried, her eyes fluttering open and closed. "It hurts."

"Oh, baby," I said, cradling her upper body in mine. "I know, sweetheart. Shhh ..."

"How many?" I asked Catherine.

"I don't know. I think she stepped in a nest. She was just standin' near the edge of the creek and started screamin'. I saw a flurry of snakes, but I didn't see how many! Three? Four, maybe? Mr. Snyder just snatched her up and started runnin'."

"Are ya bit?" I asked, turning to the stranger.

"No, ma'am. I'm fine," he said.

Sara's breathing was short and raspy, and there wasn't a damned thing I could do. I knew she couldn't survive this. A grown man might survive a single bite from a young snake, but Sara was only two and had taken three bites I could see. Once again, I was completely powerless.

The stranger stood awkwardly near the door, not knowing what he should do. I nodded at him. "Thanks for your help. We're good now. You can go on your way."

"Ma'am." The stranger nodded then turned to leave.

"Catherine, take the little ones into the other room and start dinner. They don't need to see this."

Catherine herded Grace and Jack out of the room. When they were gone, I scooped Sara's tiny body into my arms and carried her to the rocking chair. Cradling my baby close to my heart, I sat and rocked slowly back and forth.

My brain stopped working. I couldn't think beyond the next second. The only thing I knew was there was nothing I could do. My sweet Sara wouldn't live to see her next birthday.

*Creak-creak-creak-creak.*

The sound of my own chair reminded me of my mother's grief so many years before.

Sara didn't move or utter another word. If not for the shallow rise and fall of her chest, I might've thought she was already gone.

"It's okay, baby," I said, smoothing her hair away from her face. "Mama's got ya. Just go to sleep, and everything'll be okay."

Still Sara didn't move, nor open her eyes to acknowledge my words. I watched and waited, but didn't have to wait long. Within moments, she slipped quietly into death.

Unwilling to let her go just yet, I continued rocking back and forth. Time moved slowly. I gazed down into the peaceful face of my beautiful girl and remembered the first time I'd looked upon her. She was gone; returned to Will for safekeeping. Now he'd watch over her.

I don't know if it was five minutes or five hours; but, after some time, Catherine came in and sat down on the bed across from me.

"She's gone?" she asked, chocking back a sob.

I nodded. My throat had closed over my own sob, and I wasn't able to form words just yet. So I rocked back and forth, holding my baby. After some time, I took a deep breath and asked what I needed to know. "Tell me what happened."

"I'm not sure," she whispered. "I took the little ones down to the creek to fish. That man—Mr. Snyder—he was down there fishin', too. The boys were splashin' around in the shallow water, but Sara was just standin' by the edge of the water. Ya know how she's afraid of water, so she just stood there, watchin'. I turned my back for a quick second, and she started screamin'. I thought one of the boy's was teasin' her or somethin', but I caught a quick look at them snakes splashing in the water just before they disappeared. Cottonmouths! I don't know how many, but a bunch of 'em! I was so scared, I froze. When I finally rushed to grab her outta the water, Mr. Snyder was already there. He shouted at me, askin' which way to the house, and I just pointed and we ran."

Catherine was fully sobbing now, but I had my arms full of Sara, and I wasn't ready to let go. "It's okay," I said.

"It's all my fault!" Catherine sobbed. "I took 'em to the creek. I should've been standin' right next to her! I should've done something!"

"There wasn't anything ya could've done."

Catherine's sobs echoed those in my heart. We sat for several more moments before I remembered I had three more children unaccounted for.

"Where are the other children?" I asked.

"I fed 'em and Mr. Snyder, then put 'em to bed. There wasn't much in there. Just some bread, butter, and some left over ham from the sow. I figured that'd be enough."

"That was fine." I nodded. "Where's Mr. Snyder now?"

"Outside. He's just passin' through, lookin' for work. I said he could bed down in the barn for tonight, if he wanted, since he helped so much with Sara."

"That's fine. But he'll need to be gone first thing tomorrow morning. I don't have enough to feed all y'all as it is. I can't take another."

"I know. I told him."

Catherine and I sat in silence, each consumed in our own thoughts. After some time, she asked, "So what d'we do now?"

"We're gonna need to bury Sara. Can ya take the truck and go get Joseph and Daniel? We're gonna need 'em to dig us a hole, maybe out under that big tree in the back part of the house."

"We're not gonna bury her in town with Daddy?"

"We don't have any money, Catherine. We're just gonna have to do the best we can with what we have, and right now we have nothin'."

"Can we do that?"

"Doesn't matter. We don't have any other choice. I'd like to get it done tonight. I don't want Gracie, Jack and Ethan seein' her. Not like this. It's bad enough to bury their daddy and a baby they didn't know. They don't need to see us bury Sara, too."

"Are ya sure that's the right thing to do?"

"Ah hell, Catherine! I don't know what's right or wrong anymore! Right now I'm just doin' my best to stay afloat and tread water. Now, will ya please go get the boys, or am I gonna have to do it?"

"I'll go."

DANIEL AND JOSEPH arrived together, about forty minutes later, and found me still sitting in the rocking chair with Sara in my arms.

Daniel fell to his knees and choked back a sob. "Oh, God! Not Sara!"

I couldn't speak. It was hard enough dealing with my own pain and Catherine's; I couldn't stand to see the boys cry, too. I used every ounce of my energy holding back the tears. I wouldn't cry. The boys needed me strong. For the first time, I knew exactly how my own mama felt when my baby brother died. The pain in my heart was physical—like a knife cut straight through to my soul. I wanted nothing more than to lie down and go to sleep. I wanted to give my worries to someone else, and just disappear inside my head as my mama had done. But I wouldn't. I knew what that did to a child, and I wouldn't do that to my own children. So I held onto my sanity by the tips of my fingers.

"We're so sorry," Joseph said, kneeling in front of me. He smoothed Sara's soft cheek and pushed her baby-fine hair behind her ear. "What d'ya want us to do?"

"I need y'all two to dig a hole in the backyard, maybe out underneath that big tree. That man—Mr. Snyder, the one that carried her in?—Catherine says he's bunkin' out in the barn. See if he can help ya."

"We're not gonna take her to town for burial?" Daniel asked.

Losing my patience, I snapped. "Ya know as well as I that I don't have money for that! What'm I supposed to do?"

Daniel placed his hand on my shoulder and squeezed gently. "No, you're right. I wasn't thinkin'." Turning to Joseph, he said, "C'mon. Let's get it done."

The boys—now grown men—left me alone with Sara's tiny body still in my arms. For the next two hours, I rocked back and forth in that rocking chair, praying this was all some awful dream.

# CHAPTER TWENTY-NINE

I didn't sleep at all that night; I'm sure none of us did. Watching the sunrise out my window, I pulled myself out of bed. We'd stayed up late burying Sara under the old apple tree in the back yard. The full moon had shined down on us, providing light, as we each said a few words about Sara. Mr. Snyder joined us. He hadn't known her, and we didn't know him, but he'd helped us when we needed him, and we were thankful.

I cringed as my feet touched the cold, wood floor. I had business to attend, and I wanted to get it done before the children awoke.

Digging through the dresser, I pulled out one of Will's old shirts and a pair of overalls. I slipped them on, one leg at a time, accommodating for the length by rolling the cuffs over a few times. Though clean, they still smelled like Will—woodsy, like the outdoors. I took a deep breath and again wished he were here.

In the back of the closet was Will's old hunting rifle. I'd used it a few times, but I'd hidden it in the closet to keep it away from the babies. Checking for bullets, and finding an adequate supply, I tiptoed out of the house and walked down to the creek with the rifle clutched tightly in my hands.

I'm not sure what I expected, but I'd hoped to find that cottonmouth nest. I'd planned to blow those slimy beasts to tiny pieces. Instead I found nothing but the creek and grass. Still, I stood on the edge of the bank waiting.

I'd just shot the second snake in three hours when Mr. Snyder joined me, his presence startling me.

"Did ya get any?" he asked.

"Just two."

"How many more are ya plannin' to get?"

"I don't know. As many as I can, I guess."

"Ya know," Mr. Snyder said, carefully choosing his words. "I know a little bit about what you're goin' through."

Really? He couldn't be a day older than twenty, yet he stood there saying he knew what I was going through. Anger overtook me, and I wanted to punch him. How dare he suggest he knew what I was going through!

"Ya ever lost a child, Mr. Snyder?" I asked, attempting to control the venom in my voice.

He paused before replying. "No, can't say as I've ever lost a child, but—"

"Then how can you possibly claim to know how I'm feelin' right now?"

"I lost my best friend to a rattlesnake bite some years back. I'd say that's pretty close. We was kids together—more like brothers than best friends. There wasn't a thing I could do. Before I knew it, he was gone."

"Just like my Sara," I whispered.

He nodded. "Just like your Sara."

Mr. Snyder gently took the rifle from my hands. "C'mon. Your little ones are worried about ya, and they've been askin' questions about the baby. That older girl of yours has her hands full, and she's not sure how to handle their questions. She needs ya. They all do."

Mr. Snyder was right. I could stand there all day shooting at cottonmouths, but what good would it do? I'd likely never find the ones that killed my Sara. My children needed me, and it was time to start behaving like their mother.

THE DAYS FOLLOWING Sara's death were hard. Will's passing had been difficult on all of us, but the loss of Sara took our grief to a new dimension. To the children, Sara had been not only their baby sister, but their playmate; and Catherine and Grace had been like surrogate mothers to her. To me, Sara was my baby—the last of Will's children. The last of Will.

Catherine took Sara's death the hardest. She had trouble forgiving herself, insisting she could've done something or should've been paying better attention. She was inconsolable.

Mr. Snyder—Troy, as we began calling him—stayed on far longer than expected, and Catherine took to him immediately. He was a drifter looking for a place to put down roots, and had taken a shine to Catherine as well. I knew I'd have to watch this. We knew nothing about Mr. Snyder, and Catherine was far too young to be thinking about a beau. But Mr. Snyder had been helpful, and the harvest would be coming in soon. Joseph and Daniel convinced me to let him stay, saying they'd need help with the harvest. We couldn't pay him, but Mr. Snyder insisted all he really needed was shelter over his head and food in his belly. He said he was sick of drifting, and just needed a connection to people. He didn't have any more money than we did—which is to say he had nothing—so his contributions would be the help he provided for the harvest, and any meat he could put on the table through hunting. We asked him to stay, and gave him the mostly-empty barn for sleeping. This proved a good decision, and he immediately took over much of the hard labor Will had once done.

Troy Snyder was only a couple years older than the twins, and the three young men fell into fast friendship. He had big plans and great ideas, and no idea or scheme was too grand. He and the twins sat up late many nights, sitting at my kitchen table, making plans for the farm. His ideas were too good to be true, but he was sincere, and we were desperate. We'd take hope anywhere we could find it.

I liked Troy Snyder, but I worried about his presence. Experiencing her first real crush, Catherine followed him whenever possible. Troy was patient, and careful of her feelings, but I watched them closely. I knew any relationship between them would only lead to heartache.

The first of May came, and plans for harvest were kicked into high gear. The problem was, we still hadn't had enough rain, and crops were dying in the fields. Instead of lush stalks of wheat, there was nothing but dry, cracked earth in every direction. Not all of the crops failed, but enough that we knew we wouldn't get the bumper crop we needed. Most everywhere you looked was suffering the same. Some places were so dry the ground was cracked with two-to-three-inch wide gaps extending deep into the earth below. We wondered how far down those cracks went. Some nights I dreamed of the ground opening up and swallowing us into the pits of Hell. Even in my dreams, Hell was better than Oklahoma at that time.

The dust storms that had begun the two previous years picked up with more frequency, leaving dirt and poverty the only constants in our lives. That, and hunger. We'd cut back on our food rationing to ensure the children were properly fed. More than a few nights every week, I went to bed hungry. It was more important for the children to have food for their growing bodies, so I gave much of my share to them.

Removing the dust and dirt from our home was a constant process. We began hanging wet blankets over the windows and doors to catch as much of the dirt as we could. If it helped at all, it was minimal. We went to bed each night, then arose each morning to find an imprint on the sheets of where our heads had lain, the area around it stained by the constant dust and dirt that had settled during the night. Some families tied sheets between the headboard and footboard to catch the dust falling over their bodies while they slept. There were just too many of us. We didn't have enough extra blankets or sheets, and certainly no money to buy them.

The dirt outside the home was beyond imagination. Down by the creek was a thicket of sand plum bushes, the entire colony sagged heavily with the weight of the dirt covering it. Even the animals couldn't escape. Those housed in barns received some relief, but the livestock living in the fields suffered most. They had no shelter from the constant dirt in the air. The dust settled deep into their lungs, eventually killing them. Even people were falling ill from what became known as dust pneumonia. It was an awful way to die.

As May moved into June, we were hit with even more devastating news. Of the twenty-five head of cattle Joseph and Daniel had saved to sell come August, seventeen had died.

July came, and with it came Gene Blanchard. I knew it was coming, but I dreaded seeing his car lumbering down the path toward our home. I'd hoped he might forget about me with all his other responsibilities. But luck never seemed to be on my side.

Gene stepped out of his car and approached me with a sleazy grin on his pock-marked face. As always, his dark hair was slicked back, and his mustache was trimmed neatly. His suit was immaculately cleaned and pressed, despite the sweltering heat of the Oklahoma sun, or the constant dirt in the air. His big belly protruded over the tops of his pants, and the buttons of his shirt strained where they met. He was obviously enjoying better times than we were.

"Victoria," he said, eyeing me up and down. "You're lookin' good."

"Gene." I nodded. "What can I do for ya?"

"Just thought I'd check in on ya and see how things are goin'—how the crops are comin' along."

"And what did you discover?" I asked.

C.H. ARMSTRONG

"Not much yet. Mind if I take a look around?"

"Yes, I mind."

Gene lifted a mocking brow. "Why is it ya always have to make things so difficult?"

I shrugged. "Just protectin' what's mine."

Standing under the hot sun, Gene pulled a handkerchief from his pocket and wiped his brow. When he finished, his eyes met mine and his mouth tipped in a creepy smile. "Let's just push this animosity aside for a few minutes, and be straight with each other. Okay?"

"Go ahead," I prompted.

"Your loan'll be called in come next month. That means you've got two or three weeks to pull the money together, and I don't see near enough crops to make that happen. Unless you've got some money hidden away I don't know about, I'm thinkin' you're not gonna make that payment. D'ya know what happens when ya don't make that payment?"

I crossed my arms over my chest. "I'm sure you'd love to tell me."

"The bank takes possession of the things ya own. First we come for the small things, like your truck. No truck, ya can't get to town very easily. You're cut off, socially, from those who can help ya, and gettin' groceries is that much harder. Next we come for the farm equipment. No farm equipment, then no chance of farmin'. Now your best chance at livelihood is taken away. After that, there's not much left but the house and farm itself, so the note on that gets called in."

A chill rushed down my spine at his words, but I lifted my chin in defiance. "I'm well aware of all that."

"Yeah, I'm sure y'are. I wonder, though: your family is already in dire straits. I've heard talk your kids are near starvin' already. You've lost so much weight yourself, I barely recognize ya. What's gonna happen when ya not only can't put food in those kids' bellies, but ya don't even have a place to shelter 'em at night? It ain't pretty bein' homeless in these times."

"What's your point, Gene?"

"Well, here's the thing: the bank don't really want your property, and there's not a damned thing they can do with a farm that won't produce. What they do want is the confidence to know they're gonna get their money back. I can give that to 'em. That is, if you're nice to me."

148

"Go on."

"Well," he continued. "Let's start with just bein' neighborly. I come here, and ya don't invite me in. Ya stand out in the road and block my path so I can't even get near the house. Ya make me feel as though I'm not welcome."

"That's 'cause you're not."

Gene cleared his throat. "Let's not to be too hasty, Victoria. You're not in the best position to make me angry."

"Are ya threatenin' me?" I narrowed my eyes.

"No, not threatenin'. Just offerin' you an alternative."

"And what is that alternative?"

"Ya know Maureen passed on 'bout a year ago. Had ya heard?"

"I'd heard she was ill. I didn't know she'd passed. I'm sorry for your loss." Somehow I think his wife got the better half of that deal.

"Thank you." He nodded. "But ya see, a man gets lonely without his wife. He gets used to a certain type of . . . comfort, shall we say? And when that regular comfort goes away, it makes a man rather . . . *uncomfortable.*"

The tiny hairs on the back of my neck stood up straight as Gene laughed at his own joke.

"And what is it ya want from me?" I asked.

"You're an attractive woman, Victoria. I'm just thinkin' if you were to make me comfortable now and then, I'm sure I could convince the bank to give ya some extra time on that loan of yours. Give your kids someplace to continue callin' home."

"You're disgusting."

"Maybe, but I have somethin' ya need, and you have somethin' I want. We can do each other a favor."

The idea was repulsive. But something in me told me to keep listening. "What would this entail?"

"Oh, I dunno." Gene shrugged. "Maybe a social visit from me, say, twice a month—sometime when the kids aren't here? You can lose 'em for an afternoon twice a month, can't ya? You still have that big sister of yours down the road, don'tcha? Think ya could find a way for her to keep 'em occupied?"

"I don't know." I shook with anger, and maybe even a small amount of fear. "I'd need food, too. Twice a month of 'social time' in exchange for an extension on the loan isn't enough. I need groceries. Beans, rice, canned goods, fresh fruits and vegetables. Meat, occasionally."

"Oh, I think my offer is more than generous." He smiled, but it was cold and didn't reach his eyes. "But I'm feelin' charitable. I'll negotiate a bit. I'll bring ya some groceries from town when I come out. Not much, mind. These're hard times and we're all hurtin'. But I can bring enough to fill the gap. But twice each month, I expect ya to be here with a smile on your face and ready to treat me sweet."

"I need time to think about it. I can't decide right now."

"Sorry, darlin'. This is a one-time offer. I'm a busy man, and I have other house calls to make. Make a decision, and do it quickly, or the offer's off the table."

"I don't know! I need time to think on it!"

"I'll tell ya what: you take all the time ya need, but I can't guarantee I'll still be interested when ya finally decide. Your children are hungry now. I don't have time for this, Victoria; so, when I leave, I can't promise the offer'll still be open."

Gene walked back toward his vehicle, pulled the door open, and stepped inside. Seating himself, he closed the door but leaned out through the open window. "Last chance . . . "

I didn't know what to do. I stood there, dumbly, watching as he started the car and backed down the path to the main road. I didn't want to do it. The idea of being anywhere near Gene Blanchard made my skin crawl. But I didn't have a lot of options. The kids were hungry, and the crops wouldn't bring in enough to pay off the loan, much less feed the kids.

Gene turned his steering wheel, raised his hand out the window, waved goodbye, then slowly drove toward the main road.

"FINE!" I ran after him. "FINE! JUST STOP! I'LL DO IT!"

Gene's car slowed to a stop, then backed in reverse toward me. When he pulled up next to me, he leaned out the window again. "Smart girl. I knew you'd come around. Ya just saved your children from starvation."

# CHAPTER THIRTY

GENE BLANCHARD AND I AGREED TO MEET ON the second and fourth Wednesdays of every month, which meant I had to be sure the children were out of the house. Grace and Jack returned to school in August, which left only four-year-old Ethan still underfoot. On the days I met with Gene, I sent Ethan to Julianne's for the afternoon. Though suspicious, she never asked questions. I'm glad she didn't—there was no way to explain my decision. She'd never understand. Nobody could.

The first time with Gene was the worst, leaving me physically ill. Each time afterward was a little easier, but I could feel pieces of my soul chipping away. I wondered how much more could disintegrate before there was nothing left of me. I dreaded those Wednesdays for days in advance, then mourned again for Will in the days following. In the beginning, I worried constantly about people discovering my secret. But, watching nearby families starve, and their children die, cured me of that worry. It was an era of survival, and I would survive at all costs. Morals and values came second to not dying. Still, I worried about those I loved discovering my secret. What would Mother Elizabeth say? Father Caleb? Julianne? Will's children? I knew they wouldn't understand. How could they? If it meant choosing between my children's lives or certain death, I didn't care if they understood. There was nothing I wouldn't do for my children.

Reconciling myself with this arrangement eased my guilt, but the disparity between my husband and Gene left me empty and sad. I was angry before, but debasing myself stripped my dignity.

The differences between Will and Gene were more than just physical. I'd loved Will deeply. I barely tolerated Gene. Each time with Will was a celebration. Our joining had been more than a physical act; it was an expression of love, where we each gave a piece of ourselves to the other for safekeeping. I missed those moments with Will, but I dreaded every second spent with Gene. Each moment with Gene was a small death. Where Will had been gentle and caring, Gene was selfish and hasty. Everything about Gene Blanchard repulsed me. His dark hair, carefully slicked back with not a stray strand in sight; his black eyes; his tightly trimmed mustache; his extra flesh, heavy from wealth and laziness; and even the smell of his cologne—it all left me physically ill. Will had smelled like the outdoors, a combination of sweat and leather. He smelled like a man who worked hard providing for his family. Gene reeked of privilege and excess.

Maybe the most notable difference between Will and Gene was their hands. I'd always thought you could tell a lot about a man by his hands, and how he used them. Will's hands were large and calloused from hard work, yet gentle as he held me or cradled one of our children. His hands on my skin soothed like silk. Gene's hands were smaller and softer than Will's, with no evidence of having worked a day in his life. He didn't have Will's strength, but he made up for it with force. His hands on my body chafed like sandpaper, abrasive and raw. Every last thing about Gene Blanchard made me sick.

His only redeeming value was the extension he provided on our loan, together with the few groceries he brought each visit. Not a lot, but it kept the children from starving. Though I hated Gene and our arrangement more than anything I'd ever known, the children were assured food and a roof over their heads—so long as I continued the arrangement, or until Gene became bored.

Before long, fall had passed, and 1934 was ushered in. My arrangement with Gene had moved along for nearly six months with no complications. Now, though, I was hit with the most dangerous complication imaginable. I was caught. I'd known it was a possibility. How long could a woman have carnal relations with a man and remain unburdened? I'd prayed it wouldn't happen, but there was no doubt. I'd missed my courses for two straight months. I didn't know what to do. Who could I turn to?

I held off telling anyone for as long as I could, but it's impossible to be intimate with a man and keep that information from him. I kept it secret until the middle of February, but time was running out. I'd have to tell Gene soon, or he'd figure it out on his own. He might've been a disgusting pig, but he wasn't stupid.

That second Wednesday in February, I decided to tell Gene the news. I didn't know how he'd react, or what this meant for our arrangement, but my most important concern was keeping the children fed.

Gene and I spent the afternoon "socializing," and I'd been just about as social as I was capable of being for one afternoon. Rising from the bed, I threw my robe over my shoulders and turned to him. "We need to have a serious conversation."

"Oh yeah," he asked. "What about?"

"I'm caught."

"What do you mean you're 'caught'? What the hell does that even mean?"

"It means I'm expectin' a baby. I've known for a while, but I wasn't sure how to tell ya. I'm thinkin' I'm due in early July."

"Congratulations," he said. "But why're ya tellin' me?"

"Why d'ya think I'm tellin' you?" The urge to scratch his eyes out was almost too much, so I clenched my fists by my side. "I didn't do this by myself."

"I'm sure ya didn't, but what makes ya think it's mine?"

"What? What the hell are ya sayin', Gene?" I sputtered. "Ya know damned well it's yours. Who else d'ya think could've fathered it? Ya know I've not been with anyone else!"

"I haven't the slightest idea, and I know no such thing; but, just because you're pregnant, doesn't mean it's mine."

"You son of a bitch," I whispered, too angry to speak any louder. "What'm I supposed to do?"

Gene sat up in the bed and threw his legs over the side. Grabbing for his pants, he slipped them on and buckled his belt, all while refusing to face me. "Do whatever ya want. It's not my problem. You and I had a business arrangement. I expected you to deal with any problems that might arise. My suggestion is ya find yourself someone ya can pin this on, but it ain't fixin' to be me. No way am I takin' on those brats of yours."

I was so angry, if I'd had a gun I would've shot him dead and without remorse. Instead, I took a deep breath and tried to figure things out in my head. What in the world would I do? Somehow I'd have to make Gene see reason. I didn't want to marry the man—I'd rather have died. I'm not sure what I expected of him, but it was as much his problem as mine, and I needed help.

Drawing in a deep breath, I circled the bed until I was standing directly in front of him. "Gene, this is your baby, and ya know it. Ya can't expect me to let it grow up a bastard?"

"I don't expect ya to do anything, but figure it out. If ya can't figure it out, then we've got nothin' more to discuss." Standing now, he brushed past me, knocking me out of his path as he moved toward the door. "It's been a fun ride, but I don't have the time or money for complications."

I grabbed for his arm, stilling his progress. "I can ruin you, Gene. All I have to do is tell people what you've done."

Turning back toward me, Gene studied my hand on his arm until I dropped it to my side. His eyes now meeting mine, he lifted his brow in challenge. "Ya don't really think that'll ruin me, do ya? Who'd believe ya? Most people in town will see ya as some desperate widow, just tryin' to sink your claws into me so ya can feed your kids. Hell, even your own family wouldn't believe ya. I heard your mother-in-law doesn't even believe those kids ya already have are Will's. Don't think people've forgotten she called 'em bastards at your own husband's funeral."

In that moment, I lost my mind. Looking back, I remember the sequence of events unfold as though I was an outsider watching. I threw myself at Gene with more force than I realized I had. My fist connected with his nose, and blood gushed onto the wood floor. My nails sliced down the sides of his face, leaving long scratches from temple to chin. I used everything in my possession to hurt him. How dare he leave me to pick up the pieces! He would not get away with this! I'd kill him, if it was the last thing I ever did.

Gene's fist flew out of nowhere, connecting with my lip and loosening a tooth. I spit blood onto the floor. Trying to stand, I didn't see his second swing coming. The force of it sent me flying backwards. I crashed into the bedside table and blindly lay there as everything atop it rained down upon me. The pain of that second blow left stars dotting my vision. Gene backhanded me once again, this time knocking the wind completely out of me. I gasped for breath, but the more I reached for air, the harder it was to breathe. I didn't know whether to run, fight back, or play dead. Before I could make a decision, Gene grabbed my hair and yanked me upright. Bringing my face close to his own, our noses nearly touching, he looked at me through the blackness of his dead eyes.

"Now you listen here, ya stupid bitch." Spit flew from his mouth and landed near my left eye, but I didn't dare wipe it away. I couldn't if I'd wanted to. "I don't care if this child is mine, the grocer's, or the milkman's. I will not claim it, and I'll deny any and every allegation ya make towards me. And I'm pretty confident I'll be believed. But even if I'm not, there's not a damned thing ya can do about it. Ya made your bed; now lie in it."

Gene released my hair and stepped back, leaving me to fall to the floor like a rag doll. Strands of my hair hung from his fingers, and he brushed them off carelessly to the floor, spitting on it to add further insult. "I can't believe you're so stupid! Did ya do this on purpose, thinkin' you'd trap me into marryin' ya and takin' on those brats of yours as my own?"

I shook my head. My jaw throbbed, and I wasn't sure I could even form the words.

"I'll tell ya what, Victoria." Gene narrowed his eyes and tapped his top lip with a fat finger. "I'm gonna do ya one last favor because I like ya and because we've had a good time. But don't ask me for another damned thing. Understood?"

I nodded.

"I'm gonna give ya three more months on the loan, outta the kindness of my heart. Take those three months to figure out how to come up with the money. Maybe make use of your 'special skills.' But at the end of those three months—by the second Wednesday in May—I'm done. If ya can't make the payments, then the bank'll take the house and land. Figure out what you're gonna do, but don'tcha ever contact me again, unless it relates to the payment on your loan. Got it?"

Once again, I nodded. I couldn't speak if I'd wanted. My teeth were chattering, and I could feel one wiggle against the others. I was cold all over. With those last words, Gene grabbed his jacket off the back of the rocker and left the house, slamming the door behind him.

# CHAPTER THIRTY-ONE

"OH MY GOSH, VICTORIA!" CATHERINE RACED
toward me. "What happened to your face?"

The children had just arrived home from school. I'd spent the last few
hours cleaning up the broken pieces in my bedroom, and trying to come up
with a believable story about my bruises. My right eye was badly swollen and
turning black; and my nose was nearly twice its normal size, making it difficult to breathe. I was sure it was broken.

"Mama?" Gracie's eyes filled with tears. "What happened?"

Jack stood behind his sisters, watching. His little fists clenched tight as
though he was preparing to fight whatever demon had invaded our home. I
wished, for a moment, he was older and could protect us.

"I'm okay." I attempted a smile, but raised my fingers to my split lip as
sharp pain assaulted me. "Don't y'all get all worked up. A damned armadillo
took up residence in the barn, and just about scared me to death when he
darted out in front of me. I tripped over somethin' and bashed my face against
one of the empty pens."

"Are ya sure you're okay?" Catherine stepped closer, her eyes narrowed as
she examined my lip. "Where's Ethan?"

"He's still at Aunt Julianne's. She's watchin' him today. I've been a little
shaken up since my fall, and haven't felt like fetchin' him yet. Why don'tcha
take Jack and Gracie, and go get him for me."

"Okay." Catherine studied me another moment, then took Grace and
Jack by their hands and turned reluctantly toward the door. "C'mon y'all.
Let's go get Ethan."

Breaking away from her sister, Grace ran toward me and threw her arms
around my waist. "I love you, Mama."

"Me too, baby," I replied.

With the children gone, I sat at the table and pondered my next move. I had three months, and then the house would be gone. What was I going to do? I didn't have long to think about it. The children had barely left when I heard a vehicle approaching the house. Going to the window, I pulled back the now-dry, rust-stained blanket and spotted Caroline and Olivia coming up the drive. I hadn't seen the girls since the infant boy's burial. They'd been so upset at my decision not to name him that they'd stayed away since. I'd missed them. I wondered what brought them out my way, and whether they'd forgiven me. Stepping out of the house, I waited for the truck to come to a stop.

Opening the door and stepping onto the barren ground first was Caroline from the passenger's side, followed closely by Olivia. They stood in front of me, maybe ten feet away, each of us staring at one another. None of us knew how to proceed. After an uncomfortable moment, Olivia squared her shoulders and offered me a tentative smile.

"Victoria," she said softly. "We've missed ya."

I wanted to pull them into my arms and hug them close, but I admit it—I was afraid. They had been the ones to avoid me, not the other way around. As much as I wanted their friendship and approval, I could not change how I was.

Clearing my throat, I nodded. "I've missed you, too. It's good to see ya."

Standing between Olivia and me, Caroline watched the two of us, her eyes moving back and forth as though watching a tennis match in slow motion. Blowing out a frustrated sigh, she grabbed Olivia's arm and pulled her toward me. "Good lord! Y'all two are the most hardheaded women I've ever known! We're sorry, Victoria! We love ya! Now give us a hug, and tell us ya love us as much as we love you!"

With their arms around me, I laughed. I couldn't help it. Relief overwhelmed me, and I bit the inside of my cheek to stave off tears. I tightened my arms around them. "I've missed you, too. Both of ya."

Olivia wiped away a tear and leaned back to look me in the eye. "And we're forgiven?"

Stepping out of their arms, I waved a hand. "We're family. There's nothin' to forgive. Now, what brings y'all out here?"

Noticing my bruises for the first time, Olivia gasped. "What happened to your face?"

I shook my head. "Ah, it's nothin'. Got scared by an armadillo in the barn, and I tripped on somethin' and landed face-first on some farm equipment. I'll be okay."

"Are ya sure?" Caroline reached out a hand as though to touch my face, then returned it to her side.

"I said I'm fine. Now tell me: what brings ya out here?"

Olivia and Caroline exchanged a look, their eyes speaking an entire conversation without uttering a word.

"What?" I asked. "Is somethin' wrong?"

Caroline blew out a breath and looped her arm through mine, leading me toward the house. "We need to talk. Can we go inside?"

"Of course," I said, keeping pace with Caroline as we approached the front door. "Is everything okay?"

"Everything's fine," Olivia said. "We just have some news we need to tell ya."

Holding the door open for the girls to enter, my stomach churned. Coming to see me after so long to give me "news" could only mean bad news. Seating them at the kitchen table, I sat across from my two stepdaughters and folded my hands on the table. "Okay, girls. Spit it out. What is it?"

Caroline breathed in a deep breath and let it out slowly. "We've practiced this conversation a dozen times, but I'm still not sure where to start. I have no idea how to say this."

"Now you're scarin' me. Just tell me. Start at the beginning."

Caroline and Olivia exchanged glances again, and Olivia nodded encouragement at her sister. Nodding, Caroline began. "The bank is callin' in the loan on our land. We have to be out by the end of next month."

"Oh no! What're y'all gonna do?" I asked. "How can I help?"

"There's nothin' you can do," Olivia said. "You've got enough on your hands as it is, what with the little ones and all. It's bad for everyone."

"John and Jefferson talked it over, and they don't see any other choice," Caroline continued. "We don't have any real way to make money without the farm, and this dirt is everywhere. The Halls lost their grandmother a few months back, then seven-year-old Helen two days ago."

"Oh, my God!" I said. "I knew about Old Lady Hall, but I had no idea about the little girl! The family must be beside themselves."

"They are," Olivia agreed.

"The thing is," said Caroline, "we're scared. When those black clouds come through, it chokes out everything. We can't see our own hands in front of our faces, let alone breathe. It gets in our eyes so we can't see, and even in our noses and ears. Everything tastes like dust and dirt, and I can't get the taste out of my mouth! Even when it's rained, it's more like drops of mud as it mixes with the dirt in the air. It's everywhere, and I can't stand it anymore. *We* can't stand it. And we're scared. Scared of what comes next. Scared of how we're gonna survive. Scared of our babies catchin' that dust pneumonia. There's just nothin' we can do. Not if we stay here."

My heart stopped. I knew what they would say next, but I hoped I was wrong. "What're ya sayin'?"

Long moments passed before Olivia spoke. "Ya know what we're sayin', Victoria. We have to go. We can't stay here anymore. There's nothin' for us."

"But where will ya go?"

"The men think California. They saw some papers advertisin' work there. Pickin' fruit, I think," Olivia said.

I nodded. "I'd heard about those adverts. It's hard work, pickin' all day. Back-breakin', I'd imagine."

"It is, I'm sure." Caroline nodded. "But it's work. And there's no dirt and dust. The children could breathe better, and work means food and clothing. And shoes. Ellen's four now, and she needs shoes badly. I can't let her walk around barefoot, what with the heat in summer and the cold in winter. She hasn't had new shoes in so long the tops of her feet are grownin' humps—her bones just have no room to grow in the shoes she's got, and we can't afford to get her new ones."

"Oh my God." I massaged the bridge of my nose, hoping to stave off the headache forming between my eyes.

There was nothing I could say. It was hard for all of us, but I had enough kids in enough different size shoes that they all had a pair that fit. I'd taken to wearing some of Will's old boots, and given mine to Catherine since her feet were smaller. She gave hers to Jack; then Jack gave his old ones to Ethan. We made do.

Clothing was a different matter. Most of us had started using old flour sacks to make and repair clothing for the children. It wasn't nice, but it was serviceable, and the flour companies had even started putting floral patterns on them. Every stitch of fabric was saved and reused. If it wasn't large enough to make into clothing, we used it to patch existing clothing. Sometimes we'd piece it together to make quilts. I hated those quilts. In later years when the hardships of these days passed, I refused to have a patchwork quilt in my home. I never wanted to see one again.

"So ya see, we gotta go," Olivia said. "To survive. We can't stay here anymore."

"We came to see if you'd go with us," said Caroline. "We're packing as much as we can now, and John expects us to head out in about another week or ten days."

"So soon?"

"There's no reason to stay. We can't pack much anyway, what with all of us in the truck," Olivia said. "Will ya go with us? Please?"

My world stopped turning. I was losing my family. They were leaving, and I couldn't go with them.

"I can't," I whispered. "I don't have two nickels to rub together. There's no way you'd fit me and the babies in your truck, along with what belongings you'll need to take. I'd have to bring our truck, too, and there's not enough money for it. I'd only make it as far as Weatherford, and then only if I was lucky."

Caroline and Olivia exchanged yet another look, once again communicating full thoughts without saying a word.

Olivia cleared her throat. "Joseph and Daniel are goin' with us. They can't make a livin' on their share of the land, and they don't want us to go without 'em."

My breath left my body. I was losing my boys, too! Not only did I love them as my own, but how could I save the farm without their help?

"There's one more thing," said Olivia.

I shook my head. "I'm not sure I wanna hear it. I'm not sure I can handle hearing more."

"Ya have to. We wanna take Catherine with us," Olivia said.

"No!" My voice echoed throughout the small room. "Ya can't take Catherine! Ya can't!"

"She's seventeen, Victoria. She's old enough to make up her own mind. Troy Snyder's coming with us. He says he's gonna marry her."

160

"Oh no, he's not! Over my dead body! She's just a child, and he's . . . he's . . . he's a drifter! He's nothin'! He doesn't have a penny to his name! He can't have Catherine. I won't allow it."

Caroline and Olivia watched me with twin expressions of sympathy.

"I don't think you're gonna have much choice," Olivia replied. "You've been so busy with all that's goin' on around here that you've not been payin' attention to what Catherine's been up to. She's in love with him. Surely you've seen the way she looks at him."

"I did." My shoulders fell. "I'd noticed, but I thought it was just a crush. She's only seventeen."

"You were barely eighteen when ya married our daddy," Caroline said.

"That was different."

"How?" asked Caroline. "You were eighteen, but Daddy was in his early forties. At least Troy's closer to her age. They already have a lot in common, and they enjoy each other's company. If ya didn't have so much on your plate, you'd've noticed that."

"Does Catherine know this—that you're leavin'?" I asked. "Does she know Troy's goin' with ya? That he's plannin' to marry her?"

"Not about California." Caroline shook her head. "I don't know if she knows Troy wants to marry her, but I don't think she'd be surprised. If he asks her to go with him, I feel sure she'll go."

"But you're breaking up this family," I said.

"We don't have any other choice," Olivia replied. "We don't wanna go; we have to. We can't live here anymore. Maybe someday things'll be better, and we can come back; but right now we gotta go."

"So that's it, then? Ya just leave, and take half my family with ya when ya go?"

"It's our family, too," Olivia said. "And you're our family. We love you. We love the babies. We'll see y'all again sometime. But we have to do this to survive. I know ya understand—or at least ya will when you give it more thought. We just can't stay."

Silence descended upon us, as we each waited for someone else to say something—anything. Finally, I came to the only decision I could.

"Fine," I said. "When d'ya plan on tellin' Catherine?"

"We saw her headin' over to Aunt Julianne's with Jack and Gracie as we were comin' up the drive. We could just stay and tell her when she gets back—if that's okay with you," Caroline said.

"Doesn't seem like I have much choice, do I?"

"Ya always have a choice, Victoria," said Olivia. "But we hope you'll support us in this, because we don't really have any other alternative."

I offered the girls a small smile. It pulled on my busted lip, but I knew I needed to give them some reassurance. "Just give me time. I'm angry right now, and I'm not sure how to understand all of this. But, talk to Catherine when she gets back. If she wants to go, I won't stop her. If she doesn't wanna go, you'll have to get through me to take her. But do not tell her Troy Snyder plans to marry her. Let him do that in his own time, if he wants to. Tell her he plans on goin' along, if ya want, but let her make the decision to follow her own heart; regardless of what Troy wants."

"Fair enough," said Caroline.

There was nothing fair about it. I was losing my family. When Will died, I had nine children with a tenth on the way. We were now down to eight, and I was losing five more.

THAT NIGHT I cried for the first time since before Will's funeral. I'd been so strong through Will's death, then the miscarriage, and even with Sara. I'd kept a stiff upper lip as I suffered through my arrangement with Gene Blanchard and then his beating. I'd even been strong when I learned I'd be bringing another child into this world; this one with no father, and doomed to be called a bastard. But this was too much.

Caroline and Olivia sat down with Catherine shortly after her return and shared their plans. She'd struggled with the decision until she heard Troy Snyder was going with them. That's all the information she needed. She'd been pulled between her older siblings and the younger ones, unsure of what to do; but knowing she might lose Troy was more than she could take. She didn't know what her future with him might be, but she loved him enough not to let him leave without her.

I had lost, and the knowledge that my family was being torn apart was too much to bear. I sobbed long into the night. I was tired of being strong. I promised myself I'd take this one last moment to grieve; then I'd wake up tomorrow, and greet the day with courage.

# CHAPTER THIRTY-TWO

ON FEBRUARY 25, 1934, MY FAMILY MOVED TO California and left us behind. I'm still not sure how they got everybody in one truck, but they did. Joseph and Daniel sold their own for extra cash, and everyone packed into the back of Olivia and Jefferson's. Eight adults and four children, along with what provisions they could take with them. It seemed impossible, but they made room. Until the very last minute, I wondered whether I could go with them; but I knew better. I'd have to sell our truck just for the cash, and then there'd be nowhere for us to ride. Then there was the fact I was pregnant. I hadn't told anyone yet; I didn't know how. Their leaving made it easy to keep the secret just a while longer. So I watched them load the truck and prepare to move west.

As they were about to leave, Joseph came over and took both of my hands into his own. Bringing them to his lips, he kissed my knuckles. "Thank you, Mama. For everything. You're the best thing that ever happened to our daddy. You've been a good mother to all of us."

My eyes widened at his words. "Joseph! You've never called me that before. You know I'm not your mother. You're old enough to remember your own mother."

He nodded. "I do. And she was a wonderful mother. And so are you. You're our mother in every way that counts. Daniel and me were only twelve when ya married Daddy. We needed a mother, and ya filled that role—for all of us. You've loved us, and treated us like your own; even after ya had the little ones. You never made any of us feel like 'us versus them.' That couldn't've been easy. Even after Daddy died, ya still took care of us. I love you. We all do.".

Tears misted my eyes. "Thank you."

"He's right." Catherine stepped from behind me and weaved an arm through mine. "I don't really remember my own mama much, but I remember you. I remember ya sitting up with me when I was sick, and kissin' my bruises when I got hurt. I called you Victoria because that's what you and Daddy asked. But, in my heart, you've been my mama for a long time."

"In all of our hearts," Caroline said, joining us with Olivia from my other side. "You've been our best friend, our sister, and our mother, all wrapped into one. We've shared our secrets and our dreams with you."

Standing next to Joseph, Daniel chimed in. "They said it all—better that I could've. I love you. We all do."

I thought I was too stubborn to cry, but even stubbornness has its limits. The tears fell, and my heart beat so hard I thought it might jump from my chest. "I don't know what I'm gonna do without y'all."

"We'll write when we get there, and send ya the address when we settle down. We'll try to put aside any extra money we get and send it back here to help with the babies," Daniel said.

"Don't you dare! You've done enough. You've worked my share of the farm since your daddy died. I can't ask more of ya."

"We want to," said Joseph. "Daniel and me don't have families yet. Let us do this just to get ya through until times get better. We'll let ya know when we get settled. Then we'll send money back when we can. Might not be much, but it'll be our way of payin' ya back. Maybe someday, when times are better, you can come visit us. Or even move out there with us."

"Someday, maybe."

One by one, each of Will's children pulled me into their tight embraces and said their goodbyes. I hugged them, then the grandbabies, and finally John and Jefferson Janicek. When I got to Troy Snyder, I stopped him for a private word.

"The girls tell me you're plannin' on marryin' Catherine," I said.

"I am." He nodded. "If she'll have me, that is."

"Have ya asked her?"

Troy stared at his feet, his hat in his hands and his shoulders low in defeat. "Not yet. I don't have nothin' to my name right now, but I will. Soon."

Reaching out, I squeezed Troy's elbow gently. "Don't wait. Times're hard. Too much hardship and too much death. Find happiness while ya can. Ya just don't know what tomorrow's gonna bring. I don't want ya lookin' back and askin' yourself how things might've been different."

Lifting his head, Troy's eyes brightened and he smiled. "I'll think on that. Thank you."

"Take care of my girl. Be good to her and treat her right. Don't you ever lay a hand on her in anger. D'ya understand?"

"Yes, ma'am." He grinned.

"Good." I nodded once and pulled him into my arms for a hug. "Now go. Make her happy."

Troy stepped away and jumped into the bed of the truck, joining the rest of those leaving who were now packed in tightly and ready to go.

I stood there on the side of the road with Grace, Jack, and Ethan, as the truck drove down the dirt path to the main road. Reaching the road, it took a right turn and headed off toward the highway. I lifted my hand in one last wave of goodbye, but I'm not sure they saw me.

Gracie and Jack sobbed their little hearts out, but Ethan didn't quite understand. He didn't know this might be the last time he'd see his siblings.

# CHAPTER THIRTY-THREE

THE HOUSE WAS QUIET WITHOUT CATHERINE
and the twins. Though Joseph and Daniel hadn't lived with us for some time, they'd been a constant presence. Those two boys had stood between us and starvation more times than I could count. Their absence echoed through my whole body. They might as well have been dead for how far away they'd gone. I didn't know when—or even if—I'd ever see or hear from them again.

Gene Blanchard turned out to be a liar. He'd promised me three more months on the loan but, at the end of March, some men from the bank took our truck. It was our only transportation, and now it was gone.

Without the twins, and now unable to get groceries from town, the children grew hungry again. Where we'd once counted on wild game to see us through, it had been several days since we'd seen hide nor hair of anything we could eat. I had to do something. I hated it, but I needed to reach out for help.

Leaving Gracie charged with Jack and Ethan's care, I set out to see Julianne and Earl. I hated leaving the children home alone, but I didn't see any choice. They'd had so little to eat that they were losing the natural energy of children. Grace was almost nine; and, between her and Jack, who was now seven, I hoped they'd be okay with Ethan.

As I approached the Sykes's house, I was greeted by the zealous enthusiasm of their dogs. Mutt had passed several years earlier, and he'd been replaced with three large mix-breeds from a litter of strays someone had dumped off near the house. I had no patience for them. With that much energy, they must be eating better than we were, and the idea infuriated me.

Hearing the dogs' overzealous welcome, Julianne stepped out of the house. I hadn't seen her since the last time I'd dropped Ethan off, the day I'd told Gene about the baby. Truthfully, I'd deliberately avoided her. My condition was becoming noticeable, and I didn't have the words to explain it to her.

"Victoria!" Her eyes widened in surprise as she met me in the drive.

"How are ya?"

"Not so good. Can we talk?"

"Of course. Come into the house."

Sitting at the kitchen table, as we had so many times before, I wasn't sure where to start. My mind was jumbled with all the things I needed to say, but I couldn't find the words. I needed help, and I didn't know how to ask for it. If it wasn't for the children, I'd rip my own tongue out before asking for charity from others.

Julianne studied me, her brows narrowed in concern. "Are ya okay?"

"No." I shook my head. "No, I'm really not."

"Okay." She nodded, all business now. "Tell me the trouble, and I'll see what I can do."

"I need to borrow the truck. The bank came to get mine, and I need to go into El Reno to see Father Caleb."

"Oh gosh, Victoria! I'm really sorry! Of course ya can borrow the truck. I just need to clear it with Earl, but I'm sure he won't mind. You're family."

"Thank you."

A long silence followed, both of us wondering what we should say and what should be left unsaid. Julianne reached for my hands and gave them a gentle squeeze. "How're the children?"

I didn't want to answer this question, but I had to. If the children were going to eat, then I had to swallow the last of my pride.

"They're hungry," I said, my eyes meeting hers. "They've not eaten much at all in two days. We just don't have anything."

"Oh, God, Victoria! Why didn't ya say somethin'? We don't have much, but I can't watch those babies go hungry! Why didn't ya come to us?"

"Too much pride, I guess." I shrugged. "I'm embarrassed. But if this goes on much longer, I don't know what I'm gonna do. The children are hungry. My loan is overdue, and I don't know how much longer I have before the bank forces us out."

Julianne didn't speak for a long moment. I'm sure she didn't know what to say, or even how to respond. Times were tough on all of us.

"When was the last time ya ate?"

I couldn't meet Julianne's eyes, so I studied a dark spot on the wall behind her head. "I'm not here about me."

"That's not what I asked, and that's not an answer. When was the last time ya ate?"

I swallowed hard, refusing to answer.

"Look at me, Victoria. I asked ya a question and I want an answer."

My eyes met hers and the pity reflected back at me was almost too much. But I had no choice—she wouldn't stop asking until she had an answer. "Breakfast. Yesterday."

"Victoria!" Getting up from the table, Julianne found a loaf of bread and some butter. "I don't have much, but this is better than nothin'." She buttered two slices of bread and handed them to me.

Swallowing my pride was hard, but I was hungry. I took the plate from her hands. "Thank you."

"I have some potatoes you can take back for the children. That should see ya through 'til tomorrow, at least. It's not much, but it's all we have right now."

"Thank you," I whispered.

"Don't you thank me! You'd do the exact same thing for us. And I'm furious at ya right now for not tellin' me sooner."

I dipped my head in shame, and silence descended upon us. I thought hard before I said my next words. "There's more . . . somethin' else I need to tell ya, and I don't know how."

"Go on," she said. "I can't think of anything worse than y'all starvin' to death."

I closed my eyes and pulled in a breath. "I'm expectin'."

"What? How?" Julianne's eyebrows drew together in confusion. "How is that even possible?"

I looked away, unable to make eye contact. "I really don't wanna say, Julianne. Please don't make me."

"I think you'd better," she replied. "It's not like this is somethin' ya can keep secret for very long. How far along are ya?"

"Five months, give or take a few weeks."

"Victoria! What were ya thinkin'? Who's the father? Why am I just hearin' this? When will ya marry?"

"We won't. It was a mistake."

Julianne's eyes widened. "But ya have to marry him! Does he know? Surely this man doesn't want his child brought into the world without a father."

"He knows, and it doesn't matter. It was somethin' I did to feed the children and gain some time on the loan. It's ended now."

"What d'ya mean it's somethin' you did to feed . . . " Understanding washed over Julianne, and her eyebrows lifted nearly to her hairline. "Oh, Victoria! Tell me ya didn't! Were ya that desperate?"

Anger consumed me, erasing the shame. My eyes met hers and I refused to allow them to waiver. "Yes, I was. And yes, I did. I'm not happy about it, but I do it again if it kept food in my babies' bellies. And you would, too! Don'tcha dare sit there and tell me ya wouldn't! My babies are damn-near starvin', and I couldn't sit back and do nothin'. And now that it's all over, it's only gonna get worse. At this rate, they'll die if I don't do somethin'. So don'tcha dare judge me!"

Julianne sat back, her bottom lip pulled between her teeth, a sheen of tears glossing her eyes. "No," she whispered. "You're right. I'd do anything to keep my babies safe."

I didn't respond. There was nothing I could say. So we sat for long moments, each of us absorbed in our own thoughts, before Julianne broke the silence.

"What're ya gonna do?" she asked. "About the baby, I mean."

I shrugged. "What can I do? I guess I'll just do what I always do: just keep on keepin' on."

"And Mama and Daddy? What'll ya tell 'em?"

My shoulders dropped. "I have no idea, but I need to do it soon. That's why I need the truck. I need them to hear it from me before word gets out. My hope is I can make 'em understand, and they'll let us stay with 'em for a spell until I get on my feet. I don't know how much longer I have before the bank takes the house and farm."

"What can we do to help?"

"Nothin'. You're doin' enough. Loan me the truck tomorrow, if you can, and I'll take those potatoes ya offered. That's more than I can or should ask."

"What'll you do with the children when you're in town?" she asked.

I shrugged. "I guess I'll leave 'em at the house. I don't want 'em in the middle of all that's fixin' to fly around."

"I'll keep 'em 'til you get back. I'll bring the truck to ya tomorrow, and then you bring me and the children back here before ya head to El Reno. I'll keep 'em for a few hours, then we can plan the next step."

My eyes met Julianne's, and I was struck by the warmth and love they held. "Thank you. I don't know what I'd do without ya. Truly."

"Well, you're never gonna have a chance to find out." Julianne smiled. "You're my sister, and there's nothin' I wouldn't do for ya."

"And I, you," I said in response.

# CHAPTER THIRTY-FOUR

SHORTLY AFTER NINE THE NEXT MORNING, Julianne showed up with the truck. We loaded the children in the back with Julianne's two, then I dropped them all back off at her house. While they were excited to play with their cousins, my stomach was in knots at the conversation I would soon have.

The five miles into town sped by much too quickly. For the first time in years, I longed for the slow transportation of the horse and wagon we'd once used. It was much less efficient, but efficiency wasn't what I needed today. I needed more courage than I'd ever possessed. I didn't know how Mother Elizabeth and Father Caleb would take my news, but I prayed like I never had before. By all rights, they'd cast me off. My pregnancy would reflect as badly upon them as it would upon me. I prayed they'd take mercy on me for the sake of the children.

As I pulled into their drive, I remembered the first time I'd ever arrived at this house. It was so long ago. Twenty years since I'd come banging on this door asking for help the first time. Some things never change.

I'd barely stepped one foot out of the truck when Father Caleb greeted me from the front door. He clearly recognized I was driving Julianne and Earl's truck, and I could see from his expression that my presence alarmed him. Coming toward me, he pulled me into his strong embrace.

"Tell me what's wrong, Victoria. Why are you drivin' Earl's truck? Where's your own?" he asked.

"Is Mother Elizabeth home?" I asked, pulling out of his embrace.

"She's in the house. Are ya okay?"

I nodded. "I'm fine, but I need to talk to you—I need to talk to both of y'all."

"Come in then."

Father Caleb held the door open for me, and I stepped inside. Mother Elizabeth was in the kitchen, her back turned to me while she ironed a tablecloth. I studied her a moment, frantically trying to find the right words to say, but there weren't any. There were just words and more words. All of them were likely to cause issues.

"Liz," Father Caleb said. "Victoria's here."

Turning to face me, Mother Elizabeth's face lit up in a smile. "Victoria! What a surprise!" she said, setting the iron down. "Where are the children?"

Stepping toward her, I met her distance as she pulled me into her familiar arms. "Julianne has 'em. I needed to talk to y'all, and I didn't want them underfoot."

Releasing me, Mother Elizabeth stepped back and studied me. "What's wrong?"

"Can't I come see ya without something bein' wrong?" I smiled, but I'm sure she could tell it was fake.

"Of course ya can, but I can see that's not the case this time. Come sit at the table. I just made some iced tea. Would ya like some?"

"Please," I replied.

Taking a seat at the table with Father Caleb, we waited while Mother Elizabeth poured us each a glass of tea. Finally taking a seat herself, she reached across the table and took my hands into her own.

"Tell us. What's the problem?"

Taking a deep breath, I exhaled. "I need to ask a favor."

"Anything," Father Caleb replied.

"Absolutely anything," Mother Elizabeth echoed.

"Thank you." I swallowed hard. "But don't say that yet. Let me tell y'all what I'm here to ask first."

I paused, unable to find the right words to continue.

"Take your time," Father Caleb encouraged.

Squaring my shoulders, I began. "We're fixin' to lose the farm. The bank already took the truck; and I expect they'll be back any day to take the farm equipment before throwin' us out completely."

"Oh, no," Mother Elizabeth whispered.

I nodded. "The children are hungry. When the twins were here, we were barely scrapin' by. Now, we're not even doin' that. The children are hungry, and I'm gettin' scared."

"What can we do?" Father Caleb asked. "If we have it or can get it, it's yours."

"Thank you. I know this is a lot to ask, and ya must know I wouldn't ask if I could come up with any other solution. I was wonderin' if we could stay here with y'all for a while. Not long—just 'til I can get us on our feet. I thought I'd see if I couldn't find a job here in town. I'll do whatever I have to so as not to put ya out more than necessary."

"Of course ya can stay here!" Father Caleb said.

"You can have your old room back, and the children can share Jacob's old room. He's been gone a long time, and I don't expect him to come back any time soon," Mother Elizabeth said.

"It wouldn't be for very long, I hope. I know y'all are hurtin' as bad as anyone. We don't need much, and I'll get a job as soon as I can. What the kids need more than anything is a roof over their heads, and a little extra in their bellies. We hardly have anything at all right now, so just a little bit of somethin' will feel like a feast to them."

"Of course!" Mother Elizabeth said. "We don't have much, but what we do have we'll make stretch."

"Thank you." I cleared my throat, my nerves overwhelming me. "But, before ya agree, I have one more thing to tell ya. It might make ya change your mind."

"Nothin' could make us change our minds, Victoria. We love you," Mother Elizabeth said.

"This might." I took a deep breath, hoping I'd find the right words. "I'm expectin' a baby."

Mother Elizabeth and Father Caleb sat in deafening silence. Several minutes passed, and we three just sat there at the table as they considered my words. Finally, Father Caleb spoke.

"I'm sure ya understand how shocked we are to hear this. I gather ya don't plan on marryin' the father?" he asked.

"No." I shook my head. "I can't. I'm not sure I would if I could."

"But who, Victoria?" Mother Elizabeth asked. "And how could you?"

"I can't say. Please don't ask me. I won't say."

"But ya must!" Mother Elizabeth said. "Women don't go around havin' relations with men they don't plan on marryin'! What were ya thinkin'?"

I couldn't answer that question. My actions shamed me, but the only thing I regretted was the resulting pregnancy. So I sat there and said nothing.

Mother Elizabeth stood from the table and backed away. Turning her back to me, she said, "I'm ashamed of ya, Victoria. Your children are hungry, and you're busy havin' relations with some man you won't identify and refuse to marry? How could you?"

"Hang on a minute, Liz," Father Caleb said. "Sit down. Let's hear her out."

"I can't sit down, Caleb! We brought her into this home and raised her as our daughter. We gave her everything we could—the same as we did Julianne and Jacob—and then she shames herself like this. She shames *us* like this. And the children!"

"Elizabeth!" Father Caleb raised his voice, as I'd never heard him do before. "You'll sit down this instant and hear her out. I have a feelin' this is more than what it appears. So sit down, close your mouth, and listen to Victoria. Now."

Anger radiated off of Mother Elizabeth until I could almost touch it. Taking her seat at the table, she said one word: "Talk."

"I don't know what to say," I said. "I'm expectin' a baby, and I neither can—nor would—marry the father. My children are hungry, and we desperately need help."

"There's more to this you're not tellin' us, Victoria. I wanna hear the rest of it," Father Caleb said.

"I can't. Please don't make me tell ya anything more."

"D'ya love him?" Mother Elizabeth asked.

"No."

"Were ya forced, Victoria?" Father Caleb asked gently.

"No. I wasn't forced—not exactly, anyway."

"But still, you were forced?"

"Not physically."

"But you were forced. Not raped, it sounds like, but you were forced? I paused before answering. "In a manner of speaking."

"By whom?"

"I can't say."

"What was the benefit? Was he holdin' somethin' over your head? What did ya gain?"

I paused again, and then whispered, "Time. Time to figure out a way to come up with money for the farm. Food. Some small groceries for the children."

Mother Elizabeth turned white, and I was afraid she might collapse in her seat.

"I see," said Father Caleb.

Time stretched in the silence of the kitchen. Even Mother Elizabeth was without words, though her expression now held pity instead of anger. I could take the anger, but the pity cut right through me.

"This man . . does he know?" Father Caleb asked.

"Yes."

"And he has no intention of doin' anything at all?"

"No."

"I see." He nodded and sat back in his chair, his arms crossed over his chest. "What if I was to pay him a visit? Could he be encouraged to make this right?"

"No. And I won't tell ya who it is. He's vile. Even if he did wanna do the right thing, I'm not sure I could stomach livin' with him. I don't see as he'd be kind to my children at all, and I'm afraid their situation wouldn't change. Might even be worse."

"Did ya ask him to make it right?" he asked.

"Not exactly. I mean, I told him; but I still don't know what I expected him to say."

"What did he say?"

"I told him I could ruin him if he didn't help me; that all I'd have to do was tell people what'd happened. He said nobody'd believe me; that they'd see me as a widow tryin' to trap him into a better life for my kids. He reminded me that even Imogene had called my kids bastards at Will's funeral."

Mother Elizabeth gasped, but said not a single word.

"I see," Father Caleb said.

Several minutes lapsed as we sat at the table pondering the situation in front of us. Standing up, I said, "Thanks for listenin' to me. Think about it and let me know. Either way, I appreciate all you've done for me."

"Sit down, Victoria," Father Caleb said.

I stood there looking down at him, dumbly.

"I said, 'sit down, Victoria,'" he repeated.

Taking my seat again, I waited for him to speak.

"I'm sorry for what happened," he began, then glanced at Mother Elizabeth for confirmation. At her nod, he continued. "*We're* sorry for what happened. Obviously we're not happy. I'm sure you're not either. But what's done is done. I have an idea who might be responsible, but we'll respect your wishes on this. If it's who I think it is, you're right—the children's situation wouldn't be any better, and yours would be worse. So, here's what we're gonna do: go back to the farm and pack up what ya can in the back of Julianne's truck. Leave the furniture, except maybe the beds. Get the children together and come here. You'll stay with us for as long as ya need, and we'll figure out how to handle your condition as it becomes more apparent. I don't know how, but we'll cross that bridge when we get there. You're our daughter. We don't just stop lovin' ya because you've had to make some hard choices. How long d'ya think it'll take ya to gather everything together?"

"Not long," I replied. "Maybe a couple days at most? We don't have much, so I could probably pack it all up tonight."

"Okay. In the meantime, then, I'll go back with ya to the farm and bring the kids back here so ya can get things organized. Elizabeth'll get them enrolled over at Lincoln School tomorrow. Maybe even while I'm gone so they can start tomorrow or the next day. Can ya do that, Liz?"

Mother Elizabeth nodded. Still she hadn't said anything, so I could only imagine what she was thinking. At least she no longer seemed angry.

"Have ya had anything to eat today?" he asked.

"Yes. I'm fine," I lied.

"Good. Then let's get goin'. The sooner we get this taken care of, the sooner those children will feel better and have food in their bellies."

Standing from the table, I reached out to take Father Caleb's hand into one of my own. "Thank you. I owe you . . . again."

"Nah, ya don't," he said. "We're family. This is what family does."

I gave him a grateful smile and nodded. Turning to Mother Elizabeth, I wasn't sure what to say or what to do.

"Thank you," I whispered.

Stepping forward and pulling me into her arms, Mother Elizabeth embraced me tightly. "I'm sorry," she whispered.

WHEN I RETURNED to the farm that afternoon, all of the farm equipment was gone. There wasn't a single piece anywhere in sight. I could only surmise the bank had come for it while I was gone. Damn them! They insisted on the prompt repayment of our loans, then took away any chance of receiving it when they repossessed the equipment we needed to earn the money!

Father Caleb stopped in with me to pick up a few things for the children, then he planned to go to Julianne's and take them back to town. They'd never step inside this house again.

I dropped Julianne's truck back at her house and let the children know they'd be going with Father Caleb back to town. Then, with the kids in tow, Father Caleb dropped me off back at my home so I could begin packing.

Methodically, I went through each room in our house, collecting only those things we couldn't leave behind—clothing, Gracie's favorite blanket, Will's hat that Jack had confiscated as his own, and Ethan's favorite toy. In the back of my closet, I found my memories: Mama's Bible with the petals from those first flowers Will had given me, and the rose rock I'd picked up on the way to Julianne's the day of the tornado back in '24. And then there was Mama's wool cloak. I placed it around my shoulders. I could still smell her scent—vanilla. Even after all these years. It couldn't possibly still be there, but I knew I smelled her. Whether it was the cloak or the memory of her spirit, I knew Mama was with me in those moments as I cleared out the closet and the remainder of the house.

I slept only a few hours that night. Once deciding to leave, I was determined to get out as quickly as I could. I figured Julianne, and maybe Earl, would come for me the next day to see what help was needed. My goal was to be ready for them when they arrived.

Opening Will's dresser, I looked over the clothing I'd not had the heart to remove after his death. I'd take them with us. Though Will was gone, his clothing was still useful in a variety of ways. Piece by piece, I removed his few shirts and overalls from the drawers and packed them in burlap bags. In the top drawer, I found a half-full package of Lucky Strikes. I smiled at the memory of Will smoking those cigarettes at the end of a long day, as we sat together on the porch swing in the warmth of a summer evening. I remembered watching the lightning bugs float around us, and telling Will that the tip of his lit cigarette resembled one large lightning bug in the dark. Smiling, I slipped the cigarettes into my skirt pocket. I'd add them to my collection of memories.

# CHAPTER THIRTY-FIVE

I MUST'VE DOZED OFF SOMETIME LATE IN THE night, because I awoke the next morning in the rocking chair by my bedroom window.

Determined to finish packing before Julianne and Earl arrived, I continued my efforts from the previous night. I was almost done when I heard a truck approaching the house. Certain it was Julianne, I continued working. I knew she'd lend a hand with whatever still remained of the packing. The truck door slammed and moments later, the screen door creaked before smacking against its frame as my guest let herself into the house.

"I'm in the back bedroom!" I called out.

Seconds later, I was stopped in my tracks by a voice I'd hoped never to hear again.

"Packin' up, are ya?" Imogene Harrison stood in the doorway.

Squaring my shoulders, I stared directly at her. "What're ya doin' here?"

"Atticus saw Earl this mornin' down at the Co-op. He said you were movin' out; that ya couldn't pay the money back to the bank Will borrowed."

"It's true," I said. "They took the truck awhile back, then the farm equipment yesterday."

"Why didn't ya come to us?"

I lifted an eyebrow. "Would you've given me the money?"

"No." Imogene grinned mockingly. "But it would've been interestin' to see ya beg."

"I figured. Which is why I didn't ask." Turning my back to her, I stuffed a folded blanket into a burlap bag. "So what're ya doin' here now? Ya come to gloat?"

"Nah. I just came to make sure ya take only what's yours, and leave anything that belongs with the house or the property."

Turning back to Imogene, I set the bag down and put my hands on my hips. "Not that it matters, but why would ya even care? It's gone. The bank is fixin' to take it."

"Nah," she said. "The bank ain't gonna take it."

"What're ya talkin' about?" I asked, narrowing my eyes.

"Gene Blanchard stopped over awhile back. He said the bank was fixin' to foreclose on the land and offered to let us buy it."

My head swam. "He didn't."

"Oh yeah. He did." Imogene smiled cruelly. "He said ya were expectin' with some drifter's bastard, and ya couldn't make the payments. He wanted to give us a chance to buy it before it went to auction, or whatever it is they do with those properties they confiscate."

"What did ya do?"

She shrugged. "We said we'd buy it. Gene said you'd be out by mid-May, so we've been bidin' our time. Waitin'."

"Waiting?" Hot blood rushed to my neck and cheeks. "While your grandchildren starved? While the bank confiscated our truck and the farm equipment?"

"Oh, we have the farm equipment," she said. "That was part of the bargain. We gave 'em the check yesterday mornin'. They picked up the equipment last night and just moved it onto our land so you couldn't try to sell it off."

"I see. Then what? What're you plannin' to do with the land? It's not producin'. Nothin' is."

"Don't really matter. It will in time. We just need us some good rain. This drought can't last forever. But we wanted to see you off of it. I told ya those bastards of yours would never inherit this land, and I meant it."

Straightening my shoulders, I took a few steps toward her. "I done told ya a long time ago not to call my children bastards. Don't push me on this, Imogene."

"Just calm down. I didn't come here to fight with ya. I got what I wanted—what I've always wanted. At any rate, we paid off the bank. So the title is ours and I just wanted to be sure ya don't take anything with ya that ya ought not."

"What'm I gonna take, Imogene? I can only fit clothing and a few small items. Were ya gonna just throw us out in mid-May?"

She shook her head. "I was pretty sure we wouldn't have to, but I s'pose we would've if it'd come to that. I knew you'd figure somethin' out, though. And you did, so it's all good."

"You really need to leave before I do somethin' I'll regret," I said, taking another step toward her.

"I'm leavin'," she replied, turning to go. "Have a good life, Victoria."

I was shaking with rage. Thank God I'd not had a gun nearby. I might've shot her.

Imogene had barely driven away when another truck approached the house. This time it must be Julianne, I thought. Peeking out the front window, I spotted Earl driving with Julianne riding shotgun in the passenger seat. I stepped outside and onto the front porch.

"Mornin', Victoria." Earl opened the door on his side and stepped out. "That Imogene just leavin'?"

"Of course," I said, barely concealing my irritation.

"What'd she want?" asked Julianne.

"She came to gloat. Atticus carried back the information to Imogene about us movin'. She came out here to make sure we didn't take anything that doesn't belong to us."

"Why would she care?" Earl asked.

"Because they've paid off the loan to the bank, and had the title transferred to their names."

"They didn't!" Julianne gasped.

"They did. She was waitin' until mid-May to evict me, but decided to come out here after she heard from Atticus that we were leavin'."

"Unbelievable," she said, shaking her head.

"I'm sorry, Victoria. That just ain't right." Earl glanced at his watch. "Listen, I need to get back out to the fields or we're gonna lose our farm, too. What d'ya need carried out to the truck? I'll help ya get it packed, and then Julianne will go on into town with ya. She can bring the truck back when you're done."

"Thanks, Earl. I owe ya."

"Nah, ya don't." He smiled. "We're family. This is what family does."

"Ya sound like Father Caleb. He said the same thing yesterday."

"I'll bet he did," he said.

There wasn't much to load, and Earl had the truck packed in no time. We couldn't take the furniture, so we just took the mattresses from the beds and Mama's rocking chair. Then we tossed in the burlap bags filled with clothing and other things I couldn't stand to leave behind.

"Is that it?" Earl asked.

"I think so. I just wanna take one last walk-through to be sure I'm not leavin' anything we really need. If you'll wait, we can drop you off out by the pasture."

"Nah. I'm fixin' to get goin'. Y'all two take your time. I'll see ya when I see ya, Victoria. Be safe." Turning to Julianne, Earl pulled her close in a tight hug. "I'll see you when ya get home tonight."

"Bye, Earl," I said. "Thank you!"

"Anytime, darlin'." Earl walked down the path toward his own fields.

Julianne and I took one last pass through the house, until I decided I had everything we needed. As we were leaving, I turned to lock the door. Julianne laughed and placed her hand upon my arm. "Lockin' the door? What for?"

"I guess I hadn't even thought about it. Now that ya mention it, there's no reason to make things easy for Imogene when she comes." I finished turning the key in the lock then tossed it far into the yard behind me.

Julianne laughed. "Wish I'd thought of that."

Before getting in the truck, I turned and leaned against it to look one last time at my home of ten years. Placing my hands in my pockets, I realized I still had the packet of Will's cigarettes from the night before.

"Want one?" I asked Julianne, lighting a cigarette for myself.

"Ya know I don't smoke," she said. "I didn't realize you did either."

"Nah, I don't smoke." I shook my head. "Not usually, anyway. They were Will's. Found 'em in his dresser drawer and took 'em to remind me of him. It just seemed like the right thing to do—ya know: smoke one of his cigarettes as my way of sayin' goodbye."

We stood there for several long moments, staring at the house as the end of my cigarette burned down to a stub. Seeing that it was nearly at its end, I flicked it toward the house and watched it land on the front porch.

"Let's go then," I said, turning toward the passenger seat of the truck.

"Let's kick this pig," Julianne added, her favorite expression she'd adopted from one of the children.

Climbing into the truck and heading off toward town, we didn't see the cigarette catch fire in the dry air; but we could see the smoke behind us as we neared town. At the time, it didn't occur to us it might be my house burning in the distance. If it had, I wouldn't have gone back anyway. I hadn't planned to burn the house down, but I wasn't the least bit sorry. Or, maybe, on some subconscious level, I'd hoped it would burn. I learned later the house was gone, burned all the way to the ground. Imogene could have the land, but she'd never have my home.

Years later, when times were better and I had more money, I had Sara's body exhumed from what had been the back yard and moved to the El Reno Cemetery to rest beside Will's grave. Surprisingly, the apple tree we'd buried her under still stood. What was more surprising was the house—now leveled to nothing more than pastureland—was covered in a flat field of black-eyed Susans. I smiled in remembrance, and sent a silent prayer of thanks up to Will. I had no doubt this was his doing—Will's sign to me that we were good.

# PART FOUR

## 1935-1939

# CHAPTER THIRTY-SIX

MOVING BACK TO EL RENO WAS HARDER THAN I had imagined. I was grateful to Mother Elizabeth and Father Caleb for taking me in, but I refused to take more from them than absolutely necessary.

Finding a job was nearly impossible. Jobs were scarce, and nobody was hiring. Refusing to burden Mother Elizabeth and Father Caleb, I took in laundry from the single and widowed gentlemen in town; it was the only option available to me. The work was back-breaking and brought in very little, but every penny separated us a little further from starvation.

When I'd moved to town, I planned our stay to be short. But times were hard, and Father Caleb insisted it made more sense if we shared the same home and expenses. In that way, we both benefitted. With Father Caleb's work and my odd jobs, the children were eating regularly once again. The portions were small, and we stretched them further than in previous years, but the children were thriving.

In July of 1934, Mother Elizabeth helped me deliver David Nicholas Harrison. Small for his age, David was born with a full head of black hair, the exact shade of Gene Blanchard's. If anyone guessed his paternity, there could be no denying it. He was the image of a man I despised. And yet, despite his paternity, we all fell in love with David.

I'd agonized over his surname. It seemed wrong to give him Will's name, but there was no other choice. My last name was Harrison and, with no father of record, the child took my last name. I resolved this in my mind by remembering how difficult his road would be. The fewer differences between David and his siblings, the better he would be in the long run. Deep down, I knew Will would've understood.

I was surprised very few townspeople raised an eyebrow at David's birth. Did they not realize he wasn't Will's? I'm not sure how that was possible. Certainly there were some who hadn't known Will; but, even living five miles outside of town, we still knew quite a lot of people in the community. I'd expected some sort of backlash. Maybe they didn't care. Or, maybe they'd suspected the truth: there's nothing a mother won't do to feed her children.

After David's birth, I searched for work until I was hired as a housekeeper by Isabel and Iris Delaney. The two Misses Delaney were twins, in their late sixties, and had never married. Rumor said when Iris Delaney's beau proposed some years back, she'd refused because she couldn't bear to part from her sister. The two ladies had lived with their father in a stately home on Macomb Street until their father's death in 1930. Old Mr. Delaney was a county judge and had invested well in the stock market. He was lucky. He was among the few who'd pulled his money out before the crash in '29. When he died, he left his entire estate to his two daughters. Speculation was rampant about their net worth. Nobody knew how much money the two Misses Delaney shared, only that they always had enough, and their money made them impervious to the opinions of others. They did as they wished, and I envied them. They took me in as their housekeeper, and paid me four dollars a week. My job was straightforward: to keep their home clean, prepare their meals, and wash their laundry. In return, they were kind to me and allowed me to bring David along. Having no children of their own, they loved playing with mine and spoiled them rotten.

In February 1935, David was nearly seven months old, and I'd been housekeeping for the Delaney sisters for five months. I'd just returned home after a long day, and wanted nothing more than to take a nap before the children returned from school. I put David down to sleep and enjoyed the quiet emptiness of the home. Mother Elizabeth and Father Caleb had stepped out for the afternoon, so this alone time was a rarity. I aimed to enjoy every second of it.

David had barely fallen asleep when the front door opened. In walked Grace, Jack and Ethan, each looking more bedraggled than the next. Both boys sported bruised knuckles, busted lips, and the beginnings of black eyes. Even Grace looked battered. The sleeve of her dress was torn from the right shoulder, and her normally neat copper braids were mussed and tangled with bits of dirt and grass dangling from them.

"What in the world are y'all doin' home?" I asked. "You're about forty minutes early."

Grace and Ethan held back tears while Jack, my little man and the pro-tector of our family, stood tall and angry. Jack's arms were crossed in front of him and he stood ready for battle.

"We got expelled," he said.

"You what?" I asked. "What d'ya mean y'all got expelled? What did ya do?"

"We got into a fight," Grace explained. Her big blue eyes filled with tears.

"All of ya?" I asked.

"Them boys was mean to Gracie!" Ethan said.

"What boys?"

"Them boys!" Ethan repeated. "They were callin' Gracie bad names, and they made her cry; and then they started pushin' on her!"

"Grace?" I asked.

Grace stared at the floor, refusing to meet my eyes with her own. "They said some mean things. I'm sorry, Mama."

I turned my attention to my oldest son, and lifted a questioning eyebrow. "Jack?"

"Just what they said." He shrugged. "Gracie was cryin' on the playground. Some bigger boys were pickin' on her and sayin' mean things. They'd pushed her down and . . . well, she's my sister! They don't get to push my sister down and get away with it! I'm sorry, Mama. I didn't mean to get Ethan involved. I didn't even know he was there 'til we all got hauled into Mr. Holly's office."

Anger rushed to my cheeks in hot waves. "Y'all can't do this. Ya just can't get into fights at school. Now sit down and tell me from the beginning what happened."

Gracie shook her head. "No, ma'am."

"What'd ya say?" I was shocked. Gracie never defied me.

"No, ma'am," she repeated. "I don't wanna tell ya."

I narrowed my eyes. "Don't you talk back to me, young lady, or I'll whip your backside with a switch. I asked ya to tell me what happened, and it wasn't a request; it was an order. Now you sit your butt down here right now, and tell me what happened."

Grace crossed her arms, her pose defiant. "No, ma'am."

"Gracie, I'm warnin' ya. Don't you tell me no again, d'ya understand me?"

"Yes, ma'am. I understand. I'm sorry, Mama, but I ain't gonna tell ya."

"Jack?" I asked, turning to my oldest son.

"Sorry, Mama. Gracie's right. It don't matter."

A hot wave of anger rushed over me. "It does to me! Y'all don't get to get expelled from school and then not tell me what happened. It doesn't work that way. Now Gracie and Jack, y'all two better figure this out right now before I blister both of your backsides."

Neither answered. They were stubborn, those two. They stood there, holding their chins high, their postures defiant.

I inhaled a calming breath and turned to Ethan. "Sweetheart, will ya please tell me what happened?"

Ethan looked at me, his big blue eyes filling with tears. "I dunno, Mama. I just saw Gracie was cryin', and Jack was fightin' with these big boys; so I tried to pull 'em off Jack."

"So ya don't know what happened, but ya stepped in to help your brother and Grace?"

"Yes, ma'am," he replied.

"Thank you, Ethan. Go on into the bedroom while I talk to Grace and Jack."

Ethan left the room, and I turned back to my oldest children. "Sit down. Now."

Grace and Jack sat side by side on the sofa, shoulder to shoulder, with their two red heads nearly touching. Both sets of bright blue eyes stared back. They were courageous, my children. I had to give them credit for that.

"Now, I'm not gonna keep asking y'all the same question over 'n over again. I wanna know what happened at school today, and I wanna know right now. Don't make me tell y'all again, 'cause I will whip your butts raw if I have to ask one more time. What happened at school today?"

The children sat stoically, neither offered a single word.

Taking a deep breath, I massaged the bridge of my nose. The pain of another headache was already thumping behind my eyes. "Y'all two go on out to the back yard and bring me a switch off that big tree. Make it a good one 'cause I don't wanna send y'all back out there. You'll be sorry if I have to go get one myself."

Without a word, both children stood and walked out to the back yard, returning only a few minutes later with a thin switch, void of leaves.

I tested the switch in my hand. They'd chosen well—it was a young branch off a sapling, giving it enough elasticity not to break easily. "Okay, you two. This is your last warnin'. This is the last time I'll ask, and then I'm gonna use this switch. What caused the fight at school?"

Gracie stared down at her lap, her right hand picking at a hangnail on her left. But Jack looked right at me, not the least bit cowed, and not about to back down. I was at a loss for what more I could do other than use the switch on their backsides. With no other choice, I bent them each over the back of the sofa and swatted first Gracie, and then Jack, at least a dozen times on their rear ends.

"Are y'all two gonna tell me now?" I asked.

Gracie bit her lip and shook her head, but Jack stood tall and met my eyes. "No ma'am," he said.

"Alright, then." Pulling my arm back a second time, I swung the switch a half dozen more times until their bottoms and the backs of their legs were as beet-colored as their hair.

Gracie sobbed until I thought my heart would burst with pain, but still she refused to tell me. As for Jack, he took each lick like a boy much older than his years, refusing to back down and show weakness.

For whatever reason, these two wouldn't budge. I was frustrated and needed answers.

"If y'all aren't gonna tell me, then I'm goin' down to the school to see Mr. Holly." I blew out a frustrated breath. "I'll get to the bottom of this, but I'd much rather y'all told me."

"Please don't do that, Mama!" Grace exclaimed. "Don't go talk to Mr. Holly."

Finally! I turned to Grace. "I need ya to give me a good reason not to, Gracie. I've had about enough of your defiance for one day."

Jack stepped between Grace and me, his body shielding his sister's. "Ya really don't wanna do that, Mama. Please don't."

Throwing my hands in the air in frustration, I strode purposefully toward the door and gathered my cloak. I would get answers; if not from the children, then from their principal.

"Jack, I've had just about enough! I'm gonna get to the bottom of this one way or another. If y'all two won't tell me, then I have no other choice."

I opened the door, and had just stepped out onto the porch, when Grace called out. "FINE! I'll tell ya! But please don't go, Mama!"

Turning around, I closed the door and faced my children. "This is your last chance. Y'all two better tell me right now, or I'll find out another way. Then I'll come home and whip your butts again for makin' me go out and get the story from someone else."

Grace took Jack's hand, her eyes pleading. "It's okay, Jack. We have to tell her. If we don't, she'll find out anyway. I'd rather we told her than someone else."

"No, Gracie," Jack whispered.

I walked back toward the children and sat down in the chair across from them.

"Jack, I want ya to tell me what happened, and don't ya dare leave out a single detail."

Jack shook his head, but Grace squeezed his hand and nodded encouragement. "It's okay, Jack. Tell her."

Jack sat there for a long moment, deciding what to say. Finally, after what seemed like hours, his shoulders slumped in defeat. "Gracie was out on the playground when my class went out for recess. She was standin' in the middle of four big boys. They were circlin' 'round her, callin' her names—awful names. One of 'em had a stick and kept usin' it to lift her skirt. She was cryin' and battin' their hands away. She kept tellin' 'em to stop and leave her alone, but they wouldn't! I went to help her, but they ignored me, too. When the biggest one pushed her down, I got mad and punched him in the face. After that, I'm not really sure what happened. It just became a big brawl with everybody hittin' everybody else. They were even hittin' Gracie, Mama, and she's a girl!"

Anger raced through me so quickly my hands shook from the rush of adrenaline. "Did anyone see you? Before the fight broke out, that is. An adult?"

"Mr. Holly, I'm pretty sure. He was standin' right there on the playground and didn't do a thing to stop 'em. He didn't do nothin' until the fight broke out. Then we got pulled into his office and sent home expelled," he said.

Grace was sobbing quietly next to Jack, but I was too angry to give her sympathy. The only thing I could think of was hurting those who'd hurt my baby.

"What'd they say, Jack?"

Jack didn't answer.

I lowered my voice until he nearly had to lean in to hear me. "I'll ask ya one last time, Jack. I wanna know what they said."

Jack swallowed so hard I could see his Adam's apple bop up and down. When he spoke, his voice was lower than even mine had been, and I almost missed his words. "They called you a whore, and said Gracie was gonna grow up to be a whore just like you. They said David's a bastard and ya don't know who his daddy is. They said we were probably all bastards."

"And the other boys? Are they expelled, too?"

Jack shook his head. "No, I don't think so."

Jack had stopped talking, but I wouldn't have known either way because my ears were buzzing like a swarm of angry bees. I shook with anger. Glancing at the clock, I realized school was near to being released for the day.

"Wait here. Don'tcha dare leave those spots on that couch, or I'll whip ya both again!" Turning toward the door, I yanked it open and marched out toward the school.

Lincoln School was only a block from Mother Elizabeth's home, and I remembered it well from years gone by. Walking with purpose, I could see nothing but the three-story red brick of the gothic-style school building directly in front of me. On another day, I might have admired the regal columns on each side of the steps leading to the front door. Next to the high school, which was of a similar style on a much grander scale, it was my favorite structure in town. But today, I had no patience to enjoy its beauty as I had on so many occasions before. Today I had one mission: to find that bastard, George Holly.

I remembered George from my childhood at this same school, and my anger churned. He'd been a bully in his youth, and it seemed time hadn't changed anything. How dare he expel my children? He would not get away with this.

Stomping up each of the dozen steps leading to the school's entrance, I reached the front door just as the bell sounded. The children parted down the middle, allowing my passage. My expression must've warned of my anger.

I stepped into the hallway and was greeted by Mrs. Ellis, who had been my own third-grade teacher. "Victoria!" she exclaimed. "Can I help you?"

"Unless you can point me directly to George Holly, no ma'am. You may not," I said firmly.

"Oh!" Mrs. Ellis took a step back. "I believe he took over Mr. Allen's class today. It's the last one at the end of the hall on the right."

"Thank you, Mrs. Ellis," I said and continued down the hall.

I reached the classroom and opened the door. Standing at the back of the room, erasing the blackboard, was George Holly. He hadn't changed much since I'd known him as a child. He still reminded me of a weasel. With the switch still in my hand, I struck the desk in front of me with such force the sound reverberated throughout the room.

"George Holly. You son of a bitch!" My voice was deadly calm.

Jumping slightly, George's features held a look of both confusion and shock. "Victoria, it's been awhile. What brings ya here?"

"What d'ya think brings me here, you slimy piece of cow dung!"

I stalked toward him, like a panther after my prey. With each step, I flipped a desk over onto its side and out of my way. The room would resemble a disaster zone before I left.

"Victoria, ya really need to calm down," he said, backing away as I neared him. "What seems to be the problem?"

Now standing just about six inches from him, I grabbed him by the front of his shirt and pulled him close. "You are my problem, George." I whispered, my nose nearly touching his. "How dare you expel my children? How dare you allow four big boys to lay a hand on my Gracie?"

"Those were your kids?" he asked.

"Don't play stupid with me, you bastard. Ya know dammed well those're my kids. Ya know me and ya knew Will from way back. Don't you pretend now not to know those kids're mine! How dare you!"

I abruptly loosened my grip on his shirt, causing him to stumble backward as he stepped away from me. With the switch still in my hand, I whipped it across the nearest desk. Papers flew everywhere. "D'ya see this switch?" He nodded, so I continued. "I just used this switch to whip Gracie and Jack because they wouldn't tell me why they got expelled. They wouldn't tell me 'cause they were embarrassed. They didn't want me to know the ugly things you allow to spew out of the mouths of these vile brats you teach."

George straightened. "Now hold on a second, Victoria. This isn't my fault. I simply followed school protocol. Your kids started a fight, so your kids got expelled."

"My kids started a fight? My kids only threw the first punch. The fight had already started and you allowed it to go on. Then ya had the nerve to expel my kids? Tell me, George: what'd ya do to the other kids? Did they get expelled, or are their daddies your long-time buddies? Tell me whose kids they are—I'll stop in and see their daddies next."

"You—ya don't need to do that, Victoria."

"The hell I don't, George! You were a bully when I knew ya, and you're an even bigger bully now. But more than that, you're a coward. Let me tell ya somethin', and ya better listen real good." George swallowed hard and nodded. "You're gonna take back that expulsion on my kids, and they're gonna be here first thing tomorrow mornin' as though nothin' ever happened. I'm sick and tired of people like you pushin' me and mine around. I'll not have another minute of it! D'ya understand?"

George nodded. "Yes."

"One more thing, George. This conversation ends here. I don't wanna hear talk around town of my comin' here and why. If ya hear talk, squash it. If you're asked why I was here, tell 'em we're old friends and I came for a visit. But you will not share the details of why my kids got into a fight at school, and why they were expelled. Ya better be damn sure those little heathens don't either. Ya don't want me to come back up here again, George. Understood?"

Dazed, he nodded again.

"I'm warnin' ya: don'tcha make me come back up to this school. If I do, this switch'll be the least of your worries. And don't test me on this. I'm not the naive little girl I was when I left here after marryin' Will. I've had all I can take of you and your kind. There's nothin' I'd like better than to take my rage against all y'all out on you. D'ya understand?"

"Yes."

I stared him down a moment longer then, without another word, I turned and walked out of the classroom. With my shoulders back and my head high, I walked through the front door of the school, down the steps, and never looked back.

# CHAPTER THIRTY-SEVEN

THE NEXT DAY, ALL THREE CHILDREN RE-
turned to school without issue. The rumors about my excursion spread across town and, with each telling, the story became bigger and more sinister. I'd become a legend overnight. People were whispering, "You'd rather bite a wildcat in the ass than mess with one of Victoria Hastings Harrison's children." The phrase made me laugh, but the sentiment was spot-on. I was tired of bullies. I was tired of always fighting to be on top. In my anger, I'd flipped the tables and was soon seen as unpredictable. They didn't know what I was capable of, or what I might do next. With that one action—done purely in anger, and with no forethought—I'd secured my children from the scorn of David's birth.

The end of February brought snow showers, but it was nothing like I'd ever seen before or since. Instead of beautiful flakes of white powdering the streets, the snow fell in dark flakes of gray and black like ashes falling from the sky. The dirt and dust now overtook what should've been the purity of fresh snow. We wondered how much more we could take of the nothingness that had become our world. Everything was barren. There just wasn't ever enough rain to moisten the earth. If ever I had wondered what Hell looked like, I wondered no more. This was surely Hell on Earth.

Spring brought warmer temperatures, but still no measurable rain. What rain did come, came down in dark droplets tinged with dirt. Everywhere you looked was just pure ugly. Though spring had arrived, the beauty had been choked out by the dry, dusty earth.

April of 1935 arrived and, with it, a day I will never forget. Now, almost sixty years later, I still awaken at night, terrified from a recurring dream that takes me back to that time and place.

It was Palm Sunday, and we'd all gone to church that morning. The early part of that day was pleasant. If not for the dirt and dust, the day might've been gorgeous. In spite of the barren ground, the sun was shining and brought us hope for better days ahead. We'd returned from church and eaten a light meal, then Father Caleb headed out with several other men to hunt jackrabbits. They'd heard the fields east of town were overrun, so a party of men gathered to remove them. The jackrabbits often gave us some of our only meals back on the farm, but their numbers were now too large. They were eating every living thing that attempted to grow on the earth. Groups of men had gathered hunting parties in hopes of diminishing their numbers and, in the process, bring more food back for our tables—food we didn't have to pay for.

Jack and Ethan had planned to go with Father Caleb, but the two boys had squabbled endlessly since we'd left church that morning. Frustrated with the both of them, I'd punished them by keeping them home, instead giving them chores as penalty for their behavior. They'd cried and begged to go, but I'd put my foot down and refused to allow it. So Father Caleb went without them.

Around the middle of the afternoon, some hours after Father Caleb had gone, I'd sent the kids out into the backyard. They'd worked hard and I needed them out from under my feet. A short time later, Grace came inside alone.

"Thought ya wanted to play outside," I said to her.

"I did, but it's gettin' chilly. And the birds are actin' funny."

"What d'ya mean?" Mother Elizabeth asked.

Gracie shrugged. "They're chatterin' and actin' all nervous-like. Kinda like they do before a tornado comes through, but the weather ain't right for it."

"Where're the boys?" I asked Gracie.

"In the backyard, playin' kickball."

"Out with you," Mother Elizabeth said, opening the door to escort Grace outside. "It's too nice to be inside. Go."

I followed Grace outside to check on the boys, but a flock of birds caught my attention immediately. Grace was right; they were acting strangely.

"Mother Elizabeth." I poked my head back inside the house. "Come out and look at these birds, will ya? Have ya ever seen 'em act like this before?"

Mother Elizabeth stepped onto the stoop behind me. She studied the birds a moment, then shook her head in amusement. "Well, what d'ya know. That is odd. They seem nervous."

"Mama," Ethan grabbed my arm and tugged. "What's that?"

My eyes following the direction of Ethan's pointed finger, I stared at the blackened sky some miles away. Moving our direction was what appeared to be a large cloud; but, instead of being white and puffy, it was pitch black. I stared for a long moment, but couldn't quite grasp what I was seeing.

Standing behind me, Mother Elizabeth gasped. "Oh, my God! Victoria—get the children inside. Quick! That's a dust cloud! A dust storm is movin' at us and fast."

Gathering the children, we ran into the house. I dispensed orders as fast as I could come up with them. "Ethan! Go in the back bedroom and stay with David. He's probably still sleepin'. Try not to wake him up! Grace—find as many washrags as you can, and put them in a pot of water. Make sure to put a lid on it!"

"Yes, ma'am." Gracie and Ethan rushed to do my bidding.

"Jack, help me get some blankets and sheets wet. We need to hang 'em over all the doors and windows, especially the ones closest to the back bedroom. We gotta cover every crack we can. Hurry! We don't have much time! Those clouds are movin' in quick."

"What can I do?" Mother Elizabeth asked from behind me.

"Find some blankets to hang over the top of David's crib. Let's try to keep him as covered as possible. Maybe make sure we have a couple more dry blankets we can huddle under if we have to."

"Caleb—" Mother Elizabeth began.

"I'm sure he's fine. He'll have seen those clouds comin' in and found shelter."

Moving quickly, we worked together to prepare the room, but there just wasn't enough time. Within minutes, the light dimmed around us and time was running out. One moment, the house was filled with light; the next moment was nothing more than shadows.

"Everybody into the back bedroom!" I shouted. "We need to stay together! Gracie—where is that pot of wet washrags?"

"Right here, Mama," she said.

"Go—take 'em into the bedroom. I'll be right there."

Herding everyone in, I'd just closed the door when the entire house went black, like the darkest night. There wasn't a speck of light anywhere. There was no relief for the darkness. We'd run out of time. The wet blankets dropped uselessly from my hands. I couldn't see the door to hang them if I'd wanted. The ones we normally kept hanging would have to suffice.

"Mama?" Ethan cried out.

"Right here, baby."

"I can't see you. I can't see anything!"

"Grace?" I asked.

"Yes, Mama?"

"Ya have those wet rags?"

"Right here," she replied.

"Okay, everybody, listen closely: Gracie, start talkin' and don't stop. We can't see anything, but our ears work fine. Gracie's gonna talk and everybody else is gonna move slowly toward her voice 'til you can touch her. Gracie, can you tell me where y'are?"

"Right beside David's crib," she replied.

"Okay, then. Keep talkin'. The rest of y'all start movin' toward the sound of Gracie's voice."

The wind howled outside. Moving carefully, we blindly made our way over to Grace until each of us was touching someone else. We huddled together on the floor and waited. The dust and dirt entered through the tiniest crevices, filling the air with its heaviness. It was so thick we couldn't even see our own hands in front of our own faces. We closed our eyes to keep the dirt out, but it filled our noses, ears, and even our mouths.

"What're we gonna do, Mama?" asked Jack. "Where's Grampa?"

"Grampa's gonna be just fine," said Mother Elizabeth. "We're just gonna sit here and wait this out. Gracie, see if you can wring out some of those washrags and pass 'em around. Let's get them put over your faces to keep the dust out."

David began crying from the crib next to me. He must've been terrified. We were all afraid, but we were all old enough to understand. David was just an infant. Feeling around in the dark, I reached inside and lifted his tiny body onto my lap.

"Does anybody know if there's an extra blanket nearby?" I asked. "I need one to cover David's head."

"I saw one in the crib, Mama," Grace said.

"Can you try to find it for me, Gracie?"

Grace moved for long moments before finding the blanket. "Here, Mama," she said, holding it out for me in the dark.

I reached toward her voice and took the blanket from her hands. I placed it over David's head, then took a wet cloth from Grace.

"Did everyone get a wet rag?" I asked. "I want those over your faces. Don't breathe without it."

David's crying pierced through the darkness, but there wasn't anything I could do about it. I worried about him. With each breath, he inhaled more of the dirt deep into his lungs. I tried to keep a rag over his face, but he fought me and cried harder. The best I could do was keep the blanket firmly over his head and hope for the best.

Grace cried next, followed by Ethan's sobs.

"Y'all two stop that cryin'," I said. "I can only stand one baby cryin' at a time, and I can't do a thing about him. But y'all two are old enough to stop."

"Sorry, Mama," Grace said through tears.

"Don't be so hard on 'em, Victoria," Mother Elizabeth scolded. "They're scared."

"We're all scared. I need 'em to be strong."

The wind howled, and the dirt swept through the room. I'm not sure how long we sat in the pitch black of that bedroom, but I'm sure it must've been at least four or five hours. I sat until my legs fell asleep and my back ached. David dozed off from time to time, but the older children were wide awake. They alternated between tears and complete silence. This must be Hell, I thought. Only an angry God would send so much destruction. I thought surely He must've come to Earth, collected his most ardent believers, and left us behind.

In years since, I've been asked how I maintained a faith in God when we were all so miserable, and each day seemed more miserable than the last. This is the truth: belief kept me strong. I knew Will was somewhere better than here. If I didn't believe in God, then what did that mean for Will? I knew Will was out there somewhere, watching over us and guiding me when I was most desperate. If there was no God, then there could be no Will. The latter wasn't something I was willing to accept.

After several hours, the wind died down, and the blackness turned to gray. Once again we could see the shadowed outlines of each other in the darkness. We sat still longer, not knowing if the storm would return. When we were each fully visible, I gazed around the room. Everything was covered in dirt, literally an inch or more thick. It looked like someone had taken buckets full of dirt and just tossed them throughout the room. When we emerged outside, we found the streets covered as well. In some places, the dirt had drifted into large piles like snowdrifts on a winter day. Birds lay dead in the street, as well as the neighbor's dog. I thought about Father Caleb. I'd told Mother Elizabeth he'd be fine; that he'd have seen the dust coming and would've found a place for shelter. What if he hadn't?

Looking out onto the street, I saw cars covered in dirt and tires buried a foot deep. How could we possibly overcome this destruction? Was it even possible? Would there ever come a day when I'd look out at my beloved homeland and not see death, devastation, and destruction? I prayed for that day with everything I had. In the meantime, we set to work cleaning up.

The biggest and worst dust storm of our generation blew in almost forty-six years to the day when people all over the world had flocked to these same lands to claim property of their own in the Oklahoma Land Run of 1889. Now, some of these same families would leave just as quickly. Our Oklahoma land was no longer beautiful and prosperous. It wasn't fit for human survival.

# CHAPTER THIRTY-EIGHT

PALM SUNDAY OF 1935 BECAME KNOWN AS
Black Sunday. A party of twenty-seven men had gone hunting for jackrabbits
that day, and only six returned. Father Caleb was not among them. Survivors
said the storm caught them all by surprise and too far from any reasonable means for shelter. Soon they were stranded and blinded by the darkness. With no sense of direction, they couldn't tell up from down, and were
doomed to wait out the storm with only the clothing on their backs to cover
their faces. It wasn't enough. The heavy dust entered their lungs, smothering
them slowly. I can only think it must've been an awful way to die. Those who
survived succumbed to dust pneumonia shortly thereafter, resulting in the
deaths of two more in the following days. The remaining four lived to tell the
tale, but they never discussed it. Ever. The guilt of surviving, when so many
others had died, haunted them until their deaths some years later.

Mother Elizabeth was distraught. Hoping to ease the pain by sharing
it together, Julianne and her children stayed with us for a while afterward.
Unfortunately, the house was small and tensions were high, so their stay was
short. Jacob was notified of his father's death, but poverty and the distance
between us made it impossible for him to return home. He'd married his high
school sweetheart the year before, then followed his wife's people to Missis-
sippi for a better life. Without Jacob and Julianne, Mother Elizabeth's grief
became mine to shoulder. Twice she'd taken me in and cared for me, and now
it was my turn to care for her.

Father Caleb's death reduced our income significantly, forcing us to rely
on only those four dollars I received each week from cleaning the Misses
Delaneys' home. Though Father Caleb had saved well and had stashed away
some money for emergencies, I avoided using it. We might have a bigger
emergency. Once again I turned to laundering others' clothing. Grace and
Mother Elizabeth were a huge help with this piece, but they could only do so

much between Mother Elizabeth's grief and Grace's inexperience. At night, when everyone was fast asleep, I picked up the pieces they'd left behind. Some days I existed on only two hours of sleep. I seldom got more than four. I reminded myself that there must be better days ahead, so I held onto that hope with everything I had.

The harder I worked, the angrier and more short-tempered I became. Eventually, even the children avoided me when they could. It was just was well. I was in no mood for conversation. I was living minute by minute, and day by day.

The months following Black Sunday were filled with more of the same poverty and dirt we had come to know. I longed for the days when the grass grew green and lush. I fervently wished for the miles of those gorgeous stalks of golden wheat dancing in the wind. So many people were losing hope, but I held on with everything I had.

September 20, 1935 arrived, and I celebrated my thirtieth birthday. I use the word "celebrated" very loosely. There was no celebration, and no money for a celebration if we'd desired one. The day passed like any other. It had been months since I'd enjoyed more than a few hours of sleep at night, and I was feeling old and haggard.

The next day I spent the entire day cooking and cleaning for the Delaney sisters. It was early evening when I returned home, and I was looking forward to a hot bath before I began the household chores requiring my attention.

"Hey," I said to Mother Elizabeth as I walked into kitchen.

Her back to me, Mother Elizabeth placed the dish she'd been rinsing in the dry rack and turned to me, her hands going for her ever-present apron tied around her waist to dry them. Facing me now, her smile of welcome turned to a frown of worry. "You look tired."

"Yeah. Long day," I said, setting a sad head of cabbage on the kitchen table, a gift from the Misses Delaneys' garden. "Where are the kids?"

Mother Elizabeth picked up the cabbage and examined it, then set it back down before sitting down herself. "Sit down, Victoria, before ya drop."

I did as instructed, grateful to be off my feet.

"Grace is down at Joanna's house," Mother Elizabeth said. "Jack's workin' at Mrs. Nelson's, doin' some odd jobs for her—I expect him home pretty soon, I'd imagine. And Ethan's not feelin' well, so I put him in bed early."

I massaged the bridge of my nose. "What's wrong with him?"

"Nothin', probably. He was playin' at the Hudsons' house with their boys and got bit by their nanny goat. I looked at the bite, and it looks fine. Broke the skin a little, and I suspect he'll have a bruise, but I cleaned it up and he should be fine."

"Then why is he sick?"

"Ah, it's nothin'. He wouldn't stop complainin' about the bite and how much it hurt, so I sent him to bed. He'll be better in the mornin'."

I nodded. "And David?"

"Down for the night."

"Already? It's still early."

"He's been cranky all day, and has a bit of a cough. I put him to bed early, hopin' he'd sleep off whatever he's comin' down with."

"Thank you." I sat at the table trying to find the energy to move.

"Ya hungry?" she asked.

"Yeah. What is there?"

"I made a pot of beans from that bag we bought the other day. No meat, but it's not too bad. Should I get ya a bowl?"

"Thank you, yes." I laid my head in my folded arms on the table. I was so tired, but still had so much to do.

"What time did ya say Gracie'd be home? I could use her help with the laundry."

"Soon." She set a bowl in front of me and glanced at the clock on the wall behind me. "In the next half hour, I'd imagine."

I took a bite of beans. Chewing slowly, it took everything in me to swallow and not spit them out. I hated beans. I hated the look of them, the smell of them, the texture of them in my mouth—everything. And, with no meat, there was nothing to distract from the flavor of straight beans. But I ate them because I was hungry. They were cheap and, as bad as we had it, I knew it could be worse. It had been worse. So I ate every bite of those beans without complaint.

Finishing the last bite, I stood to take my bowl to the sink. "Let me get this bowl washed, and then I'll look in on Ethan before I get started on the ironing. Did you and Gracie finish the wash?

"All but one load." Mother Elizabeth took the bowl from my hands. "I'll get this. You go check on Ethan, and just worry about the ironin'. Gracie and I'll finish the laundry in the mornin'. The last load should be just about dry."

"Thank you."

Leaving the bowl with Mother Elizabeth, I headed toward the children's bedroom. There I found Ethan, lying under the covers with only the top of his head peeking out from underneath. I watched him for a moment, admiring the little tufts of his golden blond hair. The rhythm of his breathing told me he was still awake.

"How're ya feelin'?" I asked, ruffling his hair.

"Not good." He frowned, his bottom lip pushed out in a pout.

"I heard ya got bit by the Hudsons' nanny goat? What happened?"

"I was just sittin' on Donny Hudson's bike, and it came up behind me and bit me on the shoulder. I didn't do nothin', I swear! It just bit me outta nowhere!"

"Gramma says it still hurts?"

Ethan nodded. "Every time I move."

Taking a seat on the edge of his bed, I pulled the blanket back. "Lemme take a look."

"Owie!" Ethan cried as I carefully rolled him toward his stomach.

"I'm sorry, baby. I need you to lie on your stomach so I can see better. " I lifted the back of his shirt and studied the bite, but it looked unremarkable. A black bruise was forming around the perimeter, but Mother Elizabeth had cleaned it well and it didn't look too serious. He would heal.

"That's quite a bite," I said. "But you're a tough boy. You'll heal."

"But it hurts really bad," Ethan said, his throat clogged with tears.

"I imagine it does. That'll teach ya to stay away from that nanny goat."

"I hate that nanny goat," he pouted. "I didn't do nothin' to her! And now I hurt every time I move."

"Then don't move." I smiled.

Ethan gave me a small smile, acknowledging my joke.

"You just rest," I said, tucking blankets around him. "Get some sleep, and I bet you'll feel better in the mornin'."

"I'll try."

"G'night, baby. See ya in the mornin'."

"Love you, Mama."

"Me too," I replied, closing the bedroom door behind me as I left the room.

THE NEXT MORNING came far too early, and I was still exhausted from the day before. I'd been up until nearly 4:00 a.m. finishing the ironing from the previous day. It was now Sunday, and I'd planned to take the children to church with Mother Elizabeth, but Ethan's shoulder still hurt where he'd been bitten. I checked it periodically throughout the night, but it seemed fine. The bite was healing normally, though the area surrounding it was now fully bruised. Mother Elizabeth took the children to church without me, and I stayed behind with Ethan and started the day's laundry.

By mid-afternoon, Ethan was no better. He whined constantly about the pain, but he had no other symptoms, aside from pain at the location of the bite. I was losing my patience with his chronic whining.

Dinnertime came, but Ethan didn't feel like coming to the table, so I brought his dinner to him on a tray.

"Knock-knock," I said, entering the bedroom. "I brought you some cabbage soup."

Ethan attempted a smile. "I'm not hungry."

"Not hungry?" I lifted a surprised eyebrow. "How can you not be hungry? You're always hungry."

He shrugged then winced at the movement.

Setting the tray on a nearby table, I took a seat next to him on the bed and smoothed my palm over his forehead. "You're a little warm. Why don't ya sit up and try some soup. It'll make ya feel better."

Ethan shook his head. "I don't wanna. I'm not hungry, and it hurts too much to move."

Where the bite hadn't concerned me, Ethan's lack of appetite did. I'd hoped sleep was the answer, but he wasn't improving. If anything, he seemed worse. I sighed, knowing I'd have to take him to Dr. Heusman. I didn't have money to spare, but I'd find it somewhere.

*Tomorrow morning,* I thought. *If he's still not better tomorrow morning, I'll take him to Dr. Heusman.*

"Okay, then," I told Ethan. "You're missin' out. I'll just leave the tray right here, and you let me know if you change your mind, okay?"

"Okay, Mama," Ethan said, but his eyes were already closed and his voice was flat.

I left the room on quiet feet, hoping the extra sleep would do him good, and that whatever bug he'd caught would pass soon.

I WAS WASHING the dinner dishes, while Mother Elizabeth prepared the children for bed, when we received a visitor. Opening the front door, I found our neighbor, Jasper Hudson, standing on the front step.

"Jasper," I said. "Come in. What can I do for ya?"

"Victoria." Jasper entered and removed his hat. "I can't stay but a minute. I have some news, and ya need to know it soon."

"What's wrong?" I waved toward the sofa. "Have a seat."

Jasper took his time, his head low and his shoulders slumped in defeat. "Tessa tells me your boy got bit by that nanny goat we have?"

"Yeah," I said, sitting on the chair across from him. "Ethan. He came home yesterday with a nasty bite on his shoulder. Said she just bit him— swears he didn't do anything to provoke her."

"Victoria, you need to get him over to Doc Heusman." Jasper's eyes met mine. "That goat died this evenin'. Vet thinks she was rabid."

My heart dropped. I sat there a moment, not understanding. I couldn't even find the words to ask what I didn't understand. My brain just stopped functioning.

"Victoria?" Jasper said. "Did ya hear what I said? Ya need to take your boy to see Doc Heusman. That goat probably had rabies. Hydrophobia."

I stood, and the world swam in a wave of dizziness. Lending his arm for support, Jasper seated me back in the chair I'd just vacated. "Ya need to sit down. Ya look like you're gonna pass out."

I complied and tried to collect my thoughts. "Rabies?" I looked at Jasper for confirmation. "How is that even possible? It's a goat, for Pete's sake!"

Jasper shook his head, his hands distorting the shape of his hat in his distress. "I don't know, but the vet's pretty damned sure it was rabies. He's got her right now, and is havin' her tested. We won't know for a few days but, when he heard your boy'd been bit, he sent me over here to let ya know. If it's rabies, that boy's gonna need a doctor right away."

"Okay," I said, still too stunned to stand. "Okay—thanks. Thank you."

"Are ya okay?"

"Fine." I nodded. "Yes."

"Is your mama here?" Jasper's eyes scanned the room. "I hate to leave ya like this."

"She's gettin' the children ready for bed. I'll be okay. Thanks for comin'."

"We're real sorry, Victoria. I don't know what to say, except how sorry we are."

"Thank you." I nodded, but couldn't meet his eyes. I was trying too hard to slow down the thoughts racing through my brain.

*People die from rabies.*

The thought ran through my head like a chant.

*My Ethan is going to die.*

Jasper saw himself out, and I remained on the sofa. Rabies! I couldn't understand how that could happen. Still not thinking clearly, I stood and walked toward the front door. I needed Dr. Heusman. Money or not, I had no choice.

I DON'T REMEMBER leaving the house, or the short walk to Dr. Heusman's. But, standing on his front porch, knocking like I had so many years before, left me with a sense of déjà vu. But, unlike that day so many years before, this time the front door opened and I found myself facing Mrs. Heusman.

"Victoria." She smiled. "This is a surprise."

"Mrs. Heusman." I nodded. "I need to see Dr. Heusman. Is he in?"

If my abrupt greeting insulted her, she didn't react. Instead she held the door open wide and motioned me to enter. "Of course. Come in. Have a seat, and I'll go get him. He won't be but a moment."

"Thank you." I sat in the closest chair.

Moments later, Dr. Heusman greeted me. "Victoria? Is everything okay?"

"No." I stood and met him in the middle of the room. "Ethan—my boy. He got bit by a nanny goat yesterday over at the Hudsons'. Jasper came by to tell me the goat died. The vet thinks she was rabid."

Dr. Heusman's eyes widened. "I see. And Ethan? How is he?"

"I thought he was fine, but I'm not sure anymore. The bite was clean, and it looks like it's healing normally. It broke the skin and left a nasty bruise, and there's nothin' ominous about it. But Ethan's not been feelin' well ever since. He's says it hurts to move, so he's been stayin' in bed and hasn't eaten much. I thought maybe he was milkin' it for attention, but now I'm not so sure."

"Did you clean the wound well?" he asked.

I nodded. "I think so. Mother Elizabeth took care of it."

"This happened yesterday?"

"Yes. Early afternoon, I think."

Dr. Heusman tapped his first finger on his top lip. "I'm sorry, Victoria. If it's rabies—and I suspect it might be—there's nothin' I can do for him here. You'd have to take him to Oklahoma City, and it would be an expensive trip. And we're not talkin' about a quick trip, either. He'd need daily shots for about three weeks, all of which would have to be done at a hospital. They may even decide to hospitalize him. Frankly, I don't think you can afford it and, even if you could—and if they could provide an antidote—his chances of survival aren't great. By the time ya got the money together to get him there, it'd probably be too late."

Rage rushed through me. Standing, I pulled myself to my full five feet eleven inches. Lifting my chin, I stared Dr. Heusman in the eye. "You can either help me or you can't, Dr. Heusman. You decide. I won't let my boy die. I don't care how much it costs—I'll find the money somewhere. But ya either help me or get the hell out of my way, and I'll find someone who can. There is no alternative. We *will* get him treatment. If ya know where and how to get that treatment for him, ya better tell me now because I don't have time to stand here while you mess around and waste time tellin' me how much it costs, and how much time has already been lost."

Dr. Heusman's chest puffed out. "Be reasonable, Victoria. Like I said, you'd have to go to Oklahoma City and I'm not even sure they even have an antidote there."

"Don't tell me what can't be done," I shouted. "Tell me what I need to do to make it happen!"

"Fine." He sighed. "I'll make some calls. Like I said, you'll have to go up to the city. It's not likely they'll have an antidote on hand, but you can pray they can get one and that it gets there on time. There's a hospital up there that takes cases from the poor families. They'd probably take you. I'll at least refer ya. But you'll have to get up there and find a place to stay. You'll be gone a few weeks. Maybe a month or more."

"Oh God." I sat on the sofa, trying to work through the money and logistics in my mind.

"Maybe I can help." Dr. Heusman's voice softened. "My wife has a sister up there, and she might take ya in for a spell. I can't make any promises, but her husband died a few years back. She's livin' alone and has extra room. The rest'd be up to you. You'd have to get there and come up with money for food and whatever expenses ya have. My wife's sister—Verlie's her name—she wouldn't have the money to feed ya though. And ya can't take all those kids of yours; there's just no room. Just you and Ethan."

I nodded. "Thank you. If you'll talk to your sister-in-law and the hospital, I'll talk to Mother Elizabeth about keepin' the kids. And I'll find the money to see us through while we're there—somewhere. How long? A month, maybe?"

"At least that, I'd think. Surely not more than six weeks."

"Okay, then." I stood and walked toward the front door. "You take care of your end, and I'll take care of mine. How much time do we have?"

"I don't know—a couple of days, maybe, at most. The sooner we get this ball rollin', the better for Ethan. Let's plan for Tuesday. I hate to wait any longer than that."


LIKE THE WALK to Dr. Heusman's house, I don't remember a single minute of the walk back home. My mind was too full of things I needed to get done. I calculated ways to come up with the money. I had no idea how much I'd need, or even where I'd find it, but I refused to allow that to deter me. I made a mental list.

1. Bus tickets to the city. I'd worry about return fare later.

2. Money for food, times one month.

3. How much, if anything, would the hospital charge us?

4. How much, if anything, would we need to pay Mrs. Heusman's sister?

"Victoria? Where'd ya go?"

"Oh!" Startled out of my thoughts, I found myself standing in the kitchen of our home. I didn't even remember opening the front door. "Mother Elizabeth! You startled me!"

"I can see that. You were lost in thought. What's wrong?"

I took a seat at the table and waved for Mother Elizabeth to sit. "I went to see Dr. Heusman. I have a problem, and I don't know how to deal with it yet."

Mother Elizabeth's eyes clouded with worry. "What's happened?"

"That nanny goat that bit Ethan yesterday? Jasper Hudson said it died. They think it was rabid."

Mother Elizabeth gasped. "Oh no! Victoria—what are we goin' to do? Rabies is . . ."

I nodded. "Dr. Heusman says he can't do anything here. I'll have to take Ethan to Oklahoma City. He's gonna recommend us to a hospital that treats poor people. We'll have to stay up there, maybe a month or longer. Dr. Heusman thinks his wife's sister might give us a room, but I gotta come up with money to get there, then food and anything else we need while we're there. And I'd need you to stay with the other children. I can only take Ethan."

Mother Elizabeth didn't respond immediately. She just sat across from me, her eyes wide with shock. "Of course, ya gotta take him," she said slowly. "The other children can stay here with me. I still have some money left over that Caleb was saving. You can use that."

"How much is there?"

"I'd have to look, but I'd guess enough to eat on for a few weeks or a month, if ya eat carefully."

"What would you and the children do for food, what with me not workin' durin' that time?"

"I'll take over the housekeepin' at the Delaneys'. Then Gracie and I will keep takin' in the extra laundry. We'll get Jack to help us. There's no reason that boy can't learn to iron properly."

"That'd work." I nodded. "I still need to come up with bus tickets and a little extra money in case I need to pay for anything else." I had no idea where I'd get it.

Mother Elizabeth reached for my hands. "You're not gonna like this, but hear me out."

I lifted an eyebrow. "What?"

"Have ya thought about askin' the Delaneys for a loan? They're probably the only people in town who could loan it without it hurtin' 'em."

I shook my head. "I can't."

"Think about it. They adore your children. If they knew about Ethan, they might be willing to help. In fact, I think they'd be horrified if they knew you needed it and refused to ask."

"But that's charity. I don't take charity."

"You're willin' to use a charity hospital, and allow a stranger to put ya up. This is your boy's life we're talkin' about. I understand your pride, but ya have to put it aside right now for Ethan."

Mother Elizabeth was right. In a battle between my pride and the lives of my children, I'd always choose my children. I hated the idea of asking for charity—loan or not—but I didn't have a choice. The Delaneys not only had the money, but they had big hearts.

I blew out a breath, my shoulders falling in defeat. "Fine. I'll ask."

"Good girl," Mother Elizabeth said.

I crawled into bed that night, my head swimming with plans for how to proceed. I would not let my boy die like his daddy. Not this one—the only one who looked like Will.

# CHAPTER THIRTY-NINE

THE NEXT TWO DAYS WERE HECTIC. AFTER cleaning for the Delaney sisters that following day, I swallowed my pride and asked for a loan. Their generosity was humbling. Neither paused a heartbeat, and offered me what I needed and more. I nearly cried with relief, and promised I'd repay every dime and then some.

Dr. Heusman made arrangements with the hospital for Ethan, and his sister-in-law opened her home, at no cost, but with the understanding we'd cause her no financial hardship. She had the extra room, but she could afford nothing more. We'd leave for the city on Tuesday, September 23rd, and Ethan's first appointment was that next day.

The wait left me anxious. We didn't know how long Ethan had before his condition was irreversible, so each moment we waited left me jittery.

I purchased bus tickets, packed our meager belongings, and we were on our way to Oklahoma City. As agreed, Mother Elizabeth stayed behind with the other children. It had been three days since Ethan was bitten, and very little had changed. Though the wound was healing nicely, Ethan's pain continued and, in fact, seemed worse. By the time we left, he cried constantly that he could "feel" the noise throughout his entire body. Just the day before, Jack had been bouncing a ball up against the house, and Ethan had cried for a full hour after I finally made Jack stop. He swore he felt each sound, like an electric shock through his body, every time the ball ricocheted off the house. We needed to get him treatment, and we needed to get it done soon.

We arrived in the city in late afternoon, and walked the five blocks from the station to the home of Mrs. Verlie Watkins. By this time, Ethan was in no shape to walk on his own, so I carried him the entire way. By the time we arrived, the muscles in my arms and back burned.

Mrs. Watkins was a small woman in her fifties with long, white hair pulled back into a low chignon. When we arrived on her doorstep, she welcomed us like old friends.

"Come in!" Immediately, her eyes landed on Ethan and compassion washed over her. "Oh that poor baby! Let's take him straight back to the bedroom so he can rest."

Leading us to the spare bedroom, Mrs. Watkins talked non-stop, and it was difficult to keep up with her. "It's just so lovely to meet you, Mrs. Harrison. My sister has told me so much about you and that poor baby. You just make yourself at home, and don't you worry about a thing! They're gonna take good care of him here, I just know it."

Thank you." I set Ethan on the bed she'd prepared for us. "I can't thank you enough for allowin' us to stay with ya. I'm just so embarrassed to intrude on your hospitality."

Mrs. Watkins waved a hand in dismissal. "Not at all! I feel like I know ya already. Your mama was my dear friend when I was newly married."

"You knew my mama?" My eyes widened. "In that case, ya must call me Victoria."

"Victoria, then." She smiled. "And, yes. I remember when your mama first moved to town after marryin' your daddy. She was a beautiful woman, and she was head over heels in love. We didn't know each other long, but we were fast friends."

"I had no idea."

"Well, I imagine you wouldn't. This was several years before you were born, and my husband and I moved here not long after we married. But yes, I knew your mama long before you were born, and I remember the many hopes and dreams she had for her children."

"Thank you for telling me that," I replied.

With Ethan now settled in bed, I snugged the blankets around him and followed Mrs. Watkins back out into the front room. There we talked long into the night as she regaled me with stories of my mother and father. Sitting there with her, I felt my parents close to me. Her stories brought to life the young people they had been, reminding me of the love they'd shared. That night, I went to bed nervous about what the days would bring, yet content for the first time in ages.

WEDNESDAY MORNING, I woke early and well-rested. Glancing at the clock, I realized it was the longest stretch of sleep I'd had in months. I must've slept a full six or seven hours.

Rising from bed, careful not to disturb Ethan who'd slept beside me all night, I dressed quietly and eased the bedroom door open. As I stepped into the hall, I was assaulted by the distinct fragrance of bacon frying. My shoulders slumped. In all the excitement of the day before, I'd forgotten to buy groceries for breakfast! I wondered if I'd have time to run out for a few items before Ethan awakened.

"Good mornin'," I greeted Mrs. Watkins as I entered the kitchen.

"Mornin', Victoria." She smiled brightly. "Breakfast is almost ready, if you'd like some."

I shook my head. "Oh, I couldn't. But thank you. I promised I wouldn't be a financial burden. I was hopin' I might have time to run out and get a few things while Ethan's still sleepin'."

"Nonsense!" She waved a hand in dismissal. "I don't have much, but I can share. Y'all two eat this morning, then stop by the grocer later this afternoon and I'll let you make my breakfast tomorrow."

I nodded. "Thank you. If you're sure, that's exactly what I'll do."

"I am sure," she declared. "Now sit. Breakfast is ready."

We ate in comfortable silence, then I awoke Ethan to feed him and prepare him for his appointment. He ate very little, and cried out at every sound or the slightest movement. His discomfort left me feeling helpless; but, until the doctor saw him later that morning, there was nothing for it.

A short while later, I carried Ethan the seven blocks to the doctor's office. It wasn't a long walk, but the distance felt like miles with Ethan in my arms. I could only be thankful it wasn't Jack or Grace, as there was no way I could've carried either of the older children the distance necessary. It wasn't an ideal situation, but we had to make do. I didn't have a car, and—so long as I was able—I was determined not to use the extra money I'd brought along for emergencies.

Once arriving at the hospital, we waited nearly an hour for the doctor to see Ethan. As time passed, my patience became shorter and shorter, and Ethan's constant whining wasn't helping. Just when I was ready to insist upon seeing *any* doctor, we were taken back to meet our designated physician.

Dr. Dale Greene was a huge man and nothing I'd expected. Taller than Will had been, he must've measured a full six feet six inches. He had wavy brown hair, brown eyes, straight teeth, and a deep cleft in the center of his chin. He was barrel-chested and strong, his image completely incongruent with what I had expected of a doctor.

"Mrs. Harrison?" he asked in greeting.

I nodded. "Yes, sir."

"I'm Dr. Greene. This must be Ethan?"

Ethan nodded, his eyes huge as he took in the doctor's large stature.

Dr. Green turned his full attention to Ethan. "I hear you got bit by a nanny goat?"

Ethan nodded. "Yes, sir."

"Well, let's take a look at this bite." Helping Ethan remove his shirt, he studied the marks on his shoulder. "Hmm. Doesn't look like she ate much. You must not taste very good."

Ethan giggled, the first semblance of laughter I'd heard from him in days.

Dr. Greene gently replaced Ethan's shirt, pulling his arms carefully through the armholes one at a time. "Okay, then. Can you tell me what happened, exactly?"

Ethan's eyes widened and he stared at me. Understanding his silent plea, I explained the events of that weekend and Ethan's behavior since the bite.

Dr. Greene listened attentively, making notes on his clipboard as I spoke, and asking questions when he needed clarification. When I finished, he took a seat in his chair and scratched the back of his neck as though trying to think through what he wanted to say. After a moment, he leaned forward and rested his elbows on his knees.

"So here's what I think," Dr. Greene said. "I spoke to Dr. Heusman this morning, and the results on the nanny goat were positive. She was infected, and may have passed that infection on to Ethan."

I knew this was coming, but I covered my mouth with my hand to keep from crying out. My eyes filled with tears, but I held them in. Tears wouldn't help right now; Ethan needed my strength. Taking a deep breath, I moved my hands to my lap and clasped them together. "Okay, so what d'we need to do?"

"For starters, we need to get Ethan started on the rabies vaccine. Based upon my cursory exam, and the information provided by you and Dr. Heusman, he's already showing signs of infection so time is running out. I anticipated this might be the outcome, so we've already ordered the vaccine, but it's coming from Kansas City and won't be here until Friday."

"Friday?" I gasped. "That's too long, isn't it?"

"I'm not sure. I hope not."

"You hope not?" I accused. "Why do you have to get it from Kansas City? Why don't ya have it here already?"

"We don't see enough cases of rabies to keep the vaccine in stock, and it's expensive. But I think we've caught it in time. The vaccine should be here by Friday morning. In the meantime, you need to take him home and make sure he gets plenty of rest. We'll set up an appointment for Friday afternoon and begin the shots. He'll need one daily for the next three weeks, so you'll have a standing appointment every day at the same time until we've finished the protocol of injections."

"Every day?" How in the world was I going to carry Ethan the seven blocks every day? "But—can't I just take it with me and give it to him at home?"

"I'm sorry, Mrs. Harrison. The injections are . . . tricky." His eyes moved to Ethan, gauging how closely he was listening. He lowered his voice. "I must warn you, it's a very painful process. Excruciating, I'm told."

I swallowed hard. "How so?"

Dr. Greene lowered his voice to a whisper. "The needle goes straight into the stomach. We'll need to strap him down so he's unable to move during the procedure. Do you have someone you can bring with you to help? It's not an easy procedure to watch."

"No." I shook my head "It's just me."

"I'm sorry," he said softly. "I wouldn't have him go through the process if I wasn't certain rabies was a real threat. We could wait and see if more symptoms develop; but, the longer we wait, the more likely we'll need to admit him, and the less likely we are to have success with the treatment. I don't mean to scare you but, statistically speaking, the odds of recuperating are against him. I'm hoping we'll be lucky and discover we've caught it in time, but we won't know for sure until we've begun the injections."

"Where do ya do it?" I asked.

"Right back here. We have a room for procedures requiring restraint. I think it would be the best place for him. He looks okay right now, but we'll need to keep an eye on him. If his condition deteriorates, we'll have no choice but to admit him. For now, let's plan on you bringing him in each day."

"Thank you," I said with relief.

Dr. Greene and I talked for several moments longer, and then we were released to go home with an appointment for Friday afternoon at 3:00. Ethan's treatments would begin then, and we hoped for a swift recovery. I wouldn't allow myself to consider what would happen if he didn't. I'd lost Sara and the baby with no name; I would not lose Ethan.

FRIDAY TOOK FOREVER to arrive, but we were soon on our way to the hospital for the first of Ethan's appointments. Like before, we were seated in a small waiting area until Dr. Greene was free to see us. Finally at 3:35, he greeted us and we were escorted to a small room with a chair inside resembling one used by today's dentists. I placed Ethan in the chair, and a nurse arrived to strap down his arms, legs and hips. When she was done, his eyes were wide with fear; but there were no gaps open for him to wiggle loose.

Seeing my six-year-old boy strapped to that chair was almost more than I could endure. Though we had talked at length on Wednesday about this procedure and all it entailed, nothing prepared me for what I was about to see.

Using a needle about six inches long, Dr. Greene inserted it directly into Ethan's stomach, then slowly depressed the plunger. Ethan's screams pierced the small room. Though he struggled against his binds, he could find no escape. His face turned a deep purple until the veins in his forehead were visible. For a moment, I was a coward and looked away before forcing myself to bring my attention back to the moment and my son's distress.

The injection seemed to last for hours, but it couldn't have been longer than a minute. Ethan's sobs ripped my heart down the center. I felt as though I'd violated a sacred trust with my son. I'd allowed strangers to strap him into a chair and torture him while I stood by and watched. Yet I had no choice. The alternative was certain death. The idea of doing this every day for the next three weeks overwhelmed me, and I swayed toward the chair beside me before falling into it.

Squeezing my eyes shut tight, I breathed in a shallow breath. I tried for a deeper breath, but my throat seemed to close up and my oxygen was limited. My body shook, but I knew I had to pull myself together for Ethan.

It took me a moment to realize the room was now quiet. My eyes shot to Ethan who lay statue-still with his eyes closed. I gasped, and tripped on my feet as I ran to his side. "Ethan!"

"Shh," the nurse squeezed my elbow gently. "He just wore himself out and lost consciousness trying to fight the restraints. He'll come to in a few minutes."

Swallowing, I nodded and took a step away while the nurse unstrapped my son from the chair.

Dr. Greene took my elbow and helped me find the seat I'd vacated. "I'm sorry that was so painful to watch, Mrs. Harrison. If you'll tell me where you've parked, I can have someone help you out to the car with him."

"I haven't," I said, my voice barely a whisper. I cleared my throat. "That is to say, I didn't bring a car. I don't have one. We walked."

"You walked?" Dr. Greene lifted an eyebrow. "How far?"

"Seven blocks."

"Well, he can't walk seven blocks home, Mrs. Harrison."

"I know that," I snapped back. "I carried him."

"The entire seven blocks?"

"Yes, Dr. Greene." I gritted my teeth to keep from yelling. "The entire seven blocks. I didn't know it was going to be this bad, and I didn't have any other choice."

Dr. Greene thought on my words for a long moment then replied. "I'll take you home. Are you able to get transportation to and from the appointments after today?"

"No." I shook my head. "I don't have the money, and I don't have anyone I can borrow a car from. I can take a bus for the short term, but even that money will run out if we're ridin' here and back twice a day. Will Ethan be able to make the walk in a week or two once the injections start workin'?"

"No. Even once he's finished the injections, he'll still be too weak for that kind of walk for a while. What if you only had to ride the bus one way? Could you afford the bus ride just one direction?"

I thought on this for a moment and did a mental calculation of the costs. "I might could do that. We'd have to be careful on our other expenses, but I think it'd work."

"Okay, then. I'll take you home today. We'll set your appointments up so that they're my last of the day, and then I'll give you a lift home after his injection."

My face flamed with humiliation. Once again, I was taking charity from a stranger. And once again, I had no choice. I would swallow my pride in the best interests of Ethan.

Together we took Ethan back to Mrs. Watkins's home, then Dr. Greene carried my son upstairs to the room we shared. For the next three weeks, this would become our reality: late afternoon appointments for injections, followed by charity rides home from the good doctor.

We soon settled into a pattern. Each morning I awoke early and did simple housecleaning for Mrs. Watkins as payment for our keep. Then, each afternoon, I took Ethan by bus to the hospital.

For his part, Ethan was quieter than normal. He complained constantly about the pain in his shoulder, but he was slowly regaining some of his energy. The shots, on the other hand, were horrible. Each one robbed him of what little energy he had. He'd return home each night and sleep for a couple hours before having dinner, then drift back off to sleep for the night.

# CHAPTER FORTY

"DR. GREENE IS QUITE HANDSOME," MRS. WAT-kins said to me the next week. For nearly a week, he'd been bringing us home and carrying Ethan to his room at the end of every visit.

"I really hadn't noticed." I shrugged. It was a lie, but it was mostly the truth. It would be impossible to ignore how attractive Dale Greene was, but my priority was Ethan and getting back to El Reno.

"Well, he's certainly noticed you," she smiled.

"What d'ya mean?"

"Ya haven't noticed the way he looks at you? I'm sure it's not every child he brings home from the hospital, personally. If I didn't know better, I'd think he was interested in ya, Victoria. It wouldn't be the worst thing in the world, would it?"

"No." I shook my head. "It wouldn't be the worst thing in the world, but I'm sure you're mistaken."

"Maybe I am, but I don't think so. Think on it a bit. A man like Dr. Greene is in a position to take some of your worries away. You're still young and attractive, and he seems interested. It wouldn't take much encouragement from ya, I wouldn't think."

"Encouragement from me for what?"

"For him to become more interested. He's single with no children. I heard he'd been married some years back, but he and his wife never had any children. She died young—broke her neck falling down the stairs, I think. I'd heard he was devastated. That was some time ago, and he's still a young man."

"Ya think he'd be interested in a woman with four children?" I asked.

"I don't know but, if I were you, I'd explore it some. Encourage him a little if he seems interested."

"I'll think on it, but I think you're wrong. He'd be crazy to take on a widow with four children. What would he gain?"

"A family," she said simply. "At his age, he's not likely to wanna start brand new, but he can have an instant family by marryin' someone with children young enough to accept him as their father. Ethan is certainly young enough, and ya have a baby at home. I don't think the other two are too old yet to accept him, do you?"

"Probably not, but this is ridiculous. He's Ethan's doctor. He's just bein' kind. I won't do anything to interfere with Ethan's care."

"Just keep an open mind, dear," she replied.

OVER THE NEXT several days, I couldn't get Mrs. Watkins's words out of my head. Each day Dr. Greene—Dale, as he'd insisted I call him—carefully loaded Ethan into his car and brought us home, then gently carried him up to the bedroom to rest upon our bed. He never said or did anything inappropriate or forward, yet I had begun to consider the possibility that Mrs. Watkins might be right.

The following Wednesday marked the halfway point for Ethan's injections. Dale and I had enjoyed an easy relationship, taking the drive home to converse about a variety of different subjects. In the space of about ten days, we'd become friends of a sort. I enjoyed his company and, while I was ready to go home, I'd begun to resent the idea of saying goodbye.

"Ya know, Victoria," he said that afternoon. "We're almost through with the injections."

I smiled. "I'm glad. I never imagined how hard these were gonna be. He's takin' 'em well, but it's sapped all of his energy. He sleeps all day."

"I figured as much. Between the poison from the rabies and the pain from the injections, he's pretty worn out."

"I'll be ready when it's all over so he can get back to his normal self, doin' the things he loves to do."

"What about you, Victoria?" he asked. "What will you do?"

"Me?" I laughed. "I guess I'll go back to what I was doin' before we came here. The kids have been with my mother, and I'm sure they're ready to see me return and pick up some of the workload."

"Let me take you out this evening," he offered. "I can take you to dinner and, maybe, dancing. I get the impression you don't have much time for fun back at home."

"Oh, I couldn't." My face flushed with heat. "I don't have anyone to stay with Ethan. But thank you."

"Sure you can. Just say yes. You can ask Mrs. Watkins to stay with Ethan. The worst of his pain is gone, and he's not as sensitive to sound. He'll sleep anyway, and you can step away for a little bit and enjoy yourself. Get away for an evening. Let me show you what it's like to have fun."

I shook my head. "I really couldn't ask Mrs. Watkins. She's been kind enough to allow us to stay with her. She didn't sign on to be a babysitter."

"Ask her," he urged. "I bet she'd be delighted."

"I'll think about it," I said as we pulled into the driveway.

As had become our custom, Dale carried Ethan up to the bedroom and tucked him into bed. Following behind him, I tucked Ethan a little tighter then followed Dale out to the front room to bid him goodbye.

"How's the baby?" Mrs. Watkins asked.

"Much better," Dale said. "His mother, on the other hand, could use a night out."

"Oh?" she asked.

"Dale, that's enough," I said.

"Yes." He turned his charm full force on Mrs. Watkins. "I'd like to take her out to dinner, but she swears she has no one to keep Ethan."

"Well!" Mrs. Watkins huffed and placed her hands on her hips. "What in the world am I? I can stay with the boy for a couple of hours!"

"Mrs. Watkins, thank you. But—"

"Don't you give me any buts, young lady!" she interrupted. "I've told ya time and again I'd be happy to stay with Ethan while you step out for a bit. I'm beginnin' to feel as though ya don't trust me with the boy!"

My eyes shot wide. "Oh, no! It's not that at all! I just don't wanna take advantage. You've given us a place to live these last several weeks. I couldn't ask for more."

"I insist," she said. "Go. Let Dr. Greene take ya out. Enjoy yourself while ya can. Ethan and I will be fine. He'll sleep anyway, I'm sure."

I felt so torn. On the one hand, I wanted to get out. I was sick of worrying, and I just wanted one evening without worries. On the other hand, I felt like I was taking advantage of Mrs. Watkins. Before I could respond, however, Dale answered for me.

"There you go, Victoria. It's settled." Dale looked at his watch. "It's almost 6:00 now. How about I come back for you at 7:30? Give you some time to settle down and change?"

"Fine," I said, not sure whether I was angry or thrilled.

With an impish grin, Dale said his goodbyes to Mrs. Watkins. I was left standing in the middle of the front room, wondering what in the world I'd agreed to do.

AN HOUR LATER, I stood in front of the small closet in the guest bedroom and realized I had nothing appropriate to wear. I didn't have much anyway, but what I had was worn and dated; certainly not appropriate for an evening of dinner and dancing.

"I can't go." I turned to Mrs. Watkins, who'd insisted upon helping me get ready. "I have nothin' to wear. You'll have to tell him when he gets here because I just can't."

"Don't be ridiculous." She moved toward me and crowded me aside as she selected a dress from the closet. "This blue dress is lovely. Just put a sweater over it, and you won't notice the wear quite so much."

"I haven't got a sweater that isn't more worn," I told her.

"Maybe not, but I do." Leaving the room, she returned only moments later with a lovely cream-colored sweater that looked nearly new.

"Oh no." I put my hand palm up in front of me. "I can't. It looks like it's never been worn."

"It's been worn, and you most certainly can. I insist." Bringing her other hand out from behind her back, she held out a string of pearls. "I also grabbed these to go with it. They were my mother's, and I think they'll look lovely together."

I shook my head. "Oh no! I couldn't!"

"Oh yes, you can. I insist." Turning me away from her, she placed the strand around my neck and secured the clasp. "There. Now finish gettin' ready. He'll be here shortly."

As Mrs. Watkins left the room, I stared at my refletion in the mirror and touched the pearls around my neck. My eyes misted with gratitutde at her kindness. They *were* beautiful, and the addition lent elegance to my simple attire. Blowing out a breath, I donned the sweater she had left behind and assessed my appearance one last time. Seconds later, I heard Dale's voice from the front room. He had arrived promptly and my time was up.

Crossing into the main room, my breath caught as I saw Dale standing in the entry. I was so used to seeing him in his white coat that I hadn't realized how handsome he would appear in a well-made suit.

Dale smiled at my appearance. "Victoria. You look lovely. Are you ready?"

"Thank you." I grinned. "Ready as I'll ever be, I guess."

"Then let's go." To Mrs. Watkins he said, "We shouldn't be too late."

"Take your time and have fun. I'll still be here. I'll go to bed if I'm tired, so just take your time and enjoy yourselves."

With those words, I was whisked out the door and into Dale's waiting vehicle.

# CHAPTER FORTY-ONE

DALE TOOK ME TO AN ELEGANT RESTAURANT, and I dined out for the second time in my life. It was impossible to not remember Will and the day we were married. I'd been so young then, not to mention naive. Though I was only twelve years older now, life had aged me drastically.

Conversation with Dale was easy. He was intelligent and far more worldly than anyone I'd ever known. If I wondered for even a minute what it was he found attractive about me, I quickly dismissed it. He seemed truly interested in my thoughts and opinions. In those few hours with Dale, I had fun for the first time since Will's death.

"Tell me about your children," he asked. "I've met Ethan, but you have three more?"

"Yes." I nodded and set my fork down. "Grace is the oldest at ten, Jack is eight, Ethan is six, and David is just fifteen months."

"So who is with the other three children while you're here?"

"My mother. My father passed away in April, so we all live together. She agreed to keep the children while I brought Ethan here. Now, tell me more about you. Marriages? Children?"

"No children." He shook his head. "My wife—Evelyn was her name—died three years ago."

"So it's been just you, alone, these last three years?"

"Pretty much. My family is all in St. Louis. I came here to Oklahoma City about ten years ago to take the job at the hospital. I see the family from time to time, but not often. Usually a few years pass in between visits."

Dale and I talked for hours. As the restaurant closed around us, we decided to take a walk rather than go dancing. I'd explained I was a terrible dancer, and he'd replied that he preferred quiet conversation anyway. So we walked in the cool of the October night until my feet ached.

At the end of our evening, Dale walked me to the front door of Mrs. Watkins's home and kissed me gently. "Let's do this again, Victoria?"

"I don't know," I replied. "I don't wanna take advantage of Mrs. Watkins. Besides that, I'll be goin' home soon. I can't see how this is a good idea."

"Let me decide if this is a good idea, okay?" He leaned down and kissed me a second time.

I returned his kiss and bid him goodnight, promising to see him tomorrow for Ethan's next injection.

AFTER THAT FIRST night out with Dale, it was impossible to tell him no. Each day he'd bring me home with Ethan, then conspire with Mrs. Watkins to take me out again. As the end of Ethan's injections snuck up on us, I realized I'd been out with Dale every night since that first night celebrating the halfway mark. I didn't love Dale, but I enjoyed his company far more than I'd enjoyed anyone's company since Will. I would be sorry to say goodbye.

"Tomorrow is Ethan's last injection," Dale said as we brought Ethan in and laid him on the bed. "Where should we go tonight?"

"Oh, so you're just gonna assume I'll step out with ya now, are ya?" I laughed.

"Would I be wrong?" He grinned.

Pausing for a moment, I replied. "No, ya wouldn't be wrong. In fact I'm quite lookin' forward to it. You decide. Surprise me."

"Oh, I intend to." His grin was sly—devious, even. "Shall I pick you up at 7:30 again?"

"I'll see ya then." I was still smiling as I watched Dale walk to his car.

I HAD TWENTY minutes until Dale arrived, and I still had no idea what to wear. I'd worn everything I owned at least three times, and my wardrobe wasn't revealing anything newer or better than it had any of the other ten times I'd stood in this same spot. I didn't hear Mrs. Watkins until she was behind me.

"So this is it, huh? Tomorrow is Ethan's last injection?"

"Yes," I said, turning to face her. "I wanted to thank you for allowin' us to stay here. I know it's cost ya more than ya planned. I just want ya to know that someday, when things are easier for us, I'll pay ya back."

"You don't owe me anything, Victoria," she said, taking my hands in hers. "You filled an empty room and ya kept me company. You gave me a chance to get to know you, the daughter of a dear friend. I couldn't ask for anything more. So, enough of that. Let's talk about you and Dr. Greene."

"What is there to talk about?"

"He's quite taken with ya."

Stepping away, I turned back toward the mirror. "He's just bein' kind. He's become a good friend, and I appreciate all he's done for Ethan."

"I don't believe that, and I don't think you believe it either."

"Well, I guess it doesn't matter what I believe." I shrugged. "Tonight is our last night. Tomorrow I'll be too busy preparin' to take Ethan home."

"You've stepped out with him every night for the last week and a half. Ya don't think that means something?"

"Sure. It means he's lonely and wanted to enjoy some time in friendly company. That's all. Don't start thinkin' it's somethin' it's not." I turned toward her. "He's a doctor, for goodness sake. He couldn't possibly want anything more than a friendship with me. I have four children, and I'm dirt poor. He's well-educated, and I just barely finished high school. He'd have nothin' to gain from marryin' me."

Smoothing the skirt on the dress I'd worn the first evening I'd stepped out with Dale, I turned to check my profile in the mirror. "Would ya mind if I borrowed that sweater again? I hate to ask, but I don't really have anything very nice. I thought I might wear this again."

"Of course," she said, leaving to find it.

Returning moments later, she placed the sweater over my shoulders just as Dale's knock sounded on the front door.

"I'll get it," she said. "You finish gettin' ready."

"Mama?" said Ethan from the bed near the corner.

"Yes, baby?" I took a seat next to him, and smoothed my palm over his forehead. "How're ya feelin'?"

"Better. Are ya goin' out with Dr. Greene?"

"Yes, darlin'. Just one last time before we go home. Is that okay if I leave ya with Mrs. Watkins one more night?"

"Uh huh," he said. "I like Dr. Greene. And Mrs. Watkins is really nice.

But I wanna go home."

"Almost, baby. Just one more shot tomorrow, and then we'll go home. Can ya be my strong boy for one more day? You've done such a good job so far."

Ethan's eyes filled with tears. "I hate those shots, Mama."

"I know, baby. But they're important. You've been so big and strong. I don't think Mama could've taken them like you have. Can ya handle just one more, and then we'll head back home the next day?"

"I guess," he said, his voice clogged with tears.

Smoothing Ethan's golden hair away from his forehead, I studied my beautiful boy. "I'm fixin' to go now. Are ya feelin' well enough to come eat dinner in the kitchen with Mrs. Watkins?"

"In a minute," he said.

"Okay, then. I'm gonna go. I'll be back in a little bit, but you'll probably be asleep."

"Love you, Mama," he said.

"Me too, baby."


D A L E  T O O K  M E to the same restaurant he'd taken me that first night; an elegant restaurant in the heart of downtown, and not too far from the hospital. My mind was filled with thoughts of tomorrow and the days ahead. I was finally going home!

"Victoria?" Dale interrupted my thoughts. "Where are you? I've said your name three times, and you're clearly somewhere else."

"I'm sorry." I smiled guiltily. "Maybe tonight was a bad idea. I have so much on my mind. I have to get Ethan through tomorrow, then check the bus schedule to go home on Saturday. I haven't even talked to my mother or the children since I've been here, so they'll be surprised to see me. Then just gettin' back to normal life . . ."

"You don't really need to go back," Dale said, taking my hands in his own. "Stay here."

A tiny gasp of laughter escaped before I could stop it. "I'm sorry, Dale. I can't stay here. There's nothin' here for me. I need to get back. Mother Elizabeth is holdin' down the fort, and she won't be able to do it by herself much longer. I have a job to go back to, and I need to make sure there's money to feed the kids. Stayin' here isn't an option."

"Sure it is. Just hear me out."

"Dale." I smiled. "I'm not like you. I don't have the ability to make the same choices you do. I have four children and my mother to care for. I gotta get back."

"What if you didn't have to do it by yourself?"

"Lots of what-ifs in this world, Dale. The fact is, this is my reality. I can't play what-ifs, or my children starve."

"Let me say this differently, then. What if someone else was to take on that burden for you? What if someone else was to make sure the children were fed and clothed?"

"Sure." I laughed. "That'd be great. What if money fell from the sky? I don't see that happenin'."

"You're not listening, so I'll try again. Marry me. I have more than enough for myself and two families. Bring the children, and move up here with me. You could stop working and stop worrying about where the money's gonna come from."

Mrs. Watkins had warned me, but his words were still a shock. I had no idea how to respond.

"Ya don't know what you're askin', Dale. I have four children. Not to mention my mother—I can't leave her behind. Then I owe money to the ladies who helped me get here. It would be too much. Ya don't know what you're gettin' into."

"Bring your mother with you. There's room. The house is large enough. Say yes. Let me marry you. You wouldn't have to worry about food or clothing. You can quit working. Let someone take care of you for a while."

"But you've not even met my children . . ."

"So, I'll do that first. Let me take you home on Saturday. I'll meet your children and your mother. I know I'll like them; but if this will set your mind at ease, I'll do it. I'm forty-three, and I not only know what I want, but I'm not getting any younger; and I'm not patient enough to wait around in hopes something better comes along. I enjoy your company. You make me laugh and . . . I'm in love with you."

"I—I don't know what to say," I replied.

"Then don't say anything yet. Let me take you home on Saturday and meet your family. See how we get along. Then give me an answer. Will you do that?"

I nodded. "I can do that, I think."

Smiling, Dale squeezed my hands. "Excellent! I knew I could win you over."

I laughed. "I'm not won over yet, but I'll give ya a chance."

We spent the rest of the meal discussing every topic imaginable. Dale made it difficult to think of anything other than what the future might hold as his wife. After dinner, he took me dancing for the first time. I'd tried to beg off, telling him what an awful dancer I was, but he wouldn't take no for an answer. With no radio at home, I neither knew the music nor the dance steps, but I enjoyed learning. Dale was patient, and had a good sense of humor.

We arrived back at Mrs. Watkins's home at shortly after midnight. Walking me to the door, Dale stopped short and pulled me into his arms. "Think about what I said. I meant every word. I think you and I would be good together."

"I will," I said, stepping away. I smiled all the way into the house and long after I'd closed the door behind me.

# CHAPTER FORTY-TWO

ETHAN'S LAST INJECTION WENT AS WELL AS could be expected. It was so hard watching my strong boy suffer the pain of the needle those three weeks, and I hoped time would heal the emotional wounds suffered by each horrific visit. We finally headed home on Saturday, October 19th—three weeks and four days since the morning we'd headed to Oklahoma City.

The ride home seemed short compared to the bus ride out. Perhaps it was faster in Dale's vehicle, or maybe I was nervous at the reception we'd receive with Dale in tow. I only knew I was ready to see my family, and get Ethan back into his own environment.

Pulling into the driveway of our home in El Reno, Dale turned to me, took my hand, and kissed my knuckles. "Are you ready?"

"I think so." I turned to wake Ethan in the back seat while Dale emerged from the driver's side and came around to open my door.

"Ethan, wake up. We're home," I said.

Content to finally be home, Ethan smiled before his eyes were even fully opened.

I had just emerged from the passenger seat when my children came piling out of the house with Mother Elizabeth following.

"You're home! How's Ethan? We missed y'all!" Their questions came all at once, one over the other, as they raced toward us.

"Careful," I said. "Ethan's still recoverin' from his last injection. Give him a day or two to regain his full strength."

"It's good to have ya home." Mother Elizabeth stepped close and placed both hands on my cheeks. "We've missed you."

"I've missed you, too—all y'all."

Stepping back, Mother Elizabeth glanced at Dale and smiled. "And who is this? I hope you're plannin' to introduce us!"

I smiled. "Mother Elizabeth, please meet Dr. Dale Greene. He's been Ethan's physician, and my friend. Dale, please meet my mother, Mrs. Elizabeth Kirk."

"Mrs. Kirk." Dale bowed and, lifting her hand, raised it to his lips and placed a brief kiss upon her knuckles. "It's a pleasure."

Mother Elizabeth flushed pink. With only a few words, he'd already charmed her. It would take even less time to charm the children.

Dale stayed through the weekend then returned to Oklahoma City early Monday morning. The night before he left, we sat on the porch swing long after the children had gone to bed. I'd both anticipated and dreaded the conversation that would follow. It was time to make a decision.

Never one to waste time, Dale asked, "So, what do you think, Victoria?"

"I think I'm happy to be home." I grinned. "I hadn't realized how much I missed the children. It's good to see Ethan back in the fold."

"Agreed. It's fun to see him interact with the others. You have amazing children, Victoria. They're like their own little universe, each protecting the other from outside forces. Ethan was clearly missing that while you were away."

"Yes," I agreed. "They've not had it easy since their daddy died. They've become inseparable since their older brothers and sisters moved away. They seem to hold tight to each other for fear of losin' one more. They're just children, but they've seen too much."

"They've grown up quickly, I take it. I'd like to make their lives easier. I want to lift the burden of their worries. And yours. Let me do that, Victoria. The children seem to like me, and I know you and I would make a great pair. Let me lift some of the burden you've lived with these last several years, and make your life easier. Marry me."

Though I'd expected this question to resurface, I didn't know what to say. I didn't love Dale. I enjoyed his company, but I wasn't sure I'd ever love him. My heart still belonged to Will, and I couldn't see a day in my future where that would change. Yet Dale could make our lives so much easier. He could ease the burden of my constant worry over money. He would make certain the children ate full meals again. How could I say no to this opportunity placed in front of me? How could I deny my children the chance at a better life? Dale could offer the boys, and maybe even Gracie, college. If not college for Gracie, at least an opportunity to marry more successfully than our current situation predicted. I didn't know if I could love Dale, but I thought I could make him happy. In the bargain, my children could have a better life. Coming to a decision, I smiled.

"When?" I asked.

"You're saying yes? Is that a yes?"

"Yes!" I grinned. "When?"

"When? Right now! Marry me right now!"

"It's late at night! I can't marry ya right this minute!" I laughed.

"Tomorrow, then."

"Tomorrow's Monday, and you have appointments. And I need time to tell the children, and get our things together. Friday? We could have a civil ceremony at the courthouse, then go back with you Friday night. Could ya get away on Friday?"

"For you, I could do anything!" Dale placed a leisurely kiss upon my lips.

It was decided. I had less than a week to prepare the children and Mother Elizabeth, then pack our things and be ready for Friday. Time and again, I asked myself if I was making the right decision. Each time, I reminded myself it wasn't only what Dale wanted, but what was best for my children. With Dale as their stepfather, they'd have opportunities Will and I had never dreamed possible.

As we said our goodbyes the next morning, Dale handed me an envelope filled with large bills. "Go shopping while I'm gone. Replace your wardrobe and the children's, and don't forget your mother. Burn the clothes you've been wearing. They're tattered and over-worn. It's time you became accustomed to looking the part of a doctor's family. I'll be back on Friday morning, and I want you to pack only your new clothing and those things you absolutely must take with you. Understood?"

I couldn't help but smile. I hated not having money, and we'd soon have enough to buy decent clothing and food. But I just couldn't burn the clothes we had worn all these years. After not having anything for so long, the idea of waste made me ill.

With a brief hug and a swift kiss, Dale was gone. I stood in the driveway for long moments after watching him drive away. After a while, Mother Elizabeth came out to join me.

"You're sure this is what you want?" she asked.

"Definitely," I replied. "It's an opportunity for all of us. Most of our friends are still livin' hand to mouth. We have a chance to escape; to live a better life."

"I don't really need to go with ya," she said. "I'm fine here."

"Oh, yes, ya do! The children need you. *I* need you. Please say you'll go with us!"

"Only if you're sure," she replied.

"I've never been more sure of anything in my life."

THE NEXT SEVERAL days flew by in a flurry of preparations. The children were excited to have new clothing, not to mention new shoes and better food on the table. Soon it was Friday morning, and Dale would arrive. We were about to begin the next phase of our lives.

We didn't pack much, as there was very little worth packing save a few well-loved mementos. With all of us moving to Oklahoma City, Mother Elizabeth loaned the use of our house to a family of nine from the church. She didn't want the house standing vacant, and the family had recently lost everything when the bank foreclosed on their property. They'd been living in the chicken coop of a nearby neighbor, and the house would give them a real place to live. We couldn't help them with food and jobs, but a home to live in, free and clear, would do for them a great deal.

Dale left enough money for me to reimburse the Misses Delaney; and it was with both a heavy heart, and no small amount of relief, that I repaid their loan. Ever gracious to the end, the two ladies embraced me and wished me happiness.

On Wednesday before the wedding, Julianne and Earl came to town for a short and unexpected visit. I was elated to see them, and had feared we'd leave before saying goodbye. With no vehicle or telephone, I'd worried I'd be telling them of our move by letter. Julianne's surprise visit came at exactly the right time.

"I can't believe you're doin' this! What d'ya even know of him?" Julianne asked.

"I know as much about him as I knew about Will before we wed," I replied. "Maybe more."

"D'ya love him?"

I didn't know how to answer this question. I didn't want to lie, but stating the truth seemed so base and callous. "He's been good to me," I said instead. "He loves the children, and they seem to've accepted him. He says he loves me. He can give the children things I could never have hoped for before. It's not about money, exactly, but the fact I won't have to worry anymore. That alone makes a world of difference."

"I can understand that," she replied. "You're sure ya wanna take Mama with ya? She can come live with us, if you're worried about her livin' alone."

"Nah." I shook my head. "I want her to come with us. She's given so much to me. This is my chance to give back."

"Sounds like ya have everything worked out. Are ya happy?"

"I think I will be."

"Then I'm happy for ya," she said, pulling me into a hug.


I DID BURN one thing before we left—those patchwork quilts. Each square of fabric brought back painful memories of what we hadn't had. I hated them, and I couldn't stand to see them another moment. Using a burn barrel in the backyard, I stood outside the night before Dale's arrival, feeding each quilt to the fire until there was nothing left but ashes.

Friday morning came faster than I'd expected. At nine o'clock sharp, Dale arrived with a huge smile and a bouquet of yellow roses. They were beautiful, but seeing them brought a pang of sorrow. I missed Will. I missed his smile and the dimple in his cheek. I missed the way he interacted with the children, and the way we'd cuddle late into the night discussing the day's events. And I missed those damned black-eyed Susans he'd always presented me. I couldn't see any flower—much less a yellow flower—without remembering Will and the black-eyed Susans.

Today I would erase the last of Will's presence from our lives, and replace it with new memories. For a moment I doubted my decision. I didn't want to forget Will. I didn't want the children to forget him. But Dale was our salvation. The children had been hungry and poor for too long. This was my chance to give them the life they deserved.

I said a silent prayer to Will, asking his forgiveness for what I was about to do. A sudden warmth and peace settled over me, and my doubt was erased.

Somehow, I knew Will approved. This is what he would've wanted for us. Squaring my shoulders, I walked with Dale toward his vehicle in the driveway.

"You ready?" Dale asked, opening my door for me. The grin on his face was contagious and I couldn't help but smile in return.

"Ready," I told him.

Leaving the children at home to finish packing, we left for the courthouse with Mother Elizabeth as our witness. At shortly after 10:00 a.m. on October 25, 1935, Dale and I were pronounced man and wife. I was now Mrs. Dale Elijah Greene.

# CHAPER FORTY-THREE

THE FIRST TWO WEEKS OF OUR MARRIAGE seemed like something out of a fairy tale. We moved to Dale's large house on the corner of Drury Lane and Nichols Road, just north of Oklahoma City-proper. Only a few years old, Nichols Hills was founded by a colleague of Dale's and consisted of beautiful large houses on vast plots of land. Having lived in poverty for so long, the extravagance of Dale's home overwhelmed us all at first. Soon, though, the children made friends at their new school, and they settled in as though they'd never known poverty.

For myself, I would never forget how poor we'd been, or the hardships we'd endured. As a result, I struggled to form relationships with our affluent neighbors. Instead, I renewed my acquaintance with Mrs. Watkins, and reintroduced her to Mother Elizabeth. The two women had known each other in passing many years before, but our proximity and my relationship with both women easily brought the two of them together as close friends.

After the first few weeks together, Dale began to change. The changes were subtle at first, and I thought it was my imagination. He didn't like the way I'd arranged my hair, or perhaps I spent too much time in conversation with the butcher. Little things. Things that were easily shrugged off but, together, should've raised a red flag. With each new incident, the changes were more pronounced. He started criticizing my speech, correcting my grammar at every turn. He began gathering the mail, insisting I not touch it until he'd gone through it. I wasn't allowed to answer the telephone; it was always to be answered by him when he was home. Once, I ran into a colleague of his I'd met at a dinner party, and he wanted a detailed description of where and how I'd happened to run into him. What was I doing at that particular store at that time of day? I cast all of his behavior up to new husband jitters. I overlooked the behavior and tried harder to appease him in an effort to relieve his concerns.

Our first big disagreement came after attending a dinner party for some of Dale's colleagues at the home of Dr. and Mrs. Lloyd Harper. I'd had a lovely time, and had enjoyed the company of the many couples present. But, on the way home, Dale found fault with everything I'd said and done.

"Did you have a nice time?" he'd asked.

"It was lovely," I replied.

"You spent a lot of time locked in conversation with Dr. Henderson."

"Yes," I agreed. "I enjoyed talking to him."

"What did you talk about?"

"You were there for most of it." I shrugged. "We talked about the children, mostly. Will's older children, that is. He had some family who moved to California a couple of years ago. We were mostly discussing where they'd relocated, and whether our two families were anywhere in the same vicinity."

"I don't like it."

I was surprised by his words. "What don't you like?"

"Any of it. Will's dead, and his kids have moved. They're no longer part of your life. They're not your kids. Never were. I don't like how intimately you were talking to John Henderson. The two of you left both his wife and me out of the conversation entirely."

"I'm sorry." I turned to face him. "We didn't mean to. It was just nice to talk to someone who understood. And really, Dale. Will's children will always be a part of my life."

"No. They're part of your old life. I don't want you to have anything more to do with them. You're my wife now."

I was stunned and had no idea what to say. I couldn't cut Will's children out of my life. True, I didn't know when I'd see them again, but I'd just received a letter from Catherine last week.

"I can't do that," I said.

"You can and you will."

"How am I supposed to do that? They're the older brothers and sisters to my children. They're a part of each other."

"That's not my problem. Find a way. And I'm done with this conversation."

I was completely beyond words. I had no idea where this was coming from or why. Dale had known about Will's children before we'd married. I decided to let the conversation go for the time being. I had no desire to fight with Dale after such a pleasant evening, and decided I'd bring it up at a later time.

The next week, we were preparing to attend a dinner to raise money for the hospital. As I finished dressing, Dale came into the bedroom. He watched me for several minutes, leaving me uncomfortable with his silence.

"I'm almost ready," I told him.

"Not quite." His eyes scanned over my body. "You're not wearing that."

"Whyever not?" I looked down at the elegant ensemble Mother Elizabeth and I had selected just for the event.

"I don't like it. It's too revealing."

Surprised, I assessed my appearance in the mirror. There was nothing revealing about the dress we'd selected. It was a lovely indigo, nearly floor-length as suited the occasion, with a sweetheart neckline and capped sleeves. The only thing the least bit questionable about it was the low v-cut in the back. But it was the height of fashion, and not the least bit promiscuous.

"I don't agree," I said. "It's all I have, so I'm wearin' it."

"Take it off." Dale's voice was eerily calm.

I laughed. "No."

"You will take it off, or I'll take it off for you."

I lifted a challenging eyebrow. I would not be bullied. I'd had enough bullying to last me a lifetime. "No."

"I said, take it off." Though his voice was calm, his body vibrated with anger. He reached up to the shoulder of the dress, and ripped it down the front.

My arms flew over my chest, shielding me from his view. "Why'd ya do that? I don't have anything else acceptable to wear! There was nothin' wrong with this one!"

"Then you won't go. I won't have my wife looking like a strumpet, not to mention talking like an ill-bred street urchin."

I was so angry that my ears were buzzing. "That is completely uncalled for."

"Yeah? Well deal with it."

Dale stormed out of the room, leaving me standing there in my torn dress and my dignity in shreds. I realized later he'd gone to the dinner party without me.

"I'M SORRY," DALE said the next morning, leaning in to kiss me. "My temper got the better of me last night. I just love you so much that I don't wanna share."

His words soothed my anger just enough for me to forgive him. The change from last night to this morning was so drastic, I wondered if I'd exaggerated in my mind how deadly the sound of his voice had been.

That afternoon, we took the children to the zoo. They loved seeing the exotic animals. Dale was kind and gracious throughout the entire day, and I again wondered if I had exaggerated our encounter the night before. How could one person go from so angry to so loving in such a short time?

Another week went by, and things seemed to resolve themselves. Dale returned to the loving man I had married, and I felt things were going well.

On a Thursday in early December, I was sitting at the kitchen table, helping Grace with homework, when Dale came in. His posture rigid, I knew immediately something was wrong but had no idea what.

"Gracie," I said quietly. "Go up to your room and finish your homework."

Getting up from the table, Grace left the room and silence descended. After several moments, Dale took from his pocket a letter and slapped it down on the table in front of me. Surprised, I looked at the return address to see it was from Joseph.

"I thought I told you there was to be no more contact with California." His voice was an ugly growl. "I thought I explained they were no longer part of your life."

"Dale, they're always gonna be—"

"Enough! I will not be undermined! I said no more contact. They are *not* your children; they're your dead husband's children. I will not compete."

"Of course you won't compete!"

"Burn it," he said.

"What?"

"I said to burn it."

"But I've not even read it yet. There might be important news in there."

"There is nothing they could say to you that would be important to your life anymore. Burn it."

I shook my head. "No."

Picking the envelope up in his hand, Dale crunched it tightly in his fist.

"I will not tell you again, Victoria. Burn it."

"No."

His closed fist hit me before I could even react, and I flew backwards out of the chair. Holding my jaw, I kept the tears at bay as best as I could.

"Get up," Dale said, extending his hand to me.

Cautiously, I placed my hand in his as he righted the chair and reseated me. "Now, I'm not asking. I'm telling. Burn the letter, Victoria. Now."

With shaking hands, I took the letter from him. I straightened out the crumpled paper and looked around for something to start a small fire. Dale reached into his jacket pocket and pulled out a set of matches. Lighting one, he handed me the match. The paper quickly took to the flame, and I jumped up to toss it in the sink before I was burned. Turning around, I looked Dale calmly in the eye. I was afraid to say anything, but I attempted to convey every bit of anger through my own steely gaze.

"Understand me now, Victoria," he said. "I will not be defied, and I will not compete. I said no contact with California, and I meant it. Do not defy me again."

Dale turned on his heel and left the room. I remained standing at the sink for long moments, shaking with suppressed rage. Or maybe it was fear. I still don't know which.

LATE THAT NIGHT, I sat quietly at the kitchen table with a cup of warm milk. I wasn't anxious to go to bed. I was still so angry with Dale that my body shook with rage. Hearing the quiet shuffling of feet, I looked up to see Mother Elizabeth coming into the kitchen.

"Can I join you?" she asked.

I smiled and nodded.

Taking a seat across from me, she studied my face. "You wanna tell me what happened to your cheek?"

I shook my head. "Not really."

"Was it Dale?"

"Ya know it was. I'm sure the whole house knows it was." Angry tears escaped from my eyes.

"Are ya okay?" Mother Elizabeth asked.

"Physically? Yes." I nodded. "Emotionally? I'm furious."

"What was it about? Maybe I can help."

"Will's children. He wants me to cut off all ties with them. He told me once before, but I ignored him. Then today, a letter came from Joseph. He made me burn it without even readin' it."

"He didn't!" she gasped.

"I'm afraid so. Will ya send a letter to them and explain? Just until I can figure things out?"

"Of course."

Mother Elizabeth and I sat silently for several moments, both of us contemplating what had happened.

"What are ya gonna do?" she asked.

"I don't know. This isn't what I envisioned when I said I'd marry him. He's just not the same person. Or maybe he is, but I never knew who he was. If I could divorce him, I would."

"Ya know you can't. The kids can't go back to bein' hungry. Not to mention, the stigma of divorce would taint all of ya."

"I know. But what do I do?"

"I don't know," she said. "I honestly don't know."

# CHAPER FORTY-FOUR

ON CHRISTMAS DAY, DALE AND I CELEBRATED
our two-month anniversary. By then, I was certain: I was expecting. With the
changes I'd seen in Dale, I had mixed feelings about this baby. We'd never
discussed children beyond that first conversation when he'd originally proposed. I wasn't entirely sure how he'd feel about becoming a father in his own
right, and at his age. Hoping for the best, I saved the news for a short time
until I could find the best way to tell him.

On New Year's Eve, Dale and I left the children at home and celebrated
with a gathering of Dale's closest friends—all doctors—at the Skirvin Plaza
Hotel in downtown Oklahoma City. The fifteen-story building was gorgeous,
and I'd never seen anything like it before. As the clock ticked down to 1936,
we stood under an ornate chandelier. Confetti fell like snowflakes upon our
heads and shoulders, while Dale kissed me to bring in the New Year.

"Happy New Year, Mrs. Greene," he said. "Here's hoping for some wonderful surprises in 1936."

"Happy New Year, Dr. Greene." I smiled, though my stomach was queasy
with fear. "Are ya ready for your first surprise?"

"You know I am! What have you got up those beautiful sleeves of yours?"

Pausing a moment, and hoping this would actually be a welcome surprise, I stretched up on my tiptoes and whispered in his ear. "I'm expectin' a
baby."

Time stood still as Dale processed my words. For a moment, I feared he
was upset. Would he welcome this news? Time stretched out until my nerves
nearly made me snap. Suddenly, Dale's face beamed with excitement. He
lifted me off the floor and spun me around in circles.

"We're having a baby!" he yelled loud enough to be heard by anyone
within twenty feet.

Immediately the congratulations came pouring in from those around us, and the joy on Dale's face relieved any fear I'd once had. He not only welcomed this baby, but he was excited. Maybe 1936 would be a good year for great things, I thought to myself. Maybe this new life I was carrying would allow Dale to put aside his insecurities and endless criticisms. Perhaps we could move forward with hope for the future.

DALE'S JOY KNEW no bounds, and the next few months flew by. For a while, it seemed as though the anger and distrust of the previous weeks had been completely forgotten. Within days, Dale insisted the extra bedroom be renovated to become a proper nursery. Walls were painted, new furniture was purchased and, before long, we had a nursery set up in shades of green and yellow to welcome our new baby.

The children were excited, more so than they had been for David's arrival. I think the relief of not having to worry about money helped in this regard. Jack was no longer needed to do odd jobs for the neighbors to supplement what I could provide, and Grace was becoming a young lady in her own right with a new interest in boys. Dale had promised to hire a woman to come in and help with the children; and, for the first time in many years, I felt the weight of the world lifted from my shoulders.

During the first several months of my pregnancy, Dale returned to the doting husband of our first days together. His anger, criticism, and distrust seemed to vanish, and I breathed easy once again. But I knew it wouldn't last.

As the pregnancy progressed, the Dale I'd come to know slowly returned. The only difference was that the physical abuse had turned verbal. What he couldn't do with his hands, he did tenfold with his words. Soon I came to dread the hour when he would return from the hospital each day.

Our daughter, Anna Christine, was born on July 22, 1936. With dark hair and eyes, she was a tiny replica of Dale, and he doted on this baby as though she hung the moon. The older children were also quite taken with her. No longer having the worries they'd once had, they enjoyed watching each stage of her growth.

Dale's devotion to Anna reached the point of extreme. If he was in the room, he monopolized her; not allowing anyone else to hold her. When she awoke at night for her feeding, he was out of the bed in seconds to see to her needs. If I hadn't been nursing, I doubt he'd have allowed me to comfort her at all. If she cried longer than a few moments, he'd accuse me of hurting her. His behavior was almost manic, and I became concerned over his state of mind.

I'd barely recovered from Anna's birth when I discovered I was expecting once again. If I was conflicted over Anna's birth, I was doubly conflicted by the news of this second baby. I'd been nursing Anna, and common understanding of the day was that doing so left me unable to conceive. Not so in my case. Because of this myth, the shock of this new pregnancy overwhelmed me.

Once again, Dale took the news with complete joy, and we made preparations for yet another new addition to our family. This pregnancy was the hardest on me, and I needed to tell Dale it would be my last. Yet I didn't dare. I couldn't begin to predict what he'd think of such a statement, but I was exhausted and knew I couldn't do this again. I was nearly thirty-two, and had been making babies for nearly fourteen years.

Dale Elijah, Jr. was born on June 7, 1937. Like his sister, he was born with a thick head of dark hair and eyes that were sure to turn dark as well. To avoid confusion with his father, we called him Elijah. Like Anna, he became the epicenter of his father's universe.

For nearly two years, life had been a yo-yo of good and bad. When Dale was in a good mood, everything looked bright and life was good. When Dale was in a bad mood, everything was awful. Between my pregnancies, Dale's jealousy, and my own discomfort in the presence of those who'd never known poverty, I'd made very few new friends. Thankfully, I'd maintained my closest friendships with Mother Elizabeth and Mrs. Watkins. Without the two of them, I'd have been totally isolated.

The children, on the other hand, were prospering. They were excelling in school; and Dale never failed to remind me that the well-being of my children was entirely in my own hands. One misstep and I was assured my children would suffer.

On a regular basis, Dale reminded me of the poverty I'd come from and how easy it would be to return. In his eyes, I was ignorant, and he made it a point to let me know that my lack of intelligence had best not reflect on our children. For every nice thing he said or did, he followed it with a gesture that felt purely evil. Each day, I wondered which Dale I would greet: the Dale I had married or the Dale I had come to know as my husband.

To the outside world, he was as kind and charming as he'd always been. On the occasions when he took me to social events, the wives of his friends raved about how fortunate I was to have such a handsome and loving husband. They all believed Dale doted on me, and that I wanted for nothing. Their praise only made me angrier.

By the time Elijah was born, I'd come to detest Dale with a hatred I'd never before known. The only reason I stayed was because of the children. I didn't doubt he'd take my children—or even kill me—if I tried to leave. Worse than that, I'd begun to hate myself, and what I had become. I hated my weakness, and that hatred made me furious. While I tiptoed around my every interaction with Dale, I began taking my anger out on anyone else around me. I was so afraid the children might set Dale off that I became a fierce disciplinarian, far more so than I'd ever been before. I would tolerate no disrespect from my children. When I told them to do something, I expected it done immediately and without any delay. The only way I could survive, and be sure my children survived, was to be sure none of us did anything to spark Dale's ire.

I learned a lot of important lessons from Dale. I learned when to back down, which was every single time we had a confrontation. I learned I would never be right. And I learned words could be more painful than an actual beating. But the most important lesson I learned from Dale was that nothing is ever truly a secret. The moment you think your secrets are buried deep, never to be disturbed, they somehow manage to wiggle their way to the surface.

My own deep dark secret was about to be revealed, and I very nearly paid the price of its keeping with my life. I had never told Dale about David's paternity.

In the beginning, it was just an oversight. Our courtship had been such a whirlwind that the timing of David's birth had never crossed my mind. Then, as the bliss of my married life turned more to nightmare—and I realized how jealous and angry Dale could become—I deliberately kept the information from him. I didn't know how he'd react, but I knew it couldn't be good. Dale had never asked, and so I'd allowed him to believe David had been Will's son. I never expected the truth would come out.

# CHAPTER FORTY-FIVE

IN OCTOBER OF 1937, AS DALE AND I CELE-
brated our second anniversary, Oklahoma was just beginning the first stages
of recovery from what became known as The Dust Bowl. President Roosevelt
instituted efforts to prevent soil erosion by planting trees, and this opened
jobs for many Oklahomans. Better still, these efforts would begin to reverse
the devastation that had resulted in the loss of crops and income for so many.
Though the drought would continue, the amount of blowing soil that had
been the bane of our existence would be reduced by more than half by the
end of 1938. While the lives of so many were about to become significantly
better, mine was about to become significantly worse.

Dale met with his Kiwanis Club every Wednesday at lunch, and it was a
meeting he looked forward to every week. In March 1938, his club welcomed
a new member: Gene Blanchard. Gene had moved from El Reno several
months earlier when he accepted a position with a bank in Oklahoma City.

Dale and Gene had become fast friends and, though I'd known his new
friend's first name, I had no idea his friend was a ghost from my past. In fact,
I didn't know until the evening Dale insisted we have dinner with his new
friend and his friend's new wife.

We'd settled on dinner at an elegant restaurant in downtown. I had
dressed carefully for the evening, hoping to make Dale proud to have me at
his side—or, if not proud, at least so as not to provoke his anger.

We arrived early and took seats to await his friend's arrival. When Gene
stepped into the restaurant with Joyanne Holly, sister to that sniveling George
Holly, my heart dropped. How was this possible? What had I done so wrong
to bring these two men together in the same room? It made no sense!

My body shook. Though I knew Gene hated me, I worried about Joyanne equally as much. She'd never been friendly, and the set-down I'd given
her brother had severed any friendship we might've shared.

As for Gene, he hadn't changed. He was still the slimy bastard he'd been when I'd last seen him on the day I'd told him I was pregnant with David.

There was no escape. I prayed to get through this evening without Dale ever learning of my previous relationship with Gene. Dale stood to greet them as they approached our table.

"Gene!" He extended his hand for a handshake. "So glad we could do this!"

Next to Gene, Joyanne gasped. "Victoria? Oh, my goodness! I haven't seen you in years! How are ya?"

I cringed at Joyanne's fake sincerity.

Surprised, Dale looked at Joyanne and then at Gene. "You've met my wife? You know Victoria?"

"We go way back," Gene said with a sly smile.

Dale glanced back and forth between the three of us, clearly trying to puzzle it all out. He waved toward the empty chairs at our table. "Have a seat, then! How long have you know each other?"

"Oh gosh," Joyanne gushed. "I'd say most of our lives! My brother's the same age as Victoria, and I believe he taught her children in school. Didn't he, Victoria?"

The expression on Joyanne's face sent fear down my spine. Her eyes narrowed in malice, it was clear she wasn't the least bit thrilled to see me. If it was possible, she'd do everything in her power to make trouble. Gene, on the other hand, was who I really worried about.

"Indeed, he did," I replied.

Was there any way to go back and start this evening over? Surely I could've feigned sickness.

"I knew her husband well," Gene said. "Will and me went way back. I was so sorry when he died. Back right after Thanksgivin' of '31, wasn't it? That's what—six and a half years ago?"

"Yes," I said. "Close to it, anyway."

"How are those kids of yours?" Gene asked. "They must be mostly grown up by now. Let's see, if I remember. Grace was your oldest. She must be about thirteen now?"

"Almost," I replied. "Next month."

*Oh, God! Please make him stop!*

There was no way to communicate how dangerous this line of questioning was. Gene was a bastard, and it was clear he was enjoying every second of making me squirm; but I couldn't imagine that, had he known how dangerous Dale could be, he would deliberately hurt me.

"Then you had the two boys. Jack and . . . Everett?"

"Ethan."

"That's right, I'm sorry. And the baby. I don't recall his name."

"David."

"Yes, that's right. David. He must be what? Four?"

"Soon," I said. "In July."

Gene was probably enjoying his little game at my expense, but I'd become truly fearful for the first time in my life. Dale was completely silent, and I could see the wheels spinning in his head as he mentally calculated the numbers. There was no way I could explain. He wouldn't believe me if I tried.

Dinner was fairly quiet with cordial talk of the weather, where Gene and Joyanne had moved, and other inane topics. I shook inside, and had difficulty following the conversation. Dale's body language said that Gene and Joyanne had done some major damage. I had no way to rectify it, so I bided my time until dinner was complete.

Saying our goodbyes and promising to do it again, we bid farewell to Gene and Joyanne Blanchard. Then I braced myself for the storm that was surely about to come.

Dale said nothing on the way home. Instead, he ground his teeth, his jaw clenched in anger. Arriving home, I checked in on the children then retreated to our bedroom to prepare for bed. Dale didn't follow me immediately. I tried not to let that concern me, and went through my nightly ritual.

It wasn't until nearly two hours later, when I had almost drifted off to sleep, that Dale entered our bedroom. Even from a distance, I smelled the alcohol immediately. He sat on the edge of our bed.

"Do you have something to tell me?" His voice was far too quiet and calm for the situation.

"What would you like to know?" I sat up and pulled the covers tightly around me.

"Everything. Everything you should've told me before we were married. Everything I should've known before we had dinner with Gene and Joyanne tonight. Everything. Leave nothing out, or by God, I'll kill you."

His words were said with such utter calm that I had no doubt he meant them. The Dale who had been in short hibernation during my pregnancies was about to re-emerge. He was like a coiled snake, and I was afraid where to place my next step for fear of the venom in his strike.

"David is . . ." I began, then changed my mind and decided to start again. "When Will died, he left the farm with a hefty loan in the hands of the bank. We were starvin' and we had no money. We didn't have money for food, much less the money to pay back the bank. We were destitute. The kind of poor you've never imagined."

"How does that have anything to do with David?"

"David was . . . an accident."

"I would guess so!"

"Yes, but not the kind you imagine. I—I needed security. I needed to be sure the kids would have a roof over their heads. We were about to lose everything. Everyone was losin' everything around us. Just the week before, a family in the next town was found squatting in an abandoned homestead because they'd lost their house and couldn't afford another. I couldn't let that happen to us."

I paused a long moment, not sure how to continue.

"I'm listening," Dale prompted.

"I couldn't let that happen to us," I repeated. "So I entered into an arrangement that would buy me some time to get the money together for the bank. And some groceries. The man who was in charge of our account—he arranged for sex in exchange for time on the loan. And he'd bring us a bag of groceries when he came. Twice a month for each month's extension."

"How long did this go on?"

"Six months, maybe?"

"Long enough to get pregnant with David," he said.

"Yes."

"And the father? Does he know?"

"Yes. I told him, but he wanted nothin' to do with us when he found out."

"What's his name?"

I sat there shaking and couldn't respond. I couldn't tell him who the father was.

"I asked you his name, Victoria. I will have an answer!"

I didn't see it coming. His fist shot out from nowhere, catching me in the side of the face and knocking me off the bed. At the edge of my vision, I saw stars and it took me a moment to get my bearings. Slowly, using the bed to assist me, I stood and took a seat on the edge.

Dale stood and walked around to stand in front of me. "Tell me his name, Victoria."

"I can't."

Once again Dale's hand flew out, this time catching me on the other side of my face and knocking me back onto the bed.

"I will have his name one way or another, Victoria. Give me his name. Now!"

"Dale," I said quietly. "I can't tell ya. You don't wanna know."

Grabbing my hair in his fist, Dale yanked me from the bed and threw me onto the floor. Still wearing shoes, he kicked me from my stomach down to my knees more times than I could count, until I was in so much pain I nearly lost consciousness. While Dale had hit me several times in the past, I'd never seen him lose control so completely. I couldn't draw a breath, and feared he might've broken one of my ribs.

"I'll not ask you again, Victoria. Answer my questions, or I'll be forced to do something we'll both regret."

I could barely see out of my left eye, and both cheeks were throbbing. Breathing was difficult. I wondered what more he could do that would cause him real regret.

"Last chance, Victoria." He stripped off his belt. "I will have the answers to my questions. Who is David's father?"

"Gene," I whispered. "Gene Blanchard."

I only remember the strap coming down once. The rest is a blur before I lost consciousness. I don't know how long I was out, but I awoke some time later on my bed with Mother Elizabeth bathing my face with cool water. At the other end of the room, sitting quietly and with the world once again on his shoulders, was Jack.

I opened my eyes then closed them to shut out the bright light of the room.

"What happened?" Mother Elizabeth asked. "Can ya tell me?"

It took me a moment to find my words. When they came out of my mouth, they were muffled between my swollen and bruised lips. "Dale. He found out about David. That he wasn't Will's."

"Oh no," she said. "He didn't know? How could ya not've told him?"

"I didn't think of it at first. Then later, I was scared what he'd do if I told him. I didn't think he'd ever find out."

"Oh, Victoria." Tears escaped from both of her eyes. "What're we gonna do?"

"I know what I'm fixin' to do!" Jack said. "I'm fixin' to kill that bastard!"

"Jack Harrison, you sit down now!" Mother Elizabeth scolded in a loud whisper. "Do not do anything to make things worse for your mother! We just need to figure this out. We don't need ya goin' off half-cocked before we figure out what to do."

"But he hit my mama!" Jack cried. "Not just hit her, but beat her within an inch of her life! He can't get away with that!"

"He won't. But we don't wanna rile him even more. So sit down, and let us figure this out!"

"Where is he?" I asked.

"He left. We heard the fight in here, and then he just left. He's been gone about half an hour," she said.

"You should go. I don't want him findin' ya here when he returns," I said. "Thank you."

"Will ya be okay?"

"I'm fine. I just need to figure things out so I know what to do when he comes back."

"Be careful, Victoria. Don't do anything hasty."

"I won't. Now go."

Coming over to the bed, Jack took my hand in his. "I'm sorry, Mama. I should've stopped him. I should've done somethin'."

"No, baby." I shook my head. "There's nothin' ya could've done. Now go, okay?"

"I love you, Mama," he said with a gentle squeeze of my hand.

"Me too, baby."

# CHAPTER FORTY-SIX

DALE WAS GONE FOR A FULL THREE DAYS. I had no idea where he was, who he was with, or even when he'd return. I began to worry—or maybe it was hope—that something had happened to him. On the evening of the third day, he returned.

I was preparing for bed when Dale surprised me by entering the room. Turning to face him, I tried to gauge his mood, but was unable to tell what he might be thinking.

"You're back," I said.

"Yes," he said. "Sit down."

Taking a seat on the edge of the bed, I waited for Dale to say his piece. I smelled the alcohol on his breath and began to worry. Dale had never been a drinker. He was mean enough without the alcohol. With the alcohol, he might be lethal.

"I've been thinking nonstop these last three days. I'm so angry, I can't even think. I loved you, and I thought you loved me. But I see now it was all a game you were playing."

"Dale, no—"

"Shut up," he said quietly. "You will not interrupt me, understood?"

I nodded.

"I can see this was all a game to you," he continued. "You saw me as your chance to get out, and you took advantage. You must've had some nice laughs at my expense. Did you think you could get out with Gene Blanchard, too, but got tossed aside instead?"

"Dale! No! I—"

The back of Dale's hand planted on my already bruised cheek, and pain radiated through my skull.

"SHUT UP! I will not warn you again!"

Tears of pain rushed out of the better of my two eyes and down my cheek. I nodded. I wouldn't say another word if I could help it.

"Things are gonna change around here. Enough of you living in luxury. We're fixin' to enter a new era with new rules. Rule number one: you may not leave this house without my express permission. If you leave this house, I will kill you. Understood?"

I nodded.

"Good. Rule number two: enough with the hired help. They're gone. I fired them before I came up here. You are now entirely responsible for the care of our children, and the upkeep of our home. I want this house kept in pristine condition. No dust, no dirt—nothing."

"But Dale, the dust—"

Again, his hand came out from nowhere, and once again it caught me near the same location as the last blow. I wasn't sure how much more I could take.

"I said shut up, and I meant it. Are you having difficulty understanding?"

I shook my head no.

"Good. The dust: I don't care how you get rid of it, but I want every trace of it gone every single day. Rule number three: money. Your allowance has been revoked. You will buy nothing without my okay. Every dime you see will come through me first. I will see your grocery list before you go, and I will send your mother with you to do your shopping. You will present me with a receipt for every purchase, and you better be able to justify every nickel you've spent. Understood?"

Again, I nodded.

"I would divorce you if I could, but you well know I can't. It would ruin my career. But know this: you are a whore, and you are dead to me. You are nothing more than an employee in my home. On occasion, I may take you to dinner parties as my wife, and you will behave appropriately. You will put a smile on your face, and, for the outside world, you will pretend we are happily married. You're good at pretending, I know."

I could do nothing more than nod my head.

"Don't you dare defy me, Victoria. I gave you everything I had, and you defiled all of it. I will not be made a fool a second time. Are we clear?"

I nodded.

With nothing more to say, Dale stalked out of our room, slamming the door behind him.

THE NEXT THREE weeks were horrible. My bruises had healed, but only on the outside. Inside, they were raw and bleeding. True to his word, Dale cut off my access to money. I had not a single penny to my name, and nowhere to access it. I didn't even try to explain Gene Blanchard to Dale again. I knew from experience it would only get me hurt. The next time, he might just kill me.

Dale began drinking on a regular basis, sometimes stumbling in stone drunk at the end of a long day. I have no idea how it didn't affect his career. I can only assume he limited his drinking to after work hours. After those first beatings, Dale began leaving his marks where nobody would ever see them, and I was careful to hide them from Mother Elizabeth and the children. With every comment, Dale made it clear that any love he'd ever had for me was replaced by hate. As the weeks moved by and the beatings continued, I fell into utter despair. At least when we were hungry, my body had been strong, and I could see a light at the end of the tunnel; but Dale's anger was changing me. I was entirely isolated from the outside world with the exception of my family. I had no resources, and began losing hope for the future, something I had never done before, even in our most desperate times. I began to dread each new day and prayed for death.

Dale's favorite pet peeves were what he called my "backwoods dialect" and the cleaning. For the latter, he'd come home every evening and run a white glove over every surface. I dusted several times a day to keep it at bay. When he could find no fault with my dusting, he'd focus on my grammar, or find other areas to criticize. There was no end to the fault he found with everything I did. The dishes weren't clean enough, the kids tracked dirt onto the floors, the closets weren't tidy enough. Each day his anger grew, and there was no reasoning with him.

It was now early May, six weeks since the dinner with Gene and Joyanne Blanchard. I was doing everything I could to keep Dale content. I'd cleaned every surface in the house until it shined, but I'd yet to do any heavy cleaning in his study. I wanted to get that done before Dale found fault with that room.

I was cleaning the floor on my hands and knees inside Dale's study, and my work had moved me into the small closet within the room. Running the damp cloth over the wood floor, I moved backward on my knees toward the other end of the closet, when my balance was thrown by an uneven board. I didn't think much of it until I took a closer look and realized the board was not only loose, but was loose by design. Looking around to make sure I was alone, I lifted the board to find a hole beneath the floor's surface. Reaching inside, I removed a small burlap bag.

I couldn't begin to imagine what could be in the bag. Did Dale know it was there? Had he hidden it? I couldn't image who else might've left it there.

Cautiously, I opened the bag to find more cash than I'd ever seen in one place at any one time. I didn't take time to count it, and I certainly didn't wish to disturb it! Quickly returning the cash to the bag, and the bag to its hiding place, I finished up in the closet and set everything to rights. I wasn't sure what I'd seen, but I knew it was something he was hiding from me. Instinctively I knew Dale wouldn't be happy to know I'd been cleaning this room.

ANOTHER MONTH PASSED, and it was now early June. There's just nothing like Oklahoma in the summer. The temperature gets so hot the sidewalks leave blisters on bare feet. I was hot and sticky from cleaning all day. My hair had fallen down from the tidy bun I'd attempted that morning, and the long strands hung around my shoulders. I appeared dirty and unkempt. Dale came home early this particular day and caught me before I'd had time to clean up. I always cleaned myself before Dale arrived home. It was one of many preparations I made to keep his ire away.

"You look like hell," he said in greeting.

"I'm sorry. You're home early. I've been cleaning all day. I've not had a chance clean up yet."

"Don't give me excuses, Victoria. Just because you're a whore doesn't mean you need to look like one. You're my wife, and you will appear presentable in case I choose to bring someone home with me."

I don't know what came over me, but I couldn't take another word. I'd taken enough abuse from him, and these last words seemed to flip a switch within me. Bringing my arm back, I reached out and slapped Dale full across the face. I'm not sure who was more surprised, me or Dale.

"Don't you ever call me a whore again," I said calmly.

In slow motion, I watched Dale erupt. He was on me before I could escape. Grabbing my hair as it trailed behind, he yanked me back toward him and began beating me with both fists. I should've been used to it by now, as I'd been beaten more than a few times in the last couple of months, but it's not something you ever get used to. My body screamed in pain.

"Don't you ever lay a hand on me again, Victoria. I will kill you," he said.

Before I could keep it from happening, Jack jumped onto Dale's back and pounded on him for everything he was worth. "Don't you ever touch my mama again!" he screamed. "Never again!"

Jack's weight was nothing to Dale. Within moments, Dale dislodged him and threw him onto the floor not far from me. He raised his fist toward Jack, and I knew Jack was too small to withstand such a blow.

"Don't!" I screamed, throwing my body over Jack's. "Dale! Please stop! Don't hurt him! He's just a boy. He's protectin' me! Please stop!"

"A boy old enough to protect his mother is old enough to take a beating if he can't make it stop," Dale said.

"Please stop," I cried. "He won't do it again! I promise!"

Dale took a deep breath. "Stand up, Jack."

Slowly, Jack got to his feet and stood defiantly before Dale.

"I've got no problem with you, son," he said. "It's your mother I have a problem with. This is your one and only warning, so listen carefully. Never again interfere between a man and his wife. This is not your fight; but, if you make it your fight, you'll regret it. Understood?"

"Yes, sir." Jack pulled his shoulders back in much the same way I always did when I needed courage.

"Now get out! Get the hell out of my sight before I change my mind."

Mother Elizabeth came quietly into the room and took Jack by the shoulders. I hadn't seen her standing there, but it was clear she'd seen everything. I was mortified. So long as this had been my secret alone, it had been my own burden to bear. But now that Mother Elizabeth knew the beatings had continued, she would make it her burden as well. I watched as she led Jack out of the room and away to safety.

# CHAPTER FORTY-SEVEN

"WE'RE GONNA NEED TO DO SOMETHIN'," Mother Elizabeth said to me the next afternoon. "This can't continue to go on. I've stood by and watched these last couple of months, but the beatings are gettin' more frequent. The combination of anger and alcohol is gettin' worse. We've gotta do somethin'."

"What can I do?" I asked. "I can't leave. I don't have any money. I can't even leave the house. If he caught me tryin', he'd kill me for sure."

"Understood, but now Jack's involved. Jack may only be a child, but he won't stand by and watch someone beat his mother. We need to figure somethin' out before Jack steps in again. Dale won't let him go away unscathed a second time."

"What'm I gonna do? Short of killin' him, I can't think of any way to make this stop. I neither have a weapon, nor am I strong enough to overtake him."

"Then be creative." Mother Elizabeth's eyes held mine. "I'm not sure we have any other choice. It's come down to you or him. Ya need to choose."

"What in the world are you suggestin'?" I whispered.

"It's not somethin' I say lightly, but this can't continue. You're right—ya can't leave or attempt to divorce him. I do believe he'd kill ya for sure if ya tried."

"Then what?"

"That's up to you, but ya need to decide soon. I'll help ya any way I can, but this has to be your decision. I just don't see any other way out. I don't believe he'll stand for Jack's interference a second time."


I THOUGHT ON Mother Elizabeth's words over the next week. I thought about the money I'd found hidden in the floorboard of the study, and vowed to check for it again as soon as I had a chance. But even if I could take it, where could we go? Besides Julianne and Earl, there was no one to turn to; and I certainly didn't want to bring Dale's wrath down upon them. The more I thought on it, the more I realized I had no other choice. I couldn't convince Dale to listen to me, and I couldn't take the chance of Jack getting in the middle again.

The only solution—the only real way out—was through death. Dale would have to die. But how? I had no weapon, and I wasn't strong enough to overpower him.

*Be creative,* Mother Elizabeth had said. My mind raced with possibilities, but I discarded them all. I'd have to come up with something clean; something that wouldn't point back to me. Anything else would leave my children destitute. They needed me, so I couldn't get caught.

The answer came to me in a dream: poison. If I could get my hands on a poison of some kind, maybe I could put it in his food. With enough poison, he'd die before he knew what hit him. But where? We didn't have poison in the house, and I couldn't buy it. If Dale saw poison of any kind on my grocery list or receipts, he'd know I was up to something. Not only that, if the police were suspicious, they'd check my purchases and my pantry to see what I had on hand.

But what if I knew someone who had poison in her cabinets? I couldn't ask someone else to be an accessory, but I already had Mother Elizabeth on my side. I couldn't leave the house, but she could. And I thought I knew where we might find the poison.

"I need ya to help me," I told her a week later, as we sat at the kitchen table after breakfast."

"Ya know I'd do anything for ya," she said.

"Mrs. Watkins. When we lived with her a few years ago, she kept rat poison in her cabinet below the sink in the kitchen. I saw it there a few times when I did some cleanin' for her. I need ya to see if ya can get some of it. But ya can't tell her and she can't find out. I'd need ya to do it quietly so she'd never know."

"I can do that. I've been invited to visit with her tomorrow afternoon. Maybe, if she steps out of the kitchen for a moment, I can take some. How much d'ya think ya need?"

"I have no idea. Maybe a tablespoon?"

"I can do that, I think. I'll hide it in a washrag, and put it in my pocket. Unless she's really low on it, she'd never know."

"Thank you for doing this," I said. "I just don't know how I'd survive without ya."

I WAS A nervous wreck the whole next day. I went through my routine of cleaning every room until it shined, all the while wondering what could be taking Mother Elizabeth so long to return. I hoped she wouldn't be caught. My stomach was in knots. At nearly three o'clock, she finally returned.

"Did ya get it?" I whispered, meeting her at the door.

"I did." Mother Elizabeth removed a washrag from her pocket, and handed it to me. I took it without looking, and placed it into my own pocket.

"How're ya gonna do it?" she asked.

"I'm makin' chicken noodle soup and fresh rolls for dinner. Dale likes my soup, especially if I make it with homemade noodles. I'll prepare the bowls like I always do, then mix in some of the poison into his bowl. I can only hope he won't taste it."

"That should work," she replied. "While you serve up the bowls, I'll take 'em to the table. I don't think he'll suspect anything, but he'd suspect less of me puttin' a dish in front of him than he might you. Just to be on the safe side."

"Thank you."

That evening, just before releasing Dale's bowl, I sprinkled in the entire contents of the poison Mother Elizabeth had collected, and mixed it well. Sitting down at the table, I smile demurely and attempted to behave as normally as I could. I'd thought this through carefully. As a doctor's wife, I'd heard Dale talk about the symptoms for all types of diseases. I'd decided I could lead the authorities in the direction of a heart attack. In his mid-forties, Dale was certainly old enough to have sustained a heart attack, especially with as stressful as his line of work had become.

As was our custom, the table was utterly silent; the only sound was the clinking of our spoons upon the ceramic bowls. Not a full ten minutes into the meal, Dale's coloring turned gray and his hands began shaking.

"I don't feel well," he said.

"What seems to be the problem?" I asked, standing up to help him. "Can I get ya somethin'? A wet rag, maybe?"

"No. I'm just—I'm dizzy, and my heart is racing."

"What can I do?" I asked, truly concerned. I may have wanted him gone, but the actual act of killing a man isn't easy.

"I think—I think maybe I should lie down."

"Jack," I said. "Please help me walk your stepfather up to his bed."

Jack rose and walked around me to Dale's other side. There he placed his shoulder and arm around his stepfather's back, and together we walked slowly with Dale between us. We'd barely made it to the stairs when Dale collapsed.

"Mama?" Jack said in surprise.

"Step back. Lemme see what I can do," I said.

Kneeling beside Dale, I could see he was already gone. His heart had stopped beating, and he was completely motionless.

"Oh, my God!" I said. "Oh, my God! Jack. Gracie. Take the children outta here. Please. Now! Don't come back 'til I call you!"

"What can I do?" Mother Elizabeth rushed to my side and whispered.

"Get rid of his soup bowl," I whispered. "Wash it out, and make sure it all goes down the drain. Then bring a fresh bowl, but only fill it half way. Put it beside his place at the table so it looks like that's what he's been eatin'. Maybe make sure his handprints are on the spoon, just to be sure. And, whatever you do, don't use the same bowl! Clean it and put it back in the cabinet mixed in with the others. I'll call for emergency."

AN HOUR LATER, I was seated on my sofa playing the part of the bereaved widow, as the officers took my statement. I watched as the coroner's office removed the body of my second husband.

"And then he just clutched his chest and said his heart felt funny," I told them. "Jack came to help me get him upstairs to the bedroom, but he just collapsed onto the floor! Oh, my God! I can't believe he's gone! What are we gonna do without him?"

"I'm so sorry for your loss, Mrs. Greene," the officer said. "Is there anything we can do for ya?"

"Nothing. Not unless you can bring my husband back! There's nothin' anyone can do!"

The officers stayed for a while longer, but I was truly so distraught there was nothing more I could contribute.

I was now a murderer. My soul would be forever stained by Dale's death.

FOUL PLAY WAS never suspected in Dale's death. I hadn't known it, but he'd had a mild heart attack some five years prior, long before we had married. The coroner's office made note of the symptoms I described, paired it with information from Dale's own doctor, then filed his report with the cause of death as a heart attack.

I never knew where that money came from that was hidden in the floor of Dale's study closet. I suspect he hid it there for fear of the stock marketing crashing like it had in '29. I used a small portion of it to give Dale a proper burial as cheaply as I could do so without raising eyebrows. What remained was still enough money to see us comfortably through a full year or more, but I was surprised to find Dale had taken out an insurance policy shortly after we had married. In his own twisted way, Dale must've loved me at some point and wanted to make sure we were well cared for. The two monies combined saw us fed and clothed until the hard times of the Dust Bowl and Depression finally ended.

We remained in Dale's home until April of 1942 when I took my family back to El Reno. There we lived until the children were fully grown and moved out on their own. To my relief, they all stayed in the vicinity to raise their own families.

Mother Elizabeth died in 1967 at nearly seventy years old. We never spoke about those days or what led to the death of Dale Greene. It was our secret, and she took her end of it to her grave.

Caroline, Olivia, Catherine, Joseph and Daniel remained in California to raise their families. As the years went by, and money was more easily available, they each returned to visit us in Oklahoma every few years. In return, we took every opportunity to visit them in California. Though the miles separated us, we were still family. All of my children—David, Anna and Elijah, included—remained very close with each other. The five older children never blinked an eye at David's birth, and they embraced him as a sibling, along with my two children with Dale Greene.

Twelve children: five of Will's, four of mine with Will, one of mine with Gene Blanchard, and two of mine with Dale Greene—all of them siblings to each other, blended seamlessly as one family. This was my gift to you— my children and grandchildren. A family. Someone to always call your own. Someone to always take your side. It was the only thing I ever wanted, and far more than I ever dared hope.

I never completely recovered who I had been before I met Dale. I certainly never remarried. Life had been too hard on me, and I resented anyone whose life was easy and without strife; including my grandchildren. Sadly, as members were added to our family through marriages and births, a disconnect grew between the younger generations and myself. Jack, Grace, and even Ethan understood me—they'd lived that harsh, unbearable life alongside me. But the younger children and my grandchildren never understood. They never have been, nor would be, homeless or hungry. I don't wish them hardship but, without it, they can't comprehend how I became the woman I am. And so they criticize. They call me "the meanest woman they've ever known." They joke behind my back about the "Immaculate Conception of David." They laugh at the old woman pinching pennies, furious over a single nickel lost between the seat cushions in the car.

But I survived, and I have no regrets; and for my efforts I leave behind a large extended and loving family. Life is not easy, and sometimes you have to make a decision between "me and thee." For myself, I will always choose me.

## THE END

# ACKNOWLEDGEMENTS

My deepest gratitude to the following people:

To Michelle Halket for taking on this second edition of *The Edge of Nowhere*. I'm so thankful for your guidance.

To my husband, Troy D. Armstrong, and my children, Amber and Braden Armstrong. Your constant belief in my abilities gives me the courage to keep going.

When the original version of this novel was released in 2016, my dad was so proud. For months before his memory deteriorated with dementia, he carried a copy in his jacket pocket to show everyone he met. This second edition is dedicated to his memory.

The Dust Bowl spread far beyond Oklahoma, leaving very few states completely unaffected. Even those states not directly affected saw some of the blowing dirt that gave the Dirty Thirties its name. It was no doubt a difficult life for those who survived.

# Q&A WITH C.H. ARMSTRONG

Since the original publishing of this novel in 2016, I've been asked many of the same questions by readers. Since I've been offered the unique opportunity to publish this second edition, I'd like to take a moment to answer some of the most popular questions I am asked.

**Q: Is *The Edge of Nowhere* a true story?**
A: Yes and no. While the overall novel is a product of my imagination, many of the events included were inspired by events that actually took place. For example:

(1) Like the character of Victoria, my grandmother did marry a man some twenty years older than herself, who came to the marriage a widower with five children close in age to herself.

(2) Similar to Will, my grandfather died of an appendicitis rupture. They tried to take him into town for treatment, but they didn't have a motor-

ized vehicle and he died en route in the back of the family's wagon.

(3) Similar to Victoria, my grandmother gave birth to two children between husbands. To my knowledge, she never named their father(s), and we're not sure how those children came to be. However, we do believe there's a strong possibility those children were conceived in a manner she found necessary to survive as a widow with children to support in that difficult era.

(4) Like David, my two uncles were never seen as "other." To my knowledge, they were always embraced as equal siblings, and without prejudice. In fact, as a niece, I was completely unaware of this "secret" until I was nearly an adult, as the love shared by all of my grandmother's children was strong and unwavering. It remains the same today, nearly thirty years after her death.

(5) Like Victoria, my grandmother had a child who survived rabies— my dad. I've tried to describe the scenario as closely as it was told to me throughout my childhood, including the shots that were administered so painfully. The biggest difference is that there was no Mrs. Watkins for them to stay with, nor a Mother Elizabeth to care for the other children. They were, I believe, already in Oklahoma City as they were receiving medical attention for my dad's oldest sister, who'd been hit by a car. I'm told there was only one bed for all of them, and my dad (then about 4) had to share it with his older sister (then about nine or ten, who was bedridden and in a near body cast after the accident).

(6) Like the older siblings in the book, my grandmother's stepchildren (all but one, I believe) did move to California, as many did during this era. As times and finances improved, they returned to Oklahoma frequently to visit. While they have all long-since passed, their descendants still live there today.

**Q: Did your grandmother really have that many children?**
A: Yes. My grandfather came to the marriage with five children. Together, he and my grandmother had four children, with a fifth on the way at his passing. My grandmother then had two children between husbands before marrying her second husband and having two more children. Grand total: fourteen, including the five my grandfather brought from his previous marriage.

**Q: Did your grandmother really have an evil mother-in-law?**
A: No, not to my knowledge. However, it's my understanding she wasn't

well liked by my grandfather's brothers. The character of Imogene, while fiction, represents the brothers-in-law who failed to help her when she needed it most. In contrast, the characters of Atticus and Veronica represent the one brother and his wife who seemed to be more supportive of my grandmother.

**Q: Did Dale Greene really exist?**

A: Yes and no. Dale Greene represents my grandmother's second husband. While I know their marriage wasn't ideal, I can't really tell you whether he was as much the villain as I made him out to be in the book. From talking to aunts and uncles, I'm told he wasn't the easiest personality to live with. He also was neither a doctor, nor wealthy. He did, however, father two of my favorite aunts, who went on to parent some of my favorite cousins, so I'm reluctant to cast too many aspersions on his character.

**Q: Did your grandmother really kill her second husband?**

A: For some reason, this question always makes me laugh. No—my grandmother, to the best of my knowledge, never even imagined killing anyone. She did, however, divorce her second husband in an era when divorce was still frowned upon.

**Q: Did your grandmother really march up to the school and give the principal a set-down?**

A: Yes, but ... I'm neither sure what transpired, exactly, to make her so angry, nor whether it was the principal or a teacher. The original story, as told by my father, is that he and his brothers got a "whoopin" at school for misbehaving. Well, my grandmother could be meaner than a snake, but nobody messed with her kids (or grandkids). Like Victoria in the book, my grandmother did march up to the school, and did flip desks over as she walked through. What happened next changes a little with each telling, but the common agreement is that the set-down she gave the schoolmaster was as much physical as it was verbal. And, knowing my grandmother, that's the version I choose to believe. But, for obvious reasons, it's not the version I wrote for the book. After all, who would believe a woman in that era would be capable of giving that kind of set-down? I wouldn't believe it if I hadn't known my grandmother.

**Q:** Are there any other interesting tidbits you can share with us?

**A:** Sure!

(1) In the book, Victoria mentions her dislike for patchwork quilts and that, in better days, she refused to have them in her house. While I'm not sure this was true about my grandmother, it was absolutely true of her oldest child, my aunt Gerry. She hated them, mentioning many times in my childhood that they reminded her too much of how hard those days had been.

(2) The character of Sara represents my oldest living aunt, who is still alive and well. She was never attacked by water moccasins, though there were certainly enough in Oklahoma that it could plausibly happen.

(3) In the book, Victoria miscarries the child she was carrying when Will passed. This was entirely fiction. My grandmother was pregnant at the passing of my grandfather, but the child they'd conceived was born healthy and lived well into his 70s. He (my uncle Donny) was one of my favorites of all of my aunts and uncles.

(4) At one point after Will's death, Victoria tells Catherine that he was the "finest man I ever knew." Not knowing anything at all about my grandfather, I wrote him how I imagined him. Imagine my surprise when, during the original editing of this novel, my aunt revealed to me that those were the only words she remembered my grandmother ever speaking about my grandfather. Upon hearing them, and realizing they reinforced the image of him I'd imagined, I added that original quote from my grandmother—passed down through my aunt—to the final copy of the first edition.

C.H. Armstrong is an Oklahoma-native transplanted in Minnesota. Raised in a large family, she grew up on the stories of the sacrifices her grandmother made as a widow with fourteen children in Oklahoma during the 1930s. It was through these stories and her desire to better understand her own grandmother that the inspiration for *The Edge of Nowhere* was born.

She is also the author of *Roam*.

charmstrongbooks.com
@C_H_Armstrong

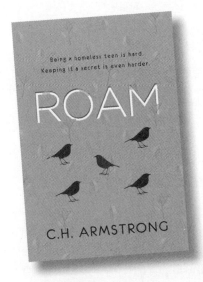

ROAM

C.H. Armstrong

YA - 978-1-77168-151-3

Seventeen-year-old Abby Lunde and her family are living on the streets. They had a normal life back in Omaha but, thanks to her mother's awful mistake, they had to leave behind what little they had for a new start in Rochester. Abby tries to be average—fitting in at school, dreaming of a boyfriend, college and a career in music. But Minnesota winters are unforgiving, and so are many teenagers. Her stepdad promises to put a roof over their heads, but times are tough and Abby is doing everything she can to keep her shameful secret from her new friends. The divide between rich and poor in high school is painfully obvious, and the stress of never knowing where they're sleeping or finding their next meal is taking its toll on the whole family.

As secrets are exposed and the hope for a home fades, Abby knows she must trust those around her to help. But will her new friends let her down like the ones back home, or will they rise to the challenge?

"Treats homelessness with respect and makes it visible." *Kirkus Reviews*

"An inspiring and heart-wrenching message." *Booklist*

Also from Central Avenue Publishing

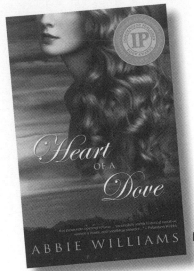

HEART OF A DOVE

Abbie Williams

Historical Fiction - 978-1-77168-014-1

The Civil War has ended, leaving the country with a gaping wound. Lorie Blake, a southern orphan sold into prostitution at fifteen, has carefully guarded her aching soul from the disgrace forced upon her every evening. Two years have passed, leaving her with little hope of anything more. Meanwhile, three men – longtime friends – and a young boy with a heart of gold are traveling northward, planning to rebuild their lives in the north and leave behind the horrors of their time as soldiers in the Confederate Army.

Fate, however, has plans of its own, causing their lives to collide in a river town whorehouse. Forced to flee, Lorie escapes and joins them on the journey north. But danger stalks them all in the form of a vindictive whorehouse madam and an ex-Union soldier, insane and bent on exacting revenge. At last, Lorie must come to terms with her past and devastating secrets that she cannot yet bear to reveal.

Heart of a Dove is the first book in a gripping, sweeping romantic saga of pain, unbearable choices, loss and true love set against the backdrop of a scarred, post-Civil War America.

"This passionate opening volume successfully melds historical narrative, women's issues, and breathless romance with horsewomanship, trailside deer-gutting, and alluring smidgeons of Celtic ESP.." - *Publishers Weekly*